Acclaim for *Satin Doll*

"Energetic, fast-paced, and provides intriguing action . . . Miller develops suspense that allows the reader to experience interesting twists in a storyline that hits on politics, romance, and class issues for a satisfying read."

—Cydney Rax, *Black Issues Book Review*

"A real page-turner! It's about wanting more, getting it, and finding that the brass ring is just that—brass. A great book club choice."

—Jenice M. Armstrong, *Philadelphia Daily News*

"Filled with sassy, humorous, and thought-provoking dialogue, *Satin Doll* is a wonderful debut."

—Kimberla Lawson Roby, author of
It's a Thin Line and *Casting the First Stone*

"Filled with intrigue, crime, love, and a surprise ending."

—Angela Brown Terrell, Gannett News Service

"*Satin Doll* is an engaging, provocative novel about a sister that decides to turn her life around and does so with style. Miller is an excellent storyteller who draws you in from page one."

—Zane, national bestselling author of
The Heat Seekers, Addicted,
The Sex Chronicles, and *Shame on It All*

Also by Karen E. Quinones Miller

I'm Telling
Using What You Got

Satin Doll

A NOVEL

KAREN E. QUINONES MILLER

POCKET BOOKS
New York   London   Toronto   Sydney

This book is a work of fiction. Names, characters, places and incidents are products
of the author's imagination or are used fictitiously. Any resemblance to actual events
or locales or persons, living or dead, is entirely coincidental.

POCKET BOOKS, a division of Simon & Schuster, Inc.
1230 Avenue of the Americas, New York, NY 10020

Copyright © 2000 by Oshun Publishing Company, Inc.
Copyright © 2001 by Karen E. Quinones Miller

Previously published in hardcover in 2001 by Simon & Schuster, Inc.

All rights reserved, including the right to reproduce
this book or portions thereof in any form whatsoever.
For information address Simon & Schuster, Inc.,
1230 Avenue of the Americas, New York, NY 10020

ISBN: 0-7434-8245-X

The author gratefully acknowledges permission from the following sources to reprint
material in their control:
    "Satin Doll," written by Duke Ellington, Billy Strayhorn, and Johnny Mercer. ©
1960 (renewed 1988) Famous Music Corporation. Reprinted by permission. All rights
reserved.
    "Satin Doll" (vocal version); words by Johnny Mercer and Billy Strayhorn; music
by Duke Ellington. Copyright © 1958 (renewed) by Music Sales Corporation/Tempo
Music, Inc. (ASCAP), and Warner Bros. Publications and Famous Music. Music
Sales Corporation administers all rights for Tempo Music, Inc. International copyright secured. All rights reserved. Reprinted by permission.
    "Satin Doll," by Johnny Mercer, Duke Ellington, Billy Strayhorn. © 1953, 1958
(copyrights renewed) by WB Music Corp., Famous Music Corporation, and Tempo
Music. All rights reserved. Used by permission. Warner Bros. Publications U.S., Inc.,
Miami, FL 33014.

First Pocket Books printing June 2003

10 9 8 7

POCKET and colophon are registered trademarks of
Simon & Schuster, Inc.

Jacket design by Tom Matt
Jacket illustration by Mark Ulriksen
and illustration manipulation by Tom Matt

For information regarding special discounts for bulk purchases,
please contact Simon & Schuster Special Sales at 1-800-456-6798
or business@simonandschuster.com

Manufactured in the United States of America

Acknowledgments

THERE ARE SO MANY PEOPLE THAT I WANT TO THANK for their support of *Satin Doll*. I need to apologize, though, before I begin—because I know I'm going to leave some people out.

Latasha Stewart—You are such a wonderful person, and a wonderful friend. I know I don't tell you often enough, but girl, you are the bomb. Thank you so much for bringing Satin Doll to the attention of your friends and colleagues in the publishing world. And I haven't forgotten that I still owe you dinner!

Delin Cormeny—thanks so much for everything, Miss Joe Cool. If there's anyone reading these acknowledgments while on an agent hunt, give Delin a call. She's super! She's with PMA Literary and Film Management in NYC.

Andrea Mullins, my editor at Simon & Schuster—man, with all the horror stories I've heard about editors at publishing houses, I had my armor donned and weapons drawn, ready to go to war. But you turned out to be such a sweetheart. Every suggestion you offered made *Satin Doll* that much better. Thank you. I hope our relationship lasts forever.

Lecia and Joel Bickerstaff, Emma Rodgers, Frances Utsey,

Acknowledgments

Janifer P. Wilson, Andre and Kim Kelton, Larry Robin, Lloyd Hart, and all of the bookstore owners around the country who were so supportive of my self-published version of *Satin Doll.* THANK YOU!

And for all the authors I've met along my self-publishing journey, but especially to Gloria Mallette *(Shades of Jade)* and Kieja Shapodee *(Written in Red Ink)*—IT'S BEEN A TRIP, AIN'T IT? Thanks for sharing so much of yourselves. I love you all.

And now here are the acknowledgments from the self-published edition of *Satin Doll*—because everything I wrote back in December 1999 still holds true today: This book could not have been written—and published—without the love and support of many.

First mention has to go to my brother, Joseph T. Quinones, my hero and my champion. Wind beneath my winds? Naw, you are my wings. I soar because of your love, Joe T.

Joseph "Jazz" Hayden . . . well, what can I say? We both know this book would not have been written if it were not for you.

Lanie Babe, you're my girl no matter what. I'll never forget how you cheered me on as I wrote this book, as you've cheered me on during so many of my endeavors. Catch all the 'tudes you want (I know you're entitled!), just remember you'll always have a friend in me.

A special "thank-you" to Maida Odom, who edited *Satin Doll* (the self-published version) under less than the best of circumstances, and did a terrific job.

Karen M. Scott. I can't believe how wonderful you've been. Thank you so much for coming in at the last minute and saving my butt. I owe you big time.

C. Carey-Jones, who designed and illustrated the wonderful book cover (for the self-published edition) of *Satin Doll.* I can't believe how lucky I was to find you!

Acknowledgments

Thank you Omar Tyree for encouraging me to self-publish, and passing along tips to do so.

And Kim Roby, who went far above and beyond the call of duty for someone she's never even met.

Thank you Jenice Armstrong, Nonie Davis, Cheryl Waddlington, Laurie Bruch, Franchella Slater, Vaughn Slater, William Thomas, Harold King, Ambre Brown, Adrian Thomas, Al Hunter Jr., Sandra Bullock, Gayle Anderson, for believing in me and egging me on.

A big THANK-YOU to the members of The Eye of Ra Bookclub, who welcomed an unknown author to their meeting. What a wonderful group of people!

Belinda and Sister, my dear sweet cousins . . . you guys have always been on my side. Thank you.

And Kitty . . . if I can do it so can you. Let me help you get it together, sis!

I save my biggest thank-you for my loving daughter, Camille Renee Quinones Miller. You've always been my biggest supporter, and I hope you know I'll always be yours. You are something special, Love Girl. Thanks for being so understanding all of those times I sat in front of a computer instead of taking you to the skating rink or the mall. You could have stood around and sulked, but instead asked if you could help. Oh man, what did I do to deserve you? I love you, Camille. I love you. I love you. I love you.

Maferefun Olodumare
Maferefun Oshun
Maferefun bobo Orisha

In Honor and Memory of My Mother
RITA "MARJORIE" BAYNE QUINONES
Shango Gumi
July 1930–April 1986

Prologue

1994

"BANG!"

The sound was loud, but not quite jarring enough to register instant recognition in her reefer-dulled brain.

It could have been a firecracker. It was loud enough, and the acrid smell of gunpowder filled the Harlem night air in the basement-level courtyard of the brownstone. But a firecracker wouldn't have caused her cocaine-dealing companion to lurch forward into a set of garbage cans, his manicured hands flailing wildly in the air. Nor would it cause a dark red spot to appear on the back of his yellow silk shirt. A spot that bubbled and grew bigger as she watched.

Another blast rang out. *Boom!* The dealer fell screaming to the ground.

The second blast followed an instant after the first, but in that time twenty-year-old Regina Harris's brain had cleared enough for her to realize her big-time spending companion was shot, and she was in danger. Regina dropped her pocketbook and flexed her body to sprint, but before she could move, someone grabbed her head from behind and slammed her face into the brick wall. Again and again.

The coke dealer was on all fours on the cement ground, gasping loudly. His eyes were wide, and his mouth dribbled a trail of bloody saliva as he tried a fast crawl out of the dark courtyard.

"Shit!" a man's voice growled.

The hold on the back of Regina's head was released, and her body folded to the ground. Her nose was numb and dripping even more blood than her mouth, making it difficult for her to breathe. Semiconscious, she watched in a daze as a man walked over to the scampering dealer, bent down and placed a gun against the back of his head, then let go with yet another resounding blast.

The dealer collapsed to the ground, deadly still.

I'm next, Regina thought, but try as she might she couldn't will herself to get up as the man walked back toward her.

Only a few feet away from her now, he pointed the gun and fired.

I'm shot. I'm dead, she thought, although she didn't feel the bullet that entered her battered body. Suddenly, the scream of a police siren filled the air. The man didn't hesitate. Gun in hand, he jumped over the courtyard railing and disappeared down the street.

"Oh, my God. Oh, my God!" From far away she recognized the hysterical voice as Tamika's. "Oh, Regina, are you dead? You dead?"

Regina painfully opened her eyes and looked at her friend's tearstained face staring down at her in horror, and replied honestly, but in a slur, "I don't know."

2

1999

IT WAS A WARM SEPTEMBER NIGHT IN NEW YORK CITY—
too warm and too nice to be in an apartment that really didn't
want her company, Regina Harris decided. The apartment longed
for a respectable young Jewish couple like the one who lived a
floor below, who were originally from Long Island and had coffee
and bagels each morning. Instead, Apartment 2A in the corner
building at 71st Street and West End Avenue was stuck with
Regina, formerly of Harlem, who breakfasted on home fries and
sausage.

Regina felt the apartment's disappointment, and spent a lot of
time trying to reassure it that she was good enough to reside in an
expensive one-bedroom flat on New York's Upper West Side.
She bought beautiful silk drapes, exotic plants and even a salt-
water aquarium with a rainbow array of fish, but the apartment

would have none of it. Even after living there for three months, she still opened her eyes each morning and struggled for a few seconds to remember exactly where she was. The apartment simply refused to be her home.

So Regina gave up trying to win it over. Since it refused to be her home, she turned it into her castle. She bought Nigerian sculptures that she placed on wicker tables, and hung framed posters of Malcolm X and Nelson Mandela on the walls. She considered buying an elaborate painting of Louis Farrakhan, but decided against it. She just knew that if she tried to hang it in the snooty apartment, the walls would crumble. The apartment still did not like her, but it finally resigned itself to the fact that she was there to stay.

But on a mesmerizing September night like this, Regina didn't care about the apartment. It was a perfect evening for roaming the streets on the Upper West Side. Peeking into darkened store windows at the latest fashions from Paris, browsing through bookstores to read a few pages from some novel on the *New York Times* bestseller list, or huddling in coffee shops surrounded by other young professionals sipping cappuccino while congratulating themselves on being young professionals. It was even a better night, she decided as she walked down the stairs, to catch the uptown Number 3 train and head to Harlem, to hang out with her childhood friends.

Regina stopped in the lobby to look at herself in the wall-length mirror, and briefly considered going back upstairs and changing her clothes. She wore a lightweight, powder blue dress that flared at her tiny waist, but failed to conceal the wide hips that were as much a part of her heritage as her caramel-colored skin. Her navy blue shoes were comfortable, but still boosted her actual five feet one inch height by an additional two inches. Her brown shoulder-length hair, which usually softly framed her oval face, was pulled back in a ponytail, making her almond-shaped eyes all the more noticeable. She decided that she wasn't dressed appropriately for a nightclub, but she was certainly presentable. She headed out the door and toward the subway.

Fifteen minutes later she emerged from the 125th Street station and breathed in the Lenox Avenue air that carried the tempting scent of fried chicken from the fish and chips joint on the corner and the clashing voices of Luther Vandross and Snoop Doggy Dog from competing music stores. She walked briskly along the sidewalk, ignoring the crackheads searching for a hit, and the God-fearing ladies wearing their Sunday best as they headed to Friday night sermons at the Pentecostal churches. She grew up in Harlem, and was so accustomed to the sights that she no longer saw them—though inwardly she craved them: The honking cars that didn't seem to realize pedestrians have the right of way. The young men on the corner catcalling out to the fly young girls. The winos on the stoops cradling their hard-earned bottle of Thunderbird. The Muslim brothers selling *The Final Call* in the middle of 125th Street. The vendors hawking bootleg videotapes of movies that premiered in theaters just the day before. It was all part of Harlem, and Harlem was in her blood.

A few months before she had called her father at his latest drug rehabilitation center and mentioned that she was considering buying a cherry red sports car. "Red," he snorted. "You can take the nigger out of Harlem, but you can't take Harlem out of the nigger."

She fumed when she heard his words. Half Puerto Rican and half black, he often assaulted others with insulting stereotypes of blacks as if to repudiate his own African ancestry. Forget the fact that he married two black women, though he later abandoned both. Still, Regina decided against buying a car. She barely shed a tear when she heard he died of a heroin overdose three months later while visiting distant relatives in San Juan.

"Well, well, look what the cat's dragged in!" Yvonne exclaimed when she opened the apartment door for Regina. "Girl, what you been up to?"

Yvonne grabbed her in a warm hug, as Regina smiled at the savory aroma of curry chicken coming out of the kitchen. Mama Tee was home and doing her thing. The three young children running around the middle of the living room floor playing tag stopped and began jumping up and down when they saw Regina.

"Aunt Regina, come play hide-and-seek with us," cried a four-year-old girl with four long, thick braids and a runny nose.

"Oh, Sissy, maybe later," Regina replied as she bent down and gave the wiggling little girl a hug, trying unsuccessfully not to get snot on her clothes. "Is your mom here, too?"

"Hey, girlie! What's up?" cried an excited Tamika as she emerged from Yvonne's bedroom wearing a robe, her face half made up, her hair in curlers. Puddin' was right behind her, wearing a hair weave that flowed almost down to her buttocks, and waving her hands to dry the polish on her long, tapered fingernails. "Yvonne didn't say you was coming out with us tonight. Darren, go wipe your sister's nose for Mommy."

Regina had forgotten it was a Friday. Five years ago she, too, had been in Yvonne's apartment readying for a night of clubbing.

Her brush with death had made her reevaluate her life. Hanging out with dope dealers and gamblers willing to pay good money to have a "pretty young thing" on their arms and in their beds, had been profitable—but the bullet that had entered her shoulder that night could just as easily have pierced her heart. It was while she was recovering in the hospital that she decided there had to be a better way to make a living. College, then long hours promoting her freelance writing career, had replaced Harlem after-hour spots in her life.

She had known Yvonne, Tamika, and Puddin' since elementary school, and the four had started hanging out when they reached their early teens. Tamika was the youngest by just a few months, but there was a childlike quality about her that made people want to cuddle her. She was the sweetest one of the crew, always quick to find the bright side of a situation.

Puddin' was the opposite of Tamika. Tall and lean, she imagined herself a Whitney Houston look-alike, and she was indeed gorgeous. The problem was her attitude. Guys were attracted to her because of her stunning looks, but after they slept with her a few times they grew less tolerant of her smart mouth and gold-digging ways. She even got on her friends' nerves with her constant primping and sarcastic remarks, but she had some good qualities. If you were outnumbered in a fight, Puddin' was the one you wanted by your side. It didn't matter if you were right or wrong, Puddin' would snatch off her wig, reach into her pocketbook for a roll of pennies to stash in her gold-ringed fist, and be the first to throw a punch on your behalf.

Regina walked back into the kitchen and gave Mama Tee a kiss. The curry smelled even stronger in the kitchen, and Regina's mouth began to water, even though she had stopped for a slice of Neapolitan pizza just an hour before. Her mother, like Mama Tee, was Trinidadian, and the smell of curry was always in the air while Regina was growing up.

"Oh, come see Mama Tee after all dis time, did you? I beginning to tink you don't love your mama no more," the gray-haired woman said in her thick Trinidadian accent before grabbing Regina in a bear hug. "You know you family, Regina. You like me own daughter." Mama Tee motioned for her to sit down in one of the aluminum chairs with red padded seats. The kitchen was spotless as usual, unless you counted the old yellow grease stains over the stove that were too high for Mama Tee to reach now that she was getting older. Potholders and red gingham dish towels hung on the green enamel walls, and fruit-shaped magnets decorated the refrigerator. Mama Tee continued to bustle around the kitchen as she told Regina—yet again—how proud she was of her for getting her college diploma and starting a career.

"You were always smart, just like my Yvonne. I'm so glad you didn't get caught up in the streets and get a bunch of babies by some no-good man," she said as she added chili powder to the pot of curry chicken that simmered on the gas-burner stove.

It had broken Mama Tee's heart when Yvonne had popped up pregnant at sixteen. Yvonne had always done well in school, and her mother bragged to friends that her daughter would get an academic scholarship to a big university. But Yvonne dropped out of school in the eleventh grade, although she eventually got her G.E.D.

"At least she's got a job and earns an honest living." Mama Tee sighed as she gingerly placed slices of yellow plantain in a large sizzling black skillet. "But dat girl's too smart to be somebody's secretary. She should have her own business. She should be a boss with her own secretary."

"Who says I won't be, Mama? Just give me some time," said Yvonne, who had suddenly appeared in the kitchen. She kissed her mother on the cheek, then popped one of the already fried plantains into her mouth.

"You better marry yourself a good man who will take care of you and your child and pay for you to go to college," said Mama Tee as she swatted Yvonne's hand away from another of the plantains. Disappointed though she was, Mama Tee loved her only child dearly, and spoiled her as an adult as much as she had done when Yvonne was a child.

"Come on, Regina. Let's get out of this kitchen before Mama starts giving me another one of her lectures." Yvonne smiled as she pulled Regina by the hand.

"You still got Mama fooled, girl. She just doesn't know what a ho you are," Yvonne whispered to Regina as the two walked down the narrow hallway. "Of course, now that you've got a degree it's different, huh?"

"It is different." Regina giggled. "Now I'm a ho with a journalism degree."

"Yeah!" Yvonne giggled. "Educated pussy!"

Yvonne was the logical one in the group. She was extremely intelligent, articulate, and had all the social graces—the mark of a good West Indian daughter. It was one of the things she and Regina had in common, being raised by Trinidadians. Unlike Regina, Yvonne was an only child with a doting mother. Growing up, she had all of the hottest toys and wore all of the latest fashion, but she was never a snob. She was Regina's closest friend, and the unofficial leader of the crew. Her home became the starting and ending point for their party nights.

The four girls crowded into the small bedroom Yvonne shared with her ten-year-old son, Zegory. A smoking electric curling iron was perched precariously on the edge of the old wooden dresser that was covered with perfume bottles and makeup jars, as well as nail polish stains and cigarette burns. The walls were decorated with a large tattered poster of Brian McKnight and pictures of Mariah Carey and Puff Daddy that had been torn out of magazines. Dynamic as Brian, Mariah, and Puff were, they couldn't hide the fact that the room, like the rest of the apartment, was badly in need of a fresh coat of paint.

Regina pushed aside some clothes and sat down on the twin bed, while Yvonne grabbed the curling iron and began making Shirley Temple coils in her long red hair.

"So, where are you guys going?" Regina asked.

"Perks," Tamika said excitedly in her squeaky little-girl voice from where she sat on the windowsill. "You coming, right? We ain't all hung out in like, forever. Come on, this'll be fun!"

"Yeah, you should come along," Yvonne said as she frowned in the mirror at a strand of hair on the top of her head that insisted it didn't want to curl. "Tamika's right, you haven't hung out with us in ages, and Perks is going to be jumping tonight."

Regina had never been to Perks, one of the more popular clubs in Harlem, but she had heard a lot about it. They had live jazz bands during the week and sometimes a blues act. On the weekend a deejay played a combination of R&B and hip-hop. It was one of the few places in Harlem that had a cover charge on the weekends, but people paid it because they knew they'd find whatever it was they were looking for—a good time on the dance floor or a bunch of new telephone numbers for their little black books. The patrons during the week were usually older, between thirty and fifty, but on the weekends the club attracted a younger group, but not a wild crowd. The two big bouncers who kept watch over the place made sure of that.

"Girl, you know Regina's too good to hang out with us now that she's a buppie," Puddin' said in her cool, sarcastic tone.

"Wrong as usual," Regina replied as she casually flipped through the latest copy of *Jet* magazine. "I've always been too good to hang out with you guys."

That got an uproarious laugh, as the young women started talking about their many adventures hanging out in clubs together, and playing on guys who tried to pick them up.

"God, we used to get into so much trouble," Regina said wistfully. "Remember the time that crazy dude at Lickety-Split spent all of his money setting up the bar trying to impress Yvonne, and then got mad when she wouldn't talk to him after he ran out of cash? He said he wasn't going to let us leave. That one of us was going to have to give him some pussy."

"Yeah, Regina," laughed Puddin'. "It's good thing the guy you were making goo-goo eyes at all night was a cop, else we weren't getting out of that bar that night. He got up and said he'd take care of you, and told us to wait outside, and then the two of them started arguing."

Puddin' started giggling so hard Tamika, in her tiny, squeaky voice picked up the story, although she was struggling to keep from laughing herself.

"Yep, and then this other guy pulls up in a Caddie and asks if we wanted a ride and we drove off with him to an after-hours spot. We get there and he pulls out all this coke and reefer, and he just knew he was getting in Puddin's pants with all that coke she was sniffing. Then when he got drunk, she rolled him for seven hundred bucks and we jumped in a cab and went to another spot to see if we could catch up with one of Regina's boyfriends and—"

"And we run right smack dab into the crazy guy we had been trying to duck in the first place. Turns out he was the bouncer at the spot," Regina cut in, though doubled up with laughter. "I thought Yvonne was going to die when she saw him. She took off so fast she broke her heel and fell facedown in a puddle of mud. She started hollering. Tamika started crying. Puddin' put up her dukes, and I was so stoned I didn't know what to do, so I stepped out in the street and tried to hail a cab."

The four friends roared with laughter at the memory. Tears rolled down Regina's face as she slid down the bed. Puddin' and Tamika were laughing so hard they had to struggle to catch their breaths. The kids started banging on the door trying to find out what was so funny, and Yvonne had to open the door and wave them away with her hand since she was laughing so hard she couldn't even speak.

"I don't know how we managed to get through that night without getting killed," Puddin' said, when she finally regained her composure. "Thank God the guy who owned the spot came out and recognized you, Gina. The only reason he stopped the guy from kicking our ass was because your boyfriend was a big-time spender, and he didn't want to lose his business."

"Oh, God, we were crazy," gasped Regina.

"And lucky," added Yvonne.

"But we had fun," said Tamika, and the foursome doubled up with laughter again.

Two hours later they were out the door and headed to Perks, but not before eating a big plate of curry chicken, beans and rice, plantains and avocado salad at Mama Tee's insistence. She wasn't going to let her girls go out drinking—and she knew they were going out drinking—without some food in their stomachs, she said. Mama Tee also made it a point to remind them that she was not the neighborhood sitter. She already raised her own child; she was not going to raise Yvonne's child, too.

"Oh Mama, don't worry, we're not going to be out too late," said Yvonne as she hugged her mother good-bye.

"Mama Tee, I understand if you're not up to watching Darren and Sissy. I'll just take them over to my aunt's and pick them up in the morning," Tamika said meekly.

"You'll do no such ting, child. Tat woman don't even like children. You know dese babies are welcome in dis house anytime. You go out and have a good time," Mama Tee said indignantly, contradicting her earlier declarations as if she were being insulted.

"Just don't make it a habit," she shouted after them as they headed down the hall. "And Yvonne, don't you come in dis house drunk tonight, you hear?"

It was early, only 11:00 P.M., when they arrived at Perks, but there was already a line of people waiting to get into the club. One of the bouncers, a short but husky man with a gold tooth, gave Regina an admiring look as she handed him ten dollars for her cover charge. She pretended not to notice his leer, but she was appreciative. She had been worried about going out dressed so simply, especially since her friends were dressed to kill. Yvonne wore a tight, low-cut black dress that showed off her large bosom, and Tamika wore a tight purple miniskirt and a sheer violet blouse. Puddin' had on electric blue spandex pants and a pale blue camisole top. Tamika, ever the sweetheart, had offered to let Regina wear another outfit she had brought over to Yvonne's, but Regina declined, saying she was five inches shorter than her friend. Puddin' wickedly added that Tamika was also twenty-five pounds heavier, but Yvonne and Regina soothed Tamika's feelings by assuring her that the weight was in all the right places, which was true.

Perks had two levels. On the ground floor was a bar and restaurant, and a number of small tables where people sat and looked good while checking each other out and deciding who they wanted to wind up with at the end of the night. Women sexily swayed their heads and shoulders to the tempo of the music, pretending that they didn't notice the men standing at the bar or against the walls looking their way. The men struck their best poses, trying to look cool or mysterious as they struggled to catch the eye of the woman of their choice.

Once a match was made, the couple would go downstairs, where there was another bar, along with a coatroom, rest rooms and a large dance floor ringed by a few small tables, and continue the flirting game.

The girls sat down at one of the ground floor tables, and Regina bought the first round of drinks. They were only there for a few minutes when they noticed three guys at the bar checking them out. One was about six feet five, with cream-colored skin, hazel eyes and curly hair. Another was almost as tall, a bit on the husky side, with a chocolate complexion, and a goatee and large white teeth that he kept flashing in the girls' direction. The third man was thin, about six feet tall, with medium-brown skin and protuding ears. Regina noticed that he was the most sullen in the group, and showed no interest in checking out the women. When the hazel-eyed guy raised his glass toward their table in a mock toast, his sullen friend made a remark and turned toward the bar. Regina couldn't hear what he said, but his body language communicated that it wasn't flattering. She decided she didn't like him.

The guys didn't look like they were from Harlem; they were preppy and clean-cut. Although they appeared too old to be college students, they had that university look about them—the look that said they thought they had more on the ball than anyone in the place.

Tamika was excited and giggly. But then she was always getting excited about attention from men, which was pretty funny, since she never gave any of them her telephone number. Tamika's boyfriend, Chink, was in prison, and although she still liked to go out, Tamika was faithful. But Regina noticed that Yvonne and Puddin' were slyly checking the guys out. They looked like they had money and jobs, and that made them hot prospects in Harlem.

The trio waited until Yvonne paid for a second round of drinks before they approached the table, a fact that did not go unnoticed by Regina.

"Mind if we sit with you young ladies?" the hazel-eyed man asked. Yvonne shrugged her shoulders; Regina could see she was intending on playing it cool until she got more information, but Puddin' gave them the go-ahead. Regina twirled the stirrer in her rum and Coke and said nothing. She had told her friends that she was only going to stay for a couple of drinks anyway, and since there were four women and only three men, she decided to do everyone a favor and even the number as soon as she finished her drink.

She had to prepare for a meeting with an editor from *Cosmopolitan* in a few days, and she needed to get up early to do some research on the Internet. She remained aloof, slightly turning in her chair and occasionally looking at her watch, alerting the guys that she was uninterested and unavailable.

The hazel-eyed guy's name was Robert, and he seemed to be

the spokesman of the group. The goatee guy was David, and the sullen man was introduced as Charles. Charles smirked as the girls introduced themselves in return.

"What did I tell you?" he said to David.

"Our friend here is clairvoyant. He said he knew one of you girls was named Tamika," said Robert with a laugh. That brought a laugh from everyone at the table except Regina. While at school in Philadelphia, she had heard the guys refer to girls as "Tamika-babes," meaning fly but stupid street women. She hadn't heard the term used in New York, but she was sure the meaning was the same.

It turned out the men were graduate students at Columbia University, and were just out on the town for the evening. They were subtly letting the girls know they were men with a bright future—good catches—and they got the reaction they expected. Yvonne leaned over in her seat so that her cleavage showed a bit more and began to playfully flirt with Robert. She had always been attracted to light-skinned men, so Regina knew he was going to be her pick. Tamika was giggling and laughing with David, who seemed pleasantly surprised at the attention. Puddin' was doing her best to strike Charles's interest. She crossed and uncrossed her legs. She licked her lips as she talked. She made suggestive remarks, accentuated by knowing looks. But Charles acted bored, occasionally looking over at his friends as if to say "How long do we really have to stay?" Regina decided she really didn't like him.

She tried to get up to leave, but Yvonne pulled her back down in the chair, and whispered for her to stay a little longer. She looked at her friend inquisitively, but Yvonne offered no explanation. She was hitting it off with Robert, and Tamika's little-girl style seemed to appeal to David, but Puddin' was still making no headway with Charles. He answered questions when asked, but initiated no conversation on his own. Then she said that he looked a little like her father. Charles smiled and asked if she considered her father handsome, and grateful for the little bit of interest shown, Puddin' began to loudly gush about how much she adored her father. Suddenly Charles guffawed loudly. "Great. An Oedipus complex."

His friends all started laughing, and Puddin' and Tamika laughed along, although they didn't catch the joke. Yvonne did, though, and she looked none too pleased. Finally, Tamika asked what an Oedipus complex was, and Robert explained that Oedipus was a Greek hero who was the only man clever enough to solve the riddle of the Sphinx.

"Look at that. I guess he's saying you're smart," Tamika told Puddin' with a smile.

"An Oedipus complex refers to a man who is in love with his mother," Regina said icily.

"Well, that, too," admitted Robert.

Tamika still didn't get it, but Puddin' did.

"I said that I adore my father, not that I'm in love with him," she said to Charles with a pretty pout designed to appeal.

Regina coolly picked up her pocketbook to leave. All evening she had noticed the sideways glances between the guys when one of her friends used a word incorrectly, something Tamika was famous for doing. It was painfully apparent that the men thought she and her friends were easy pickups, and it bothered her that the women were confirming their beliefs. Yvonne, who obviously knew what was going on, was still flirting with Robert. Tamika, who probably didn't have a clue, was prattling on to David, and Puddin' was still trying to talk to Charles even after his insulting put-down. Regina decided to leave before she said something that would ruin everyone's good time, but at that moment Charles announced that he was leaving because he had to study for an examination. Regina paused briefly, then smiled seductively, leaned over and lightly placed a hand on his arm.

"I don't mean to bother you, but could you do me one small favor?" she asked in a low husky voice lightly brushing her fingers over his muscled bicep.

"What's that?" Charles asked, finally with some interest in his voice.

"Would you wait five minutes before you go? I'm leaving right now, and I don't want anyone to see me walk out the door with someone too ignorant to know the difference between an Oedipus complex and an Electra complex."

Charles's mouth dropped open, and his friends started to laugh, which started the girls laughing.

"Yeah, that's right, Sir Brainiac. Only a man can have an Oedipus complex. A woman in love with her father has an Electra complex," said Robert in between gulps for air. "I think you just got a lesson in humility."

Regina stood up, and walked out the club without looking back, so that no one would see the big grin on her face.

And the score, she said to herself with satisfaction, *is Harlem, 1—Preppyville, 0.*

2

"OH, REGINA, HONEY, THE ARTICLE SOUNDS JUST SO fabulous. My goodness, you come up with such terrific ideas. But you know, I just don't think it's fit for our magazine, sugar."

Regina grimly munched on a stalk of celery as she sat on a bench in busy Rockefeller Center and listened to *Cosmopolitan* magazine's features editor. She lightly brushed a hand over the shoulder of her cream-colored suit to remove a leaf that had floated from God knows where—no trees were in sight—then casually put on her Gucci sunglasses. She hoped Margaret Peterson would believe it was to shield her eyes from the sun's glare. What she really wanted to do was hide her disappointment.

Regina had been trying for more than a year to get into the popular women's publication, but with no success. Each time she queried them about an article, whether by mail, telephone, or in person, honey-blond, Southern-belle Maggie would say, "I just don't think it fits our image, dear." Or, "Ooh, terrific. But we did it last year, sweetie."

Regina had offered to take Maggie to a nice Japanese restaurant for lunch while she made her latest story pitch. She hoped a good meal, and perhaps a glass of rice wine, would enhance her chances this time. But after Regina arrived, smartly dressed and ten minutes early despite a fifteen-minute delay on the subway, Maggie breezed into the office, and trilled her finger at her as she crossed the room. "Oh, Regina. I'm just so sorry, but I don't think I'll have time to have lunch with you. I don't need to tell you how crazy things can get around here. I declare, just absolutely crazy. Do you mind terribly if we just grab a quick bite around the corner?" She didn't wait for Regina to answer before she said, "Great, I knew you'd understand, sugar."

So Regina was forced to make her latest pitch while sitting on a public bench, shooing away greedy pigeons and trying to talk over the annoying clamor of the jackhammer drilling into the street a few feet away. So much for atmosphere.

"I know I've told you before, but I'm going to go ahead and suggest again that you read the magazine on a regular basis to get a feel for exactly what we're looking for, sweetie," Maggie said in a honey-toned drawl. She took a dainty bite from her cucumber sandwich and added. "You're a very talented writer, and we'd love to have you write one of our *Cosmo* pieces. It just takes time."

The usual kiss-off. Regina sighed and uncrossed her legs. One of her stockings caught on a splinter from the wooden bench, causing a run. *Great,* she thought as she watched the tiny train-track pattern speed down her leg. She tugged her skirt down to cover it, causing the run to spread farther. Rejection, a wasted lunch, and a run in her brand new pantyhose. Was it her imagination, or did Maggie, who was dressed in a chic lavender pantsuit, smirk at her stocking disaster? *I'd better get out of here before I tell her that she's added too much collagen to her lips,* she thought.

Regina stood up, smoothing the wrinkles from her skirt. At least she was going to have the satisfaction of signaling the meeting was over rather than waiting to be dismissed.

"Okay, Maggie, I really do think a story on homosexual urgings in heterosexual women would interest your readers, but you know best. Thanks for having lunch with me, though. I know you're busy." Regina smiled.

Maggie rose, and the two women shook hands warmly the way professional young women do when they don't really like each other.

"I'm never too busy for you, Regina. We want to get new voices in *Cosmo*. I want you to keep contacting me with story ideas. I know we'll be able to work together soon," Maggie said sweetly.

After the blonde sashayed off, Regina bent down and put her small spiral memo pad back into her burgundy leather briefcase she had bought as a graduation gift two years before. She could hardly afford it at the time, and splurging an extra twenty-five dollars to get gold initials embossed on the supple leather seemed an extravagance, but she'd decided that since she was stepping into the business world, she was going to step out in style.

Not that she really needed a briefcase. As a freelance writer she spent the majority of her time at her apartment in front of a computer, banging out articles, or surfing the Internet doing research, or on the telephone finding clients. *Cosmopolitan* magazine notwithstanding, she was quite successful. Just the month before she had feature-length articles in two national magazines, and a cover story in a regional publication.

Regina had majored in journalism at Temple University in Philadelphia with the intention of becoming a hotshot reporter at the *Washington Post* or some other major newspaper, but after completing student internships at the *Philadelphia Inquirer* and the *New York Times,* she decided a newsroom wasn't her cup of tea. Daily deadlines didn't give her the time to do the longer feature articles she enjoyed, and she would have to be in the business for years before she could rack up enough experience to apply for a columnist's job. In her junior year she had begun to do a few freelance pieces for small magazines and newspapers, and after a while she had begun to build a clientele. Her best-paying client was *People* magazine, which paid $500 a page. It was published weekly, and she could usually count on doing one or two articles for them a month, so she was bringing in between $1,000 and $2,000 a month working part time while still in school. Then she started writing an occasional piece for *Seventeen* magazine which paid $1 a word, and since most of her pieces were 500 words she made out pretty well. By her senior year she had decided to make freelance writing a career, if only temporarily, while she decided what else she could do with her journalism degree. By the time she graduated, she had managed to place articles in hip-hop magazines like *Vibe* and *The Source,* and had even done a few articles in larger publications like *Newsweek, Essence, Family Circle,* and *Playboy.* She was bringing in a respectable $3,000 to $5,000 a month freelancing.

However, the work wasn't steady. There were weeks when she had no writing assignments at all, but she was able to afford her apartment on the classy Upper West Side, and buy a few nice outfits. Dining out was a luxury, but she was a good cook, and her other needs were minimal, so she was doing all right for herself. She wasn't interested in dating; she had had more than her fill of men in her previous life. But still, there were plenty of men vying for her attention. One of the more persistent was Earl Masters, a married African-American editor at the *New York Times.* She flirted with Earl just enough to get writing assignments in their *Sunday Magazine,* which paid well and gave her greater name recognition in the magazine industry. She went to business lunches with the portly middle-aged editor to discuss story ideas, and once or twice to dinner, but to Earl's dismay she kept the relationship strictly business. Industry rumor had it that he slept around quite a bit, and that the very proper Maggie Peterson was one of his part-time paramours. Regina suspected that was the real reason she was having such a hard time breaking into *Cosmopolitan*.

Regina walked over to a corner ice cream stand and ordered a double scoop of Breyers vanilla ice cream to top off the raw carrots and celery she'd eaten for lunch. She only ordered the vegetables in an attempt to bond with the ever-dieting Maggie. Not that it had helped. *From my lips to that bitch's hips,* Regina said to herself as she took a bite of ice cream. *The article was perfect for* Cosmopolitan *and she knew it.*

Regina lightly swung her briefcase while eating her ice cream cone and walked toward Broadway to catch the subway home, stopping along the way to join a small crowd enjoying a lone saxophonist's rendition of Duke Ellington's *Satin Doll.* She bopped her head to the music, singing the words in her head.

> *Cigarette holder, that wigs me*
> *Over her shoulder, she digs me*
> *Out cattin'*
> *That Satin Doll*
> *Baby can we go, out skippin'*
> *Hold on amigo, you're flippin'*
> *Speaks Latin. That Satin Doll.*

A patrol car approached but didn't bother to slow down to shoo away the panhandler; to do so would have held up the traffic that was always jammed around New York City's midtown area. Regina dug a dollar out of her purse to drop in an old black top hat in front of the soloist, then moved on down the street, weaving through the hordes of businessmen rushing back from lunch.

A lady never eats or drinks in the street, she was told as a youngster. Eating while walking was worse. Licking an ice cream cone was cause for damnation. A lady never shows her tongue in public, her mother lectured her. Though Matilda Johnson Harris died thirteen years before, Regina remembered her rules and offered an obedient concession, mouthing her vanilla ice cream rather than licking the sides.

Matilda moved from Trinidad to Harlem as a teenager with her parents in the early 1940s. Though Matilda and Mama Tee knew each other as children, the two were never friends. Matilda's family "had money," and the rest of the families on 119th Street considered them snobs. The Johnsons opened a little grocery store on Lenox Avenue between 117th and 118th Street, and Matilda, an only child, received a good Catholic-school education. She attended City College for two years before misfortune befell the family. Her father died from a heart attack and unscrupulous lawyers cheated her mother out of the family bank account and the family business.

Matilda quit school and got a job as a bookkeeper in a real estate office to support herself and her mother. Two years later her mother died, and she married James Harris—half black, half Puerto Rican—and had four children. The two oldest, both boys, died hours after birth. Matilda had Brenda when she was forty-two, and Regina four years later. James taught his children a smattering of Spanish, and proudly trotted them out to count to ten in their paternal grandfather's native tongue. But when Regina was six, James left the family for a younger woman who had presented him with what he wanted most in life—a son.

"He said he wanted the Harris name to continue after him. *Hmmph!* All you have to do is look in the telephone book and see there are too many damn Harrises now," Matilda would say bitterly when she spoke of her departed husband.

Matilda took it as a personal shortcoming, and was even ashamed, that she was raising her children in a broken home. Good West Indian families stayed together. Still, she tried to raise

her daughters as good West Indian girls—demure, polite, and la-
dylike. Brenda went along with the routine while in elementary
school, but in adolescence she rebelled with a vengeance. She
started sneaking out of the house after her mother fell asleep and
hanging out on the roof drinking wine and smoking reefer with a
fast crowd. Matilda would throw her nose up in the air and say
nothing when she heard the newsy women in the building, like
Miss Libby and Miss Bernice, gossiping about Brenda, but then
would walk upstairs to their third-floor apartment and beat the
teenager with a garrison belt—one of the few things that James
Harris had left behind—for shaming the family. She even tried ty-
ing Brenda to the bed so she couldn't sneak out at night, but
Brenda became a master at slipping through the knots.

While Brenda was fresh and sassy with adults, Regina was polite and charming. She always said "Good morning" to the older
ladies in the block, and offered to run errands when their own
children were out running the streets. Regina could read at an
early age—her mother said intelligence ran in the family—and
every Sunday afternoon after church she would sit with blind
Miss Bee, who lived on the ground floor, and read her passages
from the Bible. The neighbors agreed that Regina was destined
for great things. Maybe she would be a lawyer. Or even a doctor,
they agreed.

Regina was seven years old when she showed her mean streak
in public for the first time. She was outside playing hopscotch
with her friends, while fat old Miss Libby was on the stoop of
their tenement complaining about a painful swollen corn on the
little toe of her left foot. Miss Libby was wearing sandals, because
shoes would be too painful, she told the ladies sitting in beach
chairs on the stoop. They clucked compassionately.

Miss Libby sighed with a shake of her head. "And every time
I go to the foot doctor and get it cut off it just pops back in a
couple of months."

"Chile, I don't know why you keep wasting good money on them doctors. They don't know what they doing," Miss Bernice said with a snort. "What you need to do is go to one of them root people to give you herbs to rub on it."

"Bernice, why don't you just stop with all that root stuff. You act like you're still in Savannah or something," Miss Libby snapped at the woman. "I ain't putting no smelly plants on my toe."

"I'se just trying to help, Libby," Miss Bernice said in a wounded tone. "And I heard some of them root people really know what they doing."

"I just bet you did," Miss Libby said with a sly smile. "Everybody knows you done went to that one on 115th Street to get some roots put on that woman fooling around with your Jimmy."

"And so what if I did?" Miss Bernice answered defensively, trying to hide her embarrassment as the other women on the stoop chuckled at her expense. "Someone gots to stop that woman from taking paychecks from men what's got chillen to feed at home. I hope all her hair falls out and she gets boils in her fool mouth."

"Stop getting mad at me, I wasn't trying to hurt your feelings or nothing," Miss Libby said as she raised her foot to look at her throbbing toe. "Anyway, that woman ain't nothing but a little slut. What's her name? Eva, right? She always was loose. Her mama, too. Running around here with no bra on so men could look at her titties. That whole family ain't nothing but loose women."

"Well, if that little heifer ever got in my man's face I wouldn't worry about no roots. I'd throw some lye in her face," another of the women on the stoop said with a haughty sniff.

"Girl, don't nobody want that broke-ass man of yours." Miss Libby laughed.

"At least I got a man," the woman snapped back.

"I would too if I were to settle for just any fool that got something swinging between their legs," Miss Libby shot back.

The woman opened her mouth to say something else, but then just sucked her teeth and marched into the building.

"Poor girl can't bear to hear the truth," Miss Libby said solemnly. The other women said nothing, not wanting to be the next target of Miss Libby's wicked tongue.

"And someone should tell her that her daughter is smoking cigarettes and hanging around with boys instead of going to school," Miss Libby continued. "I ain't gonna be the one to tell her because it ain't none of my business. But I swear, someone should tell her."

"I know what you mean," Miss Bernie said, nodding her head, glad that the subject had turned from her. "I done see that girl hanging around with a bad crowd."

"Hanging out with that fresh-ass Brenda," Miss Libby said with a snort. "Now that's a bad-ass little girl. You know she came home at three o'clock in the morning the other day. Stumbling up the steps all drunk. Woke up half the building. And one day I smelled reefer in her clothes. And I wonder if her prissy mama knows that girl's screwing half the men in the neighborhood."

Regina's face flushed with heat as she waited behind two girls for her next turn to hop inside the chalked lines on the sidewalk. *I hate you, Miss Libby. I hate you, you old fat woman,* she thought.

"You mark my words, that girl's going to pop up pregnant any minute now, and she ain't going to know who to blame as the father," Miss Libby continued, oblivious to the little girl's hate.

Regina suddenly broke out of the hopscotch line, and walked over to the stoop where Miss Libby sat.

"Oh, Lawd. I hope I didn't hurt your feelings, Regina," Miss Libby said, as she fanned herself with a folded copy of the *New York Post*. "I know you're not like your fast sister. I don't know why your mother don't send that child away before she gets in some real trouble."

Regina smiled and walked up real close to Miss Libby, then

brought the heel of her foot down hard on the woman's corned toe.

The old woman let out a piercing scream.

"Oh, Lord, I hope I didn't hurt your toe, Miss Libby," Regina said sweetly, emulating Miss Libby's previous tone. "I don't know why you don't just go upstairs and take care of your foot instead of minding everyone else's business."

Regina turned to the incredulous women sitting on the stoop and said innocently, "I hope everyone has a nice day," and gaily skipped upstairs.

Later that evening, the ladies from the stoop told Matilda what had happened. While admitting that "Libby ain't had no right talking about her sister like that," the women admonished Matilda that Regina shouldn't get away with attacking a grown-up.

Matilda waited until after supper to confront her younger daughter. She knocked on the girls' door and entered to find Regina—as usual—reading a book.

"Okay, my young lady. What happened?" Matilda said as she sat at the foot of the bed.

Regina poured her heart out, telling her mother how Miss Libby's mean words about Brenda had made her feel like a golf ball was caught in her throat.

"Then my head started to hurt, and I just wanted her to stop, Mommy. I hate it when people try to act like they're better than us," Regina said, as tears gathered in the corners of her eyes. "She wouldn't have said those things about Brenda if you were around, and I wanted her to know she can't say those things when I'm around, either."

Regina buried her head in her mother's lap and began to cry. Matilda comforted her, and praised her for standing up for her family.

"Family's the most important thing, Regina. And I'm very proud of you for wanting to defend you sister," Matilda said as she stroked Regina's long, thick hair. "Your family is your blood, and blood runs through the veins, always remember that. A person who turns their back on their family, turns their back on themselves."

After she calmed Regina down, Matilda went into the kitchen, removed the garrison belt from its hook, and warmed Regina's bottom.

"Because there is nothing, *nothing,* that can excuse the fact that you attacked an old woman."

It was a year later, when Regina was in the third grade, that she first met her best friend. She was reading Louise Meriwether's *Daddy Was a Number Runner,* under the desk when her teacher said she had an announcement to make. Yvonne Jamison would be joining them, she said, pointing to a skinny light-skinned girl with fat, red pigtails and a starched petticoat dress. Yvonne had attended St. Mary's Catholic School, Regina would find out later, but when her father ran off with another woman, Yvonne's mother was forced to send her little girl to public school. Regina had seen the girl in the neighborhood but they had never talked. She felt sorry for Yvonne, who stood in the front of the room biting her fingernails as she looked out at the sea of unfriendly young faces.

When Miss Robinson asked if anyone would volunteer to show Yvonne where to hang her coat, Regina raised her hand— the only child in a room of thirty to do so. Regina was Yvonne's guide for the day, and escorted her to the bathroom and lunchroom, and even walked her home that afternoon. The two found that they had a lot in common. They belonged to the same church, both their mothers were from Trinidad, both were abandoned by their fathers, and both were bookworms. They became inseparable.

It was Regina who introduced Yvonne to chubby little Tamika, a friend since kindergarten. A year later the trio met a bully named Janet Robinson. She was nicknamed Puddin' because her chocolate complexion was so smooth, and her facial features were so sweet. Puddin's temperament did not match her name. She was taller than the rest of her classmates, and picked on them incessantly. One day when Regina was waiting in line for double-dutch, Puddin' pushed in front of her. The two began fighting and Regina, who was as small for her age as Puddin' was tall for hers, had a black eye and bloodied nose by the time the teachers broke up the fight. Puddin' had to beat Regina up three times that day, and two times the next, because Regina kept coming back for more. It was a matter of principle, she said. She was right and Puddin' was wrong. Yvonne finally brokered a peace between Regina and Puddin', and eventually the hard-won respect that the two girls had for each other grew into a friendship.

Regina was an eighth-grader when the neighborhood gossips' prophecies were fulfilled and Brenda gave birth to a little girl she named Renee. The father could have been the young numbers runner on 120th Street, the sixty-six-year-old married man who worked in the hardware store on Lenox Avenue, or any one of the hundreds of men whose car Brenda climbed into on 126th Street and Park Avenue. Crack had become the scourge of Harlem, and Brenda became hooked at seventeen, turning tricks to support her habit. An hour after Renee was born in Harlem Hospital, Brenda disconnected her IV and sneaked out of the hospital in search of a hit, leaving the premature and underweight baby to the mercy of the overworked and underpaid nurses. Luckily, one of the janitors at the hospital lived in the Harrises' building, and notified Matilda that she was grandmother to a crack baby. Matilda dutifully went to the hospital every day to visit her only grandchild, and two weeks later, with lips pursed and grand head held high, she brought the child home to their tiny apartment.

"We take care of our own," Matilda would tell Regina as the two sat in the evening crocheting baby clothes after Renee dropped off to sleep. "The nurse in the hospital said the city could put that poor baby in foster care if she were too much trouble for me. How can my own blood be too much trouble?"

Three months later Matilda died of a stroke, and thirteen-year-old Regina was left to take care of herself, and her infant niece. A social worker from the Department of Public Welfare stopped by the apartment once, but luckily—or unluckily—Brenda was home at the time. With some coaching from Regina, she convinced the overworked civil servant that since she was eighteen, and legally an adult, she was capable of keeping the home together.

In reality Brenda was only interested in supporting her drug habit. It was left to Regina to find a way to pay the rent and utilities and put food on the table.

THE SMOKY SMELL of the jasmine incense she had lit that morning rushed to greet Regina as she returned to her apartment. She stopped to straighten her framed Paul Goodnight print on the foyer wall. The three brightly painted women in the picture seemed to smile in appreciation, and Regina smiled back a "you're welcome," before entering the small living room and dropping her briefcase in a corner next to a large earth-tone vase of dried flowers.

The red light on the answering machine was blinking wildly, and the digital display indicated seven messages had accumulated in the four hours she had been gone. Regina sighed as she plopped into the kente cloth-covered couch and kicked off her cream-colored pumps onto the small Indian rug. Her feet and her head ached, and the soft cushions and sweet jasmine aroma were encouraging her to take a nap.

A warm breeze from the half-open window fluttered the overgrown leaves of her hanging plant, adding to the leisurely atmosphere. Regina considered disconnecting the telephone and ignoring the answering machine's demanding flashes, but she couldn't afford to miss an important call from a magazine assigning an article on short notice. When a new writer looked like they were going to miss a deadline or handed in terribly screwed-up copy, an editor would sometimes put in a frantic call to Regina to come and save the day. *People* magazine was famous for their last-minute frenzied cries for help.

"Regina, it's me. I thought you were going to give me a call yesterday. Hurry and call me at work. I got something to tell you." Yvonne's excited voice spilled from the answering machine. The call had come in at 12:15 P.M., just minutes after Regina had left the apartment to meet Margaret Peterson.

"Regina. Are you there? I really have to speak to you. It's important. Hurry up and call." Yvonne again. 12:45 P.M.

"Regina, I know you'd better not be there ignoring me. Get away from the computer and pick up this phone. It's really important." 1:15 P.M.

The rest of the calls were also from Yvonne. She must have decided that Regina was indeed home and screening her calls, because the calls were all within fifteen minutes of each other, each begging Regina to pick up the telephone.

Hmmm . . . I wonder what's going on, Regina thought lazily as she cuddled deeper into the couch pillow. Yvonne's voice was excited but not frantic, so Regina knew no one was sick or hurt. She glanced at the clock. It was almost 4:30 now, so Yvonne was getting ready to leave work. Regina decided to wait an hour and then call her friend at home. Dozing off, she was awakened a few minutes later by the ringing telephone. The answering machine picked up before she could reach the receiver, and Yvonne's voice bellowed through the room.

"Where the hell are you, girl? Don't make me go to 71st Street and bust down your door!"

"I dare you." Regina giggled into the receiver she now held to her ear.

"Ooh! I knew you were there all along."

"No, no, I just got in a few minutes ago. What's going on?"

"Girl, you're not going to believe this, but remember those guys we met at Perks last Friday? Well, one of them has the hots for you. Bad!"

"You've been blowing up my answering machine to tell me that? I thought it was something important," Regina said as she picked at her cuticles with a nail file that had been lying on the table. "Okay, which one wants me?"

"The one you fucked up." Yvonne's grin could be felt even over the telephone.

"You're kidding, right?"

The two women started laughing.

Yvonne, Tamika, and Puddin' had stayed at Perks for two hours after Regina left; hazel-eyed Robert and sweet-smiling David had stayed with them. Charles left shortly after Regina made her exit, Yvonne said, but later returned to the nightclub and sat back down at the table. He leaned toward Robert and said something the girls couldn't hear, but which made Robert guffaw, "You want to know, you ask them."

Charles had glared at his friend, then turned to the ladies, smiled and asked, "So what's up with your friend? Does she live around here or what?"

"You know we didn't give up any info," Yvonne told Regina on the telephone. "He started asking a million questions about you, but we just told him he should have asked you when you were there. Puddin' was real pissed because she was kissing up to him all that time and he never paid her any mind, then you insult him and he acts like he's ready to eat your dirty panties. Her words, not mine." Yvonne giggled.

Charles finally gave up and left again, Yvonne said. Around

2:00 A.M., Yvonne and Robert and Tamika and David exchanged telephone numbers and went to their respective apartments. An hour later Robert called Yvonne—"He woke up Mama at three A.M. Boy, was she mad."—saying that he wanted to make sure she had arrived home safely.

"But he really only called because Charles made him," Yvonne said. "He said Charles felt left out when he found out that he and David had gotten telephone numbers and he hadn't. He said he wanted me to give him your number to pass on to Charles later, but I could hear Charles coaching him in the background," Yvonne said. "I told him no way. If Charles wants your number he has to ask you. So then he asked how Charles was going to ask you if he didn't know how to contact you. I just told him I had no idea, but he wasn't getting the number from me."

Yvonne and Regina started laughing again.

"So then get this, Regina. *Charles* calls me at home last night and offers me money if I'd give him your telephone number."

"Whaaaaaaat? You're kidding!"

"Nope. He only offered twenty-five dollars, so I just told him to kiss off. I didn't like him anyway. Cheap bastard."

"Dang. Good thing he didn't offer fifty, or I'd have been in trouble, huh?" Regina laughed.

"Girl, you know I wouldn't sell you out for fifty. I got him up to a hundred."

"Yvonne! I know you didn't sell that man my number!" Regina shouted as she jumped from the couch.

"Calm down and relax, Regina. No, I didn't. I just promised him I'd get you to agree to meet him again."

"You did what!" Regina was angry and tickled at the same time. "I can't believe you're actually pimping me for a lousy hundred bucks."

"Oh Regina, please. I didn't promise him you'd go to bed

with him, only that you'd meet him. Besides, Robert and I will be there, so it'll be kind of like a double date."

"And when and where is this double date supposed to take place?"

"I figured we may as well meet at Perks on Thursday night. They have jazz on Thursdays. That way when you and Charles start fighting I can be downstairs on the dance floor grinding my hips into Robert. Did I mention that Robert's father is a lawyer, his grandfather is a lawyer, and his great-grandfather was a lawyer? This dude has money in his family, and he's on his way to making some himself. I'm not going to let this one slip away."

Regina quietly shook her head as she smiled into the telephone. "Okay, but you'd better be careful, because not all that glitters is gold."

"Yeah, but that's okay," Yvonne replied coyly. "I also accept diamonds, pearls, and other shiny jewelry."

"Okaaaaaay. I would say you're beginning to sound like Puddin', but I'm not even going to go there on you." Regina laughed.

"But what's this about Tamika giving up her telephone number?" Regina asked. "Since when did Miss 'I'm-going-to-wait-for-Chink-forever' start giving out her digits? She usually just flirts, and then calls it a night."

"I asked her about that, too. She said she told him about her jailbird boyfriend, and he said he just wanted to stay in touch as friends," Yvonne replied nonchalantly. "I think she really likes him, though, and he really seems like a nice guy. Who knows? Maybe she's finally ready to move on."

"Hmmm . . . interesting."

"Yep, I'd say the whole evening was interesting. Anyway, is Thursday cool with you?"

"Yeah, sure, why not?" Regina said, sighing. At least she'd get a few drinks, and maybe a free dinner out of the evening. Perks had a good menu.

"Good. I'll call and set it up. Oh yeah, listen, how about going to the movies tomorrow night. Tamika and Puddin' want to see that new Denzel Washington movie, and I said I'd tag along. You got plans?"

"I do now! You know Denzel's my man. What time?" Regina said excitedly. Larry Fishburne may be sexy. Wesley Snipes might have machismo, but as far as she was concerned, Denzel Washington was the the man of all men.

"Girl, stop wetting your pants. I knew if I mentioned Denzel you'd be down," Yvonne said with a laugh. "I figured we'd meet at Tamika's around seven, then head to the movie theater on Eighty-sixth and Lexington."

"Cool. I'll see you then."

3

THERE WAS A TIME WHEN THERE WERE DOORMEN IN Harlem. Polite, smiling, uniformed doormen who stood inside the grand lobbies of the large apartment buildings and accepted deliveries, hailed taxis, and held out their white-gloved hands for their generous tips at Christmas.

That was when white folks still lived in Harlem, before they stampeded away in the early 1900s when blacks started their migration uptown. Only they weren't black or African-American back then—they were Negro or colored or worse. But whatever they were called, they were unwelcome. Most people credit—or blame—depending who's talking, real estate agent Phil Payton for bringing blacks to Harlem. In 1910, he talked a white landlord into letting "good Negroes" move into an apartment building on 134th Street. Within a matter of months all of the whites moved out of the building, leaving more vacant apartments available for black tenants.

Regina now walked down that same block, eighty years later, to get to Tamika's apartment building.

Regina didn't bother pushing the button for the elevator, since it was always broken; she headed straight for the stairs. The windows in the hall were nailed shut, and the heat inside the building was even more intense than outside. The higher she climbed, the more oppressive the heat became. She finally reached the fourth floor and walked down the hallway to the last apartment on the right. The door was slightly ajar, and she could hear Yvonne yelling *Jeopardy* answers at the television.

"Hey, girl! I didn't hear you come in," Tamika said with a grin as she looked up from the brown corduroy couch. "You're just in time for Double Jeopardy."

"I'm winning." Yvonne grinned, her eyes still on the television as she swirled her can of Pepsi. "I tell you, I need to fly to California and show Alex Trebek what's what."

Regina flopped down on the couch next to Tamika, slipping her feet out of the yellow sandals that perfectly matched the yellow and white shorts set she wore. Her unstockinged legs glistened with sweat, courtesy of the summer evening heat and the three flights of stairs she just climbed.

"I swear, Tamika, I'm not going to visit you again until that elevator is fixed. It's too hot to be climbing all those stairs," she said as she fanned herself with the newspaper she was carrying.

"The elevator *is* working," Tamika said as she turned a small whirling fan around to face Regina.

"You're kidding?"

"Nope. We've got a new landlord, and he's really fixing up the building."

"Now you tell me." Regina groaned.

The three laughed.

"Shhh . . . ," Yvonne commanded as Alex Trebek once again began to speak.

"This man was the only bachelor president of the United—"

"Who's Buchanan!" Yvonne and Regina yelled at the same time, prompting Tamika to laugh.

"Okay, Yvonne, you've finally got some competition," Tamika teased.

"I can handle it," Yvonne said defiantly as she took a long gulp of Pepsi. She leaned forward on the love seat as if ready to spring out of a starting gate while she waited for the next question.

"This nonmetallic element is one of five—along with iodine, bromine, chlorine and astatine—that are called halogens."

"Fluorine," Regina shouted.

"Wrong," Yvonne shouted.

"Wrong nothing!"

"You didn't say it in the form of a question."

"Bunk you!" Regina laughed.

"Hey, I don't make the rules. I just enforce them when I don't know the answers." Yvonne laughed in return.

"Okay, ladies! The diva has arrived." The women turned around as long-legged Puddin' strode into the room wearing a pair of denim cut-off shorts that barely covered the bottom of her buttocks.

"Yo, Puddin'. Don't you know that Daisy Dukes played out?" Yvonne said shaking her head critically. "I'm glad we decided to meet over here. Mama would have had a fit if she saw you in those shorts."

"If you got it, flaunt it," Puddin' said with a shrug of her shoulders. "Tamika, you'd better do something about that damn elevator," she said as she flopped on an old overstuffed chair. "This shit doesn't even make sense."

"It's working, Puddin'. You shoulda pushed the button."

"Damn. Why doesn't someone put up a sign or something? I walked all of them steps for nothing. Shit."

She fished a wrinkled reefer joint and a crumpled book of matches from her hip pocket, then reached for the ashtray that sat on the coffee table next to Regina.

"Dang, Puddin'! You're just going to light up without even asking where the kids are?" Yvonne frowned.

"If the kids were home I'd a heard them by now," Puddin' replied with an exhale of smoke. "Anyone want some?"

"No, thanks," Regina said.

"I wasn't asking you, Miss Goody-goody. One little gunshot wound and you turn party pooper. You'd think you got shot in the head instead of the shoulder. Wanna hit, Yvonne?"

"Nah! Mama's been on a tear lately, and I don't want her smelling that stuff in my clothes. And don't blow your smoke in my direction. I don't want to get blamed for something I didn't do."

Puddin' passed the reefer in Tamika's direction, but she, too, declined.

"You know I'm quitting," she said sheepishly.

"Cool. More for me," Puddin' said, taking another long puff.

"What made you decide to quit?" Regina asked Tamika.

"You mean she ain't tell you about her voodoo rebirth?" Puddin' said wickedly.

"Oh, Puddin', stop. It's not voodoo," Tamika said, tossing a sofa pillow at her friend.

"What's not voodoo?" Regina asked.

"Tamika went and got a reading from some Gypsy and now she's decided she's not getting high anymore. She's got religion all of a sudden," Yvonne answered.

"She's not a Gypsy. She's a priestess," Tamika protested.

"Yeah, a voodoo priestess," Puddin' teased.

"No she's not. She's a Yoruba priestess." Tamika frowned. "It's an African religion."

"Like I said. Voodoo."

"Shut up, Puddin'," Tamika snapped.

"Don't pay her any attention, Tamika. She's just trying to get you riled up," Yvonne said soothingly. "Why don't you tell Regina what your priestess said?"

"Yeah, do tell," Regina said with interest. "How did you get involved with an African priestess?"

"A girl from my job introduced me to her. She's not African, but she's in an African religion. Yoruba. She gave me a reading."

"Really? Does she use tarot cards or tea leaves or something?" Regina asked.

"No. Some kind of seashells. But she's really good."

"Really? What did she say?"

"She told me about my life. She knew that I'm a single mom. She said I don't like my job. She said I like the outdoors and that I've witnessed violence."

"No offense, Tamika. But couldn't all of that fit just about any woman over twenty-five living in Harlem?"

"We told her that," Yvonne said with a sigh.

"Okay. But she also knew that I was a twin."

"You're not a twin," Regina said.

"Yes I am. I had a twin brother but he died two days after we were born," Tamika said excitedly.

"I didn't know that."

"I never talk about it. But she knew."

"Okay. That could be attributed to a lucky guess," Regina said cautiously.

"Yeah? She also knew that my mother just died, and that I got her insurance money."

"How much of it does she want?" Puddin' teased.

"Very funny! And she also said that one of my children had a stomach operation. And you know Darren got his appendix taken out last year. So there!"

"Tell her what else she said," Yvonne said while trying to hide a smile.

"I'm not going to say anything else if you guys are just going to tease me." Tamika pouted.

"Aw, come on," Yvonne said soothingly. "We're just having fun. Tell Regina what she said about Chink."

"She said he's cheating on me."

"He's cheating on you? How can he be cheating on you if he's in jail? Is she saying Chink's turned homo?" Regina asked sincerely as Yvonne and Puddin' burst out laughing.

"No, she said it's with a woman. I specifically asked, and she said he's cheating on me with a woman."

"Come on, Tamika. They don't have women at Comstock. How can he be cheating on you?" Regina reasoned.

"I don't know. I'm just telling you what she said."

"And you believe her?"

"Well, she's right about everything else."

"Okay. Whatever. What's this woman's name and how much did she charge to tell you that your man who can't be cheating on you is cheating on you?" Regina said, throwing up her hands.

"Ravioli. Her name is Ravioli," Puddin' said, laughing hysterically. "Chef Boyardee Ravioli."

"It is not! Her name is Abiola—a-bee-O-la. It's a Yoruba name!" Tamika said angrily. "Y'all shouldn't be talking about a priestess like that."

"Oh, is some ravioli-eating little African demon going to come and spook me tonight?" Puddin' began laughing again.

"See, Puddin'? You need to stop smoking that stuff. It makes you act stupid," Tamika huffed.

"I'm the one that's acting stupid? You're the one who gave your hard-earned money to some voodoo witch."

"She's not a witch. She's a priestess. And it's not voodoo. It's Yoruba. YO-roo-ba!"

"Actually I've heard of it before," Yvonne cut in. "It's a religion from Nigeria. They worship a bunch of saints or gods or something, right?"

"They're called orishas," Tamika said. "And everyone is protected by one of the orishas even if they don't believe it. For instance, you're probably protected by Obatala, Yvonne. He's the leader of the orishas and he's the peacemaker, just like you."

"Well, you certainly seem to know about this Yoruba thing. How long have you being seeing this priestess?" Yvonne asked suspiciously.

"I've only been to her a few times. I been to a few of their services. And I bought a book and read up on it. *Tales of Yoruba Gods and Heroes.* You should check it out. It's interesting."

"Thanks, but I'll stick with Catholicism," Yvonne said dryly.

"Well, it kinda reminds me of Catholicism in a way. I mean Catholics have saints, and Yoruba have orishas. Only in Yoruba each person has an orisha protecting them. It's like, more personal, you know?" Tamika leaned forward, nodding her head as she spoke. It wasn't often that she knew more on a subject than her friends, and she was enjoying her moment.

"And who protects me?" Puddin' asked, still laughing.

"What do you care? You think it's all stupid, anyway," Tamika snapped.

"Yep. But I still wanna know."

"You're probably protected by Oya. She's the orisha that's always fighting, and likes to be mean to people for no reason."

"Now that does sound like Puddin'." Regina grinned.

"Yep. And I bet you're under Oshun, Regina. She's the goddess of love, who always has a lot of men and good luck. And people are always underestimating her because they think she's so pretty she doesn't have any brains."

"Hey, how come I don't get the goddess of love?" Puddin' protested.

"Because you're too evil," Tamika said, sticking out her tongue.

"Okay. I have the peacemaker. Puddin' has the fighter. Regina has the lover. What about you?"

"I'm under the protection of Elegba. He's the baby of the orishas, and everyone likes him and looks out for him. Just like you guys always do for me."

"Only because you don't know how to look out for yourself, Doo-Doo Head," Puddin' said, not unkindly. "I can't believe you're falling for this shit."

"It's not shit, Puddin'. Stop saying that."

"Make me."

"Oh, please. Why don't you just ignore her, Tamika? You know how she is," Yvonne said, without bothering to look up.

"Yeah. I'm Oya, the fighting goddess. If you don't watch out I'm going to kick your ass," Puddin' teased Tamika.

"Moving right along, here, are we going to sit around this hot house all night or are we going to the movies like we said?" Regina asked as she fanned herself with the newspaper. Puddin' had turned the fan toward herself and there was no breeze blowing through the windows.

"Yeah, let's get outta here. I want to make a stop down the street first, though," Puddin' said as she leaned back in the chair.

"Ran out of dope?" Tamika asked sarcastically.

"Yep," Puddin' answered matter-of-factly. "Hey, Regina, I hear you're going out with that creep we met at Perks. What's up with that? I thought you didn't like him."

"I don't. I'm just doing it to get Yvonne off my back."

"Yeah, right. Don't do me any favors. If you don't want to go out with him, don't," Yvonne said defensively.

"Don't even try it! Weren't you on my phone yesterday begging me to give him a chance? Don't be trying to switch up now, girl!" Regina shot back.

"All I'm saying is that he's probably not really such a bad guy. It won't hurt you to spend one evening with him. If nothing else you'll get a couple of free drinks out the deal, like you said. What do you have to lose?"

"The guy's a loser," Puddin' grumbled.

"Why? Because he didn't want your tired ass," Yvonne teased.

"Puddin', you don't have a problem with me going out with him, do you?" Regina asked, suddenly concerned that Puddin's pride might be hurt. The striking young woman seldom missed her intended target, and Regina wondered how she would react.

She needn't have worried.

"Problem with what?" Puddin' took a deep hit off the joint and leaned farther back in the chair, then lazily licked her lips and slowly exhaled a wispy cloud of smoke before continuing. "I didn't want him. If I did I would have scooped him up. But hey, I don't mind you sampling my rejects."

"Boy. Talk about rewriting history." Regina laughed. "But no problem. If that's how you say it is, that's how it is. Now come on. Let's get the hell out of here before I suffocate."

THE SKY WAS CLEAR when Regina emerged from her apartment building Thursday evening wearing a black minidress with a long, thin gold chain around her neck, but by the time she arrived at Perks in a taxi, a slight drizzle had begun to fall. She pulled a webbed gold scarf from her purse to throw over her head, but decided against it. There was something tender, almost romantic about the rain. The feel of the soft mist on her skin made her feel feminine and alluring. She walked into the club and smiled when she heard the soft strains of "My Funny Valentine" being played by a jazz trio. The gray-bearded piano man caught her eye and nodded as she strolled by, unconsciously swaying her hips to the music. She spotted Yvonne at a table and sat down with her friend.

"Looks like you've made a new friend," Yvonne said with a wide smile. "You look nice tonight."

"Thanks, so do you."

Yvonne wore a green silk blouse, with an olive green skirt, and her long red hair was pulled tightly into a French braid. A lipstick-rimmed glass of rum and Coke sat on the table, and a whisper of smoke rose from a cigarette that idled in the ashtray.

"I've never been here for jazz night. It's pretty nice, isn't it," Yvonne said. "This is your kind of scene. You're such a jazz fiend."

"Not all jazz. I like the big-band sound. So where are our dates?"

"Don't worry, they'll be here," Yvonne said as she signaled for the drink waitress. "May I get two more rum and Cokes, please?"

"Sure, honey. Be right back." The waitress flashed a smile that indicated Yvonne had tipped her richly for a previous drink.

"So what did Charles say when you told him I'd meet him?" Regina asked as she checked her lipstick in a compact mirror she pulled from her purse.

"Mmmm . . . don't try and front for me. You know you're flattered that he's trying to chase you down." Yvonne grinned, prompting Regina to laugh.

"Okay, I admit it. I sure didn't think he would want anything to do with me after—"

"Hold up, hold up. They just walked in the door."

Regina snapped her mirror shut, and turned slightly to see Charles taking large strides in their direction, and Robert rushing to keep up.

"Well, I see you ladies are early," Charles said, looking at Regina as he spoke. "I thought women were always supposed to be fashionably late."

"We're always fashionable, but seldom late," Yvonne said, smiling as Robert sat down next to her.

"Mind if I have a seat?" Charles asked Regina, nodding to the chair next to her.

"Not at all. How've you been?" Regina said warmly.

"Much better now that I've finally got a chance to see you again. Your friend here's been giving me a hard time. Did she tell you that I've been trying to get in touch with you?"

"She might have mentioned it," Regina teased.

Just then, the drink waitress appeared balancing her tray with one hand as she placed paper napkins in front of Yvonne and Regina. Yvonne started to hand the woman a crumpled bill, but Regina stopped her. "Oh, no. I think it's my turn to pay," she said, and very slowly reached for her purse.

"I've got it," Charles said hurriedly, reaching for his wallet.

"Well, actually these rum and Cokes are already paid for, courtesy of the band," the waitress said evenly, but with a hint of a smile.

"Huh?" Charles looked at Robert inquisitively. Yvonne lowered her head and began to titter.

"Oh, how nice," Regina said calmly, then turned to Charles and said, "Would you excuse me for a moment?" and without waiting for a reply she got up and headed for the piano player, returning a few minutes later.

"Wasn't that nice of him," she said sweetly as she slid back into her seat.

"Is he a friend of yours?" Charles asked.

"No. He noticed that Yvonne and I were sitting alone and he was just trying to be friendly," she said as she took a sip of the drink. "You know, I've always depended on the kindness of strangers."

Charles leaned his elbows on the table, cupped his face in his hands and grinned, revealing his pearly white teeth.

"Well, my dear Miss DuBois, I can certainly see how strangers might want to show you some kindness. I do declare, any fool with eyes in his head would want to show you a little kindness. You are certainly looking mighty stunning this evening, if I might say."

"Why, how kind of you, sir. And please just call me Blanche," Regina said in feigned Southern accent as she began to fan herself with a napkin. "My, it is so very hot in here."

"Cat on a Hot Tin Roof?" Robert offered.

"A Streetcar Named Desire," Charles and Regina said simultaneously. Charles threw his head back and started laughing. *He's actually rather nice,* Regina thought as she joined him. They stopped for a moment, looked at each other, and started laughing again. *And damn good-looking, even if his ears do stick out a little too far from his head.*

"Well, at least you have the right playwright," Yvonne told a crestfallen Robert.

"Actually, I'm more up on African-American writers." Robert shrugged his shoulders and reached over and took a sip from Yvonne's drink.

"Are you a fan of August Wilson?" Regina asked with a sly smile.

"Who?" Robert frowned.

"The guy who wrote *Fences* and *Jitney,*" Charles spoke up. "Award-winning African-American playwright."

"Bingo," Regina said, nodding her head and smiling in his direction.

"Okay, okay, I'm not up on plays. How about poets? Ask me anything about poetry," Robert said as he put his arm around Yvonne. "Especially black poets."

"Okay, I've got one for you. What poet originated the line, 'I know why the caged bird sings?'" Regina asked.

"That's too easy," Charles protested.

"Really?" Regina arched an eyebrow and coolly took a sip of her drink. "I bet he doesn't get it."

"Dang, Regina . . ." Yvonne frowned.

"Maya Angelou," Robert said, nudging Yvonne quiet.

"Wrong!" Regina grinned.

"Wrong?" Robert jerked his head back in surprise.

"Wrong? But . . ." Charles's brow furrowed for a moment, then he suddenly broke out with a grin. "Oh, I got it." He turned back to his friend, laughing. "You heard her. You're wrong." He laughed.

"Maya Angelou did write it," Yvonne protested. "It was the title of her autobiography."

"True. But Regina said the poet who originated the line," Charles said with a broad grin. "That was the hint."

"Well, that was a trick question, then. No fair," Robert said.

"Okay, then. Since you know now it wasn't Maya, who was the poet?" Regina asked.

"Hell if I know. Langston Hughes?"

"Nope." Regina grinned.

"Countee Cullen? Claude McKay?"

Regina shook her head.

"Okay, give me a hint. During or after the Harlem Renaissance?" Robert asked, exasperation creeping into his voice.

Charles chuckled. "Prior to the Harlem Renaissance, buddy."

"Prior? Who was prior? Phyllis Wheatley?"

Regina grinned and shook her head.

"I suppose you know?" Robert shot Charles an accusing look.

"I do. Paul Laurence Dunbar." Charles grinned at his friend.

"I am really impressed," Regina looked at Charles with new-found appreciation. "Do you know the title of the poem?"

"I can't say that I do," Charles admitted.

"It's 'Sympathy.' But that's okay. You can still hang out with me." Regina grinned.

"Oh, and I guess I'm not good enough to hang out with you."
Robert sucked his teeth.

"Forget them. You're hanging with me, anyway," Yvonne said
soothingly. "Come on, let's go downstairs and dance," she said,
pulling him up from his chair and toward the stairs.

"Was it something we said?" Charles grinned at Regina after
they left.

"Nothing they won't get over," Regina said, tilting her head
slightly to the side and smiling back at him.

"You're so bad," Charles said.

"And you're downright naughty."

"Not around you. At least not anymore. I'm not going to get
my head snapped off again," Charles said leaning back in his
chair with a smile. "I was lucky to get out of here alive the other
night."

"I don't know what you're talking about," Regina said lowering her eyes and taking another sip of her drink.

"Well, I guess I deserved it."

"You did."

"I thought you didn't know what I was talking about,"
Charles said, leaning toward Regina with a grin, and tapping her
nose with his finger. "I told you you were bad."

They laughed again for a moment, then Charles motioned for
the drink waitress.

"Chivas Regal straight up, and a rum and Coke for the lady."

"I haven't finished this drink yet," Regina protested.

"Yes, you have. I'm not going to sit here and let you sip on a
drink paid for by another man. Waitress, would you also send a
glass of your cheapest beer over to the piano player. Give him my
thanks for entertaining my date in my absence, but tell him his
services are no longer needed."

"Oh, no you don't!" Regina cried.

"Oh, yes I do," Charles said calmly, handing the waitress a

credit card and a twenty-dollar bill. "We'll be running a tab, but here's a little something for you for being such a sweetheart," he told her.

"Okay then, I'd like a Rémy Martin on the rocks," Regina said.

"I thought you were drinking rum and Coke." Charles grinned.

"That was before you decided you were in charge of my drinks," she smirked.

Charles looked at her with a smile. "Okay, but as long as I'm paying the cost, I'm playing the boss."

"Try at your own risk," Regina fired back.

Charles laughed again.

"Okay, whatever the lady wants," he told the waitress.

"Yes, sir," she said demurely, then silently mouthed "Nice," to Regina as she walked away.

Regina swirled her drink and contemplated her companion. His hair and mustache looked freshly trimmed, and he smelled of Drakkar Noir aftershave. He wore a black T-shirt with a sports coat, green khaki pants with pleats in the front, and expensive, black penny-loafers. *Handsome, very handsome,* she decided, *and sexy, too.* She had noticed the first night they met, and tonight she noticed again, the broadness of his chest and shoulders. Though his khaki pants were loose fitting, she could still see the form of powerful hips. Unlike many good-looking men, Charles seemed unaware of his looks, although he certainly was overly confident about his intelligence. He had a definite air of arrogance about him that she found a desirable trait rather than a character flaw. *I bet he's good in bed. Oh, Lord, why am I going there?* she thought. She wanted to blame it on alcohol, but she'd only had one drink. *Chalk it up to going months without sex.*

"You seem like a man used to getting his way," she said with a smile, trying to get her mind off his body.

"Really? I hope I'm not overbearing. I'm just having fun,"

Charles said, concern suddenly entering his voice. "Look, I really want to apologize for my behavior Friday. I was up two nights before cramming for a test. I don't even know why I let Robert talk me into coming out that night. Still, that was no excuse for my rudeness."

He paused, but Regina said nothing.

"Um, that was your opportunity to say, 'Skip it,' or 'I understand,' or something to that effect," he said.

"Not a chance."

"Not a chance?"

"Nope. You were beyond rude. You were patronizing. In fact, you were downright nasty. Your being stressed out over a test doesn't justify you poking fun of people, and trying to make them look stupid," she said curtly.

"Well, didn't you just do the same thing to Robert?"

"That was different. We were all playing around. You were making cutting remarks that you assumed were over our heads."

"True, but I said I'm sorry."

"I heard you."

They fell silent for a moment. The waitress came over and placed their drinks on the table, and started to walk away. Charles stopped her, and picked up Regina's half-finished rum and Coke and placed it on the waitress's tray.

"How about we start over again? Hi. My name is Charles Whitfield. I'm from Philadelphia and I'm finishing my last year at Columbia Law."

"Hello Charles. I'm Regina Harris. It's a pleasure to meet you."

"The pleasure is all mine. May I make a toast?" he asked, raising his glass.

Regina smiled and dutifully lifted her glass.

"Here's to the start of a beautiful relationship," he said.

They clinked glasses, then sipped their drinks.

"So what part of Philadelphia are you from?"

"Wynnefield. Are you familiar with Philly?"

"I graduated from Temple University."

"Really? When."

"Two years ago."

"Great, the same year I graduated from Penn," he said.

Figures he went to an Ivy League school, Regina thought. The students at the University of Pennsylvania traditionally took pleasure in looking down at their poorer counterparts at Temple University only a few miles away.

"What was your major?" he asked Regina.

"Journalism. I wanted to become a hot-shot columnist for the *Washington Post.*" Regina laughed.

"Good for you! So what are you doing now?"

"I'm a freelance writer. Mostly magazines."

"Any that I might have heard of?"

"Depends on what you read. I've been in *People* magazine, *Newsweek,* the *Times Sunday Mag,* and a few other national publications," she said, not bothering to feign modesty.

"Pretty impressive." Charles whistled. "You must be good."

"I am." Regina grinned.

"I have no doubt." Charles smiled back. "Should I ask for your autograph now or later?"

"Sorry, I don't give autographs after six P.M."

They both laughed.

"So, do you live in Harlem?" Charles asked a little too casually.

"No. I have a place on Seventy-first Street on the West Side. And yes, I have my own apartment." Regina smiled.

"Whew! You must be doing well," he said with a grin.

"What about you? What are your plans after you finish at Columbia?"

It turned out that his father was a City Councilman in Philadelphia, as well as the minister of the largest African-American

Baptist church in Philadelphia. His mother was a senior partner in a prestigious law firm. His older sister had attended medical school, but married a fellow student right after graduation. "She picked the right one, too," Charles said proudly. "The guy is a plastic surgeon and bringing in at least three hundred thousand dollars a year after taxes."

Charles said his mother wanted him to join her law firm—he had already interned there twice—but he wanted to strike out on his own.

He was also interested in politics, he told Regina, and worked on two local political campaigns in Philadelphia. "Both candidates lost. Maybe I'm a jinx." He laughed. Still, Charles said, he could see himself running for office sometime in the distant future. But only after he made his first million in law.

"Being a public servant is all well and good, and it's even prestigious, but if my mother weren't a successful attorney our family would barely have been able to make ends meet on Pop's salaries from City Council and the church," he said.

"You mean you wouldn't have been able to join the squash club or the equestrian team?" Regina teased.

"Don't knock it." Charles laughed. "And don't pretend like you haven't led the good life yourself."

"What do you mean?"

"No offense, but it's obvious that you didn't grow up in the same environment as your girlfriends. Look at you. You're educated, intelligent, well-mannered, articulate, you've got a great career, and you live in a classy neighborhood," he said with a smile and a swirl of his drink. "To top it off you're knock-out beautiful, and you carry yourself like a lady.

"Your friends, on the other hand . . ." He started to laugh.

"My friends what?" Regina's hackles began to rise, but Charles prattled on, unaware that he was treading on dangerous ground.

"I'm sure they're nice girls and all, but it's obvious that they're not in your class."

"What do you mean?" Regina frowned.

"Well, I'm not knocking your friends, but you have to admit that they're pretty rough around the edges. I mean, come on, blue spandex pants? And don't get me wrong, Yvonne's a nice person and all, but I thought her boobs were going to fall out of her dress the other night. Anyone could see they were fast women. And I'm not trying to be insulting, but anyone could look at them and know they were on the prowl."

"What's wrong with looking for men," Regina asked in an annoyed voice that Charles missed.

"Nothing. But you have to wonder what kind of men they're going to attract."

"Really? Robert doesn't seem to have a problem with the way Yvonne was dressed." Regina took another sip of her drink so Charles couldn't see the frown on her face.

Charles leaned back and took a gulp of his drink, and signaled the waitress for another round.

"Well, that's Robert. I'm certainly not interested in getting involved with that type of women."

"*That* type of women?"

"Look, I'm obviously getting you angry, and that's not my intent. Why don't we drop the subject," he said, finally picking up on Regina's change in mood. "I'm not here to talk about your friends, I'm here to talk about you. I don't even know how I started on the subject."

"No. I'm interested in what you meant by that type of women. What type is that? I'm curious," Regina asked in a softer tone, trying to con Charles into continuing.

"Well, I noticed you were the only one whose fangs didn't appear when Robert mentioned that we're finishing up law school."

"Oh," Regina said slowly. "So you think they're blood-sucking gold diggers?"

"Look at you, trying to put my words in my mouth," Charles said playfully. "No. I'm not saying that. But I do think they're looking for potential husbands with money. I guess there's nothing wrong with that, though. I just try to steer clear of women like that."

"And you get all of this from your observations the other night?"

"Well, yeah," he answered a little defensively. "If I'm off the mark, tell me, but I pride myself in being a good judge of character."

Regina looked at him, considering for a moment throwing her newly arrived drink in his face. Instead she took a deep breath and closed her eyes. *I knew this evening was going to wind up a disaster,* she thought. *He's the pompous ass I thought he was from the beginning. It's a shame he's so damn sexy.*

He reached over and put his hand atop hers on the table. "Okay, I pissed you off again. I was just being honest."

"I'm not pissed," she said lightly. "I'm just glad you don't think I'm that type of woman."

"I know you're not!" he said eagerly. "As soon as you opened your mouth the other night I knew I was mistaken about you, Regina. You've got class to spare." He caressed her face as he looked deeply into her eyes. "You're the type of woman I want to get to know better."

She placed a hand on his face in return and giggled. *This guy has no clue,* she thought. *Perhaps I should show him just the type of woman I am.*

"So, I'm your type, Charles?" she said with another giggle.

"Yep," he said with a smile that indicated he thought he had made a love connection. "You're just my type."

"Good," Regina said in a husky whisper. "Let's get out of

here. The music's too loud, and all of this smoke is bothering me."

Before he could answer, Yvonne appeared at the table, her makeup damp and her hair in disarray. "Hey, they have disco downstairs. You guys should come on down. We're having a ball," she said as she sat on the edge of the table fanning herself.

"Where's Robert?" Charles asked, scanning the now crowded club for his friend.

"In the men's room. He'll be back in a minute. C'mon Regina, walk me to the ladies' room," she said, getting up and trying to pull Regina by the arm.

"No. Charles and I were just leaving."

"Leaving? Aren't you guys having a good time?"

"We're having a fabulous time, aren't we, Charles? We just want to find a change in scenery. I'll call you tomorrow," Regina said as she picked up her purse and winked at Charles.

"Well, at least walk me to the ladies' room," Yvonne said with a puzzled look on her face.

"No. We really have to split. I'll call you tomorrow."

Yvonne looked at her friend in amazement. "Okay, you do that," she said slowly.

"Hey, Charles," Yvonne called after them as they headed to the door. "You owe me a hundred bucks."

The cool evening air hit her as she walked out the door and she shivered slightly. Charles put his arm around her shoulders and pulled her close and kissed the tip of her nose.

"Chilly?"

"A little," she said and softly pressed her body against his. He took off his jacket and threw it around her shoulders. He kissed her on the forehead, and they started walking down Manhattan Avenue. "Okay, dear lady. Where would you like to go?"

"Well, I just wanted to go someplace where we could finish

talking. You're really such a fascinating person. I could talk to you all night."

"Oh, come on," he said with a grin. "Stop stroking my ego."

"No, I'm serious. I'm having such a nice time with you. Let's just find a place where we can have a drink and finish talking, but not another smoke-filled nightclub. And not someplace too loud."

They walked silently for a moment, his arm around her shoulders, her head leaning into his body.

"Look. I don't want to sound presumptuous or anything, but my place is just a few blocks away. I have some wine and some CDs. We could go there and talk for a while, and when you're ready to leave I can put you in a cab."

When she didn't answer right away, he continued.

"I'm not trying to put the rush on you. I know you're not that type of woman. You said you wanted to finish talking and so did I. I'm sorry if I offended you."

"No, not at all," Regina said slowly. She stopped and turned her face up to his. "Charles, I know you wouldn't try anything. You're a gentleman and I trust you. I would love to go to your place and have some wine and talk."

Ten minutes later they were at his cramped but neat apartment.

"What would you like to hear," he asked after he'd seated her on a small sofa and served her a glass of white Zinfandel.

"Do you have any Duke Ellington?"

"You like jazz," he said with a smile. "Like I said, you're my kind of lady."

"Well, I like old jazz. Mostly big-band era, especially Ellington."

"Really? What's your favorite?" Charles asked as he flipped through his CDs. "No, let me guess. 'Sophisticated Lady'?"

"Actually, it's 'Satin Doll.'"

"That fits you, too. But unfortunately I don't have the Duke, but how about Earl Klugh?"

"He'll do," she said with a slight shrug and a huge smile. "If you like him, I know I'll adore him."

"Are you always so accommodating?" he asked, after he placed the CDs in the stereo and joined her on the couch.

"I try."

"I like a woman who tries."

"Then you'll just love me," she said, snuggling close to him. He brushed her hair back from her face and kissed her on the nose. "Okay, lady. What would you like to talk about?"

"I want to talk about you," she said circling the material of his T-shirt with her finger.

"What about me?"

"I want to talk about why you keep kissing my nose, and not my lips," she said as she softly rubbed his chest.

"I didn't know if you wanted me to kiss you," he answered, his breath becoming heavy.

"I want," she said softly kissing him on the lips. "I want very much."

He took her in his arms and pressed his lips hard against hers and pulled her body against his own. She disengaged her lips, then began flicking her tongue around his lips and face, while letting out soft moans as his hands moved from her shoulders to her breasts.

"Oh, Charles, this is going too fast. I don't know if we should be doing this. We've just met," she said half-pulling away from him. "I don't want you to think that I . . ."

"Shhh. I'm not thinking anything, okay? Just relax. Everything is all right," he said pulling her back and kissing her neck and shoulders. She could feel his hands feeling for the zipper in back of her dress. Suddenly her dress was pulled down past her shoulders, revealing her small firm breasts. He began kissing them softly, causing her to moan louder. Suddenly she pushed him away and jumped up from the couch, pulling her dress back over her shoulders.

"No. This is crazy. We're going way too fast," she said as she stumbled backward.

"No, no, no. It's okay. We're both grown. It's all right, baby," he said as he stood up and walked toward her. "Come on, relax."

"No, this isn't right," she protested as he pulled her into his arms. "I shouldn't be doing this."

"Baby, it's okay. I'm not going to try and force you to do anything you don't want to do, okay?" he said as he began kissing her neck again and tugging at her dress. "I just want you to do what you feel. There's nothing wrong with that, is there? Just do what you feel."

Regina let her head loll back, closed her eyes and began to moan again as his hands firmly massaged her shoulders and back.

"You want me to do what I feel?" she said between gasps as he began to lick and nibble one of her hard nipples.

"Yeah, baby, do what you feel," he said in a husky voice.

"Can I do this?" she whispered as her hand reached down and began to rub the large bulge in his pants.

"Oh, baby, yeah," Charles groaned as he continued to kiss her breasts.

"Can I do this?" she said as she expertly unzipped him and reached inside and stroked his penis, causing him to throw his head back and groan louder.

"Can I do this?" she asked as she pulled up his T-shirt and began to flick her tongue over his chest and down his stomach.

"Can I do this?" she asked again as she lowered herself to her knees in front of him and lightly kissed the tip of his throbbing penis.

"Tell me, Daddy, can I do this?" she said looking up at him with a smile on her glistening lips. "Can I do this?"

"Oh yeah, baby, do it—*please.*" Charles groaned as he grabbed her hair and directed her head to his groin.

She lowered her head again, and began kissing and flicking her tongue over his penis, finally forming her lips in the shape of an O and taking it into her mouth.

"Oh, damn!" he moaned his hips thrusting back and forth. "Oh, yeah, baby. Do it."

When she felt he was ready to explode, she stood up and looked at him with a smile. Then she stepped out of her dress and panties and stood in front of him naked. He reached for her, pulling her close in a kiss, but she pulled away and pulled his T-shirt over his head.

"Oh, God, I want you," he groaned as she began rubbing and massaging his arms and chest while kissing his neck. "Oh, damn, you're good."

"Am I, Daddy?" she whispered as she tugged at his pants which obediently fell to his knees. She gently pushed him into a sitting position on the couch, and taking her foot pushed the pants down to the floor, then away from his feet.

"Am I really good, Daddy?"

"Oh God, yes," he moaned, reaching up and pulling her down on him as he lay back on the couch.

"Mmm . . . I want it to be good for you. I want you to like it," she said as she straddled his hips and slowly lowered herself onto him, stopping when just the tip of his throbbing penis had entered her moist vagina.

"You like it, Daddy?" she teased. "You want more?"

"Oh God, yeah," he moaned.

She eased down another inch, then began slowly moving up and down on him, lowering herself just a little farther each time. "Tell me you like it, Daddy. You do like it, don't you?"

Instead of answering, Charles reached up and grabbed Regina

by the shoulders, and pushed her down as he thrust his full length into her. It was her turn to gasp and moan as he continued to thrust into her deeply, massaging her back and kissing her neck as their bodies met. Then he grabbed her body tightly close to his, and suddenly turned so that he was on top of her. He pinned her shoulders to the couch and kissed her hard on the lips, then began thrusting even deeper into her, causing her to squirm and moan in ecstasy.

This wasn't going the way she planned. She was going to tease him, bring him to the brink of orgasm and then leave, but he was making her feel so good, there was no way she was going to stop now.

She pushed her hips to meet his every thrust, sticking her tongue into his ear and nibbling his earlobe. Finally she felt his body begin to shudder, and his groans became even louder. The thrusts became deeper, stronger, faster, and she became equally caught up in the rapture. Then with a loud "Oh God!" he thrust one last time pushing so deep inside of her she felt he touched her heart. She let out a scream as her juices mingled with his in a thundering climax. A few minutes passed before either could speak. Finally he raised his head and said, "Are you okay?"

She laughed and kissed him on the forehead. "Yeah, you?"

"I've died and gone to heaven," he said and began softly kissing her around her nose and eyes. After a few minutes he got up from the couch, picked her up as if she were a baby, and carried her into the bedroom, laying her tenderly on the bed. They made love again, and again.

Charles may not have been the most skilled lover Regina ever had, but what he lacked in experience he made up for in ardor. And his attentiveness touched her. He stroked her hair and kissed her tenderly as they made love, and praised not only her lovemaking skills, but the smoothness of her skin, and the sound of her moans.

Dawn had broken by the time they finally reached exhaustion.

"I think we've earned some sleep, don't you?" he said as he covered her with the sheet. "By the way, I make a helluva good breakfast. I hope you like omelets."

When his rhythmic snores attested to the fact that he was in a deep sleep, Regina quietly climbed out of the bed and tiptoed into the living room. If she couldn't get him one way, she would find another.

She quickly put on her clothes, then reached into his pants pocket and took out his wallet. She opened it and removed the $525 cash it contained along with his four credit cards. *A platinum American Express. I'm impressed,* she thought with a smile. She placed the now empty wallet on the couch so that it was in plain sight. She crept back into the bedroom, and removed the gold watch he had placed on the dresser, along with three gold chains and a ruby ring she also found. She fished a wrinkled plastic shopping bag out of the kitchen trash and dumped the bounty inside. She went to the bathroom and combed through her hair, washed her face and reapplied her makeup. Then she took the plastic shopping bag and hooked it to the shower nozzle and pulled the shower curtain closed. With that done, she tiptoed out of the apartment and went home.

4

"YOU DID WHAT!!!??"

"Don't shout, Yvonne. I think I have a hangover," Regina grumbled as she balanced the receiver of the cordless telephone between her ear and shoulder and opened her refrigerator in search of orange juice.

The ringing telephone had awakened her, but now she was sorry she had answered, and sorrier still that she had told Yvonne about her little prank. She wasn't nursing one of those major hangovers that comes after a good drunk; she had the slight physical punishment that reminds you that you overdid it, just a bit, the night before. Her head was lightly throbbing, she was thirsty as hell, and she wanted to get back to sleep. But Yvonne refused to get off of the telephone.

"Uh-huh, you were drunk? That's why you robbed the guy?"

"I didn't rob him. I left the stuff there in his apartment. He'll find it when he goes to take a shower. What time is it, anyway?" Regina asked, noticing the stream of bright sunlight peering through the curtain.

77

"Two o'clock in the afternoon."

"Well, he must have found it by now, otherwise the police would already be knocking on your door."

"*My* door?"

"Well, he doesn't know how to contact me, so I would guess he'd get your address from Robert and send the police over to your place." Regina eyed the glass of mango juice she had just poured. Kind of dingy looking, she decided, and checked the expiration date on the bottle. Still two days to go. She took a sip and spit the sour liquid out into the kitchen sink. So much for expiration dates. She felt even more nauseous than before.

"And I would have sent them right down to Seventy-first Street so they could haul your ass to jail," Yvonne said. "Why, Regina? Just tell me why the hell do you do shit like this?"

"Because he got on my nerves. All that B.S. about this type of woman, and that type of woman. I mean he really pissed me off—" Regina tried to explain.

"And you got so pissed off at the guy you went to his apartment and *robbed* him?"

"Stop shouting! I'm right here." Regina found a bottle of grapefruit juice in the back of the refrigerator and pondered whether she should take another chance. Deciding no, she swung the door shut and padded barefoot back to the bed and climbed in. "I just wanted to show him that he doesn't know anything about what type of woman I am, you are, or anyone else is. I was striking a blow for women everywhere."

"By fucking his *brains* out?"

"Well, I was kind of horny."

"Oh cripes."

"I'm just being honest. I don't see why you're so upset, anyway. The guy's a creep. Aren't you at work? I think I hear your boss calling you," Regina said as she pulled the lightweight blanket over her head.

"My boss isn't here, so don't even try it," Yvonne said. "And the fact that Charles is a creep doesn't justify you committing a felony."

"It's not a felony. I left the stuff there. Why are you making such a big deal about this?" Regina said in exasperation.

"Just for the record, did you even take into consideration, even for a second, that *your* best friend is involved with *his* best friend?"

"Well, no. But I don't see what this has to do with you and Robert," Regina said hesitantly. *Shit, I didn't think about that. No wonder Yvonne's mad.*

"It doesn't. But you should have at least wondered if I would have to feel some repercussions behind your stuff," Yvonne thundered. "What if Robert thought I was playing the same stupid game you're playing? Huh? What if?"

"Okay, Yvonne. I'm a bad girl. I'll go to church and make confession or something. Now can I go back to sleep?"

"Go ahead. But if you wake up dead it's because Robert gave me hell and I dropped a bomb on your building."

"He's not going to give you hell, Yvonne. And if he does, have him call me and I'll tell him you had nothing to do with it. I'll even tell him that you're not speaking to me anymore."

"That might turn out to be the truth," Yvonne huffed.

"Fine. I'll call you when I wake up and you can tell me off some more."

"Okay. You better, 'cause I'm not finished with your ass."

Six hours of sleep later Regina sat at the computer in the throes of writer's block and wondered if she should use the down time to call Yvonne. *No use in putting it off,* she thought with a sigh. She reached for the telephone to call Yvonne, but dialed Tamika's number instead, hoping to find out if Yvonne was still on the warpath.

"Hello. You've reached five five five nine seven two one,"

four-year-old Darren's taped voice said over the telephone. "We not in wite now, but weel call you wite back," his little sister's voice finished. In the background Tamika's voice was prompting her to ask callers to leave their name and number, but the little girl just giggled. "Gimme the phone, Sissy!" Darren's voice took over. "Leave your name and number and we'll get right back to you." *Beep.*

"Hey, Darren. Hey, Sissy. Aunt Regina loves ya'll. Tamika, call me back when you get this message." Regina hung up the telephone and turned back to the computer. She was supposed to send a 2,000-word article on the crisis of the African-American middle class to *Time* magazine in three days, and she had barely written 300 words. She had interviewed the authors Manning Marable and Harold Cruise for the article, and done hours of additional research, but for some reason she couldn't think of anything to write. *Maybe I should ask Charles if I could interview him and some of his stuck-up middle-class friends,* she thought meanly. Still trying to find an excuse to leave the computer, she called her sister Brenda's house to see how the family was doing.

"What's up?" a young girl's voice said over the telephone. "Speak now or forever hold your peace."

Regina laughed. Every time Renee picked up the telephone she had a new line to share. It rattled Brenda's nerves that her thirteen-year-old daughter was trying to assert her independence. Of course, it wouldn't have been as funny if Renee were answering Regina's telephone in that manner, but since it was Brenda's telephone it was cute as hell.

"Speak or forever hold your peace, huh? Is that P-E-A-C-E or P-I-E-C-E?" Regina teased.

"Hi, Aunt Regina! Hey, I didn't even think about that. Which one's catchier?" Renee asked, excited at her aunt's wittiness.

"Where's your mom?"

"Out making shalat, or whatever it is they call it," Renee answered. In the last five years Brenda had become a born-again Christian, a Jehovah's Witness, a Hebrew Israelite, and now an Orthodox Muslim. She was no doubt trying to cover all bases to atone for the behavior of her youth, but her daughter was unimpressed. Renee used to tell anyone who would listen that she was an atheist, but she recently switched to calling herself agnostic, "Just in case," she explained in her most adult manner.

"Cool. So what have you been up to? How's school?"

"I hate it. Same as usual," Renee said matter-of-factly. "Where've you been? I thought you were coming up last weekend."

"I know. I'm sorry, but I got caught up with some other stuff," Regina apologized.

"Yeah, I don't blame you. I wouldn't come up to Queens if I didn't live here, either. Can't you talk Mom into moving back to Harlem? This place is a drag."

"She just wants you to grow up in a good environment," Regina said soothingly.

"Oh yeah, right. This ain't no good environment. It's no different from Harlem, except I don't have my peeps," Renee said angrily.

"Yeah, I know you miss your friends," Regina said.

"No, you don't," Renee whined. "I live all my life in Harlem and then I get dragged up here in this hellhole and it's supposed to be for my own good. This sucks."

"Life sucks, dear child," Regina said absentmindedly as she sifted through a stack of bills sitting by the computer.

"Yeah. Especially mine."

"You'll live, sweetie. Have your mom call me when she gets home."

"Wait a minute, wait a minute," Renee said frantically.

"What's wrong?"

"Aunt Regina, I'm serious. You have to talk to Mom. This is

killing me. You don't know what it's like. I'm stuck here with no friends, no one to hang out with, and Mom trying to turn me into an Arab. I hate it here," Renee whined. "I'm going crazy and no one even cares."

"Aw come on, Ray-Ray. It can't be all that bad."

"Yes it is! I hate it. Can't you talk to Mom, please? Tell her we should move back to Harlem. *Please?*"

"Come on now, Ray-Ray. Calm down. You've only been there three months. Give it a chance," Regina said, concerned now about the desperation in her niece's voice. "You're going to make friends. Just give it some time."

"No, I'm not. I thought you would understand. I don't want to live here and I don't want to live with her!"

"Ray-Ray, what the hell is wrong with you? That's your mother you're talking about!" Regina said, raising her voice.

"I know, I'm sorry. But I can't stand it. You don't know what it's like having to live like this. Why can't we all live together again? Then at least I could get to hang out with you like before," Renee said, beginning to cry. "It's like you don't love me anymore."

"Ray-Ray, come on. You know that's not true. You're still my little girl. Come on, stop crying."

"I'm not crying," Renee lied.

"Honey, you know I love you. Look. I'll come out tomorrow night and we can go to the movies, okay? Just me and you."

"Why can't I move in with you, Aunt Regina? You're the one that raised me for real. Mommy doesn't really know me. I love her and all that, but it's not like me and you."

"She's your mother, Renee—" Regina started.

"I know. I know. I told you I love her and all, but I wanna live with you. Please, Aunt Regina. It will be like old times. Please."

Regina sighed and rubbed her forehead. "Look. I tell you what. I'm not going to make any promises, but maybe if you do well in school this year you can come stay with me over the summer. Okay?"

"Why can't I come now?" Renee whined.

"Because it doesn't make sense for you to switch schools in the middle of the school year."

"It's not the middle of the school year! School just started a couple of weeks ago."

"Well, finish out the year, and if you get good grades, I'll talk to your mother about you staying with me for the summer. Deal?"

"Why do I have to wait that long?" Renee sniffed.

"Renee . . ."

"All right, deal. But it's a deal made under duress. I reserve the right to try and renegotiate, Aunt Gina."

"You can try." Regina laughed. "Tell your mother not to worry about calling me back tonight. I'll see her tomorrow when I pick you up. I'll be there around seven, okay?"

"Okay."

"I love you, Ray-Ray. Be good now," Regina said.

She hung up the telephone wracked with guilt. For the first eight years of Renee's life she was the girl's surrogate mother, her provider, her life support, while Brenda ran the streets chasing behind men and drugs.

Regina pushed the chair away from the computer, got up and lay down on the couch. There was no sense in even trying to work now; all she could think about was Renee, and the life they had had together.

Matilda had a few hundred dollars in the bank when she died that Regina withdrew, forging her mother's name on checks. There was also $3,000 of insurance money left over after the funeral. The insurance policy was in Brenda's name, but Regina had talked her sister into letting her hold the money for her so that she didn't get robbed during one of her nightly outings. Later

Brenda had violently attacked Regina when she refused to return the money. Though Brenda was older, her body was so weakened by drugs that Regina—already a good fighter—was able to best her. Regina wisely deposited the money to Matilda's account, hiding the checkbook from Brenda. But after a time—despite careful spending—the money began to dwindle. Regina had to find another way to pay the rent, groceries, and diapers. She quit school, and during the day looked for a job that would hire a thirteen-year-old girl who looked eleven and said she was eighteen. At night she cried herself to sleep, desperately missing her mother and wondering how she was going to survive.

The baby was her only source of joy. Renee was a happy child, who gurgled and cooed at Regina when she picked her up every afternoon from the kindly old woman who watched her in return for twenty dollars a week. Regina would sit her in a bassinet on top of the kitchen table while she warmed her baby food. She talked to the baby about her day as she bustled around the kitchen, and Renee always seemed to squeal at just the right times to prove she was interested. At night Regina would crawl into her mother's bed, snuggling and cuddling Renee as if she were a best-friend rag doll, and not a real life baby. Renee never tried to wriggle away. She was content in her role as comforter.

Mama Tee had offered to help out, and even baby-sat Renee a few afternoons while Regina looked for work, but one evening when Regina came to pick the baby up, Mama Tee sat the young girl down for a talk.

"You can't go on like this," she told Regina. Why not let Renee go into foster care, then Regina could move in with her and Yvonne?

"You and Yvonne can share de room," she said with a smile. "We be a family. Just the tree of us. And den you can go to school. You're too smart not be in school."

Regina politely declined, gathered up the baby and left, deciding then never to leave Renee in Mama Tee's care again. She loved Mama Tee, but she couldn't take the chance that one day she would arrive at the woman's house to find the welfare people had taken Renee away. She didn't think Mama Tee would betray her, but there was no telling what she might do, especially if she thought it was in Regina's best interest.

THE TELEPHONE RANG, rousing Regina from her thoughts of the past. She looked at the clock: 10:00 P.M. It had to be Yvonne calling. She was right.

"Girl, you're not going to believe this," she said, when Regina picked up the telephone. "Robert picked me up from work, and guess what Charles told him?"

Regina started giggling in anticipation. Whatever it was, Yvonne didn't sound mad, and that was a relief.

"What did he say?" she asked.

"*Nothing!* He didn't tell Robert shit!" Yvonne shouted.

"What? How do you know? Maybe he told Robert and Robert's just not telling you," Regina said suspiciously.

"Nope. I can read that boy like a book, already. Trust me, he didn't tell him a thing."

"Well, maybe he and Robert haven't talked today?"

"Nope. They had some fancy lunch meeting downtown today. I wanted to ask if Charles had on his watch, but I restrained myself." Yvonne laughed.

Regina laughed in return.

"He's probably too embarrassed to tell his boy," she said.

"Damn right, he's embarrassed. Boyfriend got played! He doesn't want anyone to know. I bet he's praying that you don't tell me and I don't turn around and tell Robert. He doesn't want anyone to know what a sucker he is," Yvonne said.

"So you're not mad at me anymore?"

"I wasn't mad at you before. I just think you're stupid as hell. You always have to do something outrageous to get back at someone. But that's just how you are. I just didn't want to get caught up in it," Yvonne said matter-of-factly. "But there is one thing I gotta know that I didn't ask you this afternoon," she said with a smile in her voice.

"What's that?"

"Was he good?"

"Girl, stop!" Regina laughed.

"Well, was he? Inquiring minds want to know!"

"Let's just say on a scale of one to ten he was a nine. And if I wasn't so preoccupied with how I was going to pull my little plot off, I bet he could have reached as high as fifteen."

"Damn! But I know you're not going to go back for seconds."

"Hell, no. That man has probably gone out and bought a gun, ready to shoot me if he sees me again." Regina laughed. "He may have been good, but no dick is worth dying over."

"Truer words were never said," Yvonne agreed solemnly.

5

I-HATE-MEN PARTIES ARE GIVEN WHEN A MAN HAS
done you wrong, and you call your friends to help bad-mouth
him over drinks. A Pity Party is held when a man has done you
wrong, and you call your friends over to make sure you don't
commit suicide. Regina wasn't sure what kind of party was being
held at Tamika's place that Monday night, but she stopped at a
liquor store on her way uptown, hoping for the former.

When Puddin' opened the door with a grim expression in
place of her usual smirk, Regina knew it was going to be a long,
and probably not pleasant, night.

"What happened? Why couldn't you tell me on the phone
what's going on?" Regina whispered as she entered the apartment.

"Girl, let's just say you're not going to believe this shit," Puddin' said in a disgusted tone as she walked back into the living
room with Regina trailing behind.

"Hey, girl," a weepy Tamika croaked as they entered the
room. "Sorry to drag you out like this."

"Hey yourself? Are you okay?" Regina asked as she bent down and planted a kiss on Tamika's tearstained face.

"I'm fine. Just dandy," Tamika answered, liquor evident on her breath.

Yvonne was rubbing Tamika's back, and quickly shrugged her shoulders at the question in Regina's eyes. "I don't know," she mouthed silently.

"Okay, we're all here. Let the I-Hate-Men Party begin," Puddin' pronounced as she grabbed the wine out of Regina's hands.

"I don't hate him. I just don't understand," Tamika wailed, then buried her face in her hands, her back heaving with large sobs.

"What did Chink do? Come on, sweetie. What happened?" Regina asked in exasperation as she sat down on the couch.

"Yeah, Tamika. You have to tell us what's going on if we're going to help," Yvonne added as she tried to cradle the crying young woman in her arms.

"Mmmm . . . let me tell the story, then," Puddin' said after taking a large swallow of the wine she had poured into a McDonald's glass. "She went up to see him yesterday and found out that the voodoo priestess was right."

"About what?" Regina asked. "You mean he really *is* cheating on her?"

"More like cheating *with* her. The bastard's married."

"What?" Yvonne exclaimed. Regina was speechless.

"Yep," Puddin' said, then coolly took another gulp of the wine as Tamika continued to cry. "Fucking bastard."

She handed Yvonne the bottle. "Ready for a drink?"

"If she's not, I sure as hell am," Regina exclaimed, after she regained her voice. "How did you find all this shit out?"

"We went up to see him yesterday," Tamika said between sobs. "Me, Puddin', and the kids."

"Speaking of the kids, where are they?" Regina asked.

"At my aunt's," Tamika sniffed.

"So, okay, okay. Let's start from the beginning, because I'm lost as hell," Yvonne said.

"Hmm, I think she might already have had enough to drink," Regina said as Puddin' handed Tamika a large glass of wine.

"Fuck it. She needs to get drunk," Puddin' said as Tamika gratefully took a big swallow.

Twice a month, every other Saturday, Tamika and her two kids boarded a bus for the three-hour trip to Comstock Correctional Facility to see Chink. They had been doing it for three years, since he was locked up for robbing a bank, but for some reason Tamika decided to surprise him and visit on a Sunday.

"Maybe because I had a premonition," Tamika sobbed.

"Maybe because my boyfriend is out of town and left me the keys to his car," Puddin' interjected. "She did talk me into going, though."

When they got there—"after the fucking car overheated twice on the New York State Thruway," Puddin' added—they went into the visiting room to see Chink. Only he wasn't surprised, Tamika said. He was shocked. And more than a little bit nervous.

"He asked me what I was doing visiting on a Sunday. Then we weren't there but ten minutes, and he said we should go home so the kids could get some rest," Tamika croaked as she took another gulp of wine. "I couldn't figure out why he was trying to rush us out like that. Then this . . . this . . . this woman just comes over and sits down at the visiting table like it's all right and stuff.

"Then she kisses him on the cheek, right in front of me and the kids. Like it's all right. Like we're the intruders or something," Tamika said, sobbing again. "Right in front of me and the kids."

"Damn!" was all Regina could say.

"I was out in the car sleeping. 'Cause you *know* if I was in there I woulda kicked the bitch's ass right then and there,"

Puddin' said. She sucked her teeth and added, "And I woulda kicked his sorry ass, too."

"I didn't wanna make a scene because the kids were there and all, else I probably woulda, too," Tamika whined between sobs.

"Yeah, right." Puddin' sucked her teeth again.

"Anyway, I asked him who she was, and he just said, 'This is Marilyn, she a friend of mine.' And then she said, 'A friend of yours?' like she was upset and stuff, and he told her to be quiet," Tamika continued. "I asked him what's going on, and he just said for me to take the kids home and he'd call me later."

"Oh fuck," Regina said slowly. "So what did you do?"

"There wasn't nothing I *could* do. I left."

"Y'all just went home?" Yvonne asked incredulously.

"Fuck no!" Puddin' said. "When she came out all upset and told me what happened I wasn't going no fucking where. I tried to go in to find out what the hell was up, but they wouldn't let me in because I didn't have any ID. But you know I wasn't going nowhere till we got this shit straight."

"You go, girl," Yvonne said. "So what happened?"

"Tamika started acting stupid, as usual, crying and carrying on, saying we should just leave. But I was laying for the bitch. Tamika wouldn't tell me what she looked like, but you know my boy Darren dimed her out. Darren don't play that shit. He ain't stupid like his mama."

"Come on now, Puddin'," Regina warned, but Puddin' ignored her, continuing on with the story.

"So when Darren pointed her out I went up to the bitch, and asked what she was doing visiting my girl's man, and she said that was *her* man. *Her husband!* Then the bitch started getting smart with me! Telling me I need to keep my friend outta *her* husband's face."

Puddin' was standing up, waving her long arms, rolling her eyes, and bobbing her head as she spoke. "I slid the fucking bitch. Punched her right in her fucking mouth. If I wasn't off-balance because of Sissy pulling on me I woulda made her swallow some fucking teeth."

"No, you didn't!" Regina said.

"Like hell, I didn't," Puddin' snorted. "The only reason she got a chance to run back in the prison was because I had to yell for Darren to grab Sissy off my leg." Puddin' fixed a disapproving stare at Tamika. "You'd better teach your daughter to step out the way when Aunt Puddin' gets mad. I don't want her to get hurt."

"Maybe it's a good thing Sissy was there," Tamika retorted. "I thought those prison guards were going to lock you up. You should have seen her, yelling for the woman to come out so she could finish kicking her ass. I had to pull her back in the car."

"Damnnnnn!" Yvonne said. "And I missed all this?"

"Yeah, you missed a bunch of shit." Puddin' laughed. "Then after I take Tamika home he calls her, *collect,* and tries to lie his way out of the shit, saying the bitch was his man's girlfriend and he didn't know why she had told all them lies."

"That's what he said at first, but he finally fessed up." Tamika started crying again.

Chink told her that he had found Marilyn on a prison pen-pal list a year ago, and after corresponding for a few months, she began visiting him every other Sunday. Then she started sending him money and gifts. Big money, and expensive gifts. He told Tamika that she started pressuring him to marry her. They had a June wedding, performed by the prison chaplain.

"He's been married two months now," Tamika sobbed. "I got his two kids. I stuck by him all this time. I used up my mom's insurance on his lawyers. And then he turns around and marries some white woman for her money."

"White woman!" Regina and Yvonne shouted simultaneously.

"I was going to wait to let *her* tell y'all that little tidbit." Puddin' smirked.

"Chink married a *white* woman?" Regina said in a daze.

"I thought you didn't have a problem with interracial marriages, Regina," Yvonne said through her own shock.

"I don't. But *Chink?* Mr. I-Hate-Whitey? Mr. Black-Power? Mr. I'm-a-Political-Prisoner married a white woman! You've gotta be kidding," Regina said. "Damn. Where's that bottle?"

"I have a fifth of Bacardi in my pocketbook. We might as well break that out," Yvonne said. "That bastard!"

"He never was no fucking good," Puddin' pronounced as she dug the rum out of Yvonne's purse and poured a healthy portion into her now empty McDonald's glass. "I hope she gives him AIDS and they both die."

"Don't say that. He's still Darren and Sissy's father," Tamika said dismally.

"Yeah! And her husband!" Puddin' shot back, prompting Tamika to start sobbing again.

"You better stop all that crying and pull yourself together," Puddin' grumbled. "Where were ya'll last night? I called and couldn't get no damn body. I know your ass was holed up with Robert, Yvonne. Where the hell were you, Regina?"

"I spent the weekend at Brenda's. I called as soon as I got your message."

"I've been sitting up holding her hand all night. You know I don't like this crying and shit. She should be plotting on how to kill the fuck-face bastard. Can't she sue him or something now that he's got a rich wife?"

"Puddin's right. That jerk isn't worth crying over," Regina said.

"Oh, let her cry," Yvonne said sympathetically, as she once again started patting Tamika's heaving back. "She's been through a lot of shit."

"Exactly why she should be trying to figure out how to get back at him!" Regina exclaimed.

"Fucking real," Puddin' agreed, giving Regina a high-five. "You won't catch me or Regina sitting around crying about some no-good creep. That's your bag, Yvonne. You're the queen of the Pity Parties."

"Give me a break," Yvonne snapped.

"You can get mad if you want," Puddin' said as she poured herself another drink. "I speak the truth. Anyone else ready for another shot?"

The women all held out their glasses, and Puddin' did the honors, still mouthing off as she poured the rum.

"I don't wanna see another tear, or hear another fucking wail in this house. This is an I-Hate-Men Party, not no goddamned sob party," she said after everyone had been served.

"Amen to that," Regina said, holding up her glass.

"Here you've been faithful to him all this time, writing to his ass every day, sending him what little money you got, getting your phone turned off who knows how many times because of all his fucking collect calls, and he marries some white woman?" Puddin' walked over and stood in front of Tamika, hand on hip. She leaned down and shouted in Tamika's face, "If you ain't pissed as hell, you're stupider than I thought."

"I'm not stupid!" Tamika said, slamming the drink on the coffee table. "And yeah, I'm pissed. Of course I'm pissed!"

Regina leaned over, took Tamika's hands in her own, looked in her eyes and said in a serious voice of a woman who was well on her way to being drunk, "Okay, that's a start, sweetie. Now, I want you to go with that feeling. Feel the anger. Become one with the anger. Love the anger!"

"Love the anger?" Yvonne hooted. "What's this, an intervention?"

"Call it what you want, Yvonne. I'm down with Regina," Puddin' replied with a drunken grin. "Yeah, Tamika. Love that anger. Marry that fucking anger."

Tamika looked around the room and started giggling.

"Marry the anger?" she asked.

"Well, you can't marry him, he's already married. Fuck it. Marry the anger," Puddin' said as she took another swig of her drink. "Make love to the fucking anger!"

"Oh shit, you guys are getting weird!" Yvonne howled.

"Tamika, this man just made your kids bastards," Regina said in her still serious tone. She stopped for a moment as if in thought. "Well, I guess they were bastards anyway, since ya'll weren't married. But he just made it official."

"Regina!" Tamika shouted in drunken indignation.

"Hell, you know what I mean," Regina said, then took another swig from her glass. "Don't get mad at me. Get mad at him."

"I am mad at him. I already said that."

"Say it again," Regina urged.

"I'm mad at him!"

"Say it louder!" Puddin' cried.

"I'm mad at him! I hate him!" Tamika shouted.

"That's right! Go with that feeling," Regina shouted excitedly.

"I hate Chink. Who does he think he is, anyway?" Tamika shouted, jumping up from the couch. "Fuck Chink!"

"What did you say?" Yvonne asked her, then turned to Regina and Puddin' and laughed. "Did she really say what I thought she said?"

"Yeah, she said it! Say it again, Tamika. Fuck Chink!" Puddin' yelled at the top of her lungs.

"Fuck Chink. Fuck Chink. Fuck Chink," the women all started chanting.

Two hours later, both the wine and rum were drinks of the past. Pictures of Chink and the dozens of love letters he had written were smoldering ashes in a tin wastepaper basket placed in the middle of the living room floor. The four women were sprawled out on the couch, the chair, and on the floor.

"Best damn I-Hate-Men Party ever," Puddin' said as she raised her head and attempted to look around.

"Yeah," Regina said, not bothering to open her eyes. "Let's do it again next week."

6

REGINA PUSHED THROUGH THE NOISY AND CROWDED room at the New York Association of Black Journalists annual awards banquet, trying to keep her eye on her niece, but it was a lost cause. Renee was undoubtedly near the stage in front of the large room at the Waldorf-Astoria, trying to get up close and personal with her idol, Porsche Supreme, who was onstage dancing and singing her heart out for the media elite. She might have started out as little "Bennie" on the television show *Storming the Castle,* but Porsche had grown up to be a successful hip-hop artist and author of a just-published autobiography, as well as a teenage sex symbol. Porsche kept her lyrics clean, so Regina didn't mind Renee idolizing her, but it wouldn't have mattered if she had. Renee—like most of the Harris women—had a mind of her own.

"Well, I was hoping to run into you here, Miss Harris. How are you?"

Regina turned to find Earl Masters standing with a half-filled glass in his hand, staring with admiration at her spaghetti-strapped black sheath evening gown.

"Hi, Earl," Regina said lightly, hoping he wouldn't detain her long, but at the same time trying to appear friendly. Stuffy, portly Earl was usually good for an article or two a month, and she didn't want to get on his bad side. The *Times* paid well, and on time, something that freelance writers appreciated, since it was rare.

"Are you enjoying the show?" he shouted over the loud music.

"What I can see of it." Regina laughed. "I'm surprised they decided to have her perform before the dinner and awards ceremony. Whose idea?"

Earl shrugged his broad shoulders. "I have to admit that I have no clue, even though I am on the NYABJ's executive board. I think I heard something about the chapter president wanting her to perform by seven P.M., because some ambassador or somebody has to depart the party early, but I couldn't tell you anything for certain.

"But I'll be glad to escort you closer to the stage so you can enjoy the show, my dear," Earl said, crooking his arm in invitation.

"No, no. I'm fine right here. How have you been?"

"Very well, thank you. I haven't heard from you lately. Does that mean you're too busy these days to query a lowly rag like the *Times*?" He smiled.

Before Regina could answer, Maggie Peterson appeared, wearing a sequined blue evening gown that left little to the imagination, and obviously not feeling the least bit uncomfortable about being one of very few white people at the party.

She flashed Regina a quick and phony smile, and then turned all of her attention to Earl.

"Why, Earl, how nice to see you, honey! You haven't returned any of my calls, you bad boy, you," she shouted in her overdone Southern accent. "It's enough to give a girl a complex, sugar."

"Well, we can't have that now, can we," Earl said with a lecherous grin. "I've been rather busy, but it's certainly not been my intention to neglect you, Miss Peterson."

"Well, I was feeling a little neglected, but I'm beginning to feel a little better now," Maggie responded with a pretty pout. "You'll have to excuse me if I act a little giddy, sugar. I just don't know what they're putting in these here drinks."

Regina grinned to herself, a joke she heard recently coming to mind—What's a southern belle's mating call? "My, I am *so* drunk!"—She had thought of Maggie when she'd first heard it, and it tickled her to have it played out in real life right in front of her.

"Excuse, me. I think I see my niece," Regina said, deciding to forgo the rest of the mating ritual.

"Okay, dear. Don't make yourself a stranger, though," Earl said.

"Yes, please don't," Maggie said, without looking at her.

"Now, Earl," she continued shouting, as Regina walked away. "I really wanted to tell you how much I loved that editorial in last Sunday's paper. . . ."

Regina pushed through to the front of the stage just as the show ended, and found Renee jumping and screaming along with the rest of the crowd, most of whom were old enough to be her parents.

"I'm assuming you like the show," she shouted in her niece's ear.

"Oh, man! It's banging!" Renee exclaimed excitedly. "Can you introduce me to her, Aunt Regina?"

Regina laughed. Renee assumed she knew all of the celebrities because of her line of work. But while it was true she did interview and knew quite a few, Porsche was not one of them, she informed her crestfallen niece.

"Aw shoot," Renee muttered.

"All's not lost, child. She's going to be autographing books after dinner, so maybe you'll have a chance to talk to her then."

"She is? Oh man! But I don't have my copy with me," Renee complained.

"Yes, you do," Regina replied patting her pocketbook. "Aren't I just wonderful? Now gimme a kiss."

"Bet!" Renee exclaimed, throwing her arms around Regina so forcefully the two almost fell to the floor. "Okay? Where's the food? I'm starved!"

"Right this way," Regina said as she led the excited girl to the room where dinner would be served and the awards presented. "And Ray-Ray, if you start yawning during the awards ceremony, I'll never take you out with me again. Hear?"

"Okay, okay. Just don't pinch me under the table like you did last year. I still have black-and-blue marks on my thigh."

THE LINE OF PEOPLE waiting to get their books signed stretched around the room. Regina took one look and decided she had better things to do. Renee was not discouraged, however, and patiently stood in line, chatting with the people in front and in back of her, telling them how much she loved Porsche.

"Did you see her on MTV last week?" she excitedly asked Robin Stone from *Essence* magazine. "She was the bomb. Everyone thinks Monica and Brandy are hot, but Porsche makes them look sick."

Regina looked around at New York's black media elite, in their sequins, diamonds, and pearls. Although she knew many of them personally, she couldn't get over the feeling—had never been able to get over the feeling—that she didn't belong. That if they knew the real Regina, they would run her out of the room as an impostor. *Which is ridiculous,* she assured herself for the thousandth time. *I'm just as much a part of this scene as any other.* But what if Mayor Giuliani knew he had prosecuted a number of her drug-dealing boyfriends while he was District Attorney? Would he still invite her to his annual media celebration party? Would Steve Lovelady at *Time* magazine, who was nodding at her from across the room, contract her to do articles on the crisis of the black middle class if he knew she was a former shoplifter and cocaine user, and her sister a convicted prostitute and crackhead? *Face it,* she said to herself with a giggle. *You're perpetuating a fraud.*

Renee meanwhile, finally reached the table where Porsche sat autographing copies of her book. The young girl could barely contain her excitement as she opened her copy and thrust it into the star's hands.

"Hi! Could you sign it from Porsche to her best friend, Renee?" she asked excitedly.

"Sorry, she's just signing her name," said a brusque man standing over Porsche. "We've got to keep the line moving. Come on."

Porsche smiled at Renee apologetically, and reached for the book of the next person in line.

"Well, can I just ask you one question?" Renee said quickly as the man gave her a dirty look. "Do you get along with Foxy Brown or do you just say you do for the magazines?"

Porsche laughed, and started to answer, but the man cut her off.

"Look. You're holding up the line. Move it along," he snapped.

Renee glared at the man, ready to give a sassy retort, but just then another man's arm reached over her shoulder, and she heard a smooth baritone voice say, "Hey, Tee."

"Heyyyyy, Cuz." Porsche jumped from a chair and leaned over the table to hug the man, whose arm still lingered on Renee's shoulder. "What are you doing here?"

The man laughed and gave Renee a wink.

"See that? You never know where I'm going to pop up. But could you do me a favor? I promised my little friend here that I would use my influence to get you to sign a personal inscription in her book."

"Could you sign it from Porsche to her best friend Renee?" she asked again excitedly, then made a face at the man across the table who was glaring at her.

"Sure, girlfriend, no problem," Porsche said as she hurriedly wrote. "Hey, I've got a penthouse suite here at the hotel and I'm having some friends over later tonight after this shindig is over. Can you make it?" she asked Renee's new knight in shining armor.

"Wild horses couldn't keep me away, Tee." He grinned back. "I'll see you then. I think I've held up the line long enough as it is."

"Are you really her cousin?" Renee asked the man breathlessly as they walked away from the table. "Are you famous, too, or something?"

"In my own mind," the man replied, smiling. "We're not really cousins, but our fathers went to school together, and our families are close, so we've always called ourselves cousins."

"Oh man. That's great! I wish I had a famous cousin. Or even a famous make-believe cousin. Hey, can I come with you to the party?"

The man stopped and looked at Renee and laughed, not in the condescending way some adults do, but with a warmth that suggested he found Renee genuinely amusing.

"I won't get in the way, I-promise. Hey, are you married? I'll introduce you to my aunt. She can be your date, and I can just tag along."

"Oh really?" The man smiled and raised an eyebrow. "What do you think your aunt will say to that?"

"She'll love you. Just wait, you're just her type!" Renee said, tugging the man along through the crowd as she searched for Regina.

"What's her type?"

"I don't know. But I bet you're it. There she is. Hey, Aunt Regina, I want you to meet someone."

Regina turned around and froze when she saw her niece's companion.

"Aunt Regina, this is my friend . . . Dang! I don't even know your name!"

"Hi, Charles. Fancy meeting you here," Regina said icily.

"Always a pleasure seeing you, Regina. Pick any pockets lately?" Charles said, his eyes shooting fire.

"You guys know each other? Great," Renee exclaimed, too excited about the prospect of attending Porsche's party to notice the tension in the air between them. "Aunt Regina, Charles wants us to go with him to Porsche Supreme's after-party. Can we go? Please?"

"I'm sure your aunt already has plans," Charles told Renee politely. "It was nice meeting you, Renee."

"Wait a minute, wait a minute. She doesn't have other plans, do you, Aunt Regina?" Renee pleaded while holding on to Charles's arm to prevent him from walking away.

"I'm sure Mr. Whitfield has other people to charm, Renee," Regina told her niece. "Come on. I promised your mother you'd be home by eleven and it's after ten now."

"Actually, I don't have anything to do," Charles said suddenly. "I'd love to have the two of you accompany me to the party."

"All right!" Renee shouted, jumping up and down.

Regina stared at Charles suspiciously for a moment, wondering about his sudden change of heart. She didn't know what he was up to, and didn't want to find out with Renee in tow.

"Like I said, I promised your mother we'd be home by

eleven," she told Renee, then turned to Charles and said with a polite smile that didn't reach her eyes, "Thank you for your kind offer, but we'll have to pass."

"But why? It's a Friday. I don't have school tomorrow," Renee wailed. "Aunt Regina, come on, don't do this to me."

"You don't have to stay long. I'm sure you'll both have a good time and Renee can get a chance to actually have a conversation with Porsche. I wouldn't be surprised if there are other singers there. You know they travel in packs," Charles said, smiling at Regina.

"And did I mention I got an 'A' on my English test yesterday? Aunt Regina please!!!!!!! This is a chance in a lifetime. "Pleeeeeez!!!!!!!!"

Regina sighed, then glared at Charles, who was so obviously enjoying the difficult position he had put her in.

"All right. Call your mother. If she says it's okay, we'll go. But we're only staying an hour, you hear?"

"Bet! Bet! Oh man, I can't wait." Renee started jumping up and down. "Hey Charles, you think Lord Torique and Peter Gunz will be there? They sing with her a lot. I bet they'll be there!"

"I'm sure if they're in town they will, and I'll make sure Porsche introduces you to them personally." He smiled back at the girl.

"Oh man, I've died and gone to heaven," Renee said. "Just wait until I tell the kids in school."

She scurried off in search of a pay phone, leaving Charles and Regina alone to contemplate each other.

"So you know Porsche Supreme?" Regina asked coolly.

"Family friend," Charles said with a smile. "I'm glad to be able to help Renee out, Aunt Regina."

"You can stick with Regina, thanks."

Charles grinned. "Why? I like Aunt Regina. Makes you sound like a nice warm and fuzzy person."

"And of course we both know I'm the warm, fuzzy type," Regina snapped. "Look, I don't appreciate you using my niece to get back at me."

"Puleeze! Don't flatter yourself!" Charles snapped back. "I didn't know she was your niece. She was at the table trying to talk to Tee and was getting the brush-off, so I just stepped in to get her a personal inscription. To tell you the truth, had I known the two of you were related I probably would have just minded my business."

"Yeah, right! So you didn't see us together in the room beforehand. This is just one great coincidence?"

Before Charles could answer Porsche came up behind him and grabbed his arm.

"Look. I'm getting ready to split. You coming up?" she asked, then flashed Regina a friendly smile. "Oh, I'm sorry. I didn't mean to be rude. And don't worry, I'm not trying to make a move on Charlie. We're family."

"No need to apologize," Regina answered.

"Porsche, this is Regina . . . I'm sorry, I've forgotten your last name," Charles said.

Yeah, right, Regina thought about saying, but instead extended her hand to shake Porsche's. "Regina Harris. Nice to meet you."

"Nice to meet you, too," Porsche said graciously. "I don't mean to be rude, but I have to split. Charlie, I'll see you later, right?"

"Sure. Hey, I hope you don't mind if Regina and her niece come to the party."

"No, not at all. The more the merrier," Porsche said as she moved away. "I'll see both of you later, then."

"Okay, now where were we? Oh yeah, you were on an ego trip thinking I was using your niece to get to you, right?" Charles said, when Porsche left.

"I'm just saying it's a mighty big coincidence that you show up at a party when you knew there was a strong possibility I would be here, and that of all the hundreds of people in here to befriend, you just happen to choose my niece," Regina snapped.

"Well, it does just happen to be a coincidence. I called home this afternoon and my parents said that Porsche was going to be here so I thought I'd stop in," Charles snarled back. "Not everyone is as devious and conniving as you, you know."

"And not everyone is as pompous and self-righteous as you," Regina snapped, turning her back on him.

"Oh, no, don't change the subject, Miss Harris," Charles said, reaching for her arm. "Believe it or not, I like your little niece, although now I'm hoping your unscrupulousness is not genetic. Like I said before, I didn't know she was your niece, and don't flatter yourself into thinking I want anything to do with you!"

"Lower your voice. You're making a scene," Regina hissed as she whirled back around.

"Well, we wouldn't want that, now would we?" Charles retorted, though in a lower tone. "You prefer private scenes, don't you? Scenes where you set the stage, and everybody else plays the stooge."

"And no one can play a stooge as well as you, honey," Regina said. "Natural talent? Or do you have to rehearse?"

"Honesty happens to be a natural talent, Regina. I was being honest with you the other night. But instead of you being honest and admitting you took offense at what I said, you had to plot a little scheme to make me look stupid. Do you know I called the cops when I woke up and found all my stuff gone. I trusted you in my home, and you turn around and play me like a sap."

"Well, obviously you're not as good a judge of character as you thought, hmmm?"

"Obviously not."

Just then Renee reappeared. Her mother said it was all right for her to stay, as long as she made it home before 2:00 A.M., she told Regina. The only other stipulation was that Renee get M. C. Hammer's autograph for her if he happened to be at the party.

"Like Porsche Supreme would actually invite that old has-been to one of her parties," Renee scoffed. "Hey, you think she would mind if I call her 'Tee,' too?" she asked Charles.

"I'm sure she wouldn't mind at all," Charles said. Regina noticed his tone softened while speaking to Renee.

"But why they call her Tee? Her name doesn't start with 'T'?"

Charles grinned and looked around as if to make sure no one was listening.

"Promise you won't tell anyone if I tell you?"

"I promise," Renee said excitedly.

"Well, when she was a little girl she used to say she had to tee-tee when she had to go the bathroom. And whenever she didn't make it in time she would say, 'I tee-tee, Mommy. I tee-tee.' The name just stuck."

"Oh, man. That is so wild!" Renee doubled up with laughter.

"Now, remember, you promised you wouldn't tell anybody."

"I won't. I won't."

"Good, she'd kill me if she found out I told you. But just to make sure, you have to tell me your nickname."

"Well, my family calls me Ray-Ray, but I don't mind that."

"You probably will by the time you get to college." Charles laughed.

"I'm not going to college. I'm going to be a photographer. I don't need a college degree to do that," Renee said defiantly.

"No? You'd better not tell Tee that. She's big on education, you know. You know she only tours during summer break or on weekends."

"She's in college?" Renee asked in amazement.

"Yep. Yale. And you know Chuck D has a masters degree."

"Well, yeah, everybody knows that. But I just didn't know

Porsche Supreme was in college. Why is she in college? It's not like she needs to go get a job," Renee said, her face screwed up in puzzlement.

"People don't only go to college to get a job, missy," Charles said, playfully ruffling Renee's hair. "They go because they like to learn."

Regina listened in amazement. Renee obviously liked Charles, and the feeling seemed genuinely reciprocated. *If this is an act, it's a good one,* Regina thought. He was warm and easy with Renee, not judging or smirking at her slang. Renee was usually good at detecting phonies, but she seemed enthralled with Charles, and not just because he knew Porsche Supreme.

"He's cute," she confided to Regina when he went off to retrieve their shawls. "Are you guys going to start dating?"

"*No!*" Regina snapped loudly.

"Why not? If you two got married I could tell everyone Porsche's my cousin, too," she said.

"Renee . . ."

"Okay, okay. Just thought I'd throw that out there." Renee grinned at the tone of her aunt's voice. "Kinda touchy tonight, aren't we, Aunt Gina?"

THE PARTY UPSTAIRS in the penthouse was so different from the one Regina just left it was eerie. While the members and guests of the New York Association of Black Journalists wore evening gowns and tuxedoes, most of the guests at Porsche's party wore baggy jeans or leather suits. Diamonds and pearls were replaced with thick gold chains. One girl had rainbow-streaked hair and a pierced nose and bottom lip. Some looked as if they had just gotten offstage, and some probably had. There were a number of well-known singers in the room, and a number of fledgling artists who tried to press CDs and demo tapes into the hands of anyone they thought looked like a producer. Will Smith's latest hit played loudly in the background as the guests mingled.

"Tee said Will's in California and couldn't make it," Charles said, explaining Will's absence from his good friend's party. "I don't blame him. If I had a gorgeous wife like Jada I'd probably never leave the house."

Charles kept his word. As busy as Porsche was playing hostess, she still managed time to introduce Renee to a few of the people whose lives she'd followed in music magazines. On the elevator to the party Renee told Regina all of the questions she would ask the stars, and even practiced a few witty lines out on her aunt. Now that she was actually at the party, though, Renee was speechless for the first time in her life. Most of the time she walked around in a daze, gawking. "Oh my God, Aunt Regina, there's Puff Daddy," she gushed at one point. "Oh my God, he's so *fine*. I think I'm going to die!"

Regina spent most of the time in the corner sipping a soda and feeling overdressed in her floor-length gown. Two singer wannabes stopped to talk to her, then left abruptly when they discovered she wasn't in the music business. Three others tried to convince her to pen articles about them when they found out she was a writer. One young man, who looked about eighteen, tried to get her telephone number, saying he knew he could prove he was the man of her dreams. When she told him she was at least seven years his senior, he eagerly told her he liked older women. Not a flattering statement in Regina's view.

"Enjoying yourself?" Charles asked as he munched on a bunch of Cheez Doodles cradled in the palm of his hand.

"Immensely," she replied. "And more importantly, Renee is having a ball."

They turned to look at Renee staring wide-eyed at Larenz Tate as he told an admiring crowd about his upcoming movie.

"Yeah, she is having a good time," Charles said. "She's going to have a ball making everyone jealous when she gets back to school on Monday."

"Look, I really want to thank you for inviting us. And I'm sorry about my earlier assumptions."

"You mean your assumption that I was lusting after you, and was only nice to that sweet, little girl in a feeble attempt to get in your good graces?" Charles grinned.

"Yeah, that assumption," Regina muttered. He wasn't making this easy.

"Just goes to show you shouldn't jump to assumptions," Charles said nonchalantly.

"Okay, I apologized. Can we drop it now, though?"

"Nope. I obviously can't make you feel guilty about your misdeeds the other night, so I'm going to get as much mileage out of this as I can." He grinned.

Regina smiled in spite of herself.

"You really do well with children," Regina said. "Unless it's an act, you seem to like them."

"It's not an act. I do like kids. I even do volunteer work at an after-school program up your way. Harlem, I mean. And when I was in Philly I was in the Big Brother program. I haven't gotten involved since coming to New York because I'm not staying that long, and it's not fair to enter a kid's life and then disappear. Most of them have had too much of that as it is."

"True," Regina said thoughtfully.

"See? I'm not the complete cad you've tried to make me out to be," Charles said, popping another Cheez Doodle into his mouth.

"I never thought you were a cad. Just a pompous, self-righteous ass."

"Hmmm. You were just determined to work that back in the conversation, weren't you?" Charles grinned.

"Yep." She grinned back.

"Okay, at the risk of pissing you off again—and I'm only taking this risk because there's no way I'm inviting you back to my place tonight—I just want to say that I still don't think I was out of line the other night," Charles said in a now serious tone. "When I know I'm wrong, I admit it. That's why I apologized for my behavior the first night we met. But I wasn't trying to insult your friends last week; I was just sharing my impressions. I was just being honest and open.

"And if you were so upset with my sharing, you could have just stopped me. Or you could have just walked out. You didn't have to pull a stunt like that. Especially after we made love. I think this time it's you who owes an apology."

"I wouldn't wait on one if I were you," Regina retorted.

"You know, that doesn't surprise me. You have a hard time admitting you're wrong, don't you."

"No. When I think I'm wrong about something I apologize. But I'm not going to apologize because *you* think I'm wrong," Regina said angrily. "And as far as not being insulting to my friends, you all but called them money-grubbing sluts."

"I did not! I said they were fast and on the prowl. In retrospect, I perhaps could have used a better choice of words, but I sure didn't call them money-grubbing sluts."

"So, because they were in a club and interested in meeting nice men you call them fast and on the prowl?"

"Okay, what would you call them, then?"

"Oh, I don't know. What would you call your sister?" Regina grinned meanly.

"What the hell is that supposed to mean?" Charles asked, taken aback.

"Didn't you tell me she went to medical school, but didn't finish because she snagged an up-and-coming plastic surgeon, who's now making megabucks? Well, honey, it's the same damn thing.

Except maybe my friends didn't have lawyer mommies and politician daddies to send them to medical school to find doctor husbands.

"And let me tell you something else while we're on the subject. Fast women? If that's not a pseudonym for a slut I don't know what is. Well, for your information, Tamika is twenty-six years old and has only been with one man in her entire life. But because she's in a nightclub, and doesn't dress to your 'taste,' and doesn't talk up at your 'level,' *you* label her a fast woman. Your kind makes me sick."

"My kind?"

"Yeah! Your kind, asshole. And I say that based on what you've shown me, not on the way you speak or the type of clothes you wear."

"Okay. Are you finished your little tirade now?"

"No, I'm not. Then you tell me I'm a 'lady' because I've gone to college and live in a 'nice' neighborhood. That's *not* what makes a lady. I come from the same neighborhood as my girlfriends you so smugly put down. And yes, I do consider myself a lady. But it's not because *you* think I am. I'm a lady who can fuck your brains out, and get up the next morning, put on a dress, and go have tea with the mayor's wife. Now, that's a lady. And let me tell you something else, buster. You said the other night that I'm your type of woman? Well, you don't know anything about me. You don't know what I've been through, and you don't know what I'm going through. And you sure as hell don't know what type of woman I am. *Now* I'm finished."

Charles glared at her, then started to turn away, but changed his mind.

"Okay, now it's my turn. Maybe I was wrong, maybe I was falling for some stereotypes, but you could have just said that. You didn't have to stage an Oscar award-winning event. And as far as my not knowing you, how the hell is anyone supposed to get to know you? You're so busy waiting for someone to mess up so you can pounce on them, no one gets a damn chance. You need to take that chip off your shoulder, Regina. It's very unbecoming. Now *I'm* finished," he said angrily before walking away.

Regina started to go after him, but stopped herself. She sucked her teeth and closed her eyes, then brought her glass to her forehead as if to cool herself off. *Dammit, I hate when I lose control. I told myself I wasn't going to go off on him tonight, and then I turn around and make a scene. Well, he deserved it. Shit. No he didn't. I just got mad because he was getting over on me. He waved a rubber knife at me, and I let loose a cannonball on him. What the hell is wrong with me?* She looked at her watch. 1:30. She'd lost track of time.

Regina looked around for Renee, but her mind was still on her conversation with Charles. *He may have his shortcomings, but he was a nice guy,* she thought. *He's funny, intelligent, and good-looking. And he might sometimes be a jerk, but he did have a good side. Look at the way he volunteers his time to help kids. And the fact that he even spoke to me after what I did to him last week. . . . Well, he did until a few minutes ago. Why couldn't I have just kept my big mouth shut?*

She spotted Renee out in the drawing room of the suite. The girl's eyes were still wide as saucers as she watched Queen Latifah shoot a game of pool with Missy Elliot.

"Come on, Ray-Ray. It's time for us to split."

"Already? The party's just getting started, Aunt Regina!" the girl wailed. "Can't we stay a little longer?"

"No, we can't. Come on," Regina said impatiently.

"Can't we at least tell Tee good night?" Renee asked as she obediently, though reluctantly, trotted behind her aunt who walked briskly toward the door.

"We'll send her a thank-you note tomorrow. Now come on."

"Okay, then let me just ask her for her address real quick."

"Ray-Ray—"

"Sorry Aunt Gina," Renee mumbled.

As they awaited the elevator in silence, Regina impatiently tapped her foot on the tile floor. Regina was glad Renee was tuned into her mood and kept quiet.

In the mood I'm in I'd probably snap her head off, too. What the hell is wrong with me? Regina thought, sighing inwardly. The bell dinged, signaling the elevator's long-awaited arrival, when they heard Charles's voice.

"Going without a good-bye?"

"Aw, Charles, thanks so much for taking us to the party," Renee gushed, thankful to have someone to talk to.

"Yes, thanks a lot. We had a wonderful evening," Regina said without looking at him.

"No problem. Are you driving? Can I get you guys a cab?"

"No, we're fine. I'm sure the doorman will be glad to hail us a taxi."

Charles contemplated them for a moment. Regina's eyes were downcast, but Renee looked at him hopefully.

"Look, I'm ready to leave anyway. Why don't I just give you ladies a lift home? Hold on, let me just say my good-byes."

"You don't have to do that—" Regina started, but Charles had closed the door.

Regina was silent during the long ride to Queens, but Renee kept up a steady chatter, telling Charles about all the stars she saw at the party, how jealous the kids at school were going to be, and thanking him over and over again for allowing them to accompany him to the party.

"Man, I wish I had my camera with me. I coulda taken a whole bunch of pictures. That woulda really impressed my friends. Do you have any other famous cousins I should know about?" she asked as they finally pulled in front of the two-story frame house she shared with her mother.

"No, I think that's about it," Charles said with a laugh. He jumped out of the car and walked quickly around to the other side and opened the door of his white Lexus for the ladies.

"Well, it was nice meeting you, Miss Renee. I'm glad you had a good time. Regina, do you need a ride back to Manhattan or are you staying overnight?"

"I'm going back to Manhattan. I'll be just a minute," she said quickly.

"I thought—" Renee started.

"I changed my mind," Regina cut her off as she ran up the steps and rang the bell.

"Oh! Right. Gotcha. Don't do anything I wouldn't do, okay?" Renee grinned.

A few minutes later Regina was again in the car with Charles heading back over the Van Wyck Expressway toward Manhattan. With Renee gone, the only voices came from Debra Cox's latest song playing over the radio.

"Hey. I'd like to introduce myself. My name is Regina Harris," Regina said suddenly, turning to face Charles.

A few seconds passed.

"Sooooo, we're starting over again for the *third* time?" he asked slowly, his eyes still intent on the road.

"Well, yeah. If you want to, that is," Regina said quickly. "You think this time we might be able to get it right?"

"That depends on you, doesn't it? You're the one who seems to be calling the shots," Charles said sullenly. "And for the record—just for the record—I'm not used to a woman calling the shots."

"I'm not trying to call the shots," Regina said defensively.

"Yes, you are." Charles laughed. "But if we don't change the subject we're going to get into another argument. Now, what was it you were saying about starting over again?"

Regina smiled, causing Charles to chuckle.

"You knew. You knew I'd go along with it. I don't know why, but you've managed to get under my skin. You know that, don't you?"

"Well, I was hoping," Regina answered.

"But no more games. If you get mad at something I do or say, tell me. Don't try and get back at me, okay? And I'll do the same. Deal?"

"Deal."

Twenty minutes of pleasant conversation, and a lot of smiles and laughter later, Charles pulled in front of Regina's building.

"So now I know your address. I still don't have your telephone number, which is a shame, because I'd love to call you and ask you out to dinner tomorrow night."

"Well, I don't remember you ever asking for my number," Regina teased.

"Well, I'm officially asking. Miss Regina Harris, will you do me the honor?"

"Gladly."

They paused at the steps of Regina's building, and as Regina looked up into Charles's eyes, a warm tingly feeling started at her head and rushed down to her toes. The memory of their lovemaking was enough to make her knees weak, and for a moment she considered inviting him in for a nightcap.

"You are something special, Regina," Charles said softly. He caressed her face. "I don't know what to make of you. Do you have this effect on all men?"

Regina didn't answer. She closed her eyes, savoring the touch of his hand. He was so sweet and seemed so perfect. And it would be so good to wake up to a warm loving body in the morning. She opened her eyes, shaking her head slightly to drive the thought from her mind. *Slow down, girl. You're letting him under your skin, now.*

"Sooo . . . I guess we'll see each other tomorrow?" Charles asked gently, pulling her closer to him.

"I guess we will. Well, thanks for a lovely evening," Regina said quickly before she changed her mind.

"Thank you, Lady Regina," he said, leaning down to kiss her.

But Regina broke away, and ran up the few remaining steps and slipped into the building, pausing to laughingly say, "Good night, Sir Charles. I'm sorry, but a lady never kisses on the third date."

7

"YOU MADE ME MESS UP AGAIN, LIE STILL!" CHARLES swatted Regina's bare bottom with the folded newspaper.

"Ouch! Then why don't you do your crossword puzzle on the table? I have better uses for my back," Regina grumbled.

"What can I say? Your ass inspires me," Charles said as he smoothed the paper again over her body.

Regina closed her eyes and turned her head to the side, peacefully snuggling back into the pillow. They'd been dating four weeks, and had already developed a comfortable routine. Tuesday afternoons Regina grabbed a bus uptown and met Charles at the little coffee shop for lunch. Afterward they went to his studio apartment for lovemaking and napping. Thursday evenings he drove over to her apartment, where they watched *World News Tonight* with Peter Jennings, *Frasier,* then tuned into BET for music videos and *BET Tonight* with Tavis Smiley. On Friday nights they roamed hand in hand through the East Village, taking in the sights, browsing through bookstores and stopping at piano bars for a little wine and music. Saturdays were flexible. Once they went out dancing with Yvonne and Robert. Regina was surprised, and pleased, to find Charles was an excellent dancer, and they drew envious stares from other couples on the dance floor. Another time they attended a Lauryn Hill concert with Tamika and David, who also were dating regularly. But Sunday mornings—well, Sunday mornings were special. Charles served breakfast in bed. He was a whiz at omelets, although Regina had to teach him how to make home fries. Then, after eating, they made slow and lazy love. Contrary to stereotype, it was Regina who usually fell asleep afterward.

It couldn't be called a whirlwind courtship, because although the affair between Charles and Regina progressed faster than any other in which she had been involved, it had no dizzying affect on her. It was more grounded, and she savored every minute. The companionship, the lovemaking, and even the arguing—for they argued about any- and everything.

Once while riding back on a school bus from Renee's class trip to the Museum of Natural History, they got into an argument about whether dogs and wolves were in the same species. "They're all canines, and canines are a species of animal. So they're in the same species," Charles insisted.

"No, they're all in the same family or whatever, but they're different species," Regina countered.

The science teachers on the school bus sided with Charles. So did his law school-student buddies and the waiter at the restaurant later that evening. The janitor at Regina's building sided with her. So did the woman who ran the dry cleaners on the corner and the mailman the next morning. Finally Charles called Harvard University's Department of Organismic & Evolutionary Biology to put the matter to rest. "The word canine describes a genus, which has nine species, including dogs, wolves, and jackals," the professor who picked up the telephone said. Not satisfied, Charles insisted on talking to the department chair. He pulled a five-dollar bill from his wallet after he hung up and handed it to Regina, then refused to discuss the matter further.

"You guys are something else," David laughed when Regina told him about the argument later that night over drinks at a midtown nightclub. "I've never seen such a competitive couple."

"Gina's always been like that. She hates losing an argument," Tamika said, flashing Regina an affectionate smile. "You'll never see me disagree with her about anything. If she says something's a fact, that's good enough for me."

"It's not that I hate losing, I just hate people telling me I'm wrong when I know I'm right," Regina said, tossing her head.

"But it's the lengths that you go to to prove that you're right that are so outrageous," Charles said, grimacing.

"As if you should talk, buddy," David said with a chuckle. "You're the exact same way."

"Yeah. It was your idea to call Harvard." Regina smirked.

"Oh, shut up," Charles grumbled, prompting everyone to laugh.

"I guess that's what happens when two really smart people hook up," Tamika said finally.

"Well, we're not like that." David reached over and gently brushed a curl away from Tamika's forehead, then brought her hand to his lips and planted a kiss.

"That's because I'm not smart like you," Tamika said with a giggle.

"Says who?" David asked.

"You're so sweet, David. But come on, you're almost a lawyer, and I never even finished high school." Tamika looked down at the table and began tearing the small corners from her cocktail napkin. "You know I can't hang."

Regina shifted uncomfortably in her chair, and started to say something reassuring to her friend, but David spoke first.

"Baby, I've told you before. Schooling has nothing to do with intelligence. You're very smart. Just because you didn't go to college doesn't mean you're inferior to anyone, you hear me? You're more than a match for me and anyone else, too. Anyone can get book sense, but you have something that most people don't have. You have life sense. And you're the sweetest and kindest person I've ever met."

Regina was touched, but then Charles broke in.

"And anyway, why don't you just go ahead and get your equivalency diploma and go to college," he asked. There was a derisive tone in his voice that jolted Regina, and she shot him a warning look, but he ignored her.

"She should. She'd do great," David said in an almost defiant tone that told Regina that he, too, took offense to Charles's tone.

"What would you take up if you did go back to school?" Regina asked, with a sudden pang of guilt. Yvonne and Puddin' had laughed when Regina said she planned to go back to school, but Tamika had been thrilled. Yet it never occurred to her that Tamika herself might have wanted to further her education. She had always seemed so happy being a mother and a supermarket cashier.

"Well, maybe I'd study medicine," Tamika said timidly, still looking down at the table.

"You'd like to be a doctor?" Regina couldn't hide the surprise in her voice.

"Well, yeah. I guess so. I wouldn't mind being a pediatrician. I mean, I like being around children. You know that." Tamika shrugged her shoulders, then looked up at Regina as if to gauge her reaction.

"Hell, I think you'd make a great pediatrician, Tamika. I think you should go for it." Regina said sincerely.

"I told her the same thing," David said, taking Tamika's hand in his. Regina's guilt began to deepen. She had known Tamika for twenty years, and in all that time she had never asked Tamika about her dreams, and she doubted anyone else had, either. No one, it seemed, but David, who had known her only a month.

"Well, I would say we should drink to that, but I need a refresher." Charles looked around for a drink waitress, but no one was in sight. "Anyone else want anything while I'm at the bar?" he asked, rising from his seat.

"I'll have another rum and Coke," Regina said. She watched as he made his way through the crowded room to the bar. *Damn, that's a fine man*, she thought. *He's smart, he's fine, and he's mine. A bit on the arrogant side, and not as compassionate as I'd like, but no one's perfect.* She took a sip of her drink. *And there's time enough to work on him.*

Regina's thoughts were interrupted by a white woman sitting at the far end of the bar. She was passably pretty, although her makeup was flawless. Her hair was jet black, and flared around her face like a lion's mane. She was tall but a little plump. And her stare was fixed in Charles's direction. Regina glanced at Charles to see if he returned the stare, but he was standing at the bar, wallet in hand, waiting for his order.

Regina looked at the woman again, and noticed her talking to a man sitting next to her. The man got up, gathered his money from the bar, and started walking toward the door, passing Charles as he did so. As soon as Charles paid for his drinks, the woman got up. As she walked toward the door, she bumped into Charles, almost causing him to spill the drinks. As the woman batted her false eyelashes in apology, Regina jumped from her seat in alarm.

"Excuse me, may I talk to you for a moment?" she asked in a low voice, grabbing the woman by the arm as she reached the bar.

"I'm sorry. Do I know you?" the woman asked in a snooty voice as she tried to pull her arm away.

"Regina, she just bumped into me. It was an accident," Charles said.

"Come on, this will just take a minute," Regina said to the woman, ignoring Charles. She tightened her grip on the woman's arm. The woman's purse fell to the floor.

"Would you please let me go?" the woman said louder.

"Take your hands off of her!"

The woman's companion had suddenly appeared and was towering over Regina in a threatening manner. He then shoved Regina, causing her to topple backward into Charles. The glasses Charles was holding fell and shattered on the floor. Charles angrily grabbed the man by the back of the shirt.

"What the hell is your problem?" he shouted as people began to scurry away from the fracas. Instead of answering, the man turned around and delivered a solid blow to Charles's jaw causing Charles to relinquish his shirt. The man snatched the woman by the arm and tried for the door, but Regina reached out and grabbed the woman by the back of her hair, causing her to scream.

The man turned to punch Regina, but Charles, having quickly recovered, jabbed him twice in the face, and landed a haymaker to his jaw. Regina darted out of the way as the man toppled backward.

"Get away from him!" the woman screamed as she snatched a beer bottle from a nearby table and advanced toward Charles. Regina dug her hand into her shoulder bag and pulled out a pocketknife. She flipped it open and jumped in front of the woman.

"Yeah, bitch," she screamed, waving the knife. "Come on with it. I'll slit your fucking throat!"

Regina stood in a slight crouch, glaring at the woman with eyes squinted into slits. Her breathing was fast and loud.

The woman's eyes were wide as saucers, and she stood as if paralyzed, watching the slow wave of the threatening blade.

"Drop the knife," commanded a strong, male voice. Regina

took her eyes off the woman long enough to see the tall, bulky black man's face. It was the nightclub bouncer.

"Fuck you. Tell that bitch to drop the bottle," Regina hissed back.

The woman dropped the bottle without any coaxing and turned toward the bouncer, sobbing.

"I don't even know her! I was just leaving and she assaulted me!"

"Yeah, she was leaving," Regina yelled back, "with my boyfriend's wallet! Open up her purse. She dropped it in there!"

"Oh, shit," Charles said, as he patted the pocket of his jacket.

"I don't know what she's talking about," the woman said. "Look, I just want to get out of here." She reached again for her purse, picked it up from the floor, and looked at the bouncer with the best smile she could muster under the circumstances. "Look, I don't want to press charges. I just want to leave. Thanks."

"You're not going anywhere," David said, jumping in front of the woman before she could walk out.

"Would you please get out of my way?" the woman hissed, trying to step around him.

"You're just going to let her leave?" Charles asked the bouncer, incredulously.

"Would you mind if I look in your purse?" the bouncer asked the woman.

"Yes, I would," the woman answered haughtily. "I'm not going to be treated like a criminal. I'm leaving."

"Why don't you just wait until the police get here, then," the bouncer said.

"I said, I'm leaving," the woman huffed. "You have no right to stop me." Just then, Tamika, whom Regina hadn't even noticed, reached out and snatched the woman's purse from her hand and sprinted to Regina's side.

"Hey!" the woman screamed.

Tamika snapped the purse open, and pulled out a brown billfold. "Is this yours?" she asked triumphantly, handing it to Charles.

All eyes were upon him as he opened it quickly, and grunted. "She must have taken it from me when she bumped into me at the bar," he said grimly.

The bouncer grabbed the woman as she tried to sprint for the door. "You're not going anywhere. You're staying put until the police arrive."

Through the window Regina saw a black limousine pull up in front of the club. *As if the night weren't eventful enough,* she thought, as Earl Masters struggled out of the backseat. Three Japanese businessmen climbed out after him.

"We're not pressing charges," Regina said quickly as she closed her knife and dropped it back into her purse.

"Oh yes, we are!" Charles said just as quickly.

"You've got your wallet back, let's just get out of here," she said motioning for Tamika. They started walking toward the door.

"Regina," Charles cried after them.

"Will you please just come on?" she shouted back over her shoulder as she opened the door and headed out to the street.

"Earl!" Regina said rushing up to the *New York Times* editor as he stood on the sidewalk talking to his companions. "What are you doing out?"

"Lovely Miss Harris," Earl said kissing her hand. She couldn't help but notice the scent of cognac on his breath. "Fancy meeting you at a nightclub. I didn't think you ventured out after dark. I'm just showing some friends a night on the town. Are you leaving?"

Regina smiled sexily as she withdrew her hand, and placed it lightly on Earl's portly shoulders. "I certainly am. They just had some kind of awful incident in there. Would you believe some woman was caught picking a man's pocket?"

"Indeed?" Earl's eyebrow shot up. "And I had read such wonderful things about this place."

"Well, you know you can't believe everything you read." Regina giggled.

"So, I see." Earl stood on the sidewalk as if confused about what to do next. The Japanese businessmen stood next to him, obviously waiting for him to lead them into the club.

"My girlfriend and I are going to hit the Blue Note up on Broadway. Why don't you meet us there?" Regina asked quickly.

"Sounds like a wonderful idea. Why don't you two beautiful women allow us to give you a ride?" He turned his attention toward Tamika. "I'm sorry, dear, please allow me to introduce myself. Earl Masters," he said, extending his hand, then bringing Tamika's hand to his lips.

"How do you do, I'm Tamika Thomas," Tamika said nervously.

"We have a car, but why don't you guys go ahead and we'll meet you there," Regina said quickly. "Make sure you save us seats at your table."

"Dang, Regina. It's a good thing they didn't get here five minutes sooner," Tamika said after the limousine pulled away. "He really would have gotten an eyeful."

"Tell me about it. If word had gotten out about me waving a knife around in a nightclub, I could say good-bye to my professional reputation," Regina said, walking toward the corner. "And it's a good thing Charles didn't come out while I was talking to him, either. He wouldn't have known how to play it off even if he were inclined to do so, and I'm not sure he would have been so inclined. Where are the guys, anyway?"

"They're coming now," Tamika said, looking back over her shoulder. "Hey, how did you know she lifted his wallet? Did you see her when she did it?"

"Hmmph! You know I used to do the same thing myself,"

Regina answered with a half chuckle as they reached the spot where Charles's car was parked. "I don't blame the chick, I just wanted to get Charles's wallet back."

"Hey!"

They turned to see Charles and David walking toward them.

"Hey, baby," Regina said lightly, smiling up at Charles. Tamika walked over to David, who put his arm around her protectively.

"We really should stick around and press charges," Charles said urgently.

"Why? You've got your wallet back," she said, shrugging her shoulders. She moved closer to Charles and began lightly fingering his jacket. "Hey, where did you learn to fight like that? I was impressed."

"I boxed in high school," he grunted. "A better question is where did you get the knife?"

Regina pulled away and shrugged, unconsciously pulling her purse close to her body. "I carry it around for protection."

"For protection? From what?" Charles looked at her suspiciously.

"From whatever. Come on, let's go home. I'm really tired."

Later that night their lovemaking was fast and furious. Charles was usually a tender lover, and often let Regina be the aggressor, but this time he took the lead. Before Regina could even put her keys down, he was on her, almost ripping off her clothes. They made love on the living room floor, then made their way to the bedroom and started again. The sheets were soaked with perspiration and body juices by the time he finally rolled over and closed his eyes.

Thinking he was asleep, Regina got up and made her way to the kitchen to pour herself a glass of juice. She thought about what excuse she could offer Earl for standing him and his friends up. When she got back to the bedroom Charles was propped up on his elbow.

"So, let me ask you," he said as she climbed back into the bed. "Have you ever actually cut someone with that knife?"

"Why would you ask me something like that?" Regina said defensively.

"Uh-huh. There you go again, getting all indignant when I ask you anything about your past. I only asked because it looked like you knew what you were doing with that knife," he answered, moving closer to her, and looking directly into her eyes.

"I'm a good actress," she said, tracing her fingers over his chest and down toward his stomach.

He pulled her hand away and pulled her body against his. "I don't doubt that, but you haven't answered my question. Have you ever cut someone?"

She could feel him getting hard again. "Would you love me more if I said yes or if I said no?" she asked, kissing his shoulder.

"I just want you to tell me the truth," he answered, stroking her bare back.

"No, I've never cut anyone," she said, "but that doesn't mean I wouldn't if I had to."

"You would, though, huh?" He started to breathe heavier.

"What do you think?" she answered. Her hand crept down the front of his body again. This time he didn't stop her.

Regina smiled to herself as Charles drifted off to sleep Their lovemaking was exciting to him, but he had no idea how much excitement Regina had had in her life. Her mind drifted back to her teenage years, when she was still struggling to support herself and little Renee.

REGINA WAS IN MIDTOWN at Saks Fifth Avenue, applying for a sales job she knew she wouldn't get, when she met the person who would change her life. As she stood admiring a flimsy, black silk dress, with a $110 price tag, she heard a female voice behind her.

"Hey, you like that?"

Regina looked around, surprised that anyone had noticed her. She was even more surprised that the voice came from a young, blond, white girl dressed in expensive baggy Levi's and a red Calvin Klein sweatshirt.

"Um, yes. But I don't think you have my size," Regina mumbled, backing away. "Thanks anyway."

"I don't work here, but I bet they have your size. What are you? About a three petite?" the white girl asked in a low voice.

"Um, I don't know. Look, I can't afford it. Thanks, anyway," Regina tried again.

"Cool out. How much can you afford?" the girl said, as she reached out and grabbed Regina's arm in a friendly manner. "Trust me. It's okay."

"I only have fifteen dollars on me," Regina said, embarrassed.

"Fifteen. Is that all? Shit!" The girl let go of Regina's arm, but stood there for a moment. "Look. I'll give you a play anyway. You want a size three?"

"I think I'm more like a one," Regina said excitedly. "What are you going to do?"

"Don't worry. Just go ahead and walk out and meet me on the corner in five minutes, okay? Don't look back at me. Just walk right out the door now."

Regina obediently turned and walked toward the front door of the store, feeling the suspicious eyes of the burly security guard boring into her back. Suddenly fear enveloped her, and she turned and walked back to the rack of dresses to speak to the girl.

"Um, I changed my mind," she whispered timidly.

"Why? What's wrong?" the girl asked incredulously.

"I don't want to get in trouble, and I don't want you to get in trouble because of me. Thanks anyway," Regina said, turning to walk away.

"Wait!" the girl said urgently.

"What?"

"No one's going to get in trouble. I have the dress on me now. You're going to back out now?"

Regina looked the girl over in surprise. She had no pocketbook or shopping bags, and she hadn't had time to go to the dressing room to stash the dress in her clothes.

"You have it on you now? Where?" Regina whispered, excited again.

"Look. You're going to draw too much attention to me. Just go ahead to the corner and wait for me, like I said."

Again Regina walked toward the front door. This time the burly security guard stopped her.

"Excuse me. Do you mind if I take a look in your pocketbook?" he asked as he reached for the large black pocketbook that once belonged to her mother.

"Why? I didn't do anything," Regina cried, guilt lacing her voice.

"Then you shouldn't mind if I look in your bag. It will only take a minute."

Not knowing her rights, and afraid if she made a scene she would be arrested, Regina reluctantly handed over the pocketbook. Shoppers looked over in her direction, and a few curled up their lips in disgust, assuming that uptown trash had violated their expensive boutique haven. The white girl headed out the door with her nose up in the air, stopping for a moment to peer at Regina in contempt, as if she thought Regina was just another common thief ready to be hauled off by the police.

"You can go," the security guard said afterward with no apology.

"Thanks," Regina mumbled, as she rushed through the door, trying to hide her tears.

That girl was just trying to set me up, and I fell for it, Regina thought as she walked to the corner subway, wiping the tears with the back of her hand. A lady never cries in public, her mother once told her. *Mommy would be so upset with me now.* The thought made the tears stream down her face even faster.

"Yo! What's the matter with you?"

Regina blinked through the blur of tears to see the blond girl smiling as she leaned on top of the corner mailbox.

"Huh?" was all she could say.

"Huh, nothing. Come on," the girl said, motioning Regina over to a nearby building.

Regina hesitated for a minute, wondering if she should trust the girl, but shrugged her shoulders and followed. She had nothing to lose.

"Open up your pocketbook," the girl demanded.

"What? Don't even try it," Regina hissed as she pulled the pocketbook strap farther up her shoulder and balled up her fists. "I'll kick your ass from here to California!"

"What the fuck is wrong with you? I'm only telling you to open your bag to put the dress in it. You just going to carry a $110 dress in your arms on the subway?" The girl laughed. "You think the security guard in the store was bad, those subway cops will be all over your ass."

The girl knelt down on the sidewalk and pulled up her right pants leg, revealing a skinny calf covered by a large tube sweat sock that had the dress tucked inside.

"Oh, man!" Regina said in wonderment. "How did you do that with no one catching you?"

"Practice, honey. I make two to three hundred dollars a day doing this, so you know I'm good. Where's my money?"

Regina fished a twenty-dollar bill out of her pocketbook. "You got change?" she asked.

"Hey! I thought you only had fifteen."

"Well, I need money for the subway and dinner." Regina smiled. "Got change?"

"Yeah, I got change. And you got a bargain," the girl grumbled.

"What's your name? Where can I find you again?" Regina asked after the girl pulled some money from her bra and handed her five crumpled one-dollar bills.

"Why? You want to do more business?"

"Maybe."

"I'm Krystal. Give me your number, and if you tell me what you want, I'll call you when I get it, okay?"

"Umm. Okay. My name's Regina." She wrote her telephone number on the flap of an envelope from her pocketbook and handed it to the girl.

"Listen, do you work with anyone? I mean, could you use a partner?" Regina asked timidly.

"Who, you? No offense, but you were scared shitless in that store."

"No, I wasn't. I was just caught off guard. And I'm a fast learner," Regina said quickly as the wheels turned in her head. If she could earn $200 a day, even $200 a week, she would be able to refill the dwindling bank account and pay the bills. Maybe even put something aside for Renee to go to college.

"And two heads are better than one. And I could be your lookout. And we can take turns. And—"

"Forget it. Thanks for the offer. Nice doing business with you," the girl said as she pushed past Regina.

"Oh yeah," she said, turning her head around. "Next time you're going to have to give up more than fifteen bucks. I gave you a break this time."

• • •

THREE NIGHTS LATER, the telephone rang, just as Regina finished giving Renee her bedtime bath.

"Hi Regina? It's Krystal. Remember me?"

"Hey, yeah. How are you doing?"

"Doing okay, doing okay. What's up? You need anything?"

"No. I mean yeah. I mean . . . look, I really need to talk to you," Regina stammered.

"So talk."

"I'd really like to talk to you in person. It's important. My mom always said important talks should be in person," Regina said quickly.

"Important talk, huh? Okay, I'm interested. Can you come down some night?"

"I was hoping we could meet during the day?"

"I work during the day, honey. And I don't get coffee breaks."

"You work?"

"Yeah. I'm self-employed."

Regina laughed. "Okay. But, ummm . . . okay. Well, can you come uptown? I live right on 118th Street."

"You're the one who wants to do the talking. Why don't you come downtown?"

"Scared to come to Harlem?" Regina teased.

"Scared to come downtown?" Krystal teased back.

"No. It's just that . . ." Regina looked over at Renee cooing away on the couch, waiting to be put to bed, then glanced at the clock—8:30 P.M. Maybe she could get Mrs. Young, the elderly woman downstairs, to watch her for an hour or so. "Okay. How about right now? Where are you at?"

"Now? Hmm . . . it must be important. Okay. Meet me at the coffee shop on the corner of Fifty-ninth and Lex, across the street from Bloomingdale's. Bloomie's is open late tonight, and I need to get some shopping done," Krystal said laughing at her own joke.

"No problem. Just give me a half hour, okay?"

"Deal."

Thirty-five minutes later Regina walked into the coffee shop looking for Krystal. Renee was asleep in a baby carrier strapped across Regina's stomach. Mrs. Young wasn't home when Regina knocked on her door, and she was forced to bring the baby with her on her mission into the night.

"Oooh. I didn't know you had a kid. How old are you, anyway?" Krystal said after motioning Regina over to a booth.

"Old enough," Regina said tiredly as she undid the carrier and carefully laid the sleeping Renee on the seat before sliding in herself.

"Babies making babies," Krystal said with the shake of her head. "And you looked like such a goody-goody."

"See! You should never judge a book by its cover," Regina said, not bothering to correct Krystal's assumption. "I'm not a goody-goody. And I'm perfectly able to do what I need to do to get what I want."

"Yeah, okay. Sure. What's up? What do you have to talk to me about that's so important?"

Just then a waitress came by and asked if they were ready to order.

"Yes, please," Krystal said brightly. "Two cappuccinos, and she's buying," she said pointing to Regina.

"Hey," she continued. "Does the baby need milk or something?"

"No. She's asleep," Regina said as she patted Renee's back.

"Okay. Now what's up?"

Regina bit her lower lip and looked at the girl, trying to figure out where to start.

"Krystal," she finally said, placing her hand on Krystal's arm. "Let me work with you."

"Shit. I know you didn't come all the way down here to ask me that. I told you before, *no!* Drop it. Shit. I thought you had some kind of mega-order for me or something," Krystal said angrily snatching her arm away. "I thought you were okay, but it looks like you're just trying to waste my time. I'm outta here."

"Wait. I'm sorry. Let me just explain," Regina said frantically as Krystal slid out of the booth.

"There's nothing to explain. I can't help you out, and I don't know why you're bugging me about this shit!"

"I know, I know. It's just that I need some money. I don't have any money."

"Just ask your mommy. Don't waste my time."

"I can't ask my mom. She's dead," Regina blurted out. She looked straight at Krystal, then turned away as her eyes filled with tears.

"I don't have anyone I can ask. And I can't find a job. And I have to take care of the baby. And . . ." Regina broke out in large sobs that she tried to smother with a napkin from the table. The thought of failing herself, Renee, and her mother's memory, was too much for her to handle. She buried her face in her hands, not caring that people were staring as she cried her young heart out.

"Oh shit. I'm sorry," Krystal said, patting Regina on the back and handing her a glass of water from the table. "Come on. It's going to be okay."

"No, it's not going to be okay. I don't have enough money to pay next month's rent or this month's electric bill. I don't know what I'm going to do," Regina sobbed hysterically.

"Look, how much do you need? Maybe I can loan you some cash or something?" Krystal reached in her pocket and took out a roll of bills.

"And how am I going to pay you back? And what do I do when that money runs out?" Regina wailed.

"Is she okay?" the waitress asked Krystal.

"Oh yeah, she's fine. She just broke up with her boyfriend. You know how it is," Krystal said quickly, stuffing her money back into her pocket. "Can we get those cappuccinos, please?"

After the waitress walked away, Krystal stroked Regina's hair in an attempt to smother her sobs.

"Look, first rule if we're going to work together. Stop doing things that draw attention, okay?"

IT DIDN'T TAKE LONG before the people in Regina's apartment building noticed that she was dressing rather well for a motherless teenager. The knee-length skirts that Matilda had dressed her in were relegated to the back of the closet, and in their stead were designer jeans and silk blouses. Her chest had begun to sprout small firm breasts, which Regina covered with Gloria Vanderbilt brassieres and camisoles, all with matching panties. Thanks to the money she was making with Krystal, she was able to afford to make weekly trips to the hairdresser, and began to experiment successfully with makeup. Though she was still very small for her age, with Krystal's coaching, Regina no longer looked like a thirteen-year-old, but rather like a petite and tastefully dressed twenty-year-old. Her new appearance made security guards a little less suspicious when she walked into fancy boutiques, and made it easier for her to walk out with hundreds of dollars worth of clothing that she and Krystal then sold to a select number of customers—a group that came to include a number of uptown women who had expensive dreams but a limited budget.

Renee also benefited from Regina's new profession. Her room was filled with plush teddy bears and expensive toys. Regina dressed her baby niece in the latest designer fashions. Renee was the only baby on 118th Street with tiny Adidas sneakers in every color, with matching sweatsuits and headbands. On Sundays, when most of the clothing stores were closed, Regina would put Renee in her expensive stroller, and the two would parade down Lenox Avenue in matching outfits, enjoying the admiring and jealous glances from other women with their children.

When young women stopped Regina and Renee to compliment their clothing, Regina would size them up, and if they looked promising, she told them she might be able to supply them with the same type of finery at well below wholesale prices. She opened a new market for the hot merchandise she and Krystal collected—Harlem. Regina proved to be an excellent booster, but an even better businesswoman. Not wanting to bring clients to her mother's apartment, and she did still consider it Matilda's apartment, Regina arranged to take and deliver orders at a beauty parlor on 125th Street near Fifth Avenue. She felt little guilt about what she was doing. She had tried to make an honest living, but could find no job, she reasoned. If she couldn't support herself and Renee, they would wind up in foster care. Regina had read horror stories about young girls turned into slaves, and being sexually molested by wicked foster parents. While Matilda might have disapproved of her daughter's shoplifting, she would certainly prefer it to the alternative.

Between her new daytime career and her nighttime mothering efforts, Regina had little time to hang out with her friends, but the girls still managed occasional get-togethers at her apartment. Yvonne, Puddin', and Tamika all knew what Regina was doing, and passed no judgments. Like Renee, they profited from Regina's new career, because she supplied them with fancy clothes she boosted from the stores. All except Yvonne. Mama Tee made sure she had all the latest styles anyway, and would have questioned her if she walked into the house with new clothing. Puddin' and Tamika's parents didn't care. Puddin' had asked Regina if she could work with them, but Regina politely yet firmly refused. One reason was because she didn't think Puddin' would know how to handle herself if approached by a salesgirl or security guard. Another was the fact that Puddin' and Krystal didn't get along. All three of her girlfriends had met Krystal, and referred to her derisively as "the white girl" behind her back but Puddin' was downright rude to her in person. Krystal always blew it off, but Regina wasn't going to jeopardize her own relationship with Krystal by even broaching the subject.

Krystal was nineteen years old, Regina eventually learned. Originally from New Haven, Connecticut, she had run away from home when she was fifteen to escape her father, a college professor who had started sexually molesting her two years before when his wife had died in an automobile accident.

Krystal shared a two-bedroom apartment in Hell's Kitchen with a roommate who turned tricks in Times Square to pay her share of the rent. Regina was shocked when she found out that both used heroin, but Krystal assured her that her habit was under control. Besides, she told Regina, she only sniffed. It was people who shot up that wound up strung out and on the streets. To Krystal's credit, she never tried to get Regina to take hard drugs, although they did sometimes smoke pot together. It was Krystal who had given Regina her first knife as a birthday gift—a dainty pearl-handled number with a deadly four-inch blade.

ON A SATURDAY AFTERNOON, Regina and Charles drove to Philadelphia for Charles's parents' fortieth anniversary party. Regina's stomach did flip-flops during the two-hour drive down the New Jersey Turnpike, but she hid her nervousness from Charles. She had gathered, from what Charles had said about his family, that they were part of Philadelphia's black "society," who usually turned their noses up at anyone outside of their tight circle. *Best behavior,* Regina said to herself over and over during the car ride. *I've got to be on my best behavior. No getting upset at people putting on airs. No snide comments if someone makes disparaging remarks about poor people. I'm going to grin and bear it.*

Regina was used to putting on an act for people—the snobbish literary elite like Earl Masters and Maggie Peterson—but she only had to be around them for short periods of time.

But it's going to be different with Charles's parents. Heck, they might even wind up being my in-laws, Regina thought. *What if I can't stand them?*

Worse, what if they see that I'm not their kind? What if they don't think I'm good enough for their son? Regina's eyes closed into a squint, and she lifted her head high as if looking down her nose at someone.

"Well, then fuck them," she unknowingly said aloud.

"I'm sorry. What did you say, baby?" Charles asked, turning down the car stereo.

"Huh? Oh, nothing," Regina answered quickly. *Dang,* she thought. *I'm getting ahead of myself. They're probably really nice folks. And even if they're not, I don't have to like them. I just have to be polite. Oh God, I hope everything goes okay.*

Regina stifled a gasp as she entered the large stone mansion in the ritzy Wynnefield section of the city. The white wall-to-wall carpet on the first floor was so plush that even with high heels Regina felt she was walking on a cloud. A large, elegantly framed oil painting of a regal, middle-aged African-American couple—the man sitting, the woman standing behind his chair—hung in the foyer. A shiny black baby-grand piano dominated the enormous living room, and the entire house was filled with furniture screaming very old and very expensive. Well-dressed people stood in small groups, chatting, most holding drinks in their hands. Uniformed waiters flitted silently about with trays of hors d'oeuvres. *Good Lord,* Regina thought. *I knew they were well off, but I didn't know they were living this large!*

"Hi baby, I knew you'd make it."

Regina turned to find the woman from the painting warmly embracing Charles. Her dyed-blond hair was pulled back in a French twist, and she wore a blue, sequined blouse over a darker blue silk-chiffon evening skirt. Diamond teardrop earrings, a matching teardrop pendant, and a diamond bracelet topped off her outfit. *I would have thought Charles's mother to be more conservative, but girlfriend obviously wants people to know she's arrived in the world,* Regina thought as the woman turned to her.

"You must be Regina. Welcome to Philadelphia," Sylvia Whitfield said warmly, as she kissed her on the cheek. "And welcome to our home."

"Thank you, Mrs. Whitfield," Regina said demurely. "I'm so glad you invited me."

"Well, we had to meet the woman who's been keeping Charlie in New York every weekend." Mrs. Whitfield laughed. "Come on in and join the party."

Something about the way the older woman spoke and looked at her made the small hairs on Regina's neck bristle. She had expected to be sized up; after all, Charles was the Whitfield's only son, and knowing that, she had dressed accordingly. A simple white sheath dress with white satin pumps, and only the slightest hint of makeup. Her hair was swept up in a loose bun, with just a few tendrils hanging to soften the effect.

"Charles said you're originally from Manhattan. What part?" Mrs. Whitfield asked casually, as she led Regina into the large drawing room.

"Harlem," Regina said simply.

"Really? What area? I have good friends who used to live on Riverside Drive. Near 165th Street, I believe. Of course, that was before the Dominicans and Puerto Ricans took over. They've since moved to Danbury, Connecticut. My friends, that is," Mrs. Whitfield said with a laugh. "Perhaps you know them? Eloise and Darryl McCline? They're both psychiatrists. I believe Darryl is on staff with Columbia Presbyterian Hospital."

"No, I don't know them. But then, Harlem is a pretty big community," Regina said carefully. "Actually, I'm from Central Harlem."

"Central Harlem?"

"Yes, near Lenox Avenue and 118th Street." Regina kept her head forward, but glanced out the corner of her eye to see Mrs. Whitfield's expression. She wasn't disappointed. The woman's eyes widened, although she kept her voice even.

"Well, I can't say I'm very familiar with the area." Mrs. Whitfield stopped and signaled a waiter for a glass of champagne. "But you don't live there now, I suppose?"

"No. I have an apartment on the Upper West Side."

"Where on the Upper West Side?" Mrs. Whitfield asked suspiciously.

"Seventy-first and West End Avenue."

"Now that's a nice area!" Mrs. Whitfield took a sip from her glass, apparently pleased that her son wasn't traveling to the slums to visit his lady friend. "But I understand that the Puerto Ricans are even moving in there. It seems you just can't get away from them," she said with a sigh.

"Well, actually, I guess you could say that I'm part of the movement. My father was half Puerto Rican," she said in a demure tone, hiding her smile.

"Oh! Well, I hope I haven't offended you! I didn't mean—"

"No offense taken." Regina smiled warmly at the embarrassed woman. She didn't want to start off on the wrong foot with Charles's mother, but she couldn't start off by ignoring insults, either.

"So, Regina, what line of work was your father in?"

The interrogation was obviously still on, but before Regina could answer, a sophisticated young woman walked up and slipped her arm through Mrs. Whitfield's arm.

"Happy Anniversary, Mrs. Whitfield," the self-assured woman said, giving Charles's mother a light kiss on the cheek.

"Oh, Angela. I was looking for you earlier, dear." Mrs. Whitfield turned to face the woman. "Your mother called to say she wasn't feeling well. Is she okay?"

"Another migraine, but the doctor said she'll be fine."

Regina looked at the two women conversing. Had it not been for the age difference they could have passed for twins—or at least sisters. Both were tall and stately. Both had obviously dyed blond hair pulled back into a French twist. The younger woman—Angela—wore an open-back, peach-colored floor-length gown, with a light shawl draped around her shoulders. Regina felt suddenly underdressed.

"Angela, I'd like to introduce you to Miss Regina Harris of New York City," Mrs. Whitfield said, waving her hand in Regina's direction. "She's a good friend of Charlie's."

"Pleased to meet you, Regina. Is this your first time in Philadelphia?" Angela asked warmly as she extended a hand toward Regina.

"No, I went to school at Temple," Regina said graciously.

"Regina's a writer," Mrs. Whitfield said grandly. "She did that article I was telling you about in the *New Yorker*. A very well thought-out piece on the legalization of drugs."

"How interesting!" Angela exclaimed.

"Yes, Regina's a very interesting person," Mrs. Whitfield said in a distracted tone while peering across the room. "You two young ladies will have to excuse me, I think I see the deputy mayor over there in the corner."

Mrs. Whitfield flitted off, leaving Regina and Angela alone.

"So, did she give you the third-degree?"

The question caught Regina off guard, but the nonchalant tone in which it was asked caused her to laugh out loud.

"Don't worry. She does it to every woman she thinks is interested in her little boy." Angela grinned. "She's making sure no riffraff gets close to the family jewels."

"I got that impression." Regina smiled and appraised her new companion. Angela appeared friendly, but there was something about her that made Regina want to keep her at arm's length.

"Did you go through the interrogation, too?" she asked the woman.

"Me?" Angela's hand flew to her chest in mock surprise. "Heavens, no! I've known the Whitfields all my life. In fact, we're neighbors. I've been spared, thanks to our geographical proximity."

Regina laughed along with Angela, but noted that the woman hadn't taken the opportunity to say she wasn't interested in Charles.

"So, how long have you been writing?" Angela asked.

"About six years. I started while I was in school. What about you?"

"I guess I'm still trying to find myself." Angela sighed. "My degree's in early childhood education, but I don't want to be a teacher. I'm really not too keen on any career."

"No?" Regina's eyebrow shot upward.

"No. I guess I'm just the kind of woman who needs to get married and take care of a house full of children." Angela giggled. "Can you just see me barefoot and in the kitchen, so to speak?"

"Well, to each her own," Regina said lightly.

"Oh come on, admit it. Wouldn't you give up your career in a minute if someone like Charles asked you to marry him?"

"Why would I do that?" Regina asked, trying to keep her disgust from flowing into her voice.

"Why wouldn't you?"

"Hey, honey!" Regina looked up just as Charles slipped his arm around her waist.

"I see you've met Angela." He kissed Angela on the cheek,

but turned away before she could speak to him. "Come on, I want you to meet my dad."

Reverend Jerome Whitfield was in the far corner of the enormous room, amusing a small group of listeners with personal stories about the mayor. He was a loud and gregarious man whose laugh bellowed from his stomach. Dressed in a tuxedo, he looked as relaxed as if he were in jeans and a T-shirt. He shook Regina's hand warmly as Charles introduced her.

"I hear you're a writer. Charlie says you work for *Newsweek*?" he asked in a friendly tone.

"No, I'm a freelance writer, but I have had some articles published in *Newsweek*," she replied. He was as casual as his wife was formal. Like Charles, his eyes twinkled when he talked, and also like his only son, he looked directly into her eyes as he spoke, making her feel he was really interested in what she said.

"So are you planning on writing a book?"

"A book?"

"I thought all writers aspired to write a book," he said, clinking the ice in his half-filled glass of Scotch. "Surely you've got a book buried somewhere in your soul, young lady."

Regina liked him. She didn't dislike his wife, but she certainly liked him. She decided to try to spend the better part of the evening talking to him, but after only a few minutes of conversation he was whisked away by a fellow city councilman.

"Hey, Regina. I want you to meet a good friend of mine."

Charles's arm was around a grinning white man in a tuxedo with a kente-cloth cummerbund. His eyes were bright baby blue, and his hair stark black, although his face swore middle age.

"Regina Harris, this is Richard Davis, soon to be U. S. Senator Richard Davis."

"How do you do?" the man shook her hand politely, then turned to Charles. "It doesn't surprise me to find you escorting the prettiest girl at the party."

Regina fought a sudden urge to correct his "girl" for "woman." She didn't usually mind, even notice, when men referred to her as a girl, but for some reason she minded just then. It wasn't even so much the way it was said, as something about the person who said it.

"Woman, not girl, Rick. Regina's not the type of woman who takes kindly to being called girl," Charles said, as if reading her mind. He slapped his friend on the back. "You better practice your p.c. if you're going out on the campaign trail."

"My apologies, of course. No insult intended." Rick laughed. "And don't worry, the primaries aren't until May. I'll have it all down pat by then."

Dr. Siebert! The thought jolted Regina. *That's who Rick Davis reminds me of!* She could feel her stomach turn, and her face redden. He had that same superior, patronizing attitude that said, *I'm better than everybody else in the world, and certainly better than you.*

IN HER MIND she was back in the hospital after being shot. Dr. Siebert was a staff physician at the hospital. Dr. Siebert. Dr. Fucking Siebert. She couldn't remember his first name, maybe she never knew it. She had met him before. Through Little Joe, one of the dealers she used to hang out with. One of the few guys who treated her like a lady. Little Joe was a big-time dealer, and knew how to have a good time. He took her to fancy restaurants and Broadway plays, usually with an entourage.

Once he took her downtown to a party thrown by one of his lawyers, John Siebert, and it was there that she had met Dr. Siebert, the lawyer's brother. She didn't pay much attention to him at the time; she was too busy being overwhelmed by all the stars and entertainers at the party. John Siebert threw a great party, but he wasn't a good enough attorney to keep Little Joe out of jail. Little Joe and fourteen of his friends were spending the rest of their lives in the federal penitentiary in Leavenworth, Kansas. As fond as she was of Little Joe, Regina had no plans to visit. Leavenworth was too far from Harlem. Besides, she didn't want to run into his wife of twenty years.

Dr. Siebert made it a point to check on Regina often while she was in the hospital, making friendly conversation and asking if she was comfortable or needed more painkillers. On her fourth day he stopped in at 3:00 A.M., waking her up.

"Hi, I was just getting ready to leave the hospital and I thought I'd stop by to see how you're doing," he said in a strange voice. "You were thrashing around like you were having a nightmare. Are you okay?"

"I'm okay," Regina said groggily. Funny, she didn't remember having a bad dream. Though the room was dark, she noticed that he was in his street clothes.

"Are you sure? I could give you something to put you back to sleep and make sure you have good dreams." He smiled, but it was a nervous smile. He started stroking her hair.

Regina said nothing.

"You know, I've really been looking out for you since you've been here," he said, continuing to stroke her hair. "And I've let the nurses know I'm taking a special interest in your case. They know I want them to take really good care of you."

"I appreciate that," Regina said slowly, wondering where the conversation was going.

"Good, good." He moved closer to the hospital bed, so that his crotch was almost touching the railing. The bulge in his pants was unmistakable.

"I think I'm going back to sleep," Regina said as she moved away from that side of the bed.

"Okay, you do that," he said absently. Regina closed her eyes, hoping he would leave, but instead he took her hand and placed it on his crotch. She snatched it away and sat up in the bed.

"It's okay, it's okay. Calm down," Dr. Siebert said soothingly. "I don't want to upset you. I'm just a little lonely is all, and I just thought you might want to show your appreciation. You know . . . I take care of you and you take care of me."

"I think you'd better leave," she hissed.

"Okay, I'll leave. I see you're not feeling too well right now. Are you sure you don't want anything to go to sleep?" he asked quickly, backing away from the bed.

"No, just leave."

He turned away and started walking toward the door, but then turned back.

"You know, I don't want you to do anything perverted or anything. I'm not like that," he said moving back toward her. "All I want is a blow job. That's all. Just this one time. Come on. It'll just take five minutes, I promise. It's not like you've never done one before."

"You don't know what I've done before," she said in almost a whisper.

"I'm not trying to be unkind, but we both know what you do for a living, Regina. I can be really nice to you when you get out of here. Think about that."

"Get the fuck out of here, before I ring for a nurse," she said, raising her voice.

"I'm leaving," he said in a haughty voice. His mouth twisted in a frown. "But I wouldn't call the nurses if I were you. And I wouldn't mention this to anyone. After all, I just came in to check on you and then you propositioned me. I should be shocked, but then again, why would I be, considering the fact that you're nothing but a two-bit whore."

He turned around and stormed out the door.

Regina's body shook uncontrollably with rage. How dare he? She reached over to push the button to summon the nurse, but stopped. He was right. Who would they believe? A prominent young doctor, or a girl shot while hanging out with a drug dealer? She covered her face with her hands and started sobbing. How could this have happened to her? She was supposed to be somebody in life. Her mother had said she would be the one in the family to make something of herself. Be it a doctor, or a lawyer, or something.

How could she have sunk so low that some asshole would even think she'd consider giving him a blow job in a hospital? Who does that stupid doctor think he is? She cried even harder as she answered herself. He knew who he was, and he knew who she was. Street trash. And anybody can do anything they wanted to street trash.

But her mother didn't raise street trash. She'd show him. She'd show the world. She was just as good as anybody else. In fact, she was better that most, and she'd prove it. And she did. But here she was, five years later, shaking like a leaf just because something—someone—reminded her of that awful night.

"GINA, ARE YOU OKAY? You look like you saw a ghost!"

Regina blinked her eyes quickly and smiled weakly at Charles.

"Yes. I'm just, umm, thinking about . . . oh shoot, I don't remember what I was thinking about. Isn't that awful when that happens?"

The rest of the party was pretty much a blur of quick introductions and boring conversations. Regina was a little tipsy by the time she met Charles's older sister Kimberly. The plastic surgeon husband couldn't attend, she explained. He was at an out-of-town convention. And since their daughter was spending the weekend with a girlfriend in Harrisburg, she was playing the role of a single woman for a few days, she said with a wink.

Four martinis and three hours later Regina slept as Charles drove back to New York, and a recent dream seeped back into her unconscious.

She was at a theater, ready to play the lead in *Swan Lake* in front of an audience of thousands. But just as she was ready to dance, she looked down and realized she was wearing sneakers. Dirty, beat-up, smelly sneakers, with holes in the toes. Suddenly someone pushed her to centerstage, and the tinkly music stopped. Gasps escaped from the audience. Petrified and embarrassed, but not knowing what else to do, she started dancing ballet to a jazz tune only she could hear. Midway through a graceful leap, one of her smelly sneakers flew off her foot and landed in the lap of an audience member. The spotlight shifted, and she saw Charles, sitting there stone-faced, looking up at her.

The first time she had the dream, the audience, except for Charles, was a blur of unknown faces. This time, however, she could make out the people. They were all at the party she had just left. And sitting on either side of Charles were Dr. Siebert and Mrs. Whitfield.

"I CAN'T BELIEVE YOU'RE NERVOUS! It's just my sister," Regina said to Charles as they parked the car in the driveway of the old house that Brenda rented from a fellow mosque member. The paint on the house was peeling, and a railing on one side of the porch steps was missing. It didn't matter much to Brenda, though. The owner told Brenda that his parents and his grandparents were all Muslims, and swine had not been cooked in the house since his grandfather had built it in 1939.

"This is a house that has truly been blessed by Allah," Brenda had told Regina.

"I'm not nervous," Charles said as he opened Regina's car door.

"Then why are you so quiet?"

"I'm always quiet after a long drive."

Whatever, Regina said to herself, then wondered if her own nervousness was as apparent when they pulled up in front of the Whitfields' mansion in Philadelphia. It wouldn't have mattered, though, she assured herself. Charles was so excited about being home, he wouldn't have noticed.

"Hey, Sis!"

The door to the house flew open and a petite light-skinned woman with long flowing black hair—good hair, as they used to say—rushed out to greet them.

"You must be Charles. It's a pleasure to meet you after all this time. Regina always talks about you," Brenda said after she hugged her little sister.

"No, I don't, Brenda," Regina scoffed.

"Okay. Maybe not all the time. But she has mentioned your name in passing here and there. Renee talks about you all the time, though," Brenda said without missing a beat or losing her smile. "Come on in."

The three Harris women looked alike, short, thin, and light-skinned, but Brenda and Renee shared a carefree manner that was alien to Regina. Things that drove Regina to madness, her sister and her niece simply shrugged off and moved on. While Regina guarded her words carefully, and loathed revealing her feelings, Brenda and Renee both wore their lives on their sleeves. And if someone didn't notice, they gladly held their arms up for inspection.

Regina hugged her sister again while Charles slipped off one shoe, and after unsuccessfully trying to slip off the other, bent down and loosened the knot.

"Oh, good. Regina told you my rule about shoes in the house. Come on in and have a seat. Make yourselves comfortable. Renee's at the movies, but she should be home in a half hour or so."

Charles and Regina seated themselves on the cloth-covered foam mattress that served as the living room couch. Brenda prattled away as she disappeared into the kitchen to pour glasses of papaya juice. "You ever been in Queens before, Charles? Gina says you're from Philly. I was there once visiting Gina when she was in school. Did she tell you she went to school in Philly? Yeah, of course she did. I guess that's a stupid question. So, how do you like Queens?"

Returning, she handed them the juice and sat cross-legged on the floor.

"Oh, I like it. I've been here before, when I dropped Renee home from the party at the Waldorf," Charles answered cautiously.

"Isn't it nice? Gina and I grew up in Harlem, and I didn't want Renee to have to go through the stuff we went through. Harlem isn't no place for a young girl. You know what I mean? I don't know how Gina and I got out alive. Gina almost didn't. When they told me she was shot, I was sure she was dead. Allah was looking out for you, Gina. Looking out for me, too, because I probably should have been dead a long time ago with all the stuff I did. Do you guys like three-bean salad? It's my specialty."

"Brenda, Charles doesn't need to hear our whole life story," Regina said quickly, getting up from the mat.

"Oh yes, I do," Charles said just as quickly, pulling Regina back down. "You were shot?"

"You didn't tell him, Gina?" Brenda gave Regina a surprised look, who rolled her eyes back at her older sister.

"Uh-oh. I guess I've proven I have diarrhea of the mouth again. Let me go get that salad," Brenda said in a guilty voice before getting up and disappearing into the kitchen.

"You were shot? When were you shot?" Charles asked as soon as they were alone.

"Long story. Boring story. Not even worth mentioning," Regina said, averting his eyes.

"Boring? Come on—" Charles started, but Brenda reappeared from the kitchen, and placed a straw mat on the floor to be used as a table.

"See, now I've started you guys arguing. I'm sorry. I don't want you to think Gina was the bad girl in the family. I was the bad girl. Gina only got in trouble because of my irresponsibility. Allah's forgiven me, and I'm praying Gina will, too, but I don't want you to think that she was a bad girl or anything," she said, placing napkins and utensils on the mat as she spoke.

"I've forgiven you already, Bren. Now let's drop the subject. You're going to make me regret I introduced you two," Regina said, throwing her hands up in the air.

"Come on, let's eat already. You need some help bringing stuff out," she continued, shaking away Charles's arm as he tried to pull her back down again.

"I'm home!" Renee shouted as she slammed the front door. "Hey, Aunt Regina. Hey, Charles. Welcome to our humble abode. Hey, Mommy. The love of your life has returned."

Brenda's eyes widened, and she gasped as she looked at her daughter, wearing a black satin jacket with the outline of a pouncing panther.

"Renee, take that jacket off! You know we can't wear clothes with pictures of animals on them!"

"Why not?" Charles asked.

"Their religion," Regina explained.

"Her religion!" Renee shouted as she pulled off the jacket and threw it to the floor. "My damnation."

"Renee!" Regina and Brenda said simultaneously.

"Don't you dare talk like that about your mother's faith," Regina said angrily.

"That's blasphemy," Brenda added.

"Yeah, yeah. Sorry," Renee grumbled as she stooped down to pick up the jacket. "I'm going to my room. I'm not hungry anymore. See ya later, Aunt Regina. 'Night, Charles."

"Teenagers," Brenda said with a small shake of her head. "Can't live with them, can't kill them without going to jail."

Charles and Regina laughed.

"She's just feeling her oats. You know how it is, going through puberty and all," Regina said finally. "She's really a good kid."

"Hmm, I knew you were going to defend her," Brenda said absentmindedly. "Anyone want more salad?"

After dinner, Brenda put on her shawl and hurried to the corner mosque for evening prayer. When she returned she, Regina, and Charles carried on their conversation. At one point, Brenda started complaining about Renee, how she didn't realize how good she had it, living in Queens.

"Would you believe her school has a gymnasium with a swimming pool?" she asked Regina. "We had to go to that filthy pool in Central Park, and then after we were there an hour, like clockwork, they would throw everyone out because there would be a turd floating in the water."

"You're kidding! Gee, what a life," Charles exclaimed.

"Charles's parents have a swimming pool in their backyard," Regina said in teasing voice.

"You're kidding! Gee, what a life," Brenda said, prompting the three of them to laugh.

"What about the beach? If you didn't want to go to the swimming pool, couldn't you go to the beach?" Charles asked when the laughter died down.

"Oh, yeah. We went to the beach every Saturday, didn't we, Brenda?" Regina grinned. "Mom would dress us up in our little swimsuits and flip-flop sandals and give us our little Disney towels and we'd head out to the beach with the rest of the kids on the block."

She and Brenda started laughing uncontrollably.

"Yep," Brenda said between hoots. "Right down to the open fire hydrant on the corner."

"We'd spread our little towels on the sidewalk and take turns running in the water," Regina said, wiping her eyes as she talked.

"Cripes, what a childhood," Charles said, shaking his head in amazement that the two women could laugh at the memory.

"Oh, no, we had fun! Didn't we, Bren?" Regina said, still laughing. "Remember how we used to open a can on both sides, and use it to direct the water into any passing cars with the windows rolled down? The kids who couldn't come outside would cheer from the apartment windows whenever we got a victim."

"Oh yeah! Remember the time this big football-looking guy jumped out of the car with his clothes all soaked and chased everybody for two blocks? Mr. John had to come out with his gun, threatening to kill the guy before he would leave us alone."

"And this was fun?" Charles said in amazement.

"The best kind." Regina smiled. "We may not have had all the luxuries the rich kids had, but we had a blast. Maybe we didn't get to go to tennis camp, but we used to play some mean handball on the side of the school building. And remember what we used to do with sneakers, Brenda?"

"Oh, man, do I! We used to take our old sneakers, tie the laces together, and throw them over the telephone wires. One time I took some shoes Mommy just bought me and I threw them over the telephone wires. She tried to kill me." Brenda laughed. "It wasn't funny then, but it sure seems hilarious now."

"I thought it was funny then. I used to love it when Mommy beat your butt. You were always picking on me," Regina said.

"That's because you were such a goody-goody! I couldn't stand it!"

"Oh, Regina was the goody-goody in the family, huh? I can't believe that," Charles broke in.

"Well, since there was only the two of us it wasn't hard. Especially since I was such a terror," Brenda said, turning somber. "I really gave my mother pure hell."

"It was a long time ago, Bren. Look at you now, though. You have a nice house in Queens. You're raising your child. You're doing great. Mommy would be proud," Regina said soothingly. "We all messed up when we were young."

"Yeah. But I got really messed up with that crack," Brenda said, her eyes downcast. "I think that's what caused Mommy to have a stroke. Worrying about my stupid butt."

"Come on, Brenda. Stop blaming yourself. Mommy had high blood pressure, that's why she had a stroke," Regina said, leaning over and kissing her sister on the forehead.

"Well, why do you think she had high blood pressure? She had a crack addict for a daughter, and a trick-baby for a grand-daughter," Brenda said, tears welling up in her eyes.

"Oh, heck. I'm embarrassing you, aren't I, Charles? I'm sorry. I just get like this sometime. You have to excuse me," Brenda said suddenly.

"I'm fine. Umm, how about I take a quick walk and get a look around the neighborhood so you two can talk?" Charles offered, rising from the mat.

"Actually, it's kind of late. We should probably be leaving, anyway," Regina said, getting up. She ignored Charles's surprised look. "You going to be okay, Brenda?"

"Of course, of course. Look, I hope I haven't run you guys off. I'm okay now," Brenda said quickly.

"No. We've got to get out of here. I'll call you tomorrow, okay?" Regina said as she hugged her sister. "And tell Renee she'd best behave, okay?"

"SO. ARE YOU GOING TO TELL ME how you got shot?" Charles asked as he took off his pants to climb into bed.

"It's a long story, and a rather personal one," Regina said, her back toward him as she sat and brushed her hair in front of the mirror.

"Well, I think we're close enough for me to start hearing some personal stories," Charles said gently, walking over and massaging Regina's shoulders. "I want you to know you can tell me anything. It won't change my opinion of you."

"Oh? So you think I won't tell you because I'm afraid I'd plummet in your esteem?" Regina said, putting down her brush and turning in her chair.

"Uh-uh, baby. I didn't say that, and I don't want you to try and pick an argument, okay?" Charles said, pulling her up from the chair. He leaned down and kissed her, stroking her neck and shoulders as he did so. "There's got to be better ways to change a subject, don't you think?"

An hour later Regina lay spent in the bed. She snuggled against Charles's chest, enjoying the scent of the cologne that mixed with his light perspiration. A gentle evening breeze billowed the curtains, allowing moonlight to peek through and illuminate his handsome face.

"You're not sleepy?" she asked, tracing his thin mustache with her fingers.

He propped himself on an elbow.

"Gina. You know I love you, and nothing's going to change that. We shouldn't be keeping secrets from each other," he said softly. She tried to pull away, but he grabbed her and pulled her close. "Come on, baby. Why won't you talk to me about your past?"

"Because it's the past," Regina said in a whisper. "It's over and done with."

Charles held her for a few moments, saying nothing as he stroked her back. She lay still, hoping he would drop off to sleep. But he tilted her head and forced her to look into his eyes.

"Regina. Were you hooked on drugs? Is that the big secret you're trying to hide?" he asked in a low voice.

"*No!* Of course not!" Regina said, trying to break away from his grasp.

"Okay, okay, stop fighting. Calm down," he said, refusing to let go.

"Why does your mind immediately go to drugs? Regina cried. "How could you think something like that of me?"

"Look. I'm just trying to find out what all the mystery is about. Every time I ask you anything about your past you either change the subject or get defensive. A couple of weeks ago I find out that you carry a knife. Tonight I hear for the first time that you've been shot, and your sister said she was on crack. It may not be a correct conclusion, but you've got to admit it's a reasonable one. Stop fighting me," he said soothingly as she continued to try to twist out of his arms.

She could feel tears springing to her eyes, and she fought all the harder. She couldn't let him see her cry. Why was she crying anyway? It was her past to share or not. Dang Brenda for opening her big mouth. She finally broke free, jumped out of the bed, and rushed for the bathroom. Charles was quicker, and grabbed her arm before she could reach the door. He swung her around, and pulled her body against his.

"Let me go, Charles!" she cried, frantically struggling to break away.

"Not until you calm down," he said, holding her so close she could barely turn her head sideways.

"I'm calm. Now let me go," she said, unsuccessfully trying to will the tears from her eyes.

"Then why are you crying?"

"I'm not crying!"

"Then what's all this wet stuff on your face, huh?" he said, turning her face to meet his. "You know what's wrong? You have all this . . . this . . . this stuff all bottled up inside you, and you need to let it out. Why don't you trust me, baby? You know I love you. I'm in your corner, and I'm always going to be in your corner."

She couldn't hold back any longer. Large sobs wracked her body, accompanied by the already streaming tears. Though he still held her in a bear hug, she wiggled her arms free and began beating on his chest.

"I hate you! Let me go, dammit. I hate you!"

"Regina!"

"Fuck you! I hate you. I hate you," she shouted hysterically. "Let me go!"

Charles released her, and she sunk to the hardwood floor, burying her face in her hands, her back heaving with sobs.

"Why did you do this me? Oooh, I hate you," she cried.

Charles sat down on the floor next to her, watching but not touching her.

"Okay, you hate me. And what exactly is it that you think I've done to you, Gina?" he asked gently.

"You wormed your way into my life. And you're asking questions that most people don't think they can ask me. And you have every right to ask me. And I hate you because I have to answer them," she wailed, her face still buried in her hands.

"Baby, you don't have to answer anything. I'm sorry I've upset you so much. Come on back to bed," Charles said, rubbing her back.

"I don't want to go to bed!" she shouted.

"Okay, you don't have to go to bed. Just stop crying, okay?"

"I don't want to stop crying!" she shouted again. The ludicrousness of her words hit her suddenly, and she looked up to see his reaction. He tried to hide his smile, but she saw it and her face broke into a watery smile. Then she began to laugh, prompting him to laugh. She grabbed his neck, pushed him to the floor, then climbed on top of him.

"Now look what you made me do," she said looking down at him with a teary smile.

"What did I make you do? Tell me," he said, reaching his arms up around her neck.

"You made me laugh," she said as she snuggled into his chest.

"I'm a horrible person," he said, stroking her hair.

"Yes, you are."

"Do you think I'm nuts, Charles?" she asked softly, though she was still crying.

"Well, maybe slightly schizophrenic. But you wear it well," he joked.

She giggled and kissed him. A serious look then appeared on her face.

"You ready?" she asked.

"For what?"

"My life story."

They sat back up, and he held her in his arms, rocking softly as she began to talk.

HER SHOPLIFTING CAREER with Krystal was booming. Not only was she able to pay the bills but she was even able to put aside a nice amount of money in the bank. She was content hitting three or four stores a week, but Krystal was going out boosting seven days a week to feed her ever-growing heroin habit. She even convinced Regina to come out on days when the young girl would have preferred to stay uptown with Renee, but Regina went, out of loyalty. After all, if it weren't for Krystal, she and Renee would be out in the streets.

On one of those occasions, when Krystal dragged her downtown to Lord & Taylor, they were busted for boosting $5,000 worth of clothing. They hadn't known that a store detective had been watching them through a security camera.

"Oh Lawd, help us all. I just knew you was going to get yourself in trouble," Mama Tee wailed as she left the Manhattan District Court with Regina in tow. "Here I'm telling dese people I'm Matilda so I can get you out. Oh Lawd, I know they're going to find out and dese gonna trow us all in jail. Oh Lawd, help us."

"It's all right, Mama Tee, they won't find out, I promise. They don't look up death certificates or anything. How are they going to know?" Regina tried to assure the old woman as they boarded the subway and headed to Harlem. "Besides, it's all over with now. I'm on probation, and I'm not going to get in any more trouble."

Mama Tee closed her eyes and shook her head as if she still couldn't believe what was happening. She had taken a day off from her cleaning job to impersonate a dead woman, and one she never liked all that much. If God didn't get her, surely Matilda's spirit would.

"Gina, how you know dat little white girl won't tell the truth on you so she can get out of prison, child?" Mama Tee said, turning toward her young charge.

Regina lowered her eyes as she thought about her partner in crime. Krystal had been sentenced to a year in prison because it was her third offense, but she couldn't see Krystal diming her out to get a reduction in her sentence. Krystal was too loyal, and too much of a stand-up girl to do something like that.

"She won't, Mama Tee. She's not like that. As long as I stay out of trouble while I'm on probation everything will be fine. And I plan to stay out of trouble."

"Damn right you staying out of trouble. You're moving in with me and Yvonne, jest like I said you should before. Dere's no reason you and my baby can't share a room and you can walk to school together and act like fourteen-year-olds should act instead of running wild and stealing people's clothes. I don't know what's wrong with you, Gina."

KAREN E. QUINONES MILLER

Regina sat silent next to Mama Tee as the subway train whizzed uptown, and reflected on their conversation the night before. Mama Tee was more than willing to take her in, but she had made it clear that as much as she didn't want to, she would have to have the foster care people take Renee. There was no one to watch of the baby while she was at work and Regina and Yvonne were in school. And she couldn't afford to pay for child care on her meager earnings as a cleaning woman. Regina had cried and pleaded, but as much as Mama Tee's heart pained her, she wouldn't change her mind.

"It's for de best, Gina. You'll see dat when you get older," she said as she tried to take the young girl in her arms to comfort her.

"How'd it go?" Yvonne asked Regina when she and Mama Tee arrived at the apartment.

"Everyting went fine," Mama Tee answered for her. "Yvonne, did you go to the fish market like I asked you to?"

"Yes, Mama. They ran out of red snapper, but I got some cod fish."

"Hmmph. Dey always running out of red snapper. I don't know what wrong with dose people." Mama Tee strutted into the kitchen to get dinner started.

"How did it go?" Yvonne asked Regina again.

"Just like I said it would. I got a year's probation and Krystal got sent upstate." Regina sighed. She and Yvonne went into the small bedroom they shared for the past two weeks. Renee was asleep in her bassinet, but woke and started laughing in delight as Regina picked her up and held her in her arms.

"So, you're still going to go through with the plan?" Yvonne asked as she plopped down on the twin bed.

"Yep. We're leaving tonight."

"Oh man, you know Mama's going to have a fit when she sees you're gone."

"I know, but I don't know what else to do. I can't let them put my baby in foster care. They're going to make her a slave or rape her or something. You read the news. You know what happens to kids who grow up in foster care," Regina said.

"Yeah, I know. But Mama's going to have a fit."

"I'm sorry. But I've got to do this. Just please don't tell her where to find us."

"Oh girl, please. You know I'm not going to tell," Yvonne said with the toss of her red hair. "Puddin' came by while you guys were out. Everything's set."

Puddin', though only fourteen, looked as if she were much older, and Regina had enlisted her aid in finding a furnished room. Once they decided on a place, Regina had dipped into her savings account and given her money to pay the landlady two months' rent and one month's security.

"You're lucky Puddin' actually paid that woman. I thought she was going to take that money and put it up her nose. You know she's cocaine crazy now," Yvonne said.

"Yeah, but she wouldn't do that to me," Regina said absentmindedly. "Puddin' loves her friends even more than she likes her coke."

"Well, I made her give me the rent receipts just in case." Yvonne laughed. "She's our friend and all, but you never know with that fast-ass girl."

Things went as planned and Regina moved in. Once again she started doing some boosting, while looking for a job that could bring in a steady income. Regina only hit small boutiques that didn't have tight security. She knew if she was arrested again even Mama Tee couldn't save her. And then what would happen to Renee?

One night Puddin' convinced her, Yvonne, and Tamika to go with her to a club on Lenox Avenue where she heard guys with money hung out. All of the eyes in the club turned to them as the girls walked in wearing expensive clothing and jewelry, and perched themselves on the barstools.

"They're looking at us as fresh meat," Yvonne said with a laugh as the bartender rushed over to take their orders.

"I just ordered a rum and Coke and he didn't ask for ID or anything," Tamika said incredulously as the bartender turned away.

"Shit, he doesn't care. Just act like you know what you're doing and you'll be fine," Puddin' said as she looked around the bar. "Just don't do anything to embarrass me."

Within an hour the girls were surrounded by men who tried to pull them aside to talk or to offer them reefer or coke in hopes of getting them into bed. Regina watched in amusement as her friends ate the attention up. It wasn't her kind of scene, but she had to admit it was kind of exciting. She glanced at her watch: 11:30 P.M. She needed to get out of there to meet a customer who was interested in some silk lingerie she had boosted.

"Don't tell me you're ready to leave so soon."

Regina turned around to see an older man, maybe in his fifties, smiling at her. He was dressed expensively, but a little flashy.

"I've got an appointment," Regina said cautiously.

"Oh really? And I was hoping I could buy you a drink." A gold tooth gleamed at her as he smiled.

"I don't drink."

"You don't, huh? Don't tell me you're into nose candy."

"No, I don't mess around with cocaine." Regina smiled. The guy was nice, even if he was kind of corny.

"You don't drink and you don't do coke. What are you doing in this place?" he said waving his arm around the smoke-filled bar.

"I'm just keeping my girls company," Regina said pointing to Yvonne and Tamika, who were both in deep conversations with other men. Puddin' was in the corner grinding up against some guy with heavy gold chains around his neck.

"Well, they don't look like they're keeping you much company," he said, throwing his head back and laughing.

The man's name was Rico. He told Regina he didn't usually come to that particular bar but was glad to have stopped in that night for the chance to meet a fine young thing like her.

"How old are you?" he asked, looking her up and down.

"Old enough!" was her snappy retort.

"Old enough for what?" he responded with a smile.

The question caught Regina off guard and she giggled, prompting Rico to burst out into hearty laughter. "Hey, Scotty," he yelled to the bartender. "Bring me a Jim Beam's straight up, and a glass of orange juice for my pretty young friend here."

"So, do you live around here?" he asked her when their drinks arrived.

"Yeah. You?"

"Sort of," he answered, taking a small sip from his glass.

"Sort of?"

"Well, I have a couple of places."

"Why do have you more than one place?" Regina asked.

"So no matter what part of town I'm in, I'm only a few blocks from home." Rico grinned back.

Out of the corner of her eye Regina watched as Puddin' left the bar hugging up on the guy with the gold chains. *Didn't even bother to say she's leaving,* Regina thought. She glanced at Yvonne and Tamika. Both seemed pretty tipsy, but okay. And Regina had to admit she was really enjoying her conversation with Rico. He was engaging and a little mysterious and she was glad for his company. It stopped all the other men in the bar from coming up and pulling on her arm.

Suddenly, she remembered her customer and looked at her watch: 12:30. She couldn't believe how fast the time had flown. She had to get out of there or she was going to blow $150, that she needed to pay the telephone bill.

"Don't tell me you're really going to leave me?" Rico said, surprised, as Regina slid off the barstool.

"Yeah, I'm sorry. But I really have to make this appointment," Regina apologized.

"A money appointment," Rico asked with a raised eyebrow.

"Yep. I'm about to blow a hundred and fifty dollars sitting here messing with you," Regina said she reached over and picked up her purse from the bar. "It was nice meeting you, though."

"Hold on a minute." Rico reached into his pocket and pulled out a gold money clip, then threw $300 on the bar.

"What's that for?" Regina asked, suspiciously.

"For you. Now you don't have to make that other appointment."

"Well, brother, you've got the wrong impression," Regina huffed as she stepped back. "It's not that kind of appointment, and I'm not that kind of girl."

Rico threw up his hands in surrender and starting laughing. "I never said you were! I'm just enjoying our little talk, and I don't want you to leave, so I'm trying to make it worth your while to stay a bit."

Regina eyed him, and then the money. She would be able to pay the bill and put something toward the next month's rent. Still, she didn't want him to think that she was going to put out. She was still a virgin, and was going to remain so until she met her knight in shining armor, and she didn't think Rico was him.

As if reading her mind, Rico picked up the money and stuffed it in Regina's shirt pocket.

"There. Now the money's yours whether you decide to stay or go," he said as he turned back toward the bar.

Regina hesitated, then climbed back on her barstool. She leaned over and kissed Rico on the cheek.

"Thanks. You don't know how much I need it. Maybe you're my fairy godfather," she said, innocently.

"Fairy godfather?" Rico laughed. "Scotty, give me another a drink, and make it a double."

RICO DROVE REGINA, Tamika, and Yvonne home that night in his sparkling white BMW and left without even asking Regina for a good-night kiss. A few nights later Regina saw the BMW parked outside a club on Eighth Avenue, and went inside. Sure enough, Rico was at a table talking to two men dressed similarly to him. When he looked up and saw her, he waved for her to take a seat next to him. Suddenly frightened, Regina shook her head. She started to tell him she was on her way to someplace else, when he gave her a stern look and motioned again for her to take a seat. Regina smiled and sat down. The two men left seconds later.

"Okay pretty thing, tell me what you're doing in my club."

"Your club? You own it?"

"I might as well, I'm in here all the time. But I've never seen you in here," he answered as he leaned back in his chair and appraised her.

"I just came in because I saw your car outside and I wanted to say hello," Regina answered.

"And I guess you're rushing off now to make another appointment."

"Yep." Regina chuckled.

"And how much were you going to make off of this appointment?" Rico chuckled along with her.

"Two hundred."

Rico whistled in admiration, then pulled out his money clip and put four one hundred dollar bills in her hand.

"Now you don't have to make your appointment. I've got to split because I have an appointment of my own, but why don't you find your girlfriends and just hang out for a while?"

"You don't have to do that!" Regina protested, while thinking about how much she could use the money. Renee was due for shots in a few weeks.

"I'm only doing it because I don't have to. Now hurry up and give me my kiss on the cheek so I can get out of here." He grinned.

REGINA, HANGING OUT WITH RICO and getting paid well for it, became a regular thing. He never looked for her, came to her building, or called her on the telephone, because he knew she would welcome his open arms and open wallet at the club.

She came to know that he was a heroin dealer, but he never made any transactions with her around. Puddin' informed her that he had a reputation around town, and that he only dealt with bulk. Her friends were incredulous when Regina said he never approached her about going to bed with him. She enjoyed spending time with him at the club, and especially enjoyed going with him to the movies and fancy restaurants.

She never included Renee in their outings, though. Renee was her own responsibility and her own little joy and she wasn't ready to share those with anyone. The easy money that she got from Rico allowed her to spend more time with the baby, who grew into a joyous little toddler, always reaching out for her "Aunt Gina." They went to the zoo, the museums, and to the park. When she was out with Rico she had more than enough money to pay for a baby-sitter. And since her relationship with Rico was nonsexual, she always made it back home in time to spend the night with her baby-doll niece.

"I'm telling you he's like a big brother or something," Regina told her friends.

"I doubt that, but maybe he's just too old to get it up and he just wants you around him so people will think he can," Yvonne offered.

Whatever the reason, Regina was glad to be getting money without putting herself in risk of going to jail.

One night, as Rico was talking to a scantily clad, heavily perfumed woman at the bar, Regina stood by the door, uncertain as to whether she should approach him. He finally saw her and motioned for her to take a seat at one of the booths that lined the walls. She slid inside and waited until he disengaged himself from the clinging woman.

"I didn't mean to disturb you," she said as he sat next to her and sipped the drink in his hand.

"Well, you did, bitch." Regina looked up and saw the woman standing above them. Rico cocked his head to look at the woman, and she hurried away.

Ignoring the woman's scathing remark, Rico said, "Look, I gotta make a run to the Bronx. Why don't you drive up there with me, and then I'll take you to dinner?"

They pulled up to the front of a huge building on the Grand Concourse, and Regina prepared herself to wait in the car while Rico took care of his business upstairs. She was surprised when he motioned her to follow him. She was even more surprised when they got to the apartment on the third floor, and Rico took out a key and entered.

"This is your apartment?" she asked.

"Yeah. Make yourself at home." He threw his keys on the white fiberglass coffee table, and reached over to hit a button on the side of a built-in mini bar. The wall opened, revealing a large entertainment center. He picked up the remote from the bar, and the stereo started playing a Whitney Houston CD.

"Wow, this is fabulous!" Regina walked over and sat on the plush white leather couch. "Are all of your apartments like this?"

Rico grunted. "Yeah, they're all fabulous. I wouldn't settle for anything less. You like it, huh?"

"I love it!" Regina looked around the room in utter amazement. All white and sparkling. Even the entertainment center was white. She had never seen a white television set before, and such a large one at that.

"Well, why don't you move in?" Rico said nonchalantly while fixing himself a drink at the heavily stocked bar.

"Huh?" Regina couldn't believe what she heard.

"Move in. I seldom use it anyway."

"I couldn't afford this kind of rent." Regina started laughing. "This place must cost a fortune."

"Who said anything about paying rent?"

Regina looked at Rico as he put the drink down on the bar and sat down on one the barstools. *I know he's not offering to let me stay up here and him pay the rent,* she thought. She brushed her hand over the sofa again. *No one's that much of a fairy godfather.*

Suddenly he was standing above her. He pulled her up from the sofa and into his arms, kissing her hard on the mouth. She was surprised, and even more surprised that she didn't try to resist. Her first kiss! But when she felt his tongue try to slip past her lips she pulled away.

"Um, I thought you had an appointment," she said as he pulled her up against his body. The smell of his expensive cologne and the warmth of his embrace were inviting, but she wasn't prepared for all of this. She tried again to pull away.

"What about your appointment?"

"You're my appointment, Regina. We've had this appointment for weeks now, but it kept getting postponed."

"What do you mean?"

"Stop fooling around, you know just what I mean." Rico tried to kiss her again, but Regina broke free and rushed for the door.

"Rico, stop. I've got to go home," she pleaded when he grabbed her again.

"What? You've got another appointment? How much is it going to cost me this time, baby?" Rico was breathing heavily as he kissed Regina's neck.

"No! Let go of me. I'm going home!" Regina tried to knee him in the groin, but he twisted his body out of the way, without letting go of her.

"Stop fighting, Regina. Damn!" He pushed her toward the sofa.

"Let go!" she cried when he tried to push her down. She bit him on the shoulder and he grunted in pain. He then slapped her upside the head with his open hand. She screamed as red stars danced in front of her closed eyes.

"What the hell's wrong with you? You like it rough or something?" Rico slapped her again and she fell down on the sofa. He leaned down and he ripped open her blouse, then her brassiere.

"Aw yeah . . . that's what I'm talking about," he said as he tried to take one in his mouth.

"Rico, stop please! Please!" Regina tried to wiggle away, but Rico slapped her again. Her nose started bleeding and she began to choke on her sobs.

"Stop making all that noise! What's wrong with you?" Rico crept to the sofa and began unbuckling his pants. "Shut up before the neighbors call the cops."

His pants off, he slapped her again, and began choking her to stifle her cries. Then he reached under her skirt and ripped off her panties.

"Oh God, you're so fucking tight I can't even get it in. Oh fuck, this is going to be good," he grunted as he tried to push himself into her virginal slit.

"You're hurting me! Please, Rico! Please stop!" Managing to break his hold on her throat with her hand, Regina hollered at the top of her lungs. He ignored her screams and pinned her arms to the couch. He closed his eyes as he slowly pushed himself into her. "Oh God, yeah . . . this is it. Oh yeah, Regina, you're the shit. Oh yeah, baby, give it to your daddy. Give it to your daddy. Give me this tight pussy."

Regina felt as if her body was being split. Her throat was so hoarse no more sound could come out. Still she let out a shriek when Rico finally pushed himself all the way inside of her.

"Oh fuck baby, this is shit," Rico cried. "Yeah, you're going to make me come. Yeah, you're going to make your daddy come. That's right, baby. Come with your daddy. Come for your daddy."

He let out a holler, and with that it was all over. He collapsed on top of her, catching his breath, unaware of her crying. It was a full two minutes before he got up from the couch.

"What? Are you on your period or something," he asked as he looked down on the bloody sofa and his bloody groin. "Oh shit, Regina, please don't tell me you were a virgin."

SHE SAT SILENT IN THE CAR as he apologized over and over for what he had done. Her head ached and her clothes were torn, although he had wrapped her in his jacket.

"Regina, please look at me. I'm so sorry. Honest to God, baby. I didn't know you were a virgin. I thought all of those appointments you had were with men. And I didn't want to share you with anyone else," he pleaded. "I want to make you my woman. Let me take care of you. You can be my little princess. I'll buy you anything you want. Please forgive me for tonight. You know I never wanted to hurt you. I thought you were just playing hard to get. I thought you wanted me to be a little rough."

When they turned onto Lenox Avenue she quietly asked him to drop her off on the corner; she wanted to walk the rest of the way home. He sighed and let her out.

She walked home in a daze, and as she entered the kitchenette she went to the bathroom and turned the water on in the tub, dumping in a whole bottle of Calgon. Then she got in and just soaked, not scrubbing or even touching herself. She had read somewhere about a guy who slit his wrists and sat in a bathtub of warm water while all the blood drained from his body, and she thought about doing the same. It wasn't so much that she wanted to die as much as she didn't want to wake up the next morning and remember what had happened. But she couldn't kill herself. Renee would wind up in foster care. She had to live to take care of her baby.

The next night she went to the club and found Rico there at his usual table. It was obvious from the look on his face that he was surprised to see her, and he was even more surprised when she sat next to him. He took out his gold money clip and pressed $300 in her hand. She looked at the money and gave it back.

"I saw a coat downtown that was on sale for four hundred and fifty dollars."

He looked at her inquisitively but said nothing.

"Don't you think I'm worth it . . . Daddy?" She smiled and licked her lips and he started grinning.

"Here's seven hundred dollars. Buy yourself that coat and a matching hat, baby." He grinned, happy that Regina had forgiven him.

"Mmmm . . . thanks. Now could you do me one more big favor?" she asked with a flirtatious smile.

"Anything."

"Would you ask the bartender for a can opener?"

"A can opener? For what?"

"I can't tell you. It's a surprise. A real big surprise."

Rico shook his head, then walked over to the bar, returning a few seconds later with the requested can opener.

"Thanks. I'll be right back."

Regina walked out of the club and grabbed the can of red paint she had stashed outside, pried the top open with the can opener and slowly poured the contents all over the hood of Rico's white BMW. She gaily slipped away while people rushed in to tell Rico what she had done.

She never saw Rico again. Later she heard he was arrested on a federal drug conspiracy rap and sentenced to life. A few nights after the incident she dolled herself up, and walked into a club on Lenox Avenue, known as a hangout for drug dealers. At a table across from the bar, she spotted an older man who looked like he had money. She parked herself on a barstool directly across from him and smiled. She had started a new career.

One night, she convinced a cocaine dealer she had hooked up with to go to an after-hours spot where Tamika was hanging out with her boyfriend, Chink. She promised him that in return, he could do whatever he wanted to do to her later that night. Maybe even the threesome he'd been hinting at. Regina was used to everything by then, so it didn't really matter. Little did she know that someone had put out a contract on him. . . .

"I don't remember much of what happened next," she continued, refusing to look at Charles. "I vaguely remembered gunshots, then Tamika leaning over me, screaming. The next thing I knew I was in the hospital.

"I think that was a wake-up call for everybody. Someone found Brenda at a crack house and told her what happened, and she stayed in my hospital room the whole time I was there, crying about how it was her fault; how she should have been looking out for me instead of forcing me to shoulder her responsibilities.

"My bullet wound wasn't serious. I was just grazed on the shoulder, and it just left a little mark. To look at it you'd think it was just a scar from an inoculation or something. But I had a concussion, and my body was beat up pretty bad. So they kept me in the hospital for a week."

She stopped talking, thinking about the awful incident with Dr. Siebert. She couldn't bring herself to share that with Charles. It was too personal. Too humiliating.

"I knew that I had to turn my life around. I was lucky that time, but drug dealers get killed all the time, and I don't need to be around when they do.

"After I got out of the hospital, I took the G.E.D. test, just to see what I would need to brush up on to get my diploma. I couldn't believe it when I actually passed without going back to school. But it made me really realize I had some brains, and I could make something out of myself.

"Brenda entered a rehabilitation center, and even though they say there's no such thing as a reformed crack addict, she became the exception to the rule. When she finished the program she went on welfare for a while, got an apartment and moved Renee in with her.

"I did my best by Renee, and we had a lot of fun when I was bringing in money, but I was never able to provide her with a stable home life. When I was boosting I left her with a baby-sitter all day. When I was hanging out to make money, I left her with a baby-sitter all night. I tried to make the time I spent with her quality time, but I didn't really know what I was doing.

"Anyway, I decided to go to college. Don't laugh, but I picked Temple for two reasons. One, I wanted to get out of New York, but I didn't want to go too far. Two, I used to watch *The Cosby Show* and make believe Bill Cosby was my father. I never had a relationship with my own father. Maybe that's one of the reasons why I always hung out with older men, huh? You know, I really like your father, Charles. He's the kind of dad I always wanted. Him and Bill Cosby. Anyway, since Bill Cosby went to Temple, I figured I would, too.

"You pretty much know the rest. I moved back to New York after I graduated, but I didn't want to go back to Harlem. Too many bad memories. And yet, I still can't seem to stay away." Regina smiled and looked up at Charles for the first time since she had started talking. She wiped the tears from her eyes, and realized for the first time his face was also wet.

"So, there you have it," she said, gently pushing him away and getting up from the floor. "I'm not ashamed of my past, but I don't want to dwell on it. What happened, happened. It's all part of who I am, but the past is the past.

"Any questions, counselor?" she asked, her back toward him as she gripped the edge of the dresser, her eyes squeezed shut.

"Just one," he said, walking up from behind and folding his arms around her waist.

"And that is?" Regina said wearily.

He turned her around to face him and looked deeply into her eyes.

"Gina. Will you marry me?"

They stood there holding each other and crying until dawn announced the beginning of a new day.

"I DON'T BELIEVE YOU! I WANT TO SEE THE ROCK! I KNOW you've got a rock!"

"Now, Yvonne. Do you really think I'm so materialistic I would actually let my fiancé waste money on a trivial piece of jewelry when we're about to embark on a new life together?" Regina said, flashing her friend a patronizing smile. She then gracefully extended her arm over the table, slightly arching her wrist downward for effect. "By the way, how do you like this new color of nail polish? I hear it's the rage in Paris this year."

"Oh, shit! That must have cost a fortune!" Puddin' exclaimed loudly as she grabbed Regina's hand, causing the other patrons in the fancy downtown restaurant to stare. "Gimme that ring. Mama needs a new pair of shoes!"

Regina grinned and snatched her hand back. "Mama's gonna have to kick my ass to get this here thang off my finger."

"Oh, Regina, I'm so happy for you," Tamika said, leaning over the table to give her friend a hug. "You're going to make a beautiful bride. Are you going to have a big wedding?"

"We'll see. And you know you guys are going to be my brides-maids."

"Just make sure you order us green dresses." Yvonne smiled. "I look good in green."

"I just want to see if Regina has the nerve to wear a white dress," Puddin' said with a wicked smile. "Won't that be a hoot."

"Regina can wear any color she wants, Puddin'," Tamika said, shooting Puddin' a reproving look.

"If white is for virgins, Regina needs to walk down the aisle in black," Puddin' snorted. "What about you, Tamika? What color wedding dress are you going to wear when you and David get hitched?"

"Who said anything about us getting hitched?" Tamika said with a shy smile.

"It's coming, it's coming. That boy's in mad love with you," Puddin' teased.

"Well, I'm in love with him, too. But we haven't talked any-thing about marriage."

Puddin' signaled the waiter, and ordered an expensive bottle of champagne, after making sure Regina had brought her credit card.

"Your punishment for being the first one of us to get mar-ried," Puddin' said with a grin. "You know, Yvonne? I always thought you'd be the first one to get hitched."

Regina noticed a strange look flash across Yvonne's face, but couldn't identify it. Was it jealousy? Sadness? A feeling of unwar-ranted guilt swept over the new bride-to-be. Though her best friend, Regina intuitively knew Yvonne sometimes felt overshad-owed, maybe even threatened, by her. Yvonne was the smart one in the group, but it was Regina who finished college. It was Yvonne who dreamed of being a successful businesswoman, but it was Regina who had the glamorous career. Yvonne collected *Bride* magazine as a teenager, and now it was Regina poised to walk down the aisle. The fact that Yvonne had led a relatively easy life, with a mother who would do anything for her, while Regina lived the life of hard knocks, only made matters worse.

"You okay, Yvonne?" Regina asked, placing her unringed hand over her friend's.

"Yeah. I'm fine. I just had a tough weekend." Yvonne shrugged. "So, you guys set a date?"

"Not an exact date, but we're thinking June. That gives us eight months to get everything together," Regina said. "Which brings me to the bad news, guys."

She paused for a moment, taking a deep breath, then continued.

"Nothing's definite yet, but there's a good possibility that we'll be living in Philadelphia," she said.

"What?" Tamika shrieked. "You've got to be kidding, Regina. You just got back in New York a couple of years ago."

"I know," Regina sighed. "But he's accepted a position at a Philadelphia law firm, and I have the kind of career where my home base won't matter."

"Well, can't you guys live in different cities and still be married?" Tamika asked. "What's that called again? Communal marriage?"

"Commuter marriages," Yvonne corrected her.

"Yeah, one of those."

"Call me old-fashioned, but I would prefer living in the same city as my husband." Regina smiled.

"I'd be the last one to call you old-fashioned, Regina, but I know what you mean. And I don't blame you a bit," Yvonne said as she sipped her champagne.

"So you gonna move to Philly if you and Robert get married?" Puddin' asked as she took a swig of hers.

"I never said I was going to marry Robert," Yvonne snapped.

"Oh, please. You'd jump at the chance to marry that man, and we all know it," Puddin' drawled. "You ain't fooling nobody. He just ain't planning on asking your ass."

"Shut the fuck up, Puddin'," Yvonne snapped.

"Who you telling to shut the fuck up?" Puddin' asked, with the raise of an eyebrow.

"Hey, hey, hey, guys! Come on, now!" Tamika interrupted. "Yvonne, you know Puddin' is only kidding."

"Yeah, right, I'm kidding," Puddin' said sarcastically. "We know Robert's been begging to marry you and you just keep turning his rich ass down."

"Puddin', shut up!" Tamika shouted.

"What the fuck is this? Puddin'-shut-up day?" Puddin' snapped.

"To hell with this!" Yvonne shouted. She jumped up from the table and stormed off. "Excuse me while I stick my head in a shitty toilet to get some fresh air."

"Was it something I said?" Puddin' said nonchalantly as she poured another glass of champagne.

Regina got up from the table, shot a dirty look at Puddin', and headed to the rest room after Yvonne. She found her friend in the ladies' lounge, applying her lipstick in front of the mirror. Regina sat down on the red crushed-velvet couch in the lounge, waiting for acknowledgment. Yvonne dropped the lipstick tube into her pocketbook, then fished out her mascara, and started working on her eyes, ignoring her friend.

"You okay?" Regina finally asked.

"Sure, why wouldn't I be okay?" Yvonne answered without glancing at Regina.

"Oh, I don't know. Maybe because you just made a major scene, and we all know how you hate scenes?"

"Puddin' gets on my nerves," Yvonne said angrily. "She doesn't know when to shut up."

"Yes, she does. She just chooses not to," Regina said. "Something happen between you and Robert?"

"You tell me," Yvonne answered, still not looking in the mirror.

"What do you mean?"

"Shit. Never mind. Come on, I'm ready to get out of here," Yvonne snapped.

"Yvonne, what's going on? This just isn't like you," Regina said, rising from the couch and walking over to her friend.

Yvonne squinted her eyes at Regina as if to let go another barb, then leaned against the flowered wallpaper wall and placed her hand on her forehead. Tears rolled down her face, ruining her freshly applied makeup.

"Hey, what's wrong?" Regina said.

"Look, if I tell you, you have to promise not to say anything to anyone, okay? Not even Tamika and Puddin'."

"You have my word, Yvonne," Regina said, as she retrieved a piece of toilet tissue from a stall and dabbed at her friend's eye. She led the crying girl to the couch, and rubbed her back as Yvonne tried to pull herself together.

"I got a telephone call at work this morning. A woman asked for Yvonne Jamison, and when I identified myself she said she was Robert's wife," Yvonne said when she was finally able to speak.

"His what? I don't believe it!"

"Well, you'd better believe it. Oh, and she was soooo gracious! She said she had just received the receipt from the florist for a dozen roses that Robert had sent me. She said it was obvious that Robert and I must be very good friends, and she wanted to be sure to invite me to their anniversary dinner party next week. She wanted to know if she should send the invitation to my work address, or, if I preferred, she could send it to my home address, since she had gotten both from Robert's telephone book."

"I don't believe this," Regina said again.

"I told her she needn't bother to send an invitation, because my schedule wouldn't allow me to travel to Philadelphia next week. Then she said she had to run because she had to pick the baby up from the nursery, but she hoped to meet me sometime soon." Yvonne sniffed. She blew her nose, and attempted a smile.

"I've got to admit, the woman has class. She was calling me to make sure I knew that Robert was married, and that she knew where I lived and worked, but she never came out and made an accusation or threat."

Regina sat dumbfounded, not knowing what to say. Poor Yvonne. No wonder she was upset when Regina announced her engagement and Puddin' started mouthing off.

"Have you talked to Robert?"

"Yeah, I talked to him. He just said he was sorry that I had to find out that way, and that he'd make sure she didn't bother me again. Then he said he wanted to see me tonight so he could explain everything in person."

"What the hell is there to explain?" Regina asked in exasperation. "If the man's married, the man's married!"

"Yeah, I know." Yvonne sighed. She walked over to the sink and wet a paper towel and dabbed at the corners of her eyes. "And the man is definitely married."

"I guess the party's at your house tonight," Regina said slowly when Yvonne sat back down.

"Nope. I'm not having a Pity Party, and I'm not having an I-Hate-Men Party. You promised you wouldn't tell anyone, and I'm sure not going to broadcast it. I'll handle the situation my own way," Yvonne said angrily.

"What are you going to do?" Regina asked suspiciously.

"Nothing. I'm going out with Robert tonight, and I'm going out with him tomorrow night, and the night after that. I've got that man's nose open, you hear me, Regina? He may be her husband now, but he'll be mine by the time he graduates. Just wait," Yvonne said defiantly.

"Okay. I see you're out of your fucking mind," Regina said getting up from the couch and glaring down at her friend. "You know that, don't you?"

"Look, Regina, don't start that 'holier than thou' shit with me, okay?" Yvonne jumped up from the couch. "I know you. And I mean I *really* know you. You want to try and tell me you've never slept with a married man?"

"Yeah, plenty! But only for the money. And I was never stupid enough to try and make them unmarried men!" Regina shouted back.

"So now I'm stupid?"

"Stupid's not strong enough, Yvonne. I'll go back to my original premise. *You're out your fucking mind!* It doesn't even matter to you that he's lied to you all this time? Let's not even talk about the fact that he's been lying to his wife. Shit, if he wanted to play the adultery game, he should have at least let you know."

"Yeah, he should have. And maybe my best friend should have, too!" Yvonne shouted, waving her finger in Regina's face.

"What the hell is that supposed to mean?" Regina said. She raised her hand to slap Yvonne's finger away, but controlled herself and backed away.

"Don't play fucking innocent with me! Are you saying in all this time Charles never just happened to mention that his best friend is married? You mean to say in all your little jaunts to Philadelphia you didn't happen to run into Robert's wife?"

Two women entered the lounge chatting, then took one look at the situation and walked back out.

"And don't fucking come back!" an out-of-control Regina shouted as the door closed behind them.

"Gee Regina, you're regressing. One little argument and you turn into a gutter mouth ho," Yvonne said sarcastically.

"And fuck you, too, Yvonne. You know goddamn well that I would have told you if I had any fucking idea what Robert was pulling!" Regina yelled, walking toward Yvonne. "And let me tell you another fucking thing—"

"Hey! The manager's out here calling the police!" Tamika said, busting through the door. "What's going on in here?"

"Ask Miss-High-and-Mighty here!" Yvonne shouted as she brushed by Tamika.

"No. Ask Miss-Out-Her-Fucking-Mind!" Regina shouted at the door.

"Forget I asked anybody anything. Let's get the hell out here before we get arrested," Tamika said, grabbing Regina, who was shaking with anger.

The restaurant manager was standing outside the door, and nervously followed them back to the table, rubbing his hands together and glancing behind his back to see if anyone else would emerge from the ladies' room.

"I'm going to have to ask you young ladies to leave. You're disturbing the other patrons," he said with bravado that wasn't evident in his eyes.

"No problem. We were just leaving," Regina said brusquely, handing him her credit card.

"It's on the house," the manager said quickly. "Just leave."

"No, problem," Puddin' said, jumping up and grabbing her handbag from the table. "Brilliant plan, Regina. Start a scene so we don't have to pay the bill."

"Shut the fuck up, Puddin'," Regina snapped.

"I hope someone lets me know next time it's Puddin' shut-the-fuck-up day," Puddin' grumbled as they headed out the door.

"And for the record," Regina shouted back at the manager, "I want you to know that I've been thrown out of better places!"

"Damn, that's a good line!" Puddin' grinned. "Remind me to use it sometime."

• • •

"SO, HOW MANY OTHER little secrets are you keeping from me?" Regina demanded when Charles walked through her apartment door that evening. He took one look in her face, and for a moment considered walking back out. He had seen her angry before, but never like this. Her arms were crossed, and her face was bright red. She looked ready to explode.

"It wasn't my secret to share," he said as he carefully put down his briefcase.

"Oh! So you know what I'm talking about?"

"Yeah. I just left Robert," he said, taking off his jacket. "He told me what happened. Regina, it's none of our business. It's between Robert and Yvonne. Let them work it out."

"None of our business? My best friend just accused me of being in on this little scheme!" she cried. "And you knew what was going on all this whole time, Charles. The four of us went out together. You even went to Yvonne's house and ate her mother's cooking. And the whole time you knew your friend was making a fool out of her."

"What was I supposed to do? I kept telling you I didn't want to go out with them, but you insisted, remember?" he said throwing his hands up in the air. "I don't like this whole thing any better than you. I told Robert he should be honest with her."

"Well, he wasn't honest with her, and you weren't honest with me!" Regina shouted. "You could have told me!"

"Why? So you could run and tell Yvonne?"

"Damn right!"

"That's exactly why I kept my mouth shut!" Charles shouted.

"What else are you keeping your mouth shut about?" Regina demanded. "Is Tamika going to have to get a telephone call to find out David's married?"

"He's not married. And for your information, he happens to

be in love with Tamika. He's probably going to ask her to marry him," Charles said lowering his voice.

"Oh, I see. I guess I'm supposed to jump up and down for joy now. How is it you can tell me that little tidbit of information, but you couldn't tell me Robert's married?"

Charles walked to the kitchen and opened the refrigerator. He shifted items around for a moment, then turned to Regina.

"What's for dinner?"

"I beg your pardon?" she asked in angry disbelief.

"I said, what's for dinner? I'm through with this discussion."

"Like hell you are!" Regina said as she reached and slammed the refrigerator door shut.

"Fine," he said. He slipped on his jacket and picked up his briefcase.

"Where are you going?"

"Back uptown. I'm not going to stay here and listen to you rant and rave all night," he said calmly. "Call me when you calm down."

"Oh, we'll be well into the next millennium by then," Regina snapped.

"Fine. That's up to you," he said, reaching for the door.

"So, you're just going to walk out?"

"What do you want me to do, Regina?" he swung around and shouted. "I don't need all this drama."

"For starters, you can just admit you were wrong to lie to me all this time!"

"For starters, I didn't lie to you. I never said Robert was a bachelor. And I don't care what you say or think, it wasn't for me to tell you or anyone else that he's married," Charles shouted throwing his briefcase back down.

"And let me ask you something. What would you do if the roles were reversed, Regina? Are you going to stand there and tell me you would have told me if Yvonne was the one who was married?" he asked advancing toward her. "Are you going to try and tell me that lie? Why the hell do you think you're the only one who owes some loyalty to a friend? I understand you're upset, but don't take this shit out on me!"

Regina stared at him, not knowing what to say. *I wouldn't have told him,* she thought angrily. Still, she wasn't wrong to be upset. Or was she? Why did things have to be so complicated?

"So is the drama over, or do I have to go uptown to get some sleep?" Charles asked.

"You can stay. But you're sleeping on the couch."

"Like hell I am," he said, grabbing his briefcase again and opening the door. "Good night."

9

REGINA WANTED A SMALL WEDDING CEREMONY. SHE HAD no mother to cry in the front pew. She had no father to walk her down the aisle and present her to her groom. She had no more than six or seven people in the world that really meant anything to her. A small wedding would do nicely.

But she looked around at the 150 guests partying at Zanzibar Blue in honor of her wedding day, and had to grin. A large wedding wasn't so bad either.

A warm smile came over her face as she remembered the *oohs* and *ahhs* of the wedding guests at Mount Olivet Baptist Church earlier that afternoon. Her dress was custom-made by her favorite designer, Anthony Mark Hankins of Dallas, who insisted that her supple body would be wasted in a traditional wedding gown. Instead he designed a candle-glow white, off-the-shoulder gown made of satin silk duchess, with a plunging bodice, a cabbage rose on each shoulder point, and a rhinestone bird-of-paradise nestled within. The gown was a slimming sheath that sexily hugged her body, then blossomed into a starburst at the knee. There was Venetian lace in each gore of the starburst, so the wedding guests could see hints of her silk fishnet stockings, with netting so small it was barely discernible. The dress was fastened in the back by 150 shimmering rhinestone buttons, leading down to a long cathedral train of tulle. She held a bouquet of 100 lilies of the valley as she walked down the aisle to meet her groom.

She insisted, much to the proper Mrs. Whitfield's displeasure, that she walk down the aisle alone. There was no one, in Regina's opinion, who was qualified to give her away. Her father was dead, and even if he were alive, he wouldn't have earned the honor. She also rejected Mrs. Whitfield's suggestion that Reverend Whitfield give her away. In the few months she had known him, she had grown to love him, but he was still new to her life.

No, she insisted, the only one qualified to give her away was herself.

Regina held her head her high as she took small purposeful steps down the aisle in beat to the obligatory "Here Comes the Bride." She couldn't resist a smile when she saw Charles waiting for her, dressed in a white tuxedo and a white cummerbund. There was nothing sexier than a man in a tuxedo, and Charles looked sexier than most. She couldn't wait for their wedding night.

They exchanged vows, and when Charles lifted her veil for the kiss that cemented her new status as a married woman, the band began to play Atlantic Starr's "Always."

Most of the people at the wedding, and the reception, were guests of the Whitfields, but not all.

Tamika and David were there with her at the bridal table, holding hands under the tablecloth, exchanging whispers and stolen kisses, as if anyone could look at them and not know they were in love. David was the oldest of seven children, and a responsible and serious young man who seldom smiled—except when he was around his playful and affectionate Tamika. She brought out a softer side of him; he brought a sense of stability to the flighty Tamika.

Regina looked around the crowded nightclub for her other bridesmaid. Puddin' had a bow-tied man hemmed up in the corner, angling to determine how much he made as a stock manager at a small brokerage firm.

"Hey, you're not supposed to be smiling," Charles said as he kissed her on the cheek.

"Why not?"

"You're a blushing bride. You're supposed to be nervous about the prospect of sharing your bridal bed," he whispered in her ear.

"Oh, believe me, I'm just petrified," Regina said, grinning as she squeezed his thigh under the table. "In fact, I think you should meet me in the ladies' room in five minutes and give me a bridal quickie to calm my nerves."

"Regina, I'm shocked! You mean you're not a virgin?" Charles pulled back in feigned surprise.

"No, but I play one on TV."

They both laughed out loud.

It was only 6:00 P.M., but it was January, and already dark outside. Befitting the time of year, the temperature was 30 degrees, and the roads were so icy, most of her friends from New York were unable to make the trip to Philadelphia for the wedding. Puddin' and Tamika had taken the train down two days earlier. "Neither rain, snow, or hail was going to stop me from coming. I bet Tamika ten bucks you'd back out at the last minute. You're going to have to lend me some money to get back to New York," Puddin' said after the ceremony.

Charles had insisted that Robert be his best man, since he had served in that capacity for Robert. But Regina just as strongly insisted that he not sit at the head table during the reception. And someone else would have to give the first toast to the bride and groom. She didn't approve of Yvonne's affair, but there was no way she was going to have her friend suffer through dinner and drinks at the same table as Robert and his wife.

But Charles was adamant, and it was indeed Robert who raised his glass in honor of the newlyweds. Not that it mattered, since Yvonne didn't come anyway. She and Mama Tee, the closest thing Regina had to a mother, called that morning to give their regrets.

"I told her we could still get a train, but you know how Mama is," Yvonne drawled on the telephone. "She swears there would be ice on the tracks, and the train would derail."

Regina wondered if it were really Mama Tee or Yvonne who had opted not to make the trip. She and Yvonne had patched things up on the surface, but there was an underlying tension that neither chose to address.

Still, Regina couldn't believe that Yvonne would decide to boycott her wedding.

And weather notwithstanding, it was a beautiful wedding. Regina's wedding dress cost $2,000, and the wedding and reception cost another $9,000. Charles's father generously paid half the expenses. "Can't have you young folks starting out in debt," he had said. Charles wanted to decline, but Regina pressed her heel into his shoe signaling him to accept the offer.

"Will you look at Renee?" Regina said, pointing at the dance floor where her niece was seductively swaying her hips and waving her arms in time to the music. Next to her, an older, and slightly taller, young girl watched mesmerized.

"Yeah, she's teaching Jazz some new dance. The tootsie roll or something," Charles said.

"And you're okay with it?" Regina asked, looking at Charles in wonderment. She soon found out after they started dating that Jasmine, his fourteen-year-old niece, was his pride and joy. He coddled and spoiled her almost as much as Regina did Renee, and she couldn't believe he didn't mind that his "baby girl" was out on the dance floor, wiggling her little butt.

Charles simply shrugged his shoulders.

"They're not doing anything outrageous. Now if they start grabbing their private parts or start rubbing up against somebody, I'm going to turn the place out," he said with a laugh.

Charles got up to talk to friends, but Regina continued to watch the girls.

Renee did a slow twirl, one hand up in the air, the other on her hip, and a look of complete assurance on her face. Jasmine tried to imitate, but stumbled midway into her turn. Renee stopped and went over the step slowly with Jasmine, and soon the two girls were giggling and twirling away. Jasmine accidentally bumped into a woman in a brown mid-calf silk gown, and both girls stopped to apologize. The woman turned, and Regina realized it was Angela. Regina watched with interest as she engaged the girls in conversation, and breathed a sigh of relief when the three to started laugh. Intuitively, Regina knew Angela was jealous of her marriage, but the woman pretended to be overjoyed at the match, and even offered to throw a bridal shower. Regina had graciously declined.

The band started playing a Latin tune. Jasmine hopped up and down, then grabbed Angela's hand, and the two began to dance.

"Bet you didn't know I could salsa!" Jasmine shouted to Renee.

"Yeah, girl! I'm scared of you!" Renee shouted back, wiggling her shoulders and clapping in time to the music.

"Jasmine, that's not nice," Angela admonished as she continued to dance with the girl. "She was showing you how to do her dances; you should show her how to salsa."

"I beg your pardon! Show *me* how to salsa? Oh no, you didn't say that!" Renee put one hand on her hip in mock anger. "I'll have you know I was salsa-ing in my mother's stomach!"

"Well, excuse me!" Jasmine laughed and rolled her eyes.

"That's right, excuse you." Renee rolled her eyes, trying not to laugh.

Regina's eyes closed into slits as Angela grabbed Charles as he walked by, and entreated him on the dance floor with her and Jasmine. He looked over at Regina who gave a slight shrug and looked away. He began a few hesitant steps, but after a few seconds he and Angela were dancing together as Jasmine stood on the sidelines with Renee.

Charles and Angela were good, and had obviously danced together before, executing a number of perfect twirls and turns.

"Now this is how we salsa in Philadelphia," Angela shouted at Renee after completing a turn.

Renee's mouth dropped open as if in surprise. She looked as if she was going to shout a retort, but then suddenly turned toward her aunt. "I *know* you're not going to let them play us like that, Aunt Gina." She grinned.

"You handle it, Ray-Ray," Regina said with a wave of her hand. "I'm too tired."

Regina knew Angela's remark was directed at her. The woman obviously took Regina's unwillingness to dance as inability, and Angela was taking advantage of what she saw as an opportunity to show she was the better woman. Was Angela really crass enough to try and compete with her on her wedding day? She watched as Angela seductively wet her lips as she danced with Charles. Yep. She was crass enough. So much for good breeding.

"Aunt Gina!"

"Dance with Jasmine, Ray-Ray," Regina said as she pretended not to watch Charles, who was pretending not to notice Angela's suggestive come-ons as they danced. He twice tried to graciously dance off the floor, but Angela kept pulling him back.

"Aunt Gina, come on!" Renee said urgently. The young girl stood on the dance floor, her arms reaching out to Regina, a puzzled look on her face. Regina knew that Renee knew what Angela was trying, and couldn't understand why her aunt wasn't rising to the occasion. *But,* Regina smiled to herself, *timing is everything.*

Regina wearily rose from the table, then walked on to the dance floor, flashing what looked like a nervous smile at Angela.

"Oh Renee, your auntie's tired," Angela said, swaying her hips seductively as she danced with Charles.

"No, that's okay," Regina said in a sheepish tone. "I'll never hear the end of it if I don't at least give it a try."

She turned toward her niece and winked. "Ready?"

With that, Regina closed her eyes, put her hands on her waist, and on beat threw her head to one side. On the next beat she clapped her hands over her head, and she and Renee began a number of intricate steps toward and then away from each other. She expertly caught Renee's hand, gave her a sudden half-turn, then swirled her frontward, and they both leaned back into a deep dip, rose on beat, then did a triple turn together.

"Oye!" Renee shouted, as Regina clasped her around the waist from behind and the two started another series of steps accentuated by twirls and dips.

The music finally stopped, and Renee hugged her aunt as the crowd applauded. When Renee finally let go, Charles grabbed Regina and kissed her on the cheek.

"You didn't have to show me up like that," he said playfully. Regina grinned and slipped her arms around his shoulders.

"I wasn't trying to show you up, baby," she said as she kissed him. *I was showing up that bitch you were dancing with,* she said to herself.

"Wow, Regina, I didn't know you could salsa like that," Angela said as Regina headed back to the bridal table.

"And she can do a mean waltz, too . . . just in case you're wondering," Renee said sarcastically. "But that's okay, Angela. I bet you do a mean Electric Slide."

"Renee!" Regina shot her niece a warning look. She appreciated Renee's protective stance, but didn't want her to think it was okay to insult an adult.

"Sorry. I should have said *Miss* Angela," Renee said as she and Jasmine turned and walked back toward the dance floor.

"I don't like her either. She's such a snob," Jasmine said as they walked away. Regina glanced at Angela to see if she heard the girl's remark, but if she did, she pretended otherwise, as she quickly made excuses to leave the reception.

Regina had asked Charles before about his relationship with Angela, and although he initially insisted she was simply a family friend, he eventually admitted that the two had dated while in high school.

"She's a cold fish. Not my type at all," he told Regina. "She doesn't have a passionate bone in her body. She's the type who has sex only because she thinks it's required. You can tell she'd rather be out shopping."

"So you guys did have a couple rolls in the hay, then?" Regina asked, feigning jealousy.

"We had sex one time, that was enough for me." Charles laughed. "I bet if you looked up the word frigid in the dictionary, you'd find a picture of Angela."

"But isn't Angela the type of woman you're supposed to marry?" Regina replied. "I mean, coming from a good family, and all those high-society manners."

"Good family and high-society manners don't keep you warm at night," Charles said as he pulled Regina close. "Now shut up about Angela and give me some of that good loving, woman."

I guess she couldn't come between us before we were married because we were in New York, but now she's going to try and make up for lost time Regina thought. *I'm going to have to keep my eye on that one.*

"And how is the happy couple?"

Regina looked up from the bridal table and smiled at Robert Bynum, co-owner of Zanzibar Blue.

Charles stood up and shook the elegant looking man's hand. "Bobby, you guys have done a wonderful job. I can't thank you enough for squeezing us in at the last minute."

"Not a problem. I was glad to help out," Robert said as he moved away.

Getting the Zanzibar Blue was a coup. It was the hottest nightclub in Philadelphia and a local institution. Charles had taken Regina there to listen to jazz on a few of their many trips to the city, and he knew she loved it. The crowd was always mixed— black and white, rich and not so rich—all coming out to enjoy the local talent that performed at the club during the week, and the national talent who frequently played on the weekends.

Though it cost a hefty price to host the reception at the club, Charles willingly made the arrangements, trying to make up for pushing up the wedding by five months. He was starting a new job in January, and taking the bar exam in June. There was no way he could pull it all off while worrying about wedding plans. Regina suggested they marry later in the year, or even the following year, but Charles wouldn't hear of it.

He wanted to start 2000 at his new job, with his new bride, in his new home—a spacious stone house in the Chestnut Hill section of the city. His parents had made the down payment as a wedding present. The mortgage was heavy, but Charles insisted they could afford it based on his promised salary. And, he told her, there was always the huge trust he inherited from his maternal grandmother as a fallback. Regina reminded him that she would also be contributing to the household income. She laughed when Charles grinned and said he didn't want a working wife.

"Congratulations, Regina. You've managed to hook the best fish in the sea."

She looked up to see the politician she had met at Charles's parents' anniversary party.

"Hey Rich! I'm glad you could make it," Charles said, rising from his chair to shake the man's hand. "Gina, you remember Richard Davis, don't you?"

"Of course," she said extending her hand and pasting on her best phony smile. "Good to see you, Richard."

"You look radiant, Gina. My sincerest congratulations again," Richard said as he kissed her hand.

"Oh, would you be upset if I asked you to call me Regina? Gina's a pet name my family uses, but I much prefer everyone else to call me Regina," she said withdrawing her hand from his lingering lips. "I hope you don't mind."

"Not at all. Regina it is. Of course, I could just call you Mrs. Whitfield now, couldn't I?" he said, straightening up.

"You most certainly could," she said with a smile. "And oh, just for future reference, you don't congratulate the bride. You congratulate the groom."

"I beg your pardon?"

"The man is congratulated for winning a prize, namely the woman's hand in marriage."

"I see. And what do you say to the bride?"

"Just best wishes will do."

"Well, then you have my very best wishes for a happy and prosperous marriage, Mrs. Whitfield," he said with a slight bow.

"Thank you, Richard," Regina said graciously.

"So, what made you change your mind about joining your mother's firm, Charles?" Richard asked, turning to Charles. "I thought you had your heart set on going out on your own."

"I still do. I'm going to give it a year at the firm and gain some experience, maybe make a little reputation, then see about starting my own practice," Charles answered.

"I heard they offered you a job at the D.A.'s office?"

"Yeah, but that was never a real consideration." Charles laughed.

"Hmm, I don't blame you. Low pay and long hours, and no recognition. Any thought about running for office?"

"Somewhere down the line," Charles said slowly, putting his arm around Regina to draw her into the conversation. He needn't have bothered. Regina was listening intently. She didn't trust Richard Davis. Charles admired him, though. He even worked on Rich's failed Senate campaign six years before. "Rich is the one of the few politicians I know who actually seems to care about issues," he had told Regina.

Davis came from a long line of politicians. His grandfather was a former mayor. His uncle and father had served on the city council, along with Charles's father. Richard himself had served one term on the council, before becoming a deputy mayor under the first African-American who held the city's highest office.

"Why do you ask?" Charles said.

"I'm sure you've heard that Royce is stepping down from Congress?" Richard said, lowering his voice.

"I've heard rumors," Charles answered cautiously. James Royce Jr. was his godfather, and one of his father's closest friends. Richard had to know Charles knew. The question was, how did Richard know? It was supposed to be a closely guarded secret. A better question was how much Richard knew. Charles had confided to Regina that Royce had HIV, courtesy of a blood transfusion he received in an emergency appendectomy sixteen years before. Only his family and close friends knew the truth. Royce wanted to keep his medical condition from the public to avoid the nasty speculation that comes with an announcement of a disease still so closely connected to homosexuality and intravenous drug use.

"Have you considered throwing your hat into the ring?"

Regina's eyes widened, but she said nothing.

"You've got to be kidding," Charles scoffed. "I've never held political office. I've never even run for office. It would be ridiculous for me to start my career with a run for Congress."

"It might not be as ridiculous as you think," Richard said. "If I remember correctly, Royce was a young lawyer when he won the office."

"That was twenty years ago. Times were different then. The African-American community rallied around him because they wanted an African-American in Congress," Charles said.

"I'm just suggesting you give it some thought," Richard said, slapping him on the back. "If I get elected to the Senate it would be great knowing I had a smart and energetic guy like you backing me up in Washington. And I happen to know that there are very influential people here in Philadelphia who will welcome a chance to contribute to your campaign.

"Just something to think about. Give me a call when you get back from your honeymoon. We should talk," he said as he walked away.

"Charles?" Regina looked at her husband inquisitively.

"Don't worry, he's got to be joking, or trying to make himself seem more important than he is," Charles said with a scowl. "It's obvious he wants me to know that he knows what's going on, and just as obvious that he wants me to let Royce know he knows."

"I thought he was your boy?" Regina said sarcastically.

"He's a politician. A good politician, or so I've always thought. He has something up his sleeve." He shrugged.

"Hey," he said suddenly, reaching under the table, and massaging her thigh. "What about that bridal quickie?"

"Oh, Charles, you make me blush." Regina giggled, then excused herself from the table announcing she had to powder her nose, winking at Charles as she walked away.

• • •

REGINA NEVER THOUGHT she would ever marry, let alone marry a lawyer. Or a politician. But there she was, at a meeting Charles insisted she attend, listening to a group of old politicians trying to persuade her husband to run for the U. S. Congress. She was the only woman there in the office of Mount Olivet Baptist Church, where Reverend Whitfield pastored. Two days earlier the *Philadelphia Inquirer* published news from "unnamed sources" that Congressman James Royce Jr., the state's first and only African-American congressman, was dying from AIDS.

"If you think about it for a moment, Charles, it makes perfect sense," said James Royce, a stately gray-haired man who resembled the South African president, Nelson Mandela. That's if you could imagine Nelson Mandela with rolled-up sleeves, a loosened tie, drinking a glass of bourbon and smoking a cigar. "Davis went to the newspapers because he wanted to besmirch my name. He knows what people will think. Especially since I was outed."

Reverend Whitfield got up from his chair behind his large mahogany desk. "He figures he *might* win the Democratic nomination for the Senate seat, but then he would still have to worry about the November election with that hot-shot the Republicans are backing. He's got to be thinking he has a better shot at a congressional seat, especially this one. Everyone knows that whoever wins the Democratic primary for the second congressional district automatically wins in November. There's never been a Republican in this district, and there never will be."

Charles sat hunched over in his chair, elbows resting on his knees, his hands tightly folded, as he listened to the respected old men whose advice had shaped his life.

"That snake in the grass has already started campaigning and Royce hasn't even stepped down," grumbled state senator Vincent Williams. "He held a fund-raising dinner in my district, and didn't even invite me. In *my* district."

"I bet he didn't wear a kente-cloth cummerbund at that five-hundred-dollars-a-plate dinner," Reverend Whitfield said with a grimace. "With that last congressional realignment adding Mount Airy and Chestnut Hill to the district, the constituency's more than thirty percent white. Upwardly mobile whites with money. The kind that vote in every election. Those are the voters Davis is after."

"I understand all of that, but I still don't understand why me?" Charles said rubbing his face.

"Because Davis is going to try and convince people that the 'old guard' in the district are out of touch. He's not going to use the race card, he can't, because the whites in the district are too liberal for him to get away with it. It would backfire and he knows it. Plus, he'd lose any chance of getting any black votes, and he knows he'll need some to win. So he has to convince them that he best represents their interests, because he's younger and thinks like them.

"Now who do we have in the district that we can run against him? Most of the people considering running against him are over fifty and firmly entrenched in politics and the church. He'll just convince the voters they're out of touch, and damn, he might even be right," Royce said.

"So we need someone young and fresh, but someone that the old guard ward leaders and committeemen will relate to. They're not going to trust an outsider. They'd back Davis first," Royce said as he poured himself another drink from a crystal decanter usually hidden in Reverend Whitfield's desk drawer.

"You fit the bill, Charlie," Reverend Whitfield said. "It's not going to matter that you've never held office. You have a political history without having a political history. Your father's a city councilman, and your godfather's a congressman. You have name recognition. But at the same time, you're young, you're smart, and an Ivy League School graduate to boot. You're the new breed of black politician."

"Plus, you've worked with Rich. Hell, you were his campaign manager, so he's going to have a tough time trying to smear your politics without smearing his own," Williams added.

Regina could see Charles was torn. He kept glancing at her, but saying nothing, although he occasionally reached over and rubbed her shoulder as if for luck.

"Regina, you've been quiet. What do you think about all this," Reverend Whitfield asked suddenly.

"I think this is up to Charles—" Williams started.

"This will affect my wife just as much as it will me," Charles said firmly as he looked up at Williams.

"True. And we respect Regina's opinion. At least I do," Reverend Whitfield said, shooting Williams a dirty look. "My daughter-in-law happens to be one of the most intelligent women I know."

"Thanks," Regina said slowly, as she formulated a reply to Reverend Whitfield's question. She glanced at Charles, who was looking at her expectantly. For one of the very few times in her life, she didn't know what to say. She didn't cherish the thought of having her new husband involved in a grueling campaign so early in their marriage, but at the same time she sensed that Charles was more than intrigued with the idea of being a congressman. Who could blame him? Not yet thirty, and possibly on his way to Washington. She also realized how important it was to the men in the room that Charles won. The second congressional district was the only district in the state with an African-American representative. They had fought too hard, for too long, to gain representation in Washington, and they weren't going to relinquish it without a fight.

"I'm going to have to pass the buck here," she said finally. "If Charles wants to run, I'll support him all the way. I guess that goes without saying," she said as she squeezed her husband's hand. "And I'll support him if he decides not to run. But I do have one question. Where's the money going to come from?"

"Good question," Royce said. "I'll turn over my financial contacts, of course. And Henry Nicholas, who heads the Medical Workers Union, may be a good source of support. We'll go after the other unions and of course we'll be holding fund-raising events, but we're already way behind Davis. He's been raising money for his supposed Senate race for more than a year now."

"We'll be operating on a shoestring budget and it's not going to be easy. But I still think we can do it, if you're willing, son," Reverend Whitfield said, patting Charles on the shoulder. "It'll mean long hours of campaigning, knocking on doors, begging for money from people you don't know, and some you don't like. And a helluva lot of other unpleasant things that I can't even think of right now."

Charles rubbed his hand over his face again, then stood up and walked over and poured himself a drink from the dwindling decanter. He leaned against the mantelpiece, his eyes closed. He didn't say anything, but Regina knew his answer. So did his father.

Reverend Whitfield raised his glass.

"Here's to the newest U. S. Congressman from Pennsylvania, my son, Charles Whitfield."

The room applauded, while Charles simply smiled.

THE REST OF THE WEEK was a blur for Regina. Royce held a televised press conference, officially announcing his decision not to seek reelection due of his failing health, and thanking his constituents for their loyal support throughout the years. He promised to continue to serve the district as an elder statesman.

He stood at the podium flanked by his wife, Charles, Reverend Whitfield, and a group of African-American clergymen. "I want to say now, that I regret that you had to learn about my illness, not from me, but from people who hope to gain politically from my misfortune.

"I did not withhold the information because of any shame or fear of stigma, but because I felt it was a private matter, between my family and me," he said, squeezing his wife's hand.

Two hours after Royce's press conference, Davis held one of his own, announcing his candidacy for the congressional seat. He was immediately endorsed by the mayor, the Fraternal Order of Police, and the Philadelphia Chamber of Commerce.

Charles waited three days before announcing he was running.

"I've thought long and hard about this decision. I want to continue the legacy of good government and inclusion that has marked the tenure of my godfather, James Royce, Jr.," he said as he stood at the podium, Regina and his parents at his side. Royce gave Charles a ringing endorsement, as did City Councilman Whitfield, State Senator Williams, and the United Black Clergy of the Greater Philadelphia Area.

"Well, baby," Regina said, hugging Charles after the reporters left, "I hope we made the right decision."

Charles smiled and kissed his wife lightly on the lips. "It's too late to second-guess ourselves," he said. "Now we just have to get ready for the fight of our lives."

10

THE TELEPHONE ON THE NIGHTSTAND RANG LOUDLY, but since Regina was so used to the sound over the last three months of the campaign, it failed to rouse her. She didn't hear Charles answer it, nor did she awake when he jumped up from their satin-sheeted double bed, showered, and put on his clothes. Only when he leaned down to kiss her and she felt his freshly trimmed mustache tickle her face did she open her eyes.

"What time is it?" she asked enjoying the lingering scent of his aftershave on her cheek.

"Five-thirty," he said cheerfully.

"Where are you going at five-thirty in the morning?" she asked, propping herself up on her elbow and squinting at the clock.

"Five-thirty on a Sunday morning, no less," Charles said as he snapped on gold cuff links.

"God! Okay, where are you going at five-thirty on a Sunday morning?"

"I have a meeting with Royce and Robert, then off to a prayer breakfast, my dear. I'm going out to get some religion."

Robert, much to Regina's displeasure, had signed on as Charles's campaign field manager. She grudgingly admitted though, he was good. In addition to soliciting volunteers and setting up offices throughout the city, he wrangled invitations for Charles to a host of social and cultural events, giving him exposure and chances to get his message across to potential voters.

"Oh. You're going out to get religion, huh?"

"Yep. And hopefully a bunch of votes, and a bunch of money. It's a Delta shindig, and you know those wonderful sorority sisters always carry their wonderful checkbooks," he said kissing Regina again. "I'll see you tonight. I should be home around eleven-thirty or so."

Pretty much par for the course, Regina thought, burrowing down into a pillow, as he walked out the door. She only saw Charles four or five hours a day, and then usually only when she woke up in the middle of the night to find him asleep beside her. Lovemaking was reduced to a few early morning quickies, and the promise of a forty-eight-hour, two-person orgy as soon as the grueling campaign was over.

Regina occasionally went out on the campaign trail with him, but sometimes having a beautiful wife was a liability for a politician. Especially a politician as young and handsome as Charles. Women gladly pressed checks into his hand just to have an excuse to touch him. Charles, in his campaign, kissed more women than most politicians kissed babies. "Only on the cheek, though," he laughingly told Regina, "and I make sure they see my wedding band."

Things were going well for the Charles Whitfield for Congress campaign, although they gave up hope of getting an endorsement from the chairman of the Democratic Party in Philadelphia. George Overton knew openly endorsing Richard Davis would alienate the African Americans in the party, but he worked behind the scenes on Davis's behalf, pressuring his cronies to make huge financial contributions and persuading some ward leaders to throw their support behind Davis.

But Royce worked miracles of his own. During his twenty years in Congress he had become a leader in the Congressional Black Caucus, and a number of prominent African-American politicians flew into town to campaign on his godson's behalf. None of them wanted to see the only African-American congressional seat in the state relinquished to a white man.

"We black folks want to think that we've overcome. Well, I'm here to tell you there is a still lot of overcoming to do," a fiery congressman from Michigan said in a speech to the Philadelphia NAACP. "And to do that we have to have voices in Congress who are willing to stand up to the political right. We need strong young African-American men and women who are willing to get up on the floor of Congress, and remind white America that there is someone watching, and participating, and demanding a piece of the pie for African-Americans in this country."

Reverend Whitfield also called in chits for favors done during his twenty years of public service. His biggest coup was arranging a meeting between his son and the white ward leaders in Mount Airy and Chestnut Hill who were still stunned that they had been realigned into a majority African-American congressional district. The ward leaders invited Davis to the meeting, but he arrogantly declined. His chosen method of campaigning was to ignore his long-shot opponent, and he refused three invitations for a debate. Davis chose to attend a banquet given by the Roofers Union, confident that the white wards were firmly in his camp. He hadn't counted on Charles's ability to relate to affluent whites as well as to not-so-affluent blacks.

"Our issues are the same," Charles told the ward leaders. "We're all concerned about housing, crime, and education. I know many of you have children who are attending private schools. I don't blame you. I went to private schools most of my life, and if I hadn't I might not have been able to attend Ivy League colleges. If I had children I would want them to have the best education possible, and that's not to be found in public schools. But isn't that the problem? Shouldn't we be concentrating on improving public education so that we don't have to pay outrageous tuition to ensure our children can get into good colleges?"

Charles strode away with a standing ovation and the ward leaders' endorsement. Charles was dynamic, he was personable, and he knew the issues and how to articulate them. What Davis thought would be a cakewalk was turning into a real horse race.

As much as she hated to, Regina had to give Robert and Angela their due. Robert was an astute campaign manager, making sure Charles was in all the right places at all the right times, and turning on his immense charm for the swarm of media who were closely following the race. And Angela swung into action with a vengeance, almost single-handedly managing the campaign office until a horde of volunteers signed on once it became apparent that Charles had a chance of actually winning the primary election. The woman was madly efficient, making appointments, handling telephone calls, and always having a fresh pot of Charles's favorite coffee brewing in the office. When Regina teased Charles that Angela was trying to convince him that he married the wrong woman, he laughed.

"She's just trying to hitch her wagon to a star, baby. Watch, Angela's going to snare one of those up-and-coming men dropping off résumés at the office, anticipating our trip to Washington. And if anything, working with Angela has proven to me more than ever how lucky I am to have a woman like you. The woman doesn't have a mind of her own. She agrees with everything I say."

"I thought men liked women like that," Regina said suspiciously.

"Not this man. I want someone I can bounce ideas off of.

Who's not afraid to stand up to me and tell me when I'm going in the wrong direction."

Though Regina had little to do with the campaign, she was keeping busy pursuing her writing career. She drove up to New York City regularly to meet with editors and maintain her business relationships. She also started picking up contacts in Philadelphia. She was a regular contributor to the ritzy *Philadelphia* magazine, and wrote occasional pieces for the *Philadelphia Inquirer* and the *Philadelphia Daily News*. And she even benefited from Charles's congressional run. After writing a couple of Charles's campaign speeches, she began receiving requests to write political speeches for some other politicians. She also became active in the Philadelphia Association of Black Journalists. It was good for her writing career, and it certainly didn't hurt Charles that she was socializing with media people who were covering the congressional race.

The telephone rang again at 8:30, this time waking Regina, who had fallen back to sleep.

"Hey, Gina. I forgot! You're supposed to meet me downtown for the opening of that rehab center, right?" Charles said in a hurried voice.

"Oh that's right. Sure, four-thirty this afternoon?" Regina asked groggily, a little resentful about being reawakened.

"Right. I don't have the address, but call Angela in the office later on and she can give it to you. See you later, baby."

Click.

A wave of nausea swept over Regina, and she jumped out of the bed and rushed to the adjoining bathroom, barely making it to the commode before her dinner from the night before made an unsightly reappearance.

Regina brushed her teeth, then dampened a pink washcloth with cold water and wiped her face. *Dang, I'll be glad when I get over this morning sickness business,* Regina thought as she stumbled back to the bed. By her calculations she was six weeks pregnant, by the doctor's, eight weeks. She and Charles hadn't shared their good news with anyone. They wanted to make the announcement the night of the primary.

Regina arrived at the Renewed Faith Center shortly before 4:30 P.M., but Charles had not yet arrived. The director of the program, Joseph Hunter, greeted her effusively. He'd just received word that the mayor himself was going to be on hand for the ribbon cutting, he told Regina proudly, and offered to take her on a tour of the two-story building that housed the agency before the celebration started.

"We have capacity for up to twenty-five in-house patients, and the capability to treat up to seventy-five clients on an out-patient basis. We already have seventeen clients ready to start the program, most referred by social service agencies here in Pennsylvania, but a few from New York and New Jersey," Hunter boasted, as they walked through the halls that still smelled of the white paint so recently slapped on the walls.

"As part of the program, clients will be seen by social service counselors who will help them define their goals, and suggest ways to go about attaining them," the enthusiastic director said. "Kicking a drug dependency is only the first step. We plan to teach our clients life skills so they don't have to go back into the same situations they just left."

After the tour, Hunter escorted her to a large reception center where a small crowd of people milled around, eating pretzels and drinking apple cider and waiting for the mayor to arrive so they could get a piece of the enormous vanilla frosted sheet cake prominently displayed on a table in the middle of the room.

She spotted Charles in a corner chatting with the director of the city health department. He stopped talking when she walked over, and planted a kiss on her cheek.

"You look good enough to eat," he whispered in her ear after making introductions.

"Promises, promises," Regina whispered back, lightly flicking her tongue between his lips as she kissed him full on the mouth.

"Charles, Regina, good to see you both." They turned to look at Richard Davis smiling at them, his arm outstretched toward Charles for a handshake.

"Good to see you, too," Charles answered, wearing his best politician's smile. Regina smiled graciously, but said nothing. All good politicians' wives kept smiles on their faces, she was coached by Royce and Daddy Whitfield. Never give the media a reason to think a campaign was putting a strain on the home life. She spotted Denise Cornish from WRAP-News, microphone in hand, finishing up an interview with the center's director. Regina excused herself, squeezing Charles's hand before she walked away.

"Hey Niecey. How goes it?" Regina greeted her warmly.

"It goes, it goes," Denise said rolling her eyes. Regina sucked her teeth sympathetically. For Denise, covering the opening of a drug rehabilitation center was like covering a dog show. Someone had to do it, but it was usually young reporters trying to build up news clips. Denise was a ten-year veteran at the television station. Her covering such a mundane event meant she pissed someone off at the station.

Though Regina and Denise seldom saw each other outside of Philadelphia Association of Black Journalists meetings, the two women genuinely liked each other. Maybe because they both had sharp tongues and disdain for people who tried to talk down to them.

"What are you doing here? Are you writing an article?" Denise asked as she grabbed a glass of ginger ale from a nearby table.

"Nope," Regina, said pointing to her husband who was still chatting with the health director while Richard Davis stood close by. "I'm out stumping with hubby."

"Hold on, here comes the mayor," Denise said motioning her

cameraman over. "I'm going to get a quick sound bite from him, and then I'm out of here. I'll talk at you later, Regina."

Richard Davis scurried over, almost knocking Regina down as he tried to get in the camera's range during Denise's interview with the mayor. Regina cut her eyes at him, and walked back over to Charles.

"How much longer are we staying?" she asked, dutifully keeping a smile on her face.

"Just a bit longer. They're going to trot out some of their prospective clients for the mayor's speech, which, if I know him, won't last but three minutes, and then we can leave," he said. "We're having a fund-raiser at Zanzibar Blue at six, and then I have a meeting with some committeemen at seven-thirty. Want to come?"

"Sure. I don't have anything planned this evening," Regina answered.

"I thought Yvonne was coming to town tonight?"

"Is she? I hadn't heard," Regina said with indifference she didn't feel. Her best friend caught the train from New York to Philadelphia at least once a week for a quick tryst with Robert, but seldom bothered to notify her. Once she even walked into Charles's campaign office and found Yvonne sitting behind a desk answering the telephones. "Just helping out," she told Regina in explanation for her presence, but said nothing about her lack of contact with Regina. Regina knew Robert and his wife owned an apartment building in North Philadelphia, and she suspected Robert had set up a little love nest for Yvonne's visits.

"Come on," Charles said, pulling Regina's hand. "The mayor's at the podium."

Charles quickly walked over and situated himself with the other local dignitaries behind the mayor as he spoke. Regina waited on the sidelines, scanning the bored faces of the crowd half-listening to the mayor's short speech about the rehabilitation center filling a need in the community. She noticed a dilapidated looking woman with stringy, blond hair and sunken cheeks standing among the crowd, staring at her intently. The woman had the vacant look of a long-time heroin user, but there was something about her that looked familiar. Still, Regina couldn't remember where she had seen her before. The woman looked at Regina as if also struggling to place her. As recognition registered in the woman's eyes, her mouth flew open, revealing yellow rotting teeth. Regina inwardly shuddered at the sight, but she still couldn't figure out who the woman was. Maybe someone she once interviewed, she thought. She started walking over to introduce herself, but Charles was suddenly pulling her arm. She looked in the woman's direction and smiled apologetically, hoping the woman would believe she recognized her but simply didn't have time to stop and chat, but the woman didn't return the smile. Instead she sneered and mouthed "Fuck you," then flashed Regina the finger. Regina's eyes widened in disbelief, but she decided not to confront the woman. No need in making a scene. She glanced back over her shoulder as she followed Charles and his entourage out the door, and was amazed to see Richard Davis talking to the woman. She must be one of his asshole supporters, Regina decided, tossing her hair and strutting out of the door.

THREE WEEKS LATER Regina received a telephone call from Denise Cornish.

"Hey, Denise. How are you doing," she said in surprise. She didn't even know Denise had her home telephone number.

"I'm doing fine. The question is how are *you* doing?"

"I'm fine. What do you mean?" Regina asked putting down the appointment book she had been flipping through. Something was up, and it didn't sound good.

"You haven't heard? Honey, you'd better sit down, because this isn't going to be pleasant."

"I'm sitting down. What's up?" Regina said, as a sickening feeling started at the pit of her stomach.

"Richard Davis is trying to plant a story that you were arrested for shoplifting back in New York, and that you were mixed up with drugs and prostitution," Denise said straight to the point.

Regina's mind reeled, and the sickening feeling in her stomach rushed up and enveloped her body. Her bones ached. Her eyes ached. Even her teeth ached. *This can't be happening,* she thought.

"Regina? Are you there?"

Regina opened her mouth to answer, but no sound came out. She held the telephone in her hand while Denise shouted into the receiver for her attention. Finally, Denise hung up and redialed.

"Hello," Regina said, emotionlessly.

"Regina, listen. Please don't make me sorry I told you this," Denise said urgently.

"Okay," Regina said dully.

"Regina, are you okay? Oh Lord, I knew I shouldn't have told you this over the telephone."

"No, no, I'm okay," Regina said forcing herself out of her daze. She had to deal with the situation. It sure as hell wasn't going to go away. "When are you guys running the story?"

"We're not. I hope you didn't think I was calling you up for a quote," Denise said gently. "He came to me with this shit this afternoon, but I decided to pass on the story, and my producer agrees. I think it's pretty slimy, him pulling this two weeks before the primary. Especially since he doesn't want anyone to know that he's the one who supplied the information. He's a real bastard.

"But, Regina, I doubt we're the only ones he told," Denise continued. "You know someone is going to run with it. In fact, I think the *Daily News* is going ahead with it. I'm surprised they haven't called you already."

"I did get a message to call them, but I hadn't gotten around to it yet. I thought they just wanted to get a quote about the campaign or something," Regina said. "So none of this conversation is on the record, right?"

"Right. In fact, I hope you won't mention that I even told you about this. I'm coming to you as one friend to the other. I didn't think you should find out when you open the newspaper tomorrow."

"Thanks, Denise. I owe you big time. I'll give you a call tomorrow or something, okay?"

"Okay. But Regina, if you *do* decide to speak out on this . . ."

"Don't worry. I'll give you an exclusive," Regina said, smiling to herself in spite of the situation. Friend or no friend, Denise was still a reporter.

She sat on the bed after hanging up, trying to make sense of everything. How did Davis find out? Regina closed her eyes, and threw back her head in a wail. *Oh, God, it was Krystal. It was my old boosting partner I saw at the drug rehabilitation center! Krystal must've told Davis everything!*

Regina massaged her temples with the tips of her fingers, trying to ease the pounding. *This will destroy Charles's campaign,* she thought. She reached for the telephone but didn't know who to call. The logical person would have been Yvonne, but she had no idea where she was, and didn't know if she'd care.

"Hello."

"Hi David, it's Regina. Is Tamika there?"

"Sure, hold on."

Regina's fingernails dug into her hands as she waited for Tamika to get on the telephone. She didn't know what she wanted to say, she just needed to hear a friendly voice.

"Hey, girl!" Tamika's ever-cheerful voice blared through the receiver.

"Tamika, I'm in trouble," Regina blurted out.

"What's the matter! What happened?"

"Tamika. I'm dying," Regina said in a low voice. Something wet dripped onto the telephone receiver, and she realized for the first time that tears were rolling down her cheeks.

"I'm here all by myself and I'm dying." Regina started crying hysterically.

"What are you talking about?" Tamika shouted on the telephone. "Regina, what happened? Are you hurt?"

Regina could hear David in the background asking if something was wrong. She couldn't speak for a few minutes. Doubled over, she rocked back and forth on the bed, her body wracked with sobs as she held onto the telephone receiver as if it were a lifeline. The sobs turned to soft moans, then finally into howls so loud and long that her throat hurt. Her eyes were squeezed shut, and waves of black and red flooded her brain. Her chest throbbed as her lungs struggled to get air. Her free hand flew up to her head, and she started clawing at her hair. She tried to get up from the bed, knocking the telephone table over in the process. The telephone, her appointment book, and a vase of flowers spilled to the floor. She tripped on the telephone cord, and landed on the carpet, banging her head on the edge of the overturned table. She didn't even notice, the pain inside her body was so overwhelming. She tried to crawl back onto the bed, but gave up and sat on the floor in a puddle of water, her legs stretched out in front of her.

"Oh God, Regina. What happened? Should I call an ambulance?"

"Tamika, it's all closing in on me. I'm suffocating. I can't breathe," Regina finally managed to say in a hoarse voice, through sobs. "I'm all messed up. I've messed everything up,

Tamika. Do you hear me? I messed it all up. Oh, God, help me. What am I going to do?"

"Gina, I want to help you, but you have to tell me what happened," Tamika pleaded. "Are you sick? Did something happen to Charles?"

"Yeah, I happened to Charles." Regina bit her swollen lips, oblivious to the mixed taste of blood and tears flowing into her mouth. "Oh, Tamika, it's all over. It's all over."

"What's all over, Regina? Please tell me what's going on."

Through her sobs and loud gulps of air, Regina told Tamika about Krystal. About Richard Davis. And about the telephone conversation with Denise.

"How could I have been so stupid?" she shouted into the telephone. She pounded her head with her fist and bit deeper into her lip. "You think I didn't know something like this was going to happen? You think I didn't know that my past was going to bite me in the ass? Now I've ruined everything. I've ruined everything for me and for Charles."

"Oh, Gina, sweetie, you've got to calm down," Tamika said soothingly. "It seems bad now, but it's going to be okay."

"How is it going to be okay? Didn't you just hear what I just said? I've just ruined Charles's political career! He's going to hate me, and I don't blame him. I hate me, too. I just wish I was dead!"

"Regina, don't you say that! You hear me?" Tamika shouted into the telephone. "You just stay put. David and I are driving down right now."

"For what, Tamika? What are you going to do? What can anyone do? It's too late! Oh, God, Tamika. What's wrong with me? Why didn't I just stay in my place? Why did I have to crawl out of my hole and go and mess it up for everybody?" Regina started sobbing hysterically again. "What am I going to do now?"

"Listen to me, Gina! You've got to calm down. I mean it." Tamika's voice took on a demanding tone. "You didn't do anything wrong, and when you calm down you'll realize it. There wasn't any way for you to know this was going to happen. How the hell could you know Krystal was in Philadelphia? And how could you know she was going to hook up with this Davis guy? It's just a bad set of coincidences, but it's not the end of the world. You're going to make it through this."

"No I'm not," Regina sobbed.

"Yes, you are. And you know why? Because you're Regina Harris. And I don't know anyone that can deal with a bad situation better than you."

"I can't deal with this, Tamika," Regina wailed.

"Yes, you can! We've known each other all of our lives, remember? You survived your mother dying. You survived being shot. And you didn't let any of that stop you. You pulled yourself together and went to school and made something of yourself.

"Girl, you're a hero! Yeah, things are bad right now, but it's not the end of the world. It's just one more thing you're going to have to overcome. But you can do it, Regina. I know you can."

"No, Tamika, I can't. See that's the thing . . . everyone always thinks I'm so strong, but I'm really not. And this is just too much!"

"Gina, you may not be invincible, but you are strong. And this is not too much. It just feels like it right now. And you're not alone, you've got to remember that. You've got me, and Puddin', and Yvonne to help you get through," Tamika said urgently. "Haven't we always stuck together? And you have Charles, too. That man loves the ground you walk on. I think you're underestimating him, Gina."

"I don't know, Tamika . . ."

"Well, I know, okay? Trust me on this," Tamika said firmly. "Now David and I are on the way. We'll be there in two hours, okay? Should we meet you at the house?"

Regina managed a small smile. Little Tamika taking charge.

"No, you guys stay there. I'm okay."

"No, you're not. It'll take us about two hours to get there. I'll call Yvonne and Puddin' and we can pick them up on the way."

Regina was feeling better, but as she picked herself up from the floor, she glanced at the full-length mirror on the wall. The self-confident, professional woman that she knew for the past five years was gone, replaced by a tired, pitiful woman with a badly swollen face, hair sticking up all over her head. She looked like she'd been in a street fight. Regina walked to the mirror in a daze, reached her hand toward the reflection, and watched in nauseating amazement as the pathetic looking woman's hand reached toward hers. Their fingers met at the glass. Tears again rolled down Regina's face, and the haggard woman in the mirror cried in sympathy.

She showered and dressed, then looked at the gold watch Charles bought her for their three-month anniversary. It was 5:30. She picked up the telephone and dialed his cellular number. No answer. He probably let the batteries die again. She dialed Robert's cellular number, knowing he was probably with her husband.

"Hi Robert, this is Regina. Is Charles with you?"

"No, he should be at the West Philadelphia office. I'm on my way to meet him now," Robert said cordially.

"How far away are you?"

"Two blocks."

"Okay. Do me a favor? Tell him to please stay put for a moment. I've got to talk to him about something, and it's urgent," Regina said, reaching for her car keys.

"Is everything okay?" Robert asked worriedly.

Regina sighed. She briefly considered telling Robert about Denise's telephone call but decided against it.

"Just please, make sure he stays put until I get there." She avoided looking into the mirror as she left the house.

Ten minutes later she walked into the office, and found the twenty volunteers crowded around the secretary's desk, talking. All twelve telephone lines were ringing off the hook, but no one was answering them. When Angela looked up and saw Regina, she waved her hand wildly at the others and silence fell over the group. *Shit,* Regina thought. *They already know.*

"Is my husband here?" she asked with as much dignity as she could muster.

"He's in with his father and Robert," Angela said, pointing to the inner office. "I think they're having a private meeting." Then in a contemptuous tone, she said, "You can have a seat and wait if you like."

So now she thinks she can talk to me any way she chooses. She seems pretty satisfied that I'm on my way out, Regina thought huffily. But there was no use in wasting what little energy she had putting Angela in her place.

"Thank you," Regina told the woman without bothering to look in her direction. Regina walked over and opened the door without knocking. The door slammed behind her. Charles sat in a chair, his legs propped on the desk, staring at the television, which was turned off, the remote in his hand. His father leaned on the wall, his arms crossed, a look of shock on his face. Robert was pacing the floor, muttering.

Regina walked to the middle of the room, her hands held out in front of her, palms up, her eyes directed at Charles.

"I'm so sorry," was all she could say.

Charles looked at her, and she thought she saw a flash of anger on his face, but the look was gone in an instant. He jumped up and rushed over to her, taking her in his arms and pulling her close.

"Gina, you don't have anything to be sorry about," he said stroking her hair.

The intercom buzzed and Robert stomped over and pushed

the button. "I thought I said we didn't want to be disturbed, Angela," he snapped.

"Sorry, Robert. Congressman Royce is on line three, and he insisted that he be put through," the secretary whined over the machine.

Robert cursed and picked up the telephone.

"Hello? . . . Yes, we heard it on the six o'clock news . . . He's right here . . . She's right here, too . . . Hold on." He placed his palm over the receiver and looked at Regina. "The congressman wants to know if you've talked to the press?"

"I spoke to one reporter. A friend of mine, Denise Cornish from Channel Six," Regina answered, pulling away from Charles's arms.

"What did you tell her?" Reverend Whitfield asked gently.

"Nothing. I told her if I had anything to say, I'd call her back."

Robert relayed the information to the congressman, then placed his palm over the receiver again.

"He wants to know if you confirmed the story."

"No, I didn't confirm anything."

He got back on the telephone.

"No, she didn't confirm anything . . . No, Channel Three was the only station that carried it . . . When? . . . Okay, we'll be there in twenty minutes." He hung up the telephone.

"He wants us to get to his house right away," Robert said, putting on his suit jacket and looking expectantly at Charles and Regina.

"Why don't you go home and get some rest," Charles said, kissing Regina on the forehead.

"He wants her to come, too," Robert said.

"No. She needs some rest," Charles said firmly.

"I'm okay. It's probably a good idea for me to go along," Regina said wearily.

Robert opened the door to the outer office, then quickly slammed it shut.

"The buzzards are circling. There's got to be ten reporters out there waiting for us to come out," he said in shock.

Reverend Whitfield walked over to Regina and placed his hands on her shoulders.

"Are you really okay?" he asked.

"Sure," Regina said, struggling to smile.

He looked at her for a moment, then smiled in return.

"Okay. Mind giving an old man a hug?" he said pulling her close. "Listen, I want you to know that we're all in your corner here. Damn the campaign. You're the most important thing here. We're going to make sure you come out of this okay, you hear? I mean that."

Regina sniffed, trying to hold back her tears.

He gently pushed her back, holding her at arm's length and looking directly into her eyes as he talked.

"When I first saw you, I said, 'My boy's got one proud woman there.' You walked into our house with your head held high, and I've never seen it any other way. And I don't expect see it any other way now, you hear?

"I knew you had a hard childhood, that was in your face. I guess I didn't know how hard. But I want you to know that I'm prouder of you now than ever, and I'm glad you're in our family. Now, we're going to walk out there, and I'm going to have my arm around my daughter-in-law's shoulders, and to hell with the reporters. Okay?"

Regina nodded, too choked up to speak.

"Sorry, Dad," Charles grinned. "I got dibs on those pretty little shoulders."

"Charlie," Reverend Whitfield said as he slipped on his coat. "Your wife has two pretty little shoulders. You're going to have to share."

Reporters swarmed them as they walked out of the campaign

headquarters, trying to stick microphones in their faces and shouting questions. Camera flashes blinded them as they made their way to a waiting car. Robert shooed the reporters as best he could, and Charles and Reverend Whitfield acted as defensive linemen for Regina, who was in a state of shock by the time she was in the sanctuary of the automobile.

THE CONGRESSMAN GREETED THEM with a grunt and a nod when they arrived at his house thirty minutes later. He showed them into the study, and immediately got down to business.

"Okay. We're in damage control mode, here. Let's start from the beginning. How much of this stuff is true?" he asked Charles.

"I can answer that," Regina said, stepping forward. "I was arrested for shoplifting when I was fifteen. I served a year's probation, and my record was expunged."

"Did you sell drugs?" Royce asked abruptly.

"No."

"Did you do drugs?"

"Yes. I smoked reefer and occasionally sniffed cocaine."

"Did you go to any drug rehab programs?"

"No. I never developed a habit."

"What about crack?"

"I never tried crack."

"I need you to be truthful, Regina," Royce said with a raised eyebrow.

"Hey, Royce. Gina's not on a witness stand. And there's no reason to assume she's lying," Charles cautioned.

"She'd better get used to it. She's going to have to face a lot tougher questioners than me," Royce snapped.

"It's okay. I'm fine," Regina cut in before Charles could say anything else. "Like I said, I never used crack."

"Heroin?"

"No. Only reefer and cocaine."

"Okay. There are a lot of people who would consider that socially acceptable. Were you arrested for prostitution?"

"*No!*" Charles yelled, his face twisted in rage.

"No, I wasn't," Regina said quietly, placing her hand on her husband's shoulder to calm him down.

"Good. How long did you prostitute?"

"I didn't, really. I kept company with men who had a lot of money, and I occasionally accepted money from them. I guess you could call them sugar daddies."

"Were these men drug dealers, Regina?" Reverend Whitfield asked gently.

"Yes, they were," Regina said, resisting the temptation to lower her eyes.

"Just great! Anything else we should know?" Royce asked as he poured himself a shot of brandy, not bothering to offer any to his guests.

"She was shot in the shoulder, Royce," Charles angrily answered for her.

"I see. She obviously lived," Royce said, in a sarcastic tone. "Anything else?"

"I think we've covered everything," Regina said impetuously. "Would you like me to sign a statement?"

Royce glared at her, his lip curled up in contempt.

"I hope you realize that you've probably managed to ruin any chance of your husband being elected," he sneered.

Regina could feel her face redden, but before she could say anything, Charles was at her side, his arm around her shoulders.

"Quit it, Royce. She hasn't done anything. I knew about her past when I married her. If it means I don't get elected, well, then, so be it," he told his godfather.

"So be it? So be it?" Royce sputtered in disbelief. "Just like that? Have these past four months been a joke to you? What the hell is wrong with you, boy?"

"Nothing's wrong with me. My marriage just happens to be more important to me than an office in Washington. Okay?" Charles shouted, releasing Regina and advancing toward Royce. "It's about priorities, and I place my wife ahead of any political career, and if you don't like it, tough shit!"

Reverend Whitfield jumped in between Charles and Royce, holding his hands up in a conciliatory manner. "Look, we all need to calm down—" he started.

"Calm down?" Royce shouted, trying to push him out of the way. "You'd better talk some sense into this boy! This may be a game to you, but it's my life's work we're talking about."

"This is my life we're talking about!" Charles shouted in return. "And you, and Washington, and the press can all go to hell for all I care."

"Go on and crawl out of here!" Royce shouted as they walked to the door. "Go on and crawl into the same gutter that wife of yours—"

"Shut up, Royce!" Reverend Whitfield suddenly roared, whirling back toward his old friend with clenched fists. "You say one more word and by God I will shove your teeth down your nasty little throat. This whole thing has gotten out of hand. We came here to discuss damage control and instead you start attacking Regina."

He turned back toward the door, signaling Regina, Charles, and Robert to follow. "Call me when you're ready to talk sense. My son and my daughter-in-law will be staying at my house tonight. Good night."

Reverend Whitfield climbed into the front seat of the car with Robert, leaving the backseat to Charles and Regina. The car was silent except for the radio.

"Now what?" Robert asked as he pulled into Reverend Whitfield's driveway.

"Now nothing," Charles said sullenly as he reached for the lever to open the car door. "It's over."

"Maybe, maybe not. Let's all keep an open mind," Reverend Whitfield said, not moving from his seat. "Regina, you said you're friendly with that reporter, Denise Cornish?"

"Yes. I told her if we were going to make any comments we'd tell her first," Regina answered.

"Can you call her and tell her to be here at the house tomorrow morning?"

"Sure, I can," Regina said slowly. "But do you mind telling me what we're going to say?"

Reverend Whitfield turned around in the car seat and looked at Regina and Charles. "I don't know what we're going to say, but I know whatever it is we're going to have to say it fast. We can't give the press time to speculate on this whole mess.

"Get ready to drink a gallon of coffee tonight, kids," he said as he stepped out of the car. "We're going to be up all night preparing our statement. Robert, you'd better call your wife and tell her you won't be coming home tonight."

A crying Mrs. Whitfield rushed to Charles and hugged him as they walked through the door. "Are you okay?" she asked him. He assured her that he was, and she fixed a stony glare on Regina. "And how are you, my dear?"

Regina tilted her head as high as she could, and matched the taller woman stare for stare. "I'm fine, Mother Whitfield."

"So glad to hear it," Mrs. Whitfield said, crossing her arms.

"Mom—" Charles started.

"I'm sure you know that this has put a black mark on the Whitfield name. Now, that might not mean much to you, and I'm not even saying I'm blaming you for all of this, but I just want you to know that you've caused a lot of trouble," she said evenly.

"*Sylvia* . . ." Reverend Whitfield said in a warning voice.

"I have nothing else to say. I just wanted to let little Miss Thing here know how I feel," Mrs. Whitfield said triumphantly.

"Well, Mother Whitfield, I thank you for your honesty, and your support," Regina said trying to control the tremble in her voice, but her eyes lowered into slits as she began her counterattack. "And I just want to let *you* know—"

"You kids go on to the library. Sylvia, let me talk to you for a moment privately," Reverend Whitfield said, taking his wife's arm and propelling her toward the kitchen. A half hour later, they emerged, and Mrs. Whitfield went upstairs to her bedroom, slamming the door behind her.

Six hours later the plan had been hashed out. The family was to go on the air with Regina as she told the straight story about her past. The idea was to get everything out in the open and move on, hoping the voters would admire her courage and resilience rather than dwell on her past errors. It made sense. Regina just hated the idea of asking for forgiveness for things that she felt weren't necessary to apologize for. And she had a nagging feeling that everything wasn't going to go as smoothly as everyone hoped.

"Okay, let's set it up," she said with a sigh. "But how about having the interview at the church?"

"Great idea," Robert said as he jumped for the telephone to call Denise. "That'll play even better with the public. Church, religion, and all that jazz will make people feel even more forgiving."

Regina grimaced. *This is really going to be fun,* she thought.

THE INTERVIEW WAS GOING WELL. Denise, grateful for the scoop, kept her most compassionate face on as Regina sat in a chair, flanked by Charles and Mrs. Whitfield. Reverend Whitfield and Royce stood behind her as she spoke into the camera.

"I was a young orphan with no adult supervision. I'm not proud of what I did, but at the time I felt I had no choice. I was arrested for shoplifting, it's true, but I served my probation, and got into no more problems with the law. And it's true that at one time I kept company with a very dangerous crowd, but I was never a drug addict, and I never resorted to prostitution to make a living," Regina said stoically.

Charles put his arm around her and kissed her on cue.

"I want to say that I'm very proud to have Regina as my wife, and yes, I knew about her background before we married," he told Denise, who nodded her head in sympathy. "I hope the people of Philadelphia will not concentrate on Regina's past mistakes, but look at who she's become and what she's achieved despite her early misfortunes."

Regina smiled up at her husband and clasped his hand in rehearsed gratitude.

"And I just want to say that I'm proud of Regina, and even prouder of my son," Mrs. Whitfield said unexpectedly. "As he said, he knew about Regina's past, but instead of rejecting her, he encouraged her to turn her life around. He's a good man, and a good Christian, and I think the people of Philadelphia should be proud to have a man of such caliber serve as their congressman."

Regina's smile froze on her face, and she could feel Charles hands squeeze her shoulders, signaling her to be quiet. Mrs. Whitfield left as soon as the cameras shut off, ignoring Regina, but kissing Charles on the cheek before she walked out of the church.

"How dare she!" Regina thundered as soon as Denise and the camera crew left. "Are you going to let her get away with that little stunt?"

"Regina, calm down. I'm just as surprised as you," Charles said soothingly. "You know how Mother is."

"I know she hates me. That's nothing new," Regina hissed. "But she had no right to tell everyone that *you* turned my life around."

"I know, and I agree, but what's done is done. It's not a big deal," Charles said, trying to pull Regina close to him.

She slapped his arm away.

"It's not a big deal? Do you actually realize what she's done? She just got on the air and told thousands of people that if it weren't for you I'd be in the gutter," Regina shouted.

"She didn't say that," Charles said defensively.

"It's what she implied," Regina said. "She said it was because of your encouragement that I turned my life around. Getting out of the streets and into school was the hardest thing I've done in my life. I built my career step by step, and now I'm a success.

"I did it all by myself, Charles. Not with your help, or anyone else's. It's my crowning achievement. *My* achievement. And now *you* get the credit."

"You're overreacting, Regina. Cut it out," Charles snapped.

"Overreacting? Don't you understand how I feel?" Regina cried. Charles looked at Regina stonily, then walked to the door.

"I understand. I understand that my political career is on the line, and there are people, including my mother, who are fighting to get this campaign back on track," he said. "You know and I know what you've achieved, and how you've achieved it. And I'm sorry that's not enough. I'm sorry that you're afraid that someone might steal your glory. I didn't know what my mother was going to say, but I do understand why she said it. I'm sorry that you don't.

"I'll be in the car," he said as he walked out the door. "Come on out when you're ready."

As Regina looked at the closed door, her first impulse was to run out after him to finish the argument. To make him understand. She started for the door, but fell onto a couch in a corner of the room. She tried at first to stifle her wails with a cushion, but gave up as she gasped for air between her sobs. What did it matter now if someone heard her cry?

11

REGINA HAD THOUGHT HER NUPTIALS WERE BEAUTIFUL, but as she watched Tamika and David kneeling on a straw mat in front of a Yoruba priest exchanging marriage vows, she was swept up in the splendor of the African wedding ceremony.

Tamika was simply beautiful in her cream-colored satin traditional wedding garb, a *buba,* a loose-fitting blouse with long, flowing sleeves tucked into her *lappa*—four yards of matching material wrapped and tucked around her waist. On her head she wore an extravagant *gele,* reminiscent of Erykah Badu, with a short veil that came to the tip of her pert nose.

David wore a long-flowing cream-colored *igbada,* with heavy gold embroidery. Sissy and Darren, also dressed in African attire, stood on each side of the kneeling couple. The bridesmaids, Yvonne, Regina, and Puddin', wore gold satin *bubas* and *lappas*. The groomsmen, Robert and Charles, were in tuxedos, although they wore kente-cloth vests and ties.

Now, that's a perfect couple, Regina thought as David and Tamika grinned at each other as they exchanged vows. David was good to Tamika, and good for her. They had bought a fixer-up brownstone in Harlem, and for the first time Darren and Sissy had their own rooms. The two kids adored "Daddy David," and he adored them. His job at the Manhattan public defender's office was grueling, but he still found time to help them with their homework and applaud them at school plays. He set up college savings accounts for them, and went over the statements with them each month. He wanted them to know, without any doubts, that college was a definite part of their future. With David's coaching, Tamika finally took the G.E.D. test and passed, and enrolled in classes at City College in Harlem. She was thinking about becoming a doctor. *Imagine. Ditzy Tamika a doctor,* Regina thought. *But stranger things have happened. Look at me. The wife of a congressman. Or at least I will be after November.* Charles had won the Democratic primary against Richard Davis by a whisper, but he was expected to win the November election over his Republican foe in a landslide. His mother already referred to him as "My son, Congressman Whitfield."

After the priest asked for Olodumare—God—to bless the union, and for the ancestral spirits to guide their paths, he pronounced them husband and wife, and three drummers started playing a slow rhythmic melody as the couple stood up and embraced.

Amazingly, Regina heard a low baby's cry despite the drumming, and turned her neck to peer in the corner of the room where Mama Tee held two-week-old Camille. She smiled as Mama Tee cooed and rocked the infant quiet. Regina glanced at Charles, not surprised that he too had turned at the muffled sound of the baby's cry. His parental instinct was as strong as any mother's.

Camille was born on September 14, the same day as Regina's mother. Her middle name was Renee, partly because it meant "reborn," in honor of Regina's mother, and partly in tribute to her niece, whom she considered her first child. Yvonne, Tamika, and Puddin' were co-godmothers, and Robert and David were the co-godfathers.

"Yeah, I'd snatch Camille from Mama Tee if I were you," Yvonne said, walking up behind Regina. "You know she thinks that's her baby."

"She'd change her mind if she had to wake up every four hours to feed her," Regina joked back. "I haven't had a good night's sleep since she was born."

Tensions between Regina and Yvonne had eased since Camille's birth. Yvonne took her role as godmother seriously, and she showered the baby with presents. One day she appeared at the house lugging an eight-foot orange elephant with a large purple satin bow, and a trunk longer than Regina's arm. Charles pronounced it the ugliest thing he had ever seen, but placed it in the pink and white nursery along with the dozens of other toys and gifts that Camille was too young to enjoy.

"You just leave dis baby be. We doing jess fine," Mama Tee said, jiggling Camille on her lap while patting her on the back. "You go do what you s'posed to be doing, Regina."

"Okay, Mama Tee. I was just checking."

"You don't need to do no checking on dis sweet ting. She jess fine."

"Watch her, Regina. She's going to kidnap that child." Yvonne laughed.

"I should do jess tat. You taking my baby away from me. Moving to Philadelphia," Mama Tee snapped at her daughter. "You know tat man ain't gonna buy the cow you give him tat milk free."

"Mama—" Yvonne started.

"No Mama, nuttin'!" Mama said, standing up and putting Camille on her shoulder. "I raise you better dan dat, child."

Regina reached for Camille, but Mama Tee ignored her outstretched arms and walked away, her large hips swinging.

Regina looked at Yvonne, but her friend maintained an impassive expression. Regina knew her well enough, though, to know her mother's cutting words hurt. But if Yvonne wanted to act as if she were okay, Regina was going to play along. She wondered, though, what Mama Tee would say if she knew her precious daughter was moving to Philadelphia to be near a married man.

"Moving right along, Regina, what's this about an offer from the *New Yorker*?" Yvonne asked as they walked toward the large punch bowl on a table near the doorway.

"Oh, did Tamika tell you? I met with the managing editor last week. I thought they wanted to talk about a freelance piece, but they offered me a staff position. Imagine that," Regina said, trying to hide the pride in her voice.

"You go, girl. I knew you had it in you." Yvonne beamed. "I guess you're not going to take it?"

"Not a chance," Regina said firmly. "I like having my independence. And even if I wanted to get a full-time job, which I don't, I couldn't move back to New York now."

"I guess you can't, Mrs. Congressman." Yvonne grinned, raising her punch glass in mock salute. "Are you going to move to D.C. with Charles?"

"Naw. We're going to keep our house in Chestnut Hill. Charles is going to commute when Congress is in session, but he'll be spending the rest of the year in Philadelphia with us," Regina answered as she sipped her punch. She glanced around the room in search of her husband, and saw him slapping a dazed-looking David on the back. Tamika was in the corner giggling with Puddin' who, by the look on her face, was probably entertaining the new bride with one of her many dirty stories.

"Regina, I need a favor," Yvonne started slowly.

Regina unconsciously raised her right eyebrow, although she tried to keep a blank look on her face. She knew what was coming, or at least she thought she knew. Yvonne had been acting too sweet as of late.

"I still haven't had any luck landing a job in Philly. I've got my résumé out to at least a dozen companies, and I know I'll land something sometime soon, but I was planning on moving down there in two weeks. I've already signed a lease and everything," Yvonne said in a low voice, her eyes darting about as if to ensure no one was listening.

"I know this is a big favor, but do you think Charles could find a spot for me in his Philadelphia office? He does have to keep an office open in Philadelphia, right? Constituent services or something?" she asked.

"Actually, he's talking about opening two offices in Philadelphia. You know, I don't have a problem with you working in one of them, but it's not up to me."

"Yeah. But I know that he wouldn't hire me without an okay from you. It wouldn't be like I was sitting getting paid for doing nothing. I mean, I have four years secretarial experience. I type 110 words a minute. I'm computer literate, and I take shorthand," Yvonne said hurriedly.

"Hey, I don't need a résumé." Regina laughed, holding her hand up to stop her friend. "I'm not the one doing the hiring."

"I know, I know. Just put in a good word for me, okay? I really need a job." Yvonne smiled.

"Hey, Gina. Yvonne. Can you guys come over here a minute? I wanna get a picture of the wedding party," Renee yelled from across the room.

"The photographer's drunk," Renee pointed to a middle-aged man slumped over in a chair in the corner of the room.

"Renee," Regina said reprovingly.

"Okay. In-ee-bree-ated. That's the word, right? Anyway, it's a good thing I brought my camera, huh?"

As she passed nice old Mr. Watson, Regina could smell the

pungent aroma of the palm wine that Reverend Whitfield had imported from Nigeria as a wedding present for Tamika and David. Renee was right. He was dead drunk.

Tamika hugged Regina around the neck excitedly, kissing her on the cheek. "Well, we're just two old married women, now, huh Regina?"

"Two down, two to go," Regina said putting her arm around Puddin's waist.

"In your dreams. I'm gonna still be out partying while you guys are out in the porch in your rocking chairs knitting sweaters," Puddin' said as she got in place for the picture. "Hey, Yvonne. I told Tamika to just lob the bouquet to you since you're such a lousy catch."

"Since when have I been known as a lousy catch?"

"You still ain't caught Robert, have you, girl?" Puddin' said, flashing her wicked grin.

"To hell with you," Regina heard Yvonne say under her breath.

"Say cheese, everyone," Renee said as she snapped the picture.

"YOUR HUSBAND'S NOT HERE. Would you like to leave a message?" Angela snapped, as Regina entered the campaign office.

"And a big hello to you, too, Angela," Regina said coolly. "Any idea where he is? I'm supposed to meet him here for lunch."

"No," Angela said as she started flipping through the pages of *Bridal Magazine*.

Regina struggled to keep her cool. Since the Krystal affair, Angela hadn't bothered to hide her contempt. Regina suspected that it irked Angela to no end that someone with Regina's background could wind up married to Charles. After all, Angela, who had had proper breeding, and had gone to the best schools that money could buy, was still flipping through bridal magazines and waiting for Mr. Right.

"Hey, Gina. I thought I heard you out here," Charles said as he walked out of his private office.

Regina shot Angela a dirty look.

"Well, he told me not to let anyone know he was in the office," Angela snapped.

"That didn't include Regina, Angela," Charles said reprovingly. "I'm always in for my wife."

"I'm sorry, but you hadn't made that clear," Angela grumbled as she started flipping through the magazine again.

"I'm making it clear now!" Charles snapped.

Regina watched in smoldering silence, ready to jump in if Angela said another word, but the woman said nothing more.

"I really ought to just fire her," Charles grumbled later as he and Regina lunched over spinach lasagna at a nearby hotel restaurant.

"Yeah right," Regina replied. "I'll hold my breath and wait on that to happen."

"What do you mean?"

"I mean that I know you, and I know you eat it up when she walks around the office treating you like the second coming of Jesus," Regina said as she reached over and dabbed at a bit of tomato sauce at the corner of Charles's mouth.

"That's not true!"

"Yes, it is and you know it." Regina giggled and started mimicking Angela's voice. "Is your coffee okay, Charles? Would you like me to run out and get you some tea, Charles? Do you like the new curtains I made for the office, Charles?"

"Oh come on, Regina." Charles started laughing.

"Yeah, and I see how you eat it up." Regina grinned, playfully poking him on the forehead.

"I don't know what you're talking about," Charles said, kissing Regina's hand before she pulled it away. "But just give the word and she's gone."

"Nope. Your personnel matters are on you. And I do have to give it to her, she's certainly efficient. If I ever get to the point where I need a secretary I might hire her myself. She's the only one I know who can even give Yvonne a run for her money. Between the two of them you have the best managed office in Philadelphia."

"I guess that's why she and Yvonne get along so well."

"Do they?"

"Yep. They usually eat lunch together, and I think they take a gym class together or something."

Regina raised an eyebrow, but said nothing more. She had seen little of her best friend since she started working in Charles's office three weeks before. Yvonne made excuses every time she called to ask her out to lunch, saying she was busy straightening out the filing system, or running errands. Yvonne was still friendly when Regina ran into her at the office, but they did no outside socializing. She figured it was because Yvonne spent all her free time with Robert, and felt uncomfortable talking about him to Regina. Still it hurt that Yvonne found time to spend with prissy Angela, but not her.

"Hey, are we still on for tonight?"

"What's happening tonight?" Charles asked as he lifted another fork of lasagna to his mouth.

"You forgot? You're supposed to take me out for a night on the town. We've hardly gone out since Camille was born." Regina pouted. "You promised."

"I didn't forget. I plan to get you drunk and ravish that luscious body of yours." Charles leered.

"You've been so busy I didn't think you even noticed my luscious, nubile body." Regina continued to pout.

"There's only two weeks left before Election Day. I can't help but be busy. And I said luscious, not nubile."

"You'd better say nubile if you want to get some of this good stuff tonight, honey," Regina teased, lightly placing her hand on her breast after glancing around to make sure no one watching.

"If I say nubile now, will I have to wait until tonight to do some ravishing?"

"What do you mean?"

Charles grinned and reached into his pants pocket, then threw a hotel key on the table.

"Room 412. Didn't you wonder why I wanted to have lunch at a hotel?" he said bringing Regina's hand to his mouth, flicking his tongue over her fingers while hungrily eyeing her breasts.

"Luscious, luscious, luscious. Nubile, nubile, nubile," he murmured. "Now, let's hurry up and finish lunch. I'm ready for dessert."

"Waiter!" Regina shouted, waving her free hand in the air. "Check, please!"

The hotel room had a lavish king-size bed, with a champagne colored satin bedspread, but the couple didn't wait to test it. As soon as the door closed, Charles pushed Regina against the wall and began kissing her neck and shoulders. Regina moaned, and reached down and began to massage the pressing bulge in Charles's pants.

"Damn, you feel so good," Charles gasped as he unbuttoned Regina's silk blouse and unsnapped her red lace brassiere, freeing her full breasts. "Oh, God. Mmm . . . your nipples are hard already," he said as he began to suck them.

Regina started kissing Charles around the neck and shoulders, unbuttoning his shirt with one hand while continuing to rub his genitals with the other. He moaned loudly as she simultaneously stuck her tongue in his ear and unzipped his pants.

"Oh, yeah, Daddy, this is what I want," Regina whispered in

his ear as she began stroking the throbbing muscle in her hand. "You gonna give it to me, Daddy?"

"Yeah, I'm going to give it to you," Charles moaned back as he continued sucking and kissing her nipples. "I'm going to give it to you good."

"Daddy, I want it now. Give it to me now," Regina hissed.

She suddenly turned around and faced the wall, and arched her back, then pulled up her short skirt revealing red lace panties, and a black garter belt that held up her stockings. She reached behind her and started rubbing Charles's penis against her panties.

"Oh yes, Daddy . . . this is just what I want. Oh, God, I want it," she moaned.

"And I'm going to give it to you, baby. Oh fuck yeah, I'm going to give it to you," Charles said. He leaned over Regina and began biting the back of her neck as he pulled roughly at the panties, tearing them off of her.

"That's right, Daddy. Come on and take this pussy."

Charles backed away a little, and pulled down his pants, then he reached his arm around Regina and pulled her hips farther toward him so that her arms slid slightly down the wall.

"Look how wet you are," he said as he began fingering her opening. He slid one finger in, and then another as Regina threw her head back moaning and swaying in ecstasy. "Yeah, I know you want this dick, don't you, baby?"

"Oh, God, you know I do, Daddy. Oh please, give it to me."

Because he was so tall Charles had to bend his knees to position himself. He thrust himself into her so powerfully that Regina was almost lifted off her feet.

"Oh yes!" Regina screamed. "Oh, fuck, Daddy, I'm coming, right now."

Regina began twisting and writhing so wildly Charles had a

hard time staying inside of her. Finally, he put his arms under her thighs and lifted her up, while still inside her, and began pumping madly as Regina's arms flailed against the wall, searching for support.

"Oh yeah, Daddy . . . fuck me," Regina screamed, her head bobbing wildly.

"Damn, Regina . . . you're going to make me come too soon. Damn, it's so fucking hot inside you, and you're so damn tight," Charles panted. "Goddamn, girl, you've got some good pussy."

"Then fuck it, Daddy. Fuck this good pussy."

Charles abruptly pulled out of Regina, but pulled her body tightly against his.

"Hold on . . . stay still for a minute. I don't want to come yet," he said through pained gasps.

"Aw, hell no. I've waited too long to be holding still," Regina said, twisting around to face him. "I want you to come. And I want you to come again. And then I want you to come again."

She pushed him down to the floor and straddled him, her skirt still pulled up around her waist, her blouse open and breasts bared.

"Oh goddamn, Regina," Charles moaned as she lowered herself onto him. "How do you do that?"

"Do what?" she said as she began to move up and down on him.

"Do that," he said as Regina contracted her muscles around him, causing him to moan in ecstasy. "It's like you have a fucking squeeze box between your legs."

"Yeah, and it's your fucking squeeze box, Daddy," Regina said. "Come on and play it."

"Oh, fuck. You're making me come, girl," Charles said as Regina quickened her pace.

"I want you to come, Daddy. I want you to come for me."

"Yeah, and I want you to come, too, baby," Charles said, as he reached up and grabbed Regina's shoulders, pinning her pelvis to his as he thrust up with all of his might.

"Oh God, Daddy, I love you," Regina screamed. "Oh fuck, I love you."

Their bodies wildly throbbed and twitched together as they came. Finally, Charles's hands slid down from Regina's shoulders, and she collapsed onto his chest.

"God, that was good," Charles finally said after a few minutes of silence.

"Damn good." Regina laughed. She picked her head up, and began kissing him on his face while smiling.

"What are you smiling about, baby?" Charles asked. "What's on your mind?"

Regina grinned as she circled his chest, his stomach, and his lower body with her fingers. "What's on my mind? Why seconds, of course."

12

"HEY, GINA, YOUR BABY THREW UP AGAIN!"

Regina looked up from the computer screen in her home office, and pressed the intercom button on the baby monitor.

"Okay, Puddin', I'll be upstairs in a minute." Regina pushed her chair away from the computer desk, as the baby monitor came alive again.

"You don't have to come up, Aunt Gina. I'll take care of it. I'm gonna change her clothes, okay?"

Regina shook her head and smiled. Puddin' and Renee had caught a ride with Tamika and David, and were spending the weekend, which was now almost over, with Regina and Charles in Philadelphia. Puddin' had spent the nights partying and the days sleeping. Not much different from what she did at home in New York.

Renee was another story. She refused to leave the house unless it was to take her baby cousin out for her walk in the stroller. She found twenty reasons a day to change Camille's clothes, and as many excuses to use the baby brush to rearrange her curly hair. She doted on her little cousin and treated her like a doll, much as Regina had treated her when she was a baby.

"Does she really need her clothes changed, Ray-Ray?" Regina asked into the intercom. "You just changed her an hour ago."

"She got throw-up on them, Aunt Gina."

"Okay. Just put her in the yellow playsuit, then. And tell Aunt Puddin' she'd better get dressed. Tamika's going to be picking you guys up in about an hour."

"Don't sweat it, I'm up and dressed," Puddin' drawled into the intercom.

Regina turned her attention back to the 4,000-word story she was writing for *Teen People* about a fifteen-year-old Philadelphia boy who started his own software company. She was being paid $1,500 for the article—not bad for two days' work. The money was good, but she hated to see what the story would look like when it actually appeared in the magazine. *People* magazine, which owned *Teen People,* requested overly long stories from freelance writers, which the staff editors would then shape into *People*-style articles. The twenty-page manuscript she was submitting would be reduced to a page and a half of text with three pages of large glossy photographs.

Still, *People* magazine was the main contributor to Regina's personal bank account. Much to Charles's ire, she had insisted on keeping an account in her name, although she placed three-quarters of her earnings in their joint account. Charles tried to coax her into giving up writing for a while, and concentrating her efforts on being a mother. They could live off his inheritance until he started drawing his congressional salary, he said. She insisted she could be both mother and writer, and excel at both, especially since she wrote from home. There was no way she was going to give up her independence. He didn't push the issue. She knew he realized she was not going to go for his suggestion from the beginning. She was surprised he had even broached the subject. But boyfriend Charles, who was so proud of his successful girlfriend, had become husband Charles, who wanted a stay-at-home trophy wife, which was strange, since his own mother had maintained a career while raising her two children.

Regina grimaced as she thought about her mother-in-law. Their relationship, which was always rocky at best, had become so strained they avoided each other's company. Because of this, Mother Whitfield only saw the baby when she and Charles visited for Sunday brunch. They would walk in and she would rush over and take Camille from Regina and coo at her for a few minutes, then place her in Charles's arms. Daddy Whitfield, on the other hand, adored his younger granddaughter. He visited constantly, dropping off gifts, and called often to see how she was doing.

The door chime interrupted Regina's thoughts. She glanced at the clock—6:00 P.M. It was probably Tamika and David coming to pick up Puddin' and Renee for the two-hour trip back to New York.

"Aunt Gina! Aunt Tamika's here!" Renee shouted. So much for the intercom.

"Don't come up. Don't come up. I wanna see your office anyway," Tamika said as she clamored down the stairs.

"Gee, this is great. You're really hooked up," Tamika said as she looked around the wood-paneled basement. "Carpet and everything. And look at all this computer stuff!"

"I have the world at my fingertips," Regina said as she pushed the chair back from the computer and stood up and hugged her friend. "How was your visit?"

"Great. But, boy, I'm ready to go home. I have to study for midterm exams."

"Where's David?"

"He's still at his mom's house. I'm driving," Tamika said, beaming and awaiting Regina's approval.

"Lord. I hope you guys have a lot of insurance." Regina laughed. "Come on, let's go upstairs. It's time for me to knock off anyway."

Regina looked at Tamika as they walked up the stairs. She still bounced like a little girl when she walked, and she still talked a mile a minute, but she was different from the Tamika she thought she knew while growing up. She was more self-assured, and more settled. She could still be an airhead at times, but she was downright smart, actually maintaining an A-minus average in school. If there was one word to describe this new Tamika, it was content.

"Aunt Gina, do I really have to leave now? Couldn't I just take the train tomorrow? I bet I can catch an early train and still make it to school on time," Renee said as they walked into the living room.

"Your mother would have a fit if I let you go up on the train by yourself, Ray-Ray," Regina answered. "I thought I told you to put Camille in a play suit."

"I know, but she looks so good in this, don't you think?" Renee said as she fingered Camille's pink dress fringed with dainty white lace.

"Renee, are you packed up? I told David we'd be back in just a few minutes," Tamika said.

"Yeah, I'm packed," Renee said sticking her lip out.

"Good. Go get your stuff. I want to get home before it gets too late."

Renee reluctantly placed the baby in Regina's arms and started up the stairs, stopping to look back at her aunt.

"Don't even try it," Regina said before Renee could say anything. "You stayed with us all summer, and you're coming back for Christmas break. Go get your stuff and get the heck out of my house."

"You don't love me!" Renee pouted.

"You got that right. Now go get your stuff," Regina said with a laugh. She sat down in an overstuffed armchair, nestling Camille in her arms.

"Is Charles still at the office?" Tamika asked after Renee left. "He's spending a lot of time there these days, isn't he?"

"Yeah," Regina said with a sigh. "I hardly get to see him."

"Why don't you spend more time at the office, then?" Tamika asked carefully as she sat down on the white leather sofa.

"I'm just in the way," Regina said without looking up as she cradled the sleeping Camille. "Besides, the election is going to be over in a week. We'll have more time together then."

"Yeah, that's true," Tamika said in a voice that caught Regina's attention. Was that concern she heard in Tamika's tone?

"Something up?" she asked her friend, who was doing her best to avoid looking at her.

"No. Nothing. Hey, did I mention that David and I stopped by Charles's office last night?"

They were interrupted by the sound of a heavy suitcase banging down the stairway, then sliding into the wall with a thump.

"It's too heavy for me to carry," Puddin' said after she walked down the stairs, stepped over the suitcase and entered the living room. She plopped down on the love seat across from Regina. "David's going to have to carry it to the car."

"I'm going to have help you then, 'cause David's not here," Tamika said.

"Where's he at? He's not coming back to the city with us?"

"We're going to pick him up from his mom's on the way out," Tamika answered.

"Cool," Puddin' said. She propped her high-heeled feet up on the ivory coffee table in front of the couch.

"Puddin', will you get your feet off the furniture," Regina snapped. "Damn, you just can't take some people anywhere."

"You see how she treats her guests? That's why I'm not going to come visit your stink ass anymore," Puddin' said as she swung her feet around and onto the love seat.

"It's not like I really got to see your butt anyway. You've been out every night since you've been here. And get your feet off the love seat. Damn!"

Tamika giggled as Puddin' finally placed her feet on the floor and sucked her teeth.

"Anyway, Tamika. What were you saying before we were so rudely interrupted," Regina said, turning back to Tamika.

"I was just saying that we stopped by Charles's office last night."

"What made you guys do that?" Regina asked, looking sideways at Puddin' to make sure she didn't try to put her feet up again.

"We weren't planning to. We had gone to that club where you had your wedding reception—Zanzibar Blue, right?—and on our way back to David's mother's house we passed the office and noticed the lights were on, so we stopped."

"And?"

"And nothing. Charles was busy working on a speech or something and his secretary—her name's Angela, right? —was doing some filing. That's all," Tamika said, avoiding Regina's eyes.

"What time was this?" Regina asked, her attention suddenly shifting back to Tamika.

"About two-thirty in the morning."

"Come again?" Puddin' sat straight up. "Were they the only ones in the office? What the fuck is this, Gina? Don't tell me I'm going to have to stay in Philadelphia and kick your man's ass."

Regina stood up and walked over to the large white bassinet in the corner of the room, and placed Camille on the down mattress, covering her with a lightweight blanket.

"Well, he told me he was going to be working late, so I'm not at all surprised you guys found him there," she said as she straightened up.

"Oh, cool. I figured you knew," Tamika said brightly.

"I didn't know Angela was there, though." Regina leaned against the fireplace, biting her bottom lip. Tamika looked down at her hands and said nothing.

"So?" Puddin' leaned forward on the couch, a hand on her hip, and looked at Tamika expectantly.

"So, what?"

"So, you're telling me all this for a reason, Tamika. Don't start acting coy now," Regina said sharply.

"I'm not trying to be coy," Tamika said in a soft wail. "I didn't even want to bring this up. I was just going to give you a call tomorrow, but after David and I talked, he thought I should tell you, quick."

"You fucking needed David to fucking tell you to let your girl know her fucking man is banging some fucking bitch in his fucking office at two-thirty in the fucking morning?" Puddin' shouted. "What the fuck is wrong with you?"

"Give me a break, Puddin'. I'm telling her, aren't I?" Tamika snapped.

Regina looked back and forth at the two women, as if wondering what they were arguing about.

"Oh, man. I don't believe this shit," she said finally, rubbing her hand over her face. "I really can't fucking believe this."

"Oh, man, Gina. I'm not saying anything was going on, but it took them forever to unlock the door, and that girl's clothes looked a little messed up, like she just hurried and put them on."

Regina closed her eyes and shook her head. "That no-good motherfucker."

"Tamika, you're sure about this shit?" Puddin' asked. She walked over and stood by Regina.

"Yeah. And the girl looked at us like she was mad at us or

something. No guilt or anything. Now, Charles looked guilty, but Angela—that's her name, right?—she just looked mad."

"Yeah, Angela. Ole prissy slutty-ass Angela," Regina muttered, her eyes still closed.

"I could tell that bitch was a ho the first time I met her," Puddin' said. "You can just look at her and tell."

"Dang, Gina. I'm sorry." Tamika's eyes filled with tears. "But you know, like I said. It's not like we actually caught them doing anything."

"Did it smell?" Regina asked, suddenly opening her eyes.

"Huh?"

"Did it smell like pussy in the office?"

Tamika blinked her eyes quickly as if surprised, then laughed.

"Dang, Gina. Yeah, I guess it did."

"Okay, I can deal with this. I can deal with this." Regina took a deep breath and raised her hands in front of herself, chest high and palms outward. "This is not the end of the world, I can deal with this."

Tamika and Puddin' looked at each other worriedly, then back at Regina as she slowly began pacing a wide circle in the living room.

"Regina—" Tamika began.

"Just give me a minute, I'm just getting myself together. I can deal with this, I really can," Regina said, looking at neither one of them. Her pace began to quicken, and the circle began to tighten, until she was almost standing in one spot, twirling around and around.

"Yo, Regina—" Puddin' moved toward her friend, reaching to grab her.

"Look. I'm okay. I'm all right. Just give me a moment, okay?" Regina said, suddenly stopping her spin. "I mean, I said I'm okay. Don't sweat me, okay?"

"Yeah, all right," Puddin' said skeptically.

Regina sniffed, raised her head and walked over to the fire-place. She picked up a white porcelain vase and slowly turned it in her hand, as if examining it for flaws, against the light of the window. Suddenly, she pulled her arm back, and hurled it at the wall.

"Oh shit," Puddin' shouted, as the baby, roused from her sleep, began to cry.

"Aunt Gina! What happened?" Renee asked, galloping down the stairs.

"Nothing. A vase fell. Do me a favor and take Camille upstairs with you, okay?" Regina said calmly as Tamika bent down and began to pick up shattered pieces of porcelain.

"How did the vase fall?"

"It just did. Please get the baby for me, sweetie."

"Where's your broom?" Tamika asked after Renee went back upstairs.

"In the kitchen, but don't worry about it, I'll pick the rest up later." Regina faced the fireplace, and rested her hands against the mantelpiece, gulping deep breaths of air.

"Okay, I just got to figure out what I'm going to do. Okay, the first thing I have to do is kill Angela," she said after a few seconds.

"So that's the plan, huh?" Puddin' asked soothingly.

"Yeah. But maybe I should kill Charles first. I don't know. What do you think?" Regina straightened up and faced Puddin'. The seriousness of her tone was almost funny.

"Well, you could just kill them at the same time," Puddin' offered.

"Yeah, good point," Regina nodded her head and chewed her lip as if contemplating.

"Puddin'," Tamika said in a loud whisper.

Puddin' hunched her shoulders and mouthed, "What am I supposed to say?"

"Regina, you're in shock, honey. Come on and sit down," Tamika said, gently putting her arm around Regina's shoulders and leading her to the couch.

"Right. I just need to sit down and figure out what I'm going to do," Regina said as she docilely sat down. "I just need a couple of moments to think."

"Where's the booze? You need a drink," Puddin' said, heading toward the small bar in the corner of the room. "Then I say we go over there and kick that bitch's ass."

"Well, beating people up isn't going to solve anything," Tamika said as she rubbed Regina's back. "I mean, you have to do something, but I don't think that's the way to go."

"Why the hell not?" Puddin' said, walking over and trying to hand the glass of brandy to Regina, who shook her head "no." Puddin' shrugged and took a long swig for herself.

"Fuck it. Let's start with Angela. Come on, Renee can watch the baby while we're gone," Puddin' said, placing the glass on the coffee table and reaching for her handbag. "Call Yvonne and tell her to meet us there. We're going to have to bring a little Harlem to this town tonight."

"Yvonne's probably at the office with Charles and Angela. You know she's Yvonne's new buddy, right?" Regina asked, not moving.

"She is?" Tamika started to look uncomfortable again.

"Yeah, she is. What's wrong, Tamika?" Regina asked suspiciously.

"Nothing. It's just that I called Yvonne this morning, because I thought she should be here when I told you," Tamika said wringing her hands.

"And what did she say?" Puddin' asked, swinging around to face Tamika.

"She said it was probably all in my head and I should mind my business."

"Oh no, hold up one goddamn minute. No, the fuck she didn't." Puddin' jerked her head back, and put her hand out in front of her as if to block out Tamika's words.

"That's what she said," Tamika wailed as she threw up her hands.

"Did you tell her you were going to let me know anyway?" Regina asked.

"No. She almost had me talked into being quiet, but then I thought about how mad she got at you for doing the same thing, and I decided I should take the chance and let you know."

"What do you mean about me doing the same thing?" Regina demanded.

"Oh shoot, Gina. I'm not trying to make you mad," Tamika wailed again.

"I'm not mad. I just want to know what you mean."

"Well, you know Puddin' and I didn't know about Robert being married, and then when David told me I told Yvonne. She said she had already found out, and that you knew the whole time and didn't tell her," Tamika said all in a rush.

"What?" Regina screeched. "And you believed that shit?"

"I don't know! I mean, why would she say something like that?" Tamika said, jumping up from the couch and backing away from Regina.

"Because she wanted you to feel sorry for her! And to turn you guys against me! I don't believe this shit!" Regina began to pace the floor, so angry at Yvonne she almost forgot her husband's infidelity.

"Hold it, hold it! You mean to tell me that Robert's married?" Puddin' said in disbelief. "That's it. I need another drink. Fuck that. I need a joint."

"Don't you light that shit up in my house," Regina snapped as Puddin' starting rifling through her pocketbook.

"Why would she want to turn us against you?" Tamika asked.

"Because she's mad at me for getting on her case about still seeing Robert after she learned he was married."

"How come no one told me?" Puddin' demanded.

"I just kind of assumed you knew. I'm used to being the last one of us to find out something," Tamika answered, shrugging her shoulders.

"Okay, for the record, I did not know that Robert was married. Yvonne told me that day we were all in the restaurant. That's why we were arguing in the bathroom. She accused me of knowing and not telling her. And I told her she was out of her fucking mind," Regina snapped. "And I don't give a shit if you guys believe me or not!"

"Calm down, Gina. You're getting mad at the wrong people. Of course we believe you. We all know how Yvonne is," Puddin' said in a surprisingly soothing tone.

"So now what?" Tamika asked after a few seconds of silence.

"Where's Charles now?" Puddin' asked Regina.

"I guess he's in the office. He usually doesn't leave there until seven or so."

"So that means Angela and Yvonne are there, too, right?"

"Probably. Why?"

"Okay, here's the game plan," Puddin' said in a serious tone. "We all go down to the office. I grab Yvonne, pull her outside, and slap some sense into her. Tamika, you kick Angela's ass, and Regina, you grab a butcher knife from the kitchen and do a Lorena Bobbit on your no-good fucking husband."

"I'm almost tempted to say that sounds like a plan, but no." Regina chuckled.

"You got a better one?" Puddin' demanded, her hands on her hips.

"No, but I'll think of something. You guys better get on the road. David's going to think there was a car accident or something."

"No, fuck that. I'm not leaving you like this," Puddin' said, flopping down on the couch and crossing her arms.

"Puddin's right—" Tamika started.

"No. You guys go ahead home. Renee's got to be in school tomorrow."

"What are you going to do?" Tamika asked.

"I don't know," Regina said. "But don't worry, I'm going to do something. I just can't see me going down like this. I am definitely going to do something."

Regina brushed her hair away from her face, and caught a glimpse of herself in the mirror over the fireplace. Her eyes were red, although she hadn't been crying, and for the first time she noticed the slight circles under them. She placed her hand on her stomach, which had been so flat when she met Charles, and now had a slight roundness that she thought made her look more womanly. She suddenly wondered if it only made her look fat. Had she let herself go after the baby? She still got whistles when she walked down the street, and appreciative looks when she walked into a room, but maybe Charles thought she was getting ugly. Maybe that's why he was sleeping with Angela. Her head was pounding.

"Okay, Aunt Gina, you promised I can come down for Thanksgiving break, right?" Renee pleaded after kissing Regina on the cheek.

"We'll see," Regina said. "Go on and wait outside. Tamika and Puddin' will be out in a minute."

She leaned on the door after Renee walked out, and looked at Tamika, who stood in the foyer with a nervous look on her face. Regina pulled herself together and walked over and gave her a hug.

"Look. I'm sorry if I acted as if I'm mad at you. I really appreciate you telling me all of this even if I don't act like it."

"I know. I don't know what I would do in your place, Gina. What *are* you going to do?"

"I don't know. I've got to think about it for a while. I'll let you know, though. I'll give both you and Puddin' a call."

"You won't have to call me. I'm not going anywhere till we get this shit straightened out," Puddin' said, crossing her legs.

"Puddin', look. Just let me work this out, okay? Now get the fuck out my house," Regina said affectionately.

Puddin' looked at Regina for a minute, then sucked her teeth and got up from the couch.

"Okay, but just remember, I've been thrown out of better places," she said as she tugged at the large suitcase still on the floor.

"Good line. Remind me to use it sometime." Regina laughed.

"All right, girl. You know you can call me anytime, okay?" Tamika said as she kissed Regina on the cheek.

"And I don't care if you tell Charles that I told you," she said defiantly. "David's so pissed at him he wants to beat him up anyway."

"He'll have to wait in line," Regina said, trying to grin. "I'll give you guys a call tomorrow, okay? And do me one favor. Don't mention all of this to Yvonne just yet. I want to be the first one to talk to her."

"You got it," Puddin' said, hugging Regina.

"Hey, Tamika. Can I ask you something?" Regina said, after Puddin' walked out.

"Sure."

"Be honest. Is she prettier than me?"

"What? Who? Oh!" Tamika said in surprise. "Oh, hell no! That girl looks like the gutter-ho that she is. Please!"

"Okay." Regina smiled. "Just checking."

Three hours later she and Charles were at the dining room table eating a late supper. He had made a big deal about getting home early enough to see her and the baby before they went to bed. Guilt, she decided. She wanted to spit at him when he walked through the door. She wanted to slap him when he leaned down and kissed her on the forehead. But she simply smiled and asked about his day, although she couldn't resist giving a slight sniff to see if she could detect perfume, or any other odors on his clothes.

She sat watching him wolf down the smothered chicken she had prepared, and waited for an opening. She wanted to catch him completely off guard. Surprise had always been her deadliest weapon.

She jumped when the telephone rang. *Shit,* she thought. *It's probably Robert or Royce.*

She reached over and picked up the receiver.

"Let me speak to Charles."

It was Angela.

"Hello. I need to speak to Charles," Angela said when Regina said nothing.

"I'm sorry, you have a wrong number," Regina said, hanging up. The nerve of that slut. Calling her house. Asking for her husband.

"What was that all about?" Charles asked, as he helped himself to some more collard greens.

"Some woman asking for someone named Romeo," Regina snapped.

Charles looked at her inquisitively but said nothing. The telephone rang again.

"Hello?"

"Don't hang up on me. I need to speak to Charles."

"I beg your pardon?" Regina said coldly.

"I said I want to speak to Charles," Angela yelled into the telephone.

"I'm sorry. Wrong number," Regina said, and slammed the telephone down.

She glared at Charles, who hurriedly pushed his plate away and got up from the table. Before he could say anything, the telephone rang again. She reached for it, but Charles was quicker.

"Hello," he said, glancing at Regina as he cradled the telephone. His face turned red as he heard the voice on the other end of the telephone.

"I'll call you later," he said quickly.

His face contorted in anger as the voice continued to speak.

"Dammit! I said I'd call you later," he shouted and slammed down the telephone so hard the table shook. Regina crossed her arms in front of her, waiting for him to turn and face her.

"Wanna talk about this?" he asked, his back still turned to her.

"You're fucking right I want to talk about this," she spat. "How long has this shit been going on?"

Charles finally turned around. He tried to match Regina's stare, but dropped his eyes and started chewing his bottom lip.

"You fucking bastard," Regina said in a low voice as she walked over to him.

"How long, Charles? How long has this been going on?" she said.

"There's really nothing going on."

"Don't lie!"

"I mean, nothing really. I'm not saying I didn't sleep with her. I did. But it only happened twice. I'm not having an affair. It's just something that happened."

"Just something that happened?" Regina shouted.

"Gina. I slipped up. I'm sorry, baby," Charles pleaded.

"How does something like this just happen, Charles?" Regina demanded. She balled up her fist and punched him in the chest.

He caught her hands and tried to push her away. She struggled as he pinned her arms to her side. Then she leaned into him and bit him on the shoulder.

"Ouch! Dammit, Gina!" he said as he released and scurried backward, banging into the table and knocking his plate onto the floor.

"How does something like this just happen, huh? You tell me

how something like this just happens," Regina screamed hysterically, stamping her foot on the floor.

"Gina, I'm sorry. Please calm down so we can talk about this."

"What's there to talk about?" Regina shouted, advancing on him again. "I'm here playing wife and mother and you're out there fucking your Ivy-League-educated, stupid-ass secretary!"

"Regina, you're going to wake up the baby," Charles said as he walked around the table to put a barrier between them.

"Don't try and play concerned daddy! Were you thinking about Camille when you were out there greasing your dick? Where was all your fucking concern then?"

"Gina, I'm coming clean about this, but we need to talk like two adults. Will you please sit down?" Charles said, circling the table away from Regina.

"So talk. I'm listening. How the hell does something like this just happen!" Regina shouted. Just then Camille began to cry. Regina quieted down, hoping that Camille would simply drift back to sleep, but the cries from the nursery continued.

"Fucking bastard," Regina spat at Charles before running upstairs to tend to the baby.

Camille was wet and hungry. Regina changed her diaper and nightgown, then ran downstairs to warm a bottle of formula. Charles sat in an overstuffed chair in the living room, and asked if the baby was all right, but she ignored him. Camille usually fell asleep after her nighttime bottle, but tonight it was almost as if she sensed her mother's agony. It was more than twenty minutes, and lullaby after lullaby, before she finally drifted back to sleep. When Regina finally descended the steps and entered the living room she was drained. She wanted to attack Charles again, but she didn't have the emotional strength. Instead, she plopped down on the love seat and stared at her husband. She wanted to hate him, but she didn't even have the strength to do that. She leaned her head back on the cushion and closed her eyes.

"So, go ahead and talk, Charles. Tell me how all this just happened," she said wearily.

He talked. He told her that Angela started flirting with him shortly after she started working in the office, but that he had ignored her. She made it a point to bring him coffee every morning, just the way he liked it. She made suggestive remarks. She told him how lucky Regina was to have married an outstanding man like him.

"I thought it was funny at first, and I guess I found her attention rather flattering, but I swear I had no intention of getting involved with her," he told Regina as he held his hands over his face. "I mean, I've known her all my life, and I've never been attracted to her. Never! The only reason I dated her in high school was to please my mother.

"But then one night I was in my office late, and I thought everyone had left, but Angela walked in. She had a bottle of wine and two glasses, and she said she thought I needed a drink to unwind. That I had been working too hard. So I had a glass, but I swear I still didn't think anything was going to happen. We started talking, and all of a sudden she gets up and starts rubbing my crotch. I pushed her hand away, and started to get up, but then she knelt down and started unzipping my pants. The next thing I knew she was giving me a blow job."

Charles looked at Regina as if to gauge her response, but she simply looked at him with disgust, her arms folded against her chest, and said nothing.

"That's all that happened. When she finished I said I had to leave. I didn't kiss her or anything. I swear. And the next day I didn't even go to the office because I didn't want to face her. When I went in the day after that she did her best to find a way to get me alone. But I made sure there was always someone in the office with us. Somehow a few nights later we wound up alone again. I know she engineered it. When I went into my office

Yvonne was the only one left in the outer office, but when I came out Yvonne was gone and Angela was there. She said she stopped by and told Yvonne she would finish up the work. She started trying to give me a massage, but I pushed her away, and she started crying. She said I made her feel like a slut, because I let her give me a blow job and then didn't even touch her. I know it's stupid, but I kind of felt guilty. I started trying to comfort her, to get her to stop crying, and I don't know, one thing led to another, and we were making love right there in the office. But that was the last time, I swear, Gina. I never went to her house, and I never took her to a hotel or anything. That's all that's ever transpired between us."

"And when did this last time occur," Regina said angrily, her strength returning.

"Last night."

"Jesus Fucking Christ!"

"I knew Tamika was going to tell you." Charles rubbed his hand over his face, then looked down toward the ground. "Regina, I swear. It's over. It was nothing to begin with, but I swear I told her right after Tamika and David left that it was completely over. I wrote her a check for two weeks' pay and told her I'd write her a good set of references but she couldn't work in the office anymore."

"Oh, boy, I'd love to see that reference letter," Regina snorted. "Damn! I can't believe I didn't see all this was going on."

"There was nothing to see. There was no affair, no relationship. I slipped up, but she never meant anything to me, baby," Charles said, getting up and walking toward Regina.

"Stay away from me, please," Regina said looking up at him, and stopping him in his tracks. "So why did she call the house tonight?"

"I don't know. The girl's crazy. She's been calling the office all day. I gave instructions to everyone that I wasn't taking her calls.

I had no idea she was going to call here. I'm going to make sure it doesn't happen again, I swear."

"And how are you going to make sure of that?"

"I don't know. I'll put a restraining order on her or something."

"So who else knows about your little hussy?"

"No one. I haven't told anyone, not even Robert. I don't think she's mentioned it to anyone either."

"Not even Yvonne?"

Charles sat back down with a sigh. "I don't know. Yvonne hasn't said anything, but I have a feeling she knows just by the way she's been looking at me. And after that first night with Angela, Yvonne came into the office and asked me if anything new was going on in my life. I'm sure she was letting me know that she knew, but I just ignored her."

That bitch, Regina thought.

"Gina, I'm sorry. I never meant to hurt you," Charles said, looking up.

"Fuck you, Charles," Regina said jumping up, her hands balled into tight fists. "You make me sick to my stomach. You have an affair with that bitch, and then you put the blame all on her. Well, I married you, not Angela. You're the one who cheated on me, not her. She may be a whore, but you're a fucking slut."

"Gina—" Charles started.

"Gina nothing. I don't have anything else to say to you," she said as she headed up the stairs. She looked back. "One more thing. You're moving out of the house tomorrow. And if you don't, I will. And if you treasure your balls you won't try and come into the bedroom tonight. I'm feeling kind of like Lorena Bobbit."

13

"ALL I WANT TO KNOW IS WHY YOU DIDN'T TELL ME."

"Tell you what?" Yvonne asked nonchalantly. She kept her eyes lowered, but she couldn't hide her smirk as she picked at her Caesar salad.

Charles hadn't moved out, and Regina hadn't forced the issue. She stopped speaking to him for a few days, and he spent a few nights on the couch, but that was the extent of it. Charles played the role of contrite husband splendidly. He sent her a bouquet of yellow roses every day, and bought her an expensive sapphire necklace and matching earrings. She hadn't forgiven him, but she did believe that the fling with Angela was just that. He had even called Angela in front of Regina and told her to never call their house again. As Regina stood next to Charles she could hear Angela crying over the telephone, and she was surprised that instead of softening, her husband's face contorted with contempt. It was just like Charles to put all the blame on Angela. Then he started shouting at her to quit the crying and get on with her life, and slammed down the telephone. No, Charles didn't want Angela, and if she still wanted him, she was nuts. Regina consoled herself with the thought that she would definitely divorce him if he had had an actual affair, but maybe . . . just maybe, a one- or two-night stand wasn't worth throwing away an otherwise good marriage.

When Regina called to ask Yvonne out to lunch she declined as usual, but when Regina popped up in the office unexpectedly, Yvonne greeted her enthusiastically, though she stayed behind her desk. Her lunch plans had fallen through, she told Regina, so she was free for lunch, after all. She prattled on incessantly about Robert as she and Regina strode across the street to a café. Things were going so well for them, she said. She gaily held out her wrist to show Regina the diamond tennis bracelet he had given her the night before. She didn't exactly avoid Regina's eyes as they walked, but she just didn't look her way.

"Did I tell you Mama's coming down this afternoon? Oh shoot, I forgot to tell you, didn't I? I've just been so busy between the campaign and Robert," Yvonne said gaily after they were served. "And she made me promise to tell you, too. You've got to drop by this evening and say hi. She's only going to be here two days. You're not busy tonight, are you? Or do you and Charles have plans?"

She knows about the affair, Regina decided as Yvonne popped a cherry tomato into her mouth. Not only did she know. She was celebrating. Regina shivered, though the heat in the restaurant was a comfortable seventy degrees. How could it have come to this? Her best friend reveling in her unhappiness. Surprisingly, Regina felt no anger as she looked at Yvonne chewing her lettuce. Just a heavy sadness.

"Yvonne, why didn't you tell me that Charles was sleeping with Angela?"

"What makes you think I knew?" Yvonne pushed her salad away, leaned back in the booth, and tilted her head. She looked at

Regina with a smirk, as if daring her to pursue her line of questioning.

"Did you?"

"What if I say yeah?"

Regina sighed and placed the linen napkin on the table. She considered just walking out of the restaurant, but that would accomplish nothing, she decided. The problem was, she didn't know what she wanted to accomplish. For Yvonne to admit her guilt? The woman obviously felt none. Regina felt a sharp pain in her eyes as tears sprang to the surface. Charles's infidelity hurt, but Yvonne's betrayal cut her to the quick. She wanted to be angry, she really did. But she couldn't even fake it. Confusion overwhelmed her.

"Man, Yvonne, I don't believe you. I mean, after all we've been through together, I don't understand how you could do this to me," she said, leaning back in the booth and closing her eyes in a wince. She shook her head and sucked her teeth, fighting back tears. "I can't believe you'd do me like this!"

"I didn't do anything to you," Yvonne said, tossing her head defiantly.

"But you did!" Regina placed her hands on the table and leaned toward Yvonne, oblivious that her scarf had dipped into the shrimp cocktail sauce. "You're supposed to be my girl. My sister! And you know someone is making it with my husband and you don't even tell me? I mean . . . I don't even get this. I really don't. We don't roll like that!"

"We don't roll any kind of way," Yvonne snapped.

"What's that supposed to mean?"

"Oh come on," Yvonne spat, her eyes narrowing. "You think you're better than everyone else. You always did."

"Oh, Yvonne come off it," Regina said. "You don't believe that shit."

"Oh, yes I do. And the worst part is you think everyone

around you is too stupid to realize it. Well, you may have Tamika and Puddin' fooled, but I'm hip to you. I'm sick of your little superior attitude, acting all saditty like you were born into the upper class," Yvonne said, bobbing her head and gyrating her shoulders as she talked. "Well, you weren't. You were born in a ghetto! Right there on 118th Street and Lenox Avenue. A fucking tenement. Just like me."

"I know my roots," Regina said incredulously.

"But you couldn't wait to leave them behind you, could you?" Yvonne snapped.

"Give me a break! I never tried to leave anything behind," Regina hissed. She leaned forward again, placing her hands on either end of the table as if to steady herself. "And I never turned my back on my friends. No matter where I was or what I was doing, I was always there if you guys needed me. I don't know what the fuck your problem is, girlie!"

"You're the one with the problem, girlie! Yeah, you'd come slumming with me and Tamika and Puddin', but I don't ever remember getting an invitation to hang out with you when you were hobnobbing with your new high-class friends at your fancy parties," Yvonne almost shouted.

"What high-class friends? I might know some so-called 'high-class' people, but I don't like most of them. Why do you think I was always hanging out in Harlem with you guys?"

"Slumming!" Yvonne retorted.

"What?"

"Oh face it, Regina. You had one world, hobnobbing with the beautiful people, and another one with the folks you grew up with, but you took pains to make sure the two worlds didn't meet," Yvonne said with a contemptuous curl of the lip.

"So now you're saying I'm ashamed of you guys?"

"Probably that, too, but mostly you're afraid we'd out you," Yvonne threw back. "You figured if people saw us they'd figure out who you really are. And we can't have that, can we Miss High-Class Writer?"

"Oh, Yvonne, please! Give it a break," Regina said wearily. "I'm not up to this nonsense. Let's just get the check. I don't have anything else to say to you." She turned around and scanned the crowded room for the waiter. He was in the corner, jotting down an order for an elderly couple. She waved her hand in the air to get his attention, but he was oblivious.

"Yeah. I forgot. I'm not class. Well, guess what? You're not in your class either. But you know that now, don't you?" Yvonne said with a snarl. "You might have finished college and you might have a nice career, and put on airs, but you're still not class. Angela might not be smart as you, and she may only be a lowly office manager, but she's class. And that's why your husband been sneaking around with her. Class goes to class."

"I've got more class in my pinkie than that bitch has in her whole body," Regina spat. "Don't mix up class with being born into a well-to-do family."

"You know what I mean. You're not *their* kind of people. And you never will be. And how does it feel to know that your husband prefers class to a reformed slut," Yvonne retorted.

Regina jerked her head back as if she had been punched in the face. She opened her mouth, but no words came out. She blinked wildly, trying to form words, trying to form thoughts. Yvonne was deliberately trying to hurt her. And she was succeeding.

"And yeah, Gina," Yvonne continued in a sarcastic tone. "You were so quick to tell me to get rid of Robert because he was married, I don't see you dumping Charles, and he cheated on you. What's up with that?"

A lock of hair fell over Regina's eye as she shook her head slowly in disbelief. "That's what this is all about, isn't it? Damn, Yvonne. You are really messed up. Yeah, I told you that you should dump the bastard, but I told you that out of love. Out of concern for your well-being. 'Cause that's how I roll. I would never do anything to hurt you. But now you turn around and you do this shit to me? To your homegirl? Not only did you know Charles was messing around with Angela, you became her friend so you could be all up in it, didn't you? So you could watch me get hurt all up close and personal. 'Cause that's how *you* roll." Regina trembled inside with hurt, but her voice was even as she spoke.

"You just couldn't stand the fact that I married Charles, could you? It's like it was some personal failure on your part. Now you tell me, what's up with *that*? Why does my being happy bother you so much? Because you want everyone to be as miserable as you? Because Robert obviously doesn't think you're anything but a stank piece of ass?"

"Go to hell, Regina," Yvonne hissed.

"Yeah, the truth hurts, doesn't it, honey!" Regina grinned wickedly. "'Cause you *know* that even if he weren't married he wouldn't marry you! To him you're nothing but trash he picked up in Harlem. You're like a piece of filthy gum stuck to his shoe that won't come loose. And you know it, and you stick around anyway. You're pathetic!"

"Go to fucking hell!" Yvonne, eyes wide, and all but frothing at the mouth, slammed her hands on the table.

"Yeah, bitch. Jump, I dare you," Regina said with a mean laugh. "You're one sick, fucking puppy. And you're a hypocritical little bitch. If it wasn't for me you wouldn't have that job so you could be near that snob-ass bastard, and you repay me by laughing at me behind my back while some little whore fucks my husband."

Regina slammed the napkin down on the table, causing Yvonne to jump back in her seat.

"Don't worry. I didn't come here to fight with you, I came to talk," Regina said with another laugh. "But then you have the nerve to sit across from me and gloat because my husband had an affair with your friend? Then you're going to tell me that I'm the one putting on airs and abandoning my friends? Stay the fuck away from me, hear?" Regina said, pointing a finger so close to Yvonne's face she almost touched her nose. "'Cause the next time I see you I might slap those ugly freckles off your face."

Regina chuckled at the fear in Yvonne's face, then turned around and calmly signaled the waiter, who was setting glasses of water at a nearby table.

"Excuse me," she said when she got his attention. "Separate checks, please."

REGINA GLANCED AT the mail stacked on the coffee table, as she walked into the house. Maybe the check from the *New Yorker* had finally come in. They were three weeks late in payment for an article she submitted more than a month earlier. They didn't use the piece, but it was no fault of hers. They still owed her one thousand dollars for the article.

"Stacey," she called out to the baby-sitter as she picked through the bills and sales circulars. "I'm home."

"Hey, baby."

She looked up in surprise. Charles was standing in the living room doorway, a sheepish smile plastered on his face.

"I thought you were going to be out all day?" she said as she once again sifted through the mail.

"I had a break in my schedule and decided to stop by and kiss my beautiful wife," he said as he pulled her close.

Regina turned her face, so his wet kiss landed on her cheek. *He probably found out I had lunch with Yvonne and is wondering what she told me,* she thought.

"Where's Stacey?" she asked out loud.

"She took the baby out for a walk. They're taking advantage

of the break in the weather. It's not often you get sixty-degree weather in late October."

"Yeah. That's true," she mumbled, not really listening. There was a Federal Express envelope on the floor that she hadn't noticed when she walked in. It was from the *New Yorker*. She ripped it open.

"Dear Ms. Harris-Whitfield. Enclosed you will find a check for $1,500 for the article you submitted on September 2, 2000. We would like to inform you at this time that we will no longer be using your services."

It was signed by the same managing editor who just days earlier had once again offered her a staff job at the magazine.

Regina blinked her eyes, then reread the short formal letter. They would no longer be using her services? Could it be some kind of a joke?

"What's wrong?"

"Hell if I know! The *New Yorker* just decided they don't want any more of my articles," she said, waving the damning paper in the air. She slammed the letter down on the coffee table and sucked her teeth in disgust. Charles's mouth opened, and his face ashened. Regina narrowed her eyes as she saw his reaction. She then picked the letter up from the table.

"Dear Ms. Harris-Whitfield . . ."

Why would they address her as Harris-Whitfield when she submitted all of her articles as Harris? She picked up the check. "Pay to the order of Regina Harris-Whitfield."

She looked up, but Charles had disappeared into the living room. She walked up behind him as he poured himself a snifter of brandy behind the bar. She paused for a moment, trying to hold back anger she was not yet sure was justified.

"Charles, did you contact the *New Yorker* for some reason?"

He swirled the glass of brandy, and stared into the vortex as if looking for an answer that might appease her.

"Charles?"

He sighed, and turned to face her.

"I called them yesterday morning. I was trying to be helpful."

"Okay," Regina said slowly, fighting to keep her face expressionless. "What did you say?"

"I told them I was your husband, and an attorney, and that I was concerned that they hadn't paid you for services provided."

Regina bit her lip to hold back her rage.

"What else did you say?"

"That's it. I thought it would just kind of nudge them into paying you a little quicker. You've been stressed out lately, and I didn't want this whole check thing weighing on your mind," Charles said. "I thought I was doing you a favor. I didn't know they were going to fire you."

Regina walked up close to him, tilting her head to try and match his eyes. "So you were helping me because you thought I've been stressed out?"

He walked over to the fireplace to get away from her, but she followed him.

"You were doing me a favor, huh?"

"Don't start, Gina," he raised his hand. "I'm sorry about what happened. I'll call them right now and apologize if you'd like."

She rolled her eyes, "Oh no, that's okay. I think you've made enough telephone calls on my behalf."

He grabbed his briefcase and began stuffing papers inside, avoiding her angry stare. "Look, I said I'm sorry. I was trying to be helpful, and I screwed up. Okay? I've apologized. Now I've got to get out of here. I'm late for an appointment."

"Oh that's right, I forgot. You were doing me a favor, because you didn't want me stressed out. How thoughtful of you." She strode over and blocked his path to the doorway. "And it didn't occur to you that I might just be stressed because my husband is getting blow jobs in his office from some two-dollar whore, you son of a bitch? Or because my best friend knew about the whole thing and was laughing at me behind my back?" she yelled.

"Look, just let me leave, okay?" he tried to push her out of the way.

"No! It's not okay! Nothing's okay! You cheat on me, you lie, and then on top of everything else you're going to fuck with my income? Hell no, it's not okay!"

"Look, I don't have time for your little hissy fits! You're an ungrateful little witch, you know that?"

She narrowed her eyes and advanced toward him. "I'm ungrateful? How the hell am I ungrateful?" she shouted.

"I messed up, and I admit that. True, maybe I shouldn't have called the magazine, but I did it with good intentions. And face it, it's not like you need the money any damn way. I have more than enough money coming in to take care of us. But no, you have to have your stupid little independence. And yeah, I cheated on you, but what are you planning to do? Hold it against me for the rest of my damn life? I forgave you when your dirty little past almost cost me the primary, but you can't forgive me one little transgression? Get out of my way. I'm late," he said trying to sidestep her.

She took both arms and forcefully shoved him back into the room.

"You bastard! You're not going to say some shit like that and walk out the door. Why don't you admit you wanted to blow it for me with the *New Yorker*? You want me to be in a position where I'm dependent on you, don't you? Well, it's never going to fucking happen!" she said, her chest heaving and her eyes looking as if they were ready to spring from their sockets.

"And you forgave me my dirty little past? You fucking forgave me my *past*? You son of a bitch, there's nothing for you to forgive. What I did I did before I met you. I didn't do anything to *you*, so there's nothing for *you* to forgive. But you cheated on me with that bitch, remember? You have a fucking wedding ring on your hand, and you take your dick and stick it into some bitch's mouth. How can you compare something I did before I met you to you violating our wedding vows! Who transgressed against whom? Don't try and play mind games with me, motherfucker. You think I'm stupid? My name's not fucking Angela!"

Charles dropped his briefcase and tried to put his arms around her. "Look, Gina, calm down, baby—"

"Get the fuck off me," she said, knocking his hands away.

"Gina, calm down. The neighbors will hear—"

"Fuck the neighbors! And fuck you!" she screeched.

"Oh, yeah, this is perfect," he said, throwing his hands up in the air and walking back toward the fireplace.

"I'll tell you what's fucking perfect. You saying my past almost cost you the primary, and not even dealing with the fact that here you are a married man running for national office and your getting blow jobs in your fucking office. I think that's just perfect! Fucking perfection! Why don't you deal with that? But oh no, you can't deal with that, can you? Instead you have to throw my past in my face. You knew about my past; I never lied to you! If it bothered you so fucking much, why'd you marry me?"

"Because I love you, and I thought you deserved a better life!"

"A better life than what?" Regina screamed. "I was doing quite well before I met you!"

"Yeah, well not as well as all this." Charles said waving his hand around the expensively furnished room. "I've done everything I can to make you happy, Gina, and you know it. You just can't admit it. Are you finished now?"

"No I'm not fucking finished. Let's talk about your mother now and how she treats me. How you let her treat me! Like I'm a piece of garbage stinking up her precious family. And then you and that . . . that mother of yours . . . get on television and all but say that you saved me from myself. Like if it weren't for you I'd be lying in some gutter with a needle up my arm."

"What the hell does my mother have to do with this argument?" he asked in exasperation.

"Not a goddamn thing, but I'm on a roll, so try and stop me!" She stood with her hands on her hips, glaring at him.

"To hell with this." Charles pushed past Regina, knocking her off-balance, and headed out the door.

"Yo, Mr. Congressman, you forgot your car keys!" Regina said, following him out the door. She hurled the keys at the back of his head. Perfect shot.

"And you forgot your briefcase!" The flying briefcase missed Charles, but crashed against the car, causing a dent, then landed with a thud on the sidewalk. Papers spilled out on the ground.

She slammed the front door shut, then leaned against it and crossed her arms as she tried to catch her breath. "Have a good day, Mr. Congressman!" she muttered to herself. "Have a smashing good day."

First the argument with Yvonne, then the blow-up with Charles, what else could possibly go wrong today? She headed to the refrigerator for a glass of mango juice to cool herself down. The container was on the second shelf, but when she pulled it out she realized it was empty. Sucking her teeth, she put it back into the refrigerator and poured herself a glass of orange juice. As she slammed the refrigerator door shut, the telephone rang. She reached for the telephone on the kitchen wall, picked up the receiver, and hung it back up. She didn't feel like dealing with anybody. She walked into the living room, placed her glass on the end table and lay down on the couch and closed her eyes. The telephone rang again, and she considered letting the answering machine pick up, but reached over for the phone on the coffee table, picked up the receiver and and again quickly hung up.

Probably no one but that damn Charles. She heard the key turn in the lock, and peeked over the arm of the couch into the foyer, and saw Stacey push Camille's stroller through the door.

"Hey, Mrs. Whitfield. I hope you didn't mind my taking Camille out for a walk. I just wanted her to get some fresh air," the matronly woman said. "Gotta take advantage of this good weather we're having."

Regina walked over and lifted Camille from the stroller. Six weeks old and already she was the spitting image of her mother. Her complexion, which was pink at birth, had darkened to a creamy caramel. Her eyes were dark and oval-shaped, and her lashes thick and luscious. The Harrises had some strong genes. Camille looked up at Regina and smiled, then began to coo, her little hands waving wildly in the air.

"How's Mommy's little princess?" Regina nuzzled the baby's face with her nose.

"She's doing fine. She's going to sleep like a rock after all that air. Babies do that, you know," Stacey said. "I'm going to head on home now, if you don't mind. I still got time to catch *Oprah*."

"No problem. Hold on and let me grab my purse."

The telephone rang again as Regina passed it, and she nonchalantly picked it up half an inch and dropped it back down in the cradle. Stacey looked at her quizzically, but said nothing.

The baby-sitter was right. After Camille was fed and changed she drifted right off to sleep in Regina's arms. After a while Regina's eyes also started getting heavy. The telephone rang again, but she didn't bother to get up. *Let the answering machine get it,* she thought.

"Regina. It's me, Yvonne. Are you there? Regina, please pick up, this is an emergency."

Fat chance I'm going to pick up, Regina thought lazily. *Both Charles and Yvonne can go to hell.*

"Okay. When you get in call Chestnut Hill Hospital. Mama's

been in an accident." Regina picked up, but it was too late. All she got was the dial tone.

She lay Camille down in her bassinet, and searched for the telephone book. When she found it, she flipped to the number for the hospital and frantically dialed. *Oh, God, please let Mama Tee be all right,* she prayed as she waited for someone to pick up.

"Chestnut Hill Hospital," the receptionist answered.

"Hello, can you tell me if you have a Theresa Jamison checked in the hospital?"

"Hold, please." The receptionist was gone for thirty long seconds. "We do have a Mrs. Theresa Jamison. She's in the Intensive Care Unit, ma'am."

"What happened? Why is she in the hospital? What kind of accident was she in?" Regina asked all in one breath.

"Excuse me, ma'am. Can you tell me your relationship to the patient?"

"Family friend," Regina said quickly, regretting her words as soon as they left her mouth. *Shit, I should have said daughter,* she thought.

"I'm sorry, ma'am. We're not allowed to give out that type of information to anyone but family members."

Shit, shit, shit.

"May I speak to her daughter, then? Yvonne Jamison, she should be there."

"Hold on, I'll connect you to the floor and you can ask a nurse to bring her to the telephone, ma'am."

"Hello, ICU," the next voice said.

"Hi, I'm Theresa Jamison's daughter, and I wanted to check on my mother's condition."

"Hold on for a moment, I'll check."

The voice appeared again a few minutes later.

"Your mother is in critical but stable condition, Miss Jamison. Do you want to speak to your sister?"

"Yes, please!"

Pause.

"I'm sorry, Miss Jamison, but your sister is talking to a doctor right now. Should I have her call you back?"

"Yes. I mean no. I mean yes," Regina said, as her mind raced. "Tell her to call me back, but if I'm not here it means I've already left for the hospital, and I'll be there in just a few minutes. Thank you." Regina hung up before the nurse could say anything else.

She picked up the telephone again.

"Stacey, this is Regina. Can you watch Camille for a few hours. I've got an emergency."

"Sure, I can be over in about a half hour."

"No, if it's okay with you I'll drop Camille at your house. I'm leaving now, and I should be there in about ten minutes, okay?"

Regina grabbed Camille out of the bassinet, and hurriedly shushed her as she started to cry. She put her in a heavy sweater set, and wrapped her in a pink blanket.

"It's okay, sweetie. Mommy's in a hurry now. Everything's okay," she cooed to her daughter as she placed a pacifier in her mouth and headed out the door. *God, I hope everything really is okay.*

SHE SCREECHED INTO the parking lot, almost hitting an ambulance. The driver angrily shouted to her from the window, but she didn't hear him. She rushed through the automatic doors of the Emergency Room, and pushed in front of two people waiting to see the receptionist for check-ins.

"Where's ICU?" she asked, out of breath.

The nurse, a young woman who looked fresh out of college, pointed down the hallway. "Second floor. Take the elevators on the left."

Regina raced down the hall. She pushed the elevator button,

waited for a few seconds, then sprinted through the door to the stairway and up to the second floor.

"Yvonne, what happened? Where's Mama Tee?"

Yvonne sat on a chair outside the ICU room, her eyes swollen and red, and brown mascara streaks staining her face. She jumped up when she saw Regina and rushed into her arms, almost knocking her down. Regina's arms instinctively closed around Yvonne.

"Oh, God, Gina. The doctors are in there with her, and they won't let anyone in. We were in a car accident, and she hit her head and was knocked unconscious."

"It's okay, honey, calm down. What are the doctors saying? Is she going to be okay?"

"I don't know. At first they said she was, but then she started having an asthma attack a few minutes ago and they threw me out of the room. There's about ten doctors in there with her now!" Yvonne sobbed hysterically, snot mingling with the tears that streamed down her face. Regina gently pushed her into a chair, and hugged her head into her chest as Yvonne cried. She wanted to ask a doctor about Mama Tee, but she couldn't leave Yvonne in this condition. *This just can't be happening. This whole day is a bad dream. I'm going to wake up any minute now,* she thought. She looked around for some help for Yvonne, but the nurses were rushing around the unit, and the other families were dealing with their own grief.

"Come on, tell me what happened," Regina urged, still holding Yvonne in her arms.

"We were coming back from the train station. Robert let me borrow his car. We had only gone about two blocks when a bus cut us off. I slammed on the brakes, and the car behind us slammed into us. Mama's head hit the dashboard," Yvonne sobbed.

"Oh, my God. Were you hurt, honey?" Regina pulled Yvonne's

face up, and saw for the first time her bottom lip was split and bloodied.

"I'm fine. I am. I'm just worried about Mama," Yvonne replied, burying her head in Regina's neck again. She suddenly pulled away, vainly attempting to wipe the tears from her face.

"Just so you know, Robert knows about the accident," she sniffed.

"Does he?" Regina didn't know what else to say.

"Yeah. I called when we got here. I thought he'd rush down to the hospital. Stupid me."

Regina looked at Yvonne intently, but said nothing.

"All he was worried about was the car. Then when I called him out on that he said he'd be over in a few minutes. That was three hours ago. I must have beeped him a dozen times, but the bastard's not answering my pages."

"Maybe he got tied up with something?" Regina offered soothingly. She didn't want to defend Robert, but she couldn't stand the pain in Yvonne's face.

"Oh, I'm sure he's tied up. He's tied up eating dinner with his wife, I bet. I should call him at home and shock the shit out of him." Yvonne started crying again, covering her face with her hands.

"Don't do that, Yvonne. I happen to know what it's like to have a woman calling your house looking for your husband," Regina said, turning her face away from her friend.

Yvonne suddenly looked up at Regina.

"Oh, God, I'm such a shit. Look at all I've done to you, and look, you're the only one here for me. Oh, God, Regina, I'm so sorry." She grabbed Regina and started crying again. "I don't blame you if you never talk to me again, girl. But I want to tell you that I really love you even if I do act messed up. I'm so sorry, sis."

Regina stroked Yvonne's disheveled hair, not knowing what to say.

"Miss Jamison?" A young doctor stood looking down at them. *Oh, God please no,* Regina thought when she saw the sympathetic look on his face.

"Oh, God, please tell me she's okay! Oh, God please tell me my mama's okay," Yvonne wailed as she looked up at the doctor.

"Miss Jamison, Miss Jamison, your mother's fine," the doctor said, as he leaned over her and rubbed her back. "In fact, she's regained consciousness and she wants to talk to you. But you can only stay a minute. I don't think she's up to seeing anyone at this point, but she's so insistent we're afraid she might go into another attack if you don't see her. But please, only a minute."

Yvonne jumped up and rushed into the room without hearing the rest of the doctor's words, and Regina rushed in after her.

Mama Tee lay immobilized on the bed, oxygen tubing in her nostrils, and an intravenous drip in her arm. She opened her eyes wearily when they entered the room, and struggled to smile.

"Oh, Mama, Mama, I'm so sorry." Yvonne sat in a chair next to the bed and buried her head in Mama Tee's bedsheets.

Mama Tee slowly lifted her arm and stroked her daughter's head. "Mama's okay, baby. Stop all dat crying," she said wearily.

Regina leaned down and kissed Mama Tee's cheek.

"Hey, Mama Tee. How you feeling?"

"I'm feeling fine. You tell them doctors we can go home now. I wanna see my grandbaby. I don't come all dis way to be in no hospital."

"We're just going to keep you overnight, Mrs. Jamison." Regina hadn't noticed the doctor enter the room. "Now why don't you get some rest and your daughters can come back and visit you in the morning?"

Yvonne looked up wildly. "I'm not leaving. I'm staying here with my mother!"

"She'll be fine. We gave her some steroids to stabilize her breathing. It wasn't a major attack, and she'll probably be able to go home in the morning. She just needs to get some rest. We only want to keep her overnight for observation," the doctor said kindly.

Mama Tee's eyes were closed, and she appeared to be asleep. It occurred to Regina that in all of the years she knew Mama Tee she had never seen her sleep. The woman was always bustling around shopping, cooking, or taking care of a baby.

"I'll check on her in the morning. I promise you she'll be fine," the doctor said as he walked Yvonne and Regina to the door. Regina noticed the doctor's appearance for the first time. He looked young, in his late twenties or early thirties, with light-tan skin and small slanted eyes. He was tall, with wavy hair, and looked as if he were half African American and half Asian. Very handsome. *Yvonne's going to kick herself later when she realizes what this guy looks like and what she looks like at the moment,* Regina thought with a smile.

"Are you sure she's going to be okay, Dr. . . ." Regina looked at the black name tag on the man's white jacket. "Dr. Mitchell."

"She'll be fine, trust me."

"Can't we stay with her, please?" Yvonne pleaded.

"Really, Miss Jamison, the best thing you can do is to go home and get some rest yourself."

Regina walked with Yvonne to the elevators, and the two women stood in silence on the ride down to the first floor lobby.

"Hey, you want to get some coffee or something before you split?" Yvonne asked hesitantly.

"Well, Camille's at the baby-sitter's, so I really should be getting home. I promise I'll give you a call tomorrow. Or tonight if you prefer," Regina said, oblivious to Yvonne's inner turmoil.

"Oh sure, that'll be fine," Yvonne said quickly. She started walking toward the hospital exit, but then turned around to face Regina.

"Look. I can't say how sorry I am about the way I've acted.

And all those things I said to you earlier today. I know I don't have any right to ask your forgiveness, but—"

"Forget it," Regina said with a smile and a wave of the hand.

"No, I really mean it. I'm really sorry," Yvonne said, tears welling in the corners of her still swollen eyes.

"So am I. Forget it, okay?" Regina reached out and touched Yvonne on the shoulder, glad to have her friend back. "Besides, there might have been some truth in what you were saying."

Regina lowered her eyes as she continued. "I mean especially the part about me not inviting you guys to different functions and stuff."

"Girl, you know we wouldn't have wanted to go to those stuffy parties you attend." Yvonne grinned.

"But that's not the point," Regina broke in. "The point is I didn't even give you the chance to turn me down."

"Gina, stop beating yourself up about this—"

"No. I've been thinking about it all night," Regina cut her off again. "And it's not that I'm embarrassed by you guys. Well, maybe a little of Puddin' . . ."

Both women giggled, causing the attendant at the information desk to look up and frown.

"But seriously," Regina continued. "It's not that I'm embarrassed or ashamed of you guys, or of my past. I think you hit the nail on the head, though, when you said that I try to keep these two different worlds separate. That's just what I've been doing all this time."

"But why?" Yvonne sat down at the nearest seat and looked at Regina expectantly. Regina sighed, then sat down next to her.

"I'm not sure. Maybe partly because I see you all as a kind of security blanket—or a sanctuary. Somewhere I could go if all this other shit got too crazy, you know? You guys are more than just my friends, you're my home. You're my heart." Regina's eyes started getting watery as she spoke. "How could I be ashamed of you? That's like me being ashamed of myself!"

"Yeah, I know, sweetie," Yvonne said soothingly, reaching out and rubbing Regina's shoulder. "I know."

"But then the question is begged, why do I feel that I need a security blanket? These people can't hurt me. And they're certainly not better than me," Regina said urgently. "So why do I have such a hard time dealing with them?"

"Gina," Yvonne said slowly. "I think that's more on you than on them."

"What do you mean?" Regina demanded.

"Come on, you have to admit you have a chip on your shoulder when you're around people who *you* think might think they're better than you. You're constantly waiting for one of them to mess up so you can launch your attack."

"Better a chip on my shoulder than a knife in my back," Regina snorted.

"Damn, Gina! And what makes you think anyone would want to stab you in the back?" Yvonne laughed. "Girl, you've got some serious issues. And I'm not even going to pretend to know how to deal with them. But I do know you are going to have to deal with them."

"Yeah, maybe." Regina sighed as she rubbed her forehead. Her head was throbbing. *Probably because of all the excitement,* she told herself. This conversation wasn't helping. She appreciated being able to talk to Yvonne in a way they hadn't talked in months, but the subject matter was, well, uncomfortable.

"Look, I really do have to get out of here. It's getting late, and Charles is going to be wondering where I am. I didn't think to write him a note or anything." Regina stood up and brushed the wrinkles out of her skirt.

"Okay," Yvonne said, rising from the chair. "But I really have to ask you something, and I want you to be truthful."

"Sure, what's up?" Regina furrowed her brow as she looked at Yvonne.

"I've apologized, and God knows I was wrong, but I'm just wondering . . . ," Yvonne said looking Regina directly in the eyes, but choosing her words carefully.

"Wondering what?"

"Well, you're the Queen of Get-Backs. And you certainly have enough reasons to get me back . . ."

Regina threw her head back and laughed, forgetting about her headache. "Yvonne, please. You're still my girl. You know that."

"Okay, just checking," Yvonne said, kissing Regina on the cheek.

As she drove home, Regina replayed both of her conversations with Yvonne. The headache was getting worse. She had to grab some aspirin when she got home.

It was true, she did have a chip on her shoulder when she was around people who thought they were better than she. She took immense delight in putting them down, and showing them she was just as smart as they.

And why shouldn't I? Someone needs to put them in their place, she thought with a grunt.

But it was more than that, Regina admitted to herself while waiting at a red light. *I start acting defensive around anyone with money. If I'm in their presence for more than just a few minutes I start getting uptight. I can fake it in business situations, but on a social level I become a mess and start attacking everyone around me. Why the hell do I do that?*

Regina looked across the intersection and noticed a young girl shivering at a bus stop. She couldn't have been more than fifteen or sixteen, and the raggedy looking lightweight jacket she wore was no match for the late-night wind. Regina looked at her watch: 11:30 P.M. *Whoever she is, she's out kind of late,* Regina thought.

A blue Mercedes-Benz pulled up, and a man rolled down the

driver's side window and started talking to the girl, who stuck her head up in the air, intent on ignoring him.

He's probably telling her he'll give her a ride home if she'll have sex with him, Regina thought angrily. The light turned green, and Regina started to make a U-turn to rescue the girl, but just then a bus pulled up at the stop, and the girl got on.

Good, Regina thought as she watched the Mercedes-Benz pull away. *What made you think you could proposition her in the first place?* As she stopped at another red light a few blocks away, she started rubbing her forehead again.

"Wait a minute. Why did I just assume that the guy in the car was a stranger trying to pick her up?" Regina said out loud to herself. "It could have been someone she knew and was just teed off with at the time. It could have been her boyfriend. Damn, it could have been anyone. Why did I just make up a story about some rich guy propositioning a poor, young girl for a blow job?"

Regina's eyes widened at her own words. *A blow job? Where the hell did that come from? Oh man, I'm really fucked up.* A driver started angrily honking behind her, and Regina looked up to see the light had turned green. She gunned through the intersection, her mind racing as fast as her car.

Regina pulled up in the baby-sitter's driveway and turned off the ignition. She sat in the car for a few seconds before getting out and slamming the car door. "Okay, I'm getting my baby, going home and going to bed. This introspection shit is for the birds."

IT WAS AFTER MIDNIGHT by the time Regina arrived home. She had hoped Charles would be in bed, but he was in the living room waiting for her.

"Where've you been? I was worried sick," he said when she walked in with the baby. He wore black suit pants, but he was barefoot and shirtless. He looked quite sexy. His well-developed chest glistened with a light coat of perspiration, probably courtesy of the heating system, which was always up way too high. Regina felt the familiar urging well up in her, the warm feeling that started in her head and flowed down to her toes whenever she remembered their lovemaking. She could use a little snuggling, and an outlet for her pent-up tensions. Being mad at Charles had never lessened her desire for him, and it wouldn't be the first time they made wild and passionate love, then woke up not speaking. In fact, when they were angry with each other, their lovemaking took on a new intensity, as if their fighting fueled their passion.

"I've had a helluva night," she said softly as she threw her keys on the coffee table. "When did you get home?"

"Couldn't you have at least left a note? I've called all over the city looking for you. Stacey said you had some kind of emergency."

She looked at him quizzically. Robert obviously hadn't told him about the accident. Probably ashamed that he had let Yvonne borrow the car. Regina started to explain but Charles cut her off.

"I hope you remember you're supposed to be coming with me to the governor's luncheon tomorrow. Here you are coming in at one in the morning, and we're going to have to leave at nine in order to make it to Harrisburg in time. What were you thinking?"

"I'm sorry. A friend was in a car accident. I went to the hospital to see if they were okay." She decided, she didn't know why, not to mention that it was Mama Tee who was hurt.

"Did you have to stay this late?" Charles spat.

Regina's eyes narrowed. Here she had just told him that a friend was in a car accident and he didn't ask who it was, or if they had even lived or died. He was more worried about the governor's luncheon than what had happened to her. The warm passion she felt turned cold as she looked at her husband.

"Sorry, you're going to have to go to Harrisburg without me," she said, making up her mind on the subject instantly. She headed up the stairs to the nursery.

"What do you mean? This was scheduled weeks ago, and it's the last big event before the election!" Charles sputtered, following her.

"I've got to go to New York tomorrow to straighten out this mess you started with the *New Yorker,*" she said as she undressed the sleeping Camille. "Quiet down or you'll wake the baby."

"Why do you have to go tomorrow? Can't it wait until later in the week?"

"No, it can't." Regina checked Camille's diaper. Dry. Good. She turned to face Charles.

"Damn, Regina, you can't do me this one favor?"

"Don't even try it. I've offered, and even asked to come along to a number of affairs. You never want me to, remember?" She headed down the hall to the master bedroom. She kicked off her shoes, and sat on the king-size bed and rubbed her ankles.

Charles appeared in the doorway of the bedroom. "I've been trying to spare you, Gina. I thought I was being thoughtful, considering you just had the baby and all."

Regina stood up and started unbuttoning her blouse. "You don't want me with you because you don't want to take the chance that someone will remember 'my dirty little past' and bring it up in conversation. I haven't been fooled. I just haven't mentioned it. If it wasn't for the fact that the governor's wife specifically invited me, you would have found an excuse to leave me behind again."

"Then why did you say you would go?" Charles walked over and leaned on the mahogany dresser facing Regina. She turned her back on him as she slipped into a sexy red nightgown.

"Because I was going to go, but I changed my mind. I have other things to do. Sorry." She ran her fingers through her hair, then adjusted the spaghetti straps of the nightgown. She studied herself in the full-length mirror next to the bed. Nice. She flicked her tongue over her lips to add moisture, then turned to Charles.

"Why don't you take Angela? I'm sure she knows how to behave at saditty luncheons."

"Regina, don't start this shit again."

"Sorry, I couldn't resist. You know how we upset wives can be."

"Upset husbands can be hell, too, you know."

"What's that supposed to mean?"

"That means, I've been taking shit from you for these past couple of days and I'm tired of it," he said, raising his voice.

"Oh, really? And what are you going to do? Divorce me?" She laughed and slipped beneath the satin sheets. "Would you turn out the lights when you leave, please? I plan to go at about seven or so. If you want I'll wake you up before. Stacey's going to be here at nine, so feed the baby breakfast, will you? I should be home around four or five in the afternoon." She reached over and clicked off the lamp. "Good night."

THE KEY DIDN'T FIT into the lock. Regina looked at the key to make sure she was using the right one for the front door. She tried again, before noticing that the lock looked new. *What the hell?* She rang the bell and waited for Stacey to answer. After a few minutes she walked around to the back door and tried her key. No luck. She walked around the side of the house and stood on tiptoes to try to peer through the window. The lights were all out. *I can't believe Charles did this shit,* she thought.

She sat down on the porch and wondered what to do next. She could call the police, but she didn't want to go through the problem of explaining to them why she was locked out of her own house. She thought about calling Charles, but she didn't want to give him that satisfaction. She walked around to the back of the house and tried the window. Locked. She picked up a heavy flower pot, and threw it at the window, smashing the glass. The security alarm blared as she knocked the shards of glass from the pane and crawled in. She ran to the security alarm controls and punched in the code, but the alarm continued ringing throughout the house. She couldn't believe it. *The bastard even changed the alarm code.*

She saw the glare of police lights flickering through the front windows, and rushed to the door to let them in.

"It's okay, officers, I'm Mrs. Whitfield. I lost my keys, and for the life of me I can't remember the security code. I'm sorry you had to come all the way out here," she said to the two tough-looking men in blue.

One of the officers, a grizzled man who looked as if he spent his entire life on the force, looked at her suspiciously. "Mind if we see some ID, miss?"

"Just part of the policy, Mrs. Whitfield," his younger partner said hurriedly. "It's not that we don't believe you, but we have to put down in our police report that we saw your identification."

"Of course, no problem." She realized she had left her pocketbook on the back porch, and ran to the back door to retrieve it. The younger officer followed her. "Here you go, my driver's license and credit cards. Will that do?"

"Sure will. I'm sorry for the inconvenience. If you want I'll get someone to come out and turn off that alarm for you."

"No, I'm sorry for inconveniencing you. It's nice to know if there really is a break-in you men will be out here so promptly." She smiled.

Neighbors gathered outside the front of the house wondering what was going on. She stepped out on the porch and waved to them. "Everything's okay. I'm sorry for all the commotion."

"Officer Merrick turned off the alarm, ma'am," said the younger officer. "Seems he happens to moonlight for your security company. We'll be leaving if you'll just sign this report."

Regina ran upstairs after the officers left. Camille's overnight bag was gone. She rushed into the master bedroom. The closet doors were open. All of her clothes were gone, though Charles's remained. She opened the dresser drawers. Her lingerie. Her jewelry. All had disappeared.

I can't believe he did this. How dare he! Regina visibly shook as she stared around the room. She went back downstairs to the living room, and with trembling fingers she reached for the telephone.

"Hi, Stacey? It's Mrs. Whitfield. I'm just calling to check on Camille," she said with her eyes closed, praying Camille was there.

"She's fine, Mrs. Whitfield. Are you okay? You sound upset."

"I'm fine, just a little tired. Did my husband say what time he was picking Camille up?"

There was a pause on the other end of the telephone.

"Well, it was my understanding that he wanted her to stay the night."

"Of course. I'd forgotten. Okay, there might be a change in plans. I might be picking her up later tonight."

"Oh." Stacey's voice dropped in disappointment.

"Don't worry. We'll still pay for the overnight stay."

"Oh, okay. That's fine," Stacey said cheerfully.

Regina placed the telephone on the receiver. As she removed her hand she noticed the moisture on the telephone. She hadn't realized it, but she was dripping with sweat. Her hair was plastered to her head, and her hands were clammy. She rubbed her hands against her torn skirt, and her wedding ring caught on a thread. She yanked it off and threw it across the room.

She picked up the telephone and dialed Charles's cellular telephone number. He picked up after only two rings.

"Charles, this is Regina."

"I recognize your voice," he said in frigid tone.

"I'm at the house."

"Oh, really?"

"Really. I climbed through the window."

There was silence on the other end of the telephone.

"Charles, we have to talk. This has gone too far. What time will you be home?"

"Regina, look, I can't deal with all this now. I have two days until the election and I can't afford to be distracted with your shit. Why don't you go on back to New York for a while, and we'll talk after the election. I've already talked to my mother. Camille can stay with her."

Regina bit her lip to keep from yelling into the telephone. Did he really think she was going to let her precious baby stay with that bitch?

"Charles, what time will you be home? I think we should talk tonight. If you want a divorce we'll talk about that, but I just think it's imperative that we talk."

"I'm not the one who mentioned divorce, you know."

"Okay, forget it, I'll give you a call after the election. Goodbye."

"No, wait," Charles said quickly. "If you want to talk, that's fine. But I'm telling you now, I don't want to hear any shit about my mother or that bitch Angela. Let's get that straight now. And I don't want to hear anything else about the *New Yorker,* either. If we're going to talk, we're going to talk about changes *you* need to make in order for this marriage to work, you got that?"

Regina blinked her eyes in amazement. He was the one who had wronged her, over and over again, and now he was laying down rules? Her first impulse was to tell him to kiss her ass, but she fought the urge. There was no way she was going to let him get away with all this, but she needed to buy herself some time to think.

"Okay, honey," she said sweetly. "Whatever you want. Bring some flowers for the table, won't you? I want this to be a special evening."

14

THAT BASTARD. HE WANTED TO SHOW ME THAT MY LIFESTYLE was dependent on him? How dare he treat me this way!

Large red spots swam in front of her eyes, and her knees started to weaken. She stumbled to the couch, and tried to calm herself. She leaned her head back on the cushion and closed her eyes. She needed to think. *This couldn't be happening. It just couldn't.* Her head throbbed, not with pain, but with the frustration and anger she wasn't sure how to release. *He can't possibly think he can get away with this,* she thought. But what could she do? Divorce him? She could drag him through a nasty and public divorce fight. It would kill his political career. Did she really want a divorce, though? Was she really ready to abandon any hope of repairing her marriage? She squeezed her eyes tighter, but tears still formed in the corners and slid down her cheeks. She wiped them away quickly. Tears weren't the way to go. He didn't deserve them. She had to show Charles that she was in control of her own life and that he had to own up, *really* own up, to his indiscretion. It was as simple as that. She reached for the telephone and dialed Yvonne's apartment. No answer. She called Chestnut Hill Hospital. The nurse said Mama Tee was doing fine, but Yvonne wasn't there. She tried the campaign office.

"Yvonne? What are you doing there?"

"Girl, Mama Tee ran me out the hospital and told me to go to work. You know how she is. With all she's gone through she's worried about me losing my job."

"Okay, listen, can you talk?"

Regina quickly filled her friend in on what had happened, then waited for a response.

"Yvonne?" she said, after a few moments of silence.

"I'm here. I just had to pick my jaw up off the floor."

"Listen, and this is important. Are you sure Charles broke it off with Angela?"

"Positive. She was calling here every half hour for the last few days, but he kept refusing to take her calls. Then I ran into her in the gym yesterday before I went to pick up Mama Tee, and she called him all kinds of bastard for dropping her cold like that."

"And you don't think it's an act?"

"Nope. She doesn't have enough brains to pull it off. She's genuinely upset."

"Has she called today?"

"Not in the last three hours."

"You sure?"

"Yep. I'm the only one in the office today. Janet's out sick."

"Okay. You said she was at a gym yesterday. Which one?"

"Gold's Gym in Center City. Why?"

"Do you know if she goes every day?"

"I don't know about every day, but I know she's in my aerobics class. Mondays, Wednesdays, and Thursdays at five-thirty."

"So there's class today?"

"Yeah, it's Thursday. Why? What's up?"

Regina glanced at her watch. It was 4:30. She would be going against rush-hour traffic, but still it would take her thirty minutes to get to Center City.

"Does she know you and I've made up?" she asked Yvonne.

"No. Why would I tell her? Robert doesn't even know, remember?"

"Cool. Yvonne, do me a favor. Don't show up for your class today. Wait there in the office until you hear from me again," she said urgently.

"Okaaaay . . . no problem," Yvonne said. "But what are you going to do?"

"I don't know. I'm going to have to wing it. Gotta run, I'll call you soon." Regina hung up, ran upstairs, and quickly showered. Whatever it was she was going to do, she didn't want to look like she'd just climbed in a window. She slipped into a green sweatsuit, applied a coat of lipstick, deciding to forgo the eyeliner. She couldn't count on not having another crying fit, and she didn't need black rings around her eyes when she talked to Angela. *If* she talked to Angela. She still didn't know what she was going to do or say. Whatever it was, it had better be good. She might not get another chance. She grabbed her keys and ran out of the door.

He had to know I wasn't going to just sit around and take this shit, she thought as she drove toward Center City. Didn't he care that she might divorce him? Or was he just so arrogant to think she couldn't bring herself to leave him? He knew she didn't want Camille to grow up in a broken home. He also knew she had grown accustomed to a lifestyle that would be difficult to retain on her own. She made enough money for a single woman, but starting out on her own again, and this time with an infant, wouldn't be fun. She had enough money in her personal bank account to rent a small apartment in a decent neighborhood, but she would have to buy all new furniture, since they had sold the contents of her old apartment when they married. Then she would have to pay for a sitter to watch Camille while she worked.

And she would have to pay for medical insurance, which she hadn't bothered with when she was single, but it would be imperative with a baby in the household. How was she going to swing it?

He thinks he has me right where he wants me, she thought. *He knows it would be difficult for me to leave. He thinks I have to take whatever he has to dish out. He probably thinks I'll just throw a hissy fit, stop talking to him for a few days, and then simply go back to life as usual. He thinks I'm a wuss.* Tears sprang to her eyes once again, blurring her vision as she took the wild turns on Lincoln Drive. *And he has every reason to think so. He has an affair and what do I do? Do I leave him? Do I threaten him with divorce? No. Just like a nice little politician's wife, I cry and accept his gifts and apologies, and pretend to the world everything's all right. No wonder he thinks he can do anything he wants to me. I surrendered my power to him.* She pulled into the gym parking lot.

Time to reclaim her life.

She looked at her watch while she waited in the locker room: 5:25. No sign of Angela. *She's not coming,* Regina thought with a sigh. Just then, a woman in a pink designer sweatsuit rushed in. Huffing, the woman threw her gym bag into an open locker, and rushed out without bothering to lock up her belongings. Regina rushed out after her. It looked like Angela, but she wasn't sure. The woman was pulling the door to the aerobics room open when Regina called out tentatively, "Angela?"

Angela swung around and looked at her. Her eyes squinted as recognition crossed her face.

"What do *you* want?" she said roughly.

"I just thought we should talk," Regina said hesitantly.

"Oh. I thought you might have been here to work off some of that baby fat you're carrying."

The little bitch. Maybe I'm a few pounds heavier than before the baby, but I still look better than her, Regina thought, though she forced a weak smile on her face. *Okay, I know just how to handle her ass.*

"Angela, this is important. Can you spare me a few minutes?" she asked, slowly approaching the woman. "This is really hard for me, but I thought I should come and congratulate you in person, and show there aren't any hard feelings."

"What are you talking about?" Angela asked, suspiciously.

"Charles is leaving me. You've won," Regina said, in what she hoped was a plaintive tone. "He wants to be with you."

"What?" Angela said, releasing the door handle.

"I don't know why you're acting surprised. All I want to do is ask that the two of you don't fight for custody of my baby. Don't you think it would be better to wait a while and have a family of your own? Just let me keep my baby, that's all I ask," Regina said in a whiny voice.

"What the hell are you talking about?"

"You haven't talked to Charles today?" Regina asked, feigning surprise. "We're all supposed to be meeting at the house tonight. I just wanted to come over and talk to you beforehand about the custody issue. I'm sorry. I thought you already knew."

"Knew what?"

"That Charles is planning on marrying you."

Angela looked at Regina, a scowl on her face. "Oh really? He told you this? That's funny. He hasn't said a word about it to me. I haven't even been able to get him on the phone. Are you trying to play some kind of game, Regina?"

Oh, please let her be as dumb as I think she is, Regina prayed as her mind raced, trying to figure out how to reel the woman into the scheme she was perfecting as she spoke.

"I wish I were playing a game. This isn't easy for me, believe me," she said, pretending to fight back tears. "Do you think we can go into the locker room? I don't want to start crying out here in the open. I feel like enough of a fool as it is."

"Okay. So when did he tell you all this?" Angela asked as the two of them sat on a wooden bench in the locker room.

Regina hung her head, trying to force tears from her eyes.

"Last night. We were making love, and he called out your name," she said burying her face in her hands, releasing fake sobs. "Then when I said something about it afterward he slapped me, and said he couldn't stand being around me. That I'm weak and fat, and that I'm not in his class. And then he said that he wanted out of the marriage."

"He called my name out?" Angela asked, impressed.

Self-absorbed bitch. Yep. She's just as dumb as I'd hoped, Regina thought with satisfaction. *This just might work, after all.*

"Then when he finally calmed down a little he said he wanted a divorce. That he wanted to marry you, Angela, and that if I knew what was best I wouldn't make a stink or he would fight me for custody of Camille. I want to keep my baby. Please let me keep my baby."

"Don't worry, Regina. I don't want your baby," Angela said soothingly. "I think it would be horrible to take a child away from its mother."

"You do? Oh, thank you! So you'll tell him that tonight?"

"Tonight?"

"Oh, that's right! You said you haven't talked to him yet! He said he was inviting you over to the house so we can all talk this out. You know, how we're going to handle the press with the up-coming election and all. He said we should get together so we can get our stories straight. You know how logical Charles is."

"Yes. Of course," Angela said, seemingly lost in thought. "But wait a minute. Why hasn't he called me, then?"

"I don't know. Have you been home?" Regina said, hoping to hear the right answer.

"No. I've been out looking for a job," Angela answered.

"Well, you know how careful Charles is. He probably

wouldn't leave a message on your answering machine. Remember what happened with Clinton and Gennifer Flowers."

"Yes. Of course. That would make sense," Angela said haltingly.

"I think he's at the North Philadelphia office. Why don't you call him?" Regina asked. "Or just go over there, I don't know. Could you do me a favor? Don't let him know I spoke to you, okay? He's mad enough as it is," Regina said, pretending to cry again. "I don't want to make matters any worse than I already have."

"Don't worry. I won't say a word. I'm going to go talk to him now. I'll see you later," Angela said, jumping up and going to the door. "And, really don't worry about it. I'll talk to him about the baby thing."

"Thank you so much. You're really sweet," Regina murmured as the woman disappeared through the door. Regina waited five minutes, to make sure Angela wouldn't double back to get the gym bag she left in the locker. Then Regina went to the pay telephone in the lobby.

"Yvonne. Angela's on her way to the office. I need you to do me a big favor. Tell her that Charles left a message for her to meet him at the house at eight o'clock tonight."

"What? What the hell are you doing?" Yvonne asked incredulously.

"I'm setting both of the bitches up. Just back me up, okay? Tell her that Charles called her house all day and couldn't get her. Tell her he just left the office five minutes before she arrived, and he left the message with you in case she called. And whatever you do, don't give her his cell phone number or pager."

"Regina, you know I'm going to get fired if I do this, right?"

"Yeah, I know. But Yvonne, please. I can't let him get away with this shit anymore."

"Okay. I owe you one, anyway. But your ass is going to have to support me until I find a new job."

25

OF COURSE, ANGELA WOULD HAVE HAD TO RUIN *everything*, Regina thought angrily as she poured a bit of grapefruit juice into the tall glass of vodka. She had told Angela to be there at 8:30 P.M., but instead she showed up at 7:30, undoubtedly anxious to celebrate her victory in the hard-fought battle over Charles.

In her mind, Regina had planned the evening down to every excruciating detail: Charles would assume she was angry at his pranks earlier in the day. But instead of being accosted by the self-righteous shrew he expected, he would be greeted by a seductive siren seemingly ready to meet his every desire. She would have his favorite meal prepared—roast duck with orange sauce and wild rice—and Moët poured into two of the crystal wineglasses he had bought for their three-month wedding anniversary. She would spray perfume on five gold tapered candles placed in an antique brass candelabra on the table, and a warm illuminating fire would blaze in the fireplace. Her hair would be loosely swept up, with a few wisps escaping down the nape of her neck, and she would wear the revealing royal blue dress that always turned Charles into an animal. Billie Holiday's sultry song, "My Man," would seep from the stereo. When she and Charles were halfway through their food, wine, and sexy murmuring, the door-bell would ring, and she would get up, graciously open the door, and smilingly invite Angela inside the sanctuary of their love. The look of shock on Charles's face when he came face-to-face with "the other woman" would be worth all of the trouble she was go-ing through to make the evening happen.

But Angela had ruined it all by arriving early. Regina was dressed, and the fire place was lit, but the food was still cooking and the table had not yet been set. Regina inwardly glared at the woman, although outside a smile was painted on her face.

"I love these paintings!" Angela gushed. "They fit the house so well. Charles must have bought them while he was away at school. Isn't that an Ernie Barnes original?" she asked, pointing to a large framed picture over the fireplace. "I don't know if I mentioned it, but I minored in art at college."

"It's an Annie Lee, but I can certainly see how you would get the two confused," Regina said, smiling as she handed Angela her third vodka and grapefruit juice. "Actually, I bought that paint-ing a few years ago, but most of the others belong to Charles. I'm sure the two of you will want to do some redecorating. Both of you have such great taste."

Angela beamed at the compliment. "Well, we probably won't make any major changes right away, but of course I will want to add my own personal touch."

"Of course," Regina replied. *Boy, is she full of herself.*

Angela continued to bore Regina as she prattled on about some imagined connection between Buddhism and Picasso's blue pe-riod. Regina smiled and nodded her head at the right times, some-thing she had perfected while attending the boring cocktail parties thrown by Charles's political friends. She silently thanked God that she had changed into her dinner clothes early, because there was no escaping Angela even for a moment. When Regina tried to excuse herself to wash her hands, she stood outside the bathroom door, talking. Regina could not shake a slight headache as she wondered how to salvage her original scheme. Damn Angela!

At exactly 8:00 P.M., Regina heard Charles's key turn in the front door. Through the opening of the slightly ajar door, Charles's arm appeared, holding a large bouquet of yellow and red roses. He then poked his head inside. His sheepish smile froze for a second, then thawed into fury when he saw the two women standing side by side.

"Get out," he said to Angela.

"What?" Angela said incredulously.

Then on cue, Regina stepped forward with a large smile on her face, and said graciously, "Why Charles, how rude. I invited Angela to join us tonight. I thought you'd be pleased."

Charles turned his glare to her.

"You fucking bitch."

"Welcome home, darling," Regina cooed.

Charles stood in front of the open door, stupefied, as Regina walked over and picked up the roses he had dropped on the expensive Oriental rug.

"She told me that you wanted me here," Angela said frantically, finally realizing that she was a pawn in an elaborate scheme. "Baby, she told me that you wanted the three of us to talk."

"I just said that since the two of you are in love I'm going to graciously step aside and let you make a go of it, *baby*," Regina said, pretending calm though her insides were churning with fear and excitement. "I told her how you cried last night and told me you wanted a divorce."

"What the hell are you talking about, Gina? I never said anything like that!"

"Really? I could have sworn you did," Regina said, her back

turned toward him as she removed a bunch of dry flowers from a dark green vase on the mantelpiece and replaced them with the roses. "My bad."

"She said you two had already worked everything out and that we were going to be adult about all this," Angela sobbed.

"What the hell is wrong with you, Regina? Why did you have to drag her into this?"

"Oh, *I'm* the villain? *I dragged* her into this, huh? Give me a break. *You* chose to step outside our marriage. *She* decided to mess around with a married man. I'm the wounded party in all this. Anyway, I think you should be happy that your soon-to-be ex-wife is so accepting of your soon-to-be next wife."

She smiled again and walked over to the bar to pour herself a glass of wine. She held it up in a toast.

"This is all just a big game to you, isn't it?" Charles shouted.

"Charlie, if she wants to step aside, then let her," Angela angrily chimed in before Regina could answer. "We can get a lawyer to work out the custody arrangement."

"We don't need a lawyer." Charles spat.

"Look, you're going to have to choose. Do you want me or her?" Angela shouted, pointing at Regina.

"Uh-uh. He doesn't have to choose. I'm voluntarily stepping out of this triangle," Regina said as she took a sip of wine.

"There is no triangle!" Charles shouted. "I don't want her!"

"Oh, really? That's what you say now, but what about last night when you said you wanted to marry her?"

"Regina, will you stop with the lies? I never said I was going to marry her, and I never said I loved her."

"Oh? And I suppose you're going to say you never called out her name when we were making love?"

"Will you *please* stop Regina? Why are you trying to soup her up?"

"I'm not trying to soup anyone up. I just think if you love

someone you should tell them," Regina said sweetly, then turned to Angela.

"He's only denying it because you're here. He's always had a hard time expressing his feelings to people he cares about." She turned back to Charles with a smile on her face. "Go ahead, honey. Tell her to her face. She deserves to hear it."

Instead of answering, Charles walked over to the mahogany coat tree, picked up Angela's coat, shoved it in her arms, and propelled her toward the open door.

"Get off of me! You think you're just going to throw me out like trash?"

"That's just what you are, okay? Now get the hell out of my house."

"You bastard, you just used me! Don't think you're going to get rid of me that easy!"

"What are you going to do? Let everyone know what a slut you are? You've slept with half the men in Philadelphia. You think anyone will care that I fucked you, too?"

Damn, Regina thought, laughing. *I wouldn't take that if I were her.*

Angela cried and swung wildly at Charles. For a second, Regina felt sorry for her rival, and considered handing her a vase to hit him with, but then thought better of it. There was no telling who Angela would choose to strike. Still, Regina had had enough of the two of them. She put down her wineglass, coolly walked over to the closet, removed a tan suede jacket, and announced that she was leaving.

"You know what? Fuck you both!" Angela screamed, storming out the door ahead of Regina.

"Is everything okay?" came a voice from the front door. It was John Clarke, the next-door neighbor.

Charles, suddenly realizing that they had been providing entertainment for the neighborhood, slammed the door in his face.

"Now, Charles, that's no way to treat your constituents two days before the election," Regina said, as she attempted to reopen the door.

"Shut up. you're not going anywhere," Charles shouted as he attempted to physically carry Regina away from the door. Regina broke free of his grip and slapped him. Shocked, Charles froze, then pulled his hand back to slap her in return.

"In all the time we've known each other you've never raised your hand to me," Regina said in a wounded voice. "And now you're going to hit me because of *her*?"

Charles dropped his hand and walked to the overstuffed leather couch, sat down and buried his head in his hands. Regina stood at the bottom of the stairs, trying to figure out a graceful way to end the dramatic scenario she had set into action.

"Where's Camille?" Charles finally asked, his head still buried.

"She's at Stacey's," Regina said, as she calmly walked over and locked the door, then sat down on the couch next to Charles. She put her hand on his arm and said pleasantly, "Are you ready for dinner, sweetheart? I fixed your favorite."

Charles stood up wearily and walked over to the stairs, turning to Regina before he ascended and simply said, "You are such a bitch." It was the second time he had called her a bitch that evening, which made it the second time he had ever called her a bitch.

Regina waited for an hour, then went upstairs and found Charles lying on top of the bed, fully dressed, his hands crossed underneath his head, his glasses off, and his eyes shut in a wince. She asked him if he was okay, but he didn't answer, so she went back downstairs and called Yvonne to tell her what had happened.

"Girl, you are too much!" Yvonne exclaimed when Regina had finished. "How do you think up these things?"

"I have no idea." Regina giggled.

"Did he really call out her name when you two were making love?"

"Of course not." Regina snorted.

"Okay, so the question is, why did he cheat on you? You think he really loves her?"

"No," Regina said slowly. "I don't think so. If he did he wouldn't have talked to her the way he did, not even for my benefit."

"Then what was it?"

"I don't know. Maybe for the excitement?"

"Maybe," Yvonne replied.

"Okay. Spill it. What's your take on it? Why did Charles have an affair with Angela?" Regina asked. She knew it was just a matter of time before Yvonne offered her opinion anyway.

"Well, I don't know. But it is curious that you and Angela are complete opposites. You're super intelligent. She's a super airhead. You come from the ghetto. She comes from the ritzy part of town."

"You forgot to mention that Angela plays doting sweetheart with Charles and I play Queen Bitch." Regina expected Yvonne to laugh at the remark, but was disappointed.

"Well, I wouldn't say you play Queen Bitch, but you do challenge him at every turn."

"So, you're saying I drove my husband into the arms of another woman?" Regina asked incredulously.

"Hell, no!" Yvonne answered quickly. "Come on, Regina. He wasn't even attracted to you until he thought you came from a background similar to his. And then, by the time he found out different, you had him hooked. He married you, but at the same time he still believes he's supposed to wind up with someone like Angela. So then he tried to make you into an Angela, but you rebelled. You wanted to be financially independent. You wanted to have your own career. I really think he thought you'd change after you got married, and especially after the baby."

"So then why doesn't he jump at a chance to get a divorce and marry someone like Angela?" Regina asked.

"Because he doesn't want someone like Angela," Yvonne said in an exasperated voice. "The only person I know who loves to argue more than you is Charles. You add excitement to his life. You're always presenting a challenge. You're stimulating, and someone like Charles loves stimulation. Angela can't compete with that. That's why he married you. And I honestly think he loves you," Yvonne said in a more somber tone. "He's probably kicking himself upside the head right now, and scared to death he's going to lose you. What I can't figure out is why you're taking this so lightly."

"I'm not taking it lightly at all," Regina said defensively. "I feel like a burden has been lifted off my shoulders after this show-down tonight."

Regina heard a rustling noise upstairs, and then footsteps descending the stairs.

"Look, I've got to go. I'll give you a call tomorrow," she whispered into the telephone before hanging up.

Charles walked into the dining room. His clothes were slightly wrinkled; his brow was furrowed. Regina couldn't help notice how tragic he looked. She felt sorry for him.

"Okay, Regina, what's next?" he said wearily.

"I'm moving," she replied innocently. "That's what you wanted, right? You changed the locks, and threw out my clothes. It's obvious you want me out of this house."

"Regina, you know it was all a joke. And I didn't throw out your clothes, they're in the attic. I don't want you out of the house, and I don't want a divorce. I was just trying to teach you a lesson."

Regina tried unsuccessfully to hide a grin as she answered. "Well, it didn't work. As you can see, I'm in control of my own life. I hope that's a lesson *you've* finally learned."

He regarded her, then leaned back against the wall and chuckled.

"Damn, couldn't you have just slashed my tires or cut up my clothes or something?" he said shaking his head.

Regina got up from her chair, walked over to her contrite husband, stood up on her tiptoes and kissed him on the chin.

"I could have, but it wouldn't have been as much fun."

The two started laughing, and he put his arms around her and pulled her close, stroking her hair. She nuzzled into his chest, and the familiar scent of his cologne soothed her. For a moment it was like old times.

"Baby, I'm sorry. I really messed up, didn't I?" Charles said as he kissed her lightly on the top of her head. "Look, if you want, we can go to marriage counseling. But I swear to you this will never happen again. Give me a chance to make it up to you."

Regina smiled weakly, and gently pulled away from him. Then she leaned back into him and kissed him softly on the lips, before slowly walking toward the stairs.

"In the words of another famous bitch, 'I'll think about it tomorrow.' Right now I'm going to bed—in the guest room."

"Baby, we can still make this marriage work, you know," Charles said plaintively.

"Charles, do you remember that saying? If it don't fit don't force it, just relax and go," Regina said as she mounted the stairs. "Well, I think it's time we both relax."

Epilogue

"I READ YOUR ARTICLE IN THE *NEW YORKER* LAST WEEK. Good stuff, Gina."

"It should have been, I spent six months waiting for those documents from the FBI. Hey, now that you're in Washington, maybe you can do something to speed things up. Freedom of Information Act or not, federal agencies hate to give up the info."

Regina sliced into her T-bone steak. Just right. She liked it when blood oozed onto the plate with each cut of the knife.

"So does Camille like the bongo drums I sent her?"

"Oh God, she loves them. But they were driving me crazy. I sent them down to Mama Tee's house, so she can bang on them all day over there. That woman has the patience of Job."

Mama Tee was a godsend, and Regina didn't know what she would do without her. Not only did she watch Camille during the day so Regina could write, she doted on the child. It was funny seeing big old Mama Tee waddle after Camille, who was just learning how to walk.

"So, have you found a house yet?" Charles asked.

"Nope, still looking. I've got to get more space. David just told me about a brownstone on his block that's up for sale. The owner just got sent up the river for ten years on a federal rap."

"Jesus, Gina. Why would you want to move Camille to a block filled with drug dealers!"

"Relax, Charles. The guy was arrested for insider trading. It's a good neighborhood. And it would be nice living on the same block as David and Tamika." Regina took a sip of red wine. Same old Charles, always jumping to conclusions. And always the worst.

"I just don't understand why you want to stay in Harlem. You can get a nice house for a lot less money in the suburbs."

"Come on, I'm not a suburb type of woman. You should at least know that by now." Regina smiled.

Charles leaned back, then shook his head and sighed. "Yeah, I do. But you did like Philadelphia. Why not come back here?"

"Been there, done that." Regina laughed. "I'm not trying to go through it again."

"Oh, come on Regina, it wasn't all that bad."

"Maybe not for you." Regina took another sip of her wine.

Charles chewed on his upper lip. He had lost some weight, making his face look a little gaunt, and making his protruding ears a bit more prominent. But he still looked good. And sexy. And the warm glow Regina felt painfully reminded her that she hadn't been with a man since their separation four months before. *Time to put down the wine,* she decided.

"Regina, are you sure you want me to sign the divorce papers."

"Positive," she said before the wine could make her reconsider.

"Come on, I wasn't all that bad." Charles frowned. "I admit I messed up, but you've got to know I wouldn't cheat on you again."

"Believe it or not, I believe you." Regina took a sip from her water glass.

"Then why won't you reconsider?" Charles leaned across the table, and took Regina's hand in his.

"Charles, it won't work. And truth be told, it's not just your fault. I shouldn't have married you in the first place."

"What do you mean?"

She gently removed her hand from his, and furrowed her brow. How could she explain? She was just beginning to understand herself, but she owed it to him to try.

"Charles, I loved you, don't get me wrong, but I think part of the reason I married you was to try and prove something. The thought of being the wife of a successful attorney, let alone a congressman, well, it was like an accomplishment. Additional proof that a bad girl could make good. It's not so much that I was trying to escape my past, as much as I was trying to prove that I had overcome it."

"Oh really? And when did you come to this realization?"

"I've been thinking about it for a while, now. Don't you see? *That's* why I was so furious when your mother got on TV and gave you credit for turning my life around. That was *my* accomplishment. I couldn't bear the thought of someone taking credit for what I did. I was always striving to succeed . . . to prove that someone who came from a background like mine could be just as good as anyone else."

"Who were you trying to prove it to? The world?"

"Yes, but more important I had to prove it to myself."

"And now?"

"It's finally hit me that I don't have to prove anything to anyone, not even myself. I was who I was. I am who I am. And it's all good." Regina smiled. "I've done some bad things, and I have a few faults, but all and all, I'm a pretty good person."

"And a pretty good mother. And a pretty good wife. And just downright pretty."

"Aw, you say the sweetest things." Regina grinned.

"True, I do. And I'd love a chance to tell you a few more sweet things, right in your sweet little ear."

"Are you propositioning me?" Regina smiled.

"Would you accept it if I were?"

Regina could feel that warm tingly feeling again. Four months really was too long a time, and she had stopped drinking the wine a little too late. But she sighed, and shook her head.

"Been there. Done that," she answered with a smile.

"Damn!"

"I didn't mean it like that." She laughed and reached over and took his hand. "It's just that I think right now our feelings are still kind of raw. I like the fact that we're friends. Let's concentrate on that, okay?"

"Shall we seal it with a kiss?" Charles asked hopefully.

"How about we simply seal it with a signature? On those divorce papers, if you don't mind."

"Yeah, yeah, yeah. Okay," Charles grumbled.

They left the restaurant together. Charles walked her to her car, an apple red Ford Mustang.

"I'll be up next week to see Camille, okay?"

"No problem. Take care of yourself, and give my love to your father. And tell your mother I said hello."

He gently pulled her into his arms, and caressed her cheek.

"Are you sure you're going to be okay driving back this late? Why don't you let me get you a hotel room?" He stroked her hair and leaned down to kiss her.

"Yo, Gina. Can we catch a ride?"

The voice startled them. Charles abruptly released Regina and spun around. Yvonne, Tamika, and Puddin' stood together on the sidewalk, grinning.

"What are you guys doing here?" Regina laughed.

"Oh, we were just in the neighborhood," Yvonne said, stepping forward and giving Regina a kiss on the cheek.

"Hey, Charles. Long time no see. Do any office managers lately?" Puddin' asked as she and Tamika brushed by him.

"Very funny." Charles curled his lip, as if to say something more, but changed his mind and turned back to Regina.

"Well, it seems your armed escort has arrived. Why don't I give you a call next week to make arrangements to see Camille."

"Let's hurry up and get in the car. It's cold out here," Tamika said without giving Charles a glance.

Regina was the only one who waved as he walked away.

"You guys are too much! What the hell are you doing here?" she asked as she piloted the car down the street.

"It was Yvonne's idea. She said you were coming down to Philadelphia to serve him with the divorce papers, and we figured that you might need some support," Puddin' said, rubbing her hands together in front of the air vent that was still blowing cold air.

"I figured it might be a kind of vulnerable time for you," Yvonne said from the backseat. "And you know we couldn't have you backsliding."

"So, we got David to drive us down," Tamika said. "He's at his mother's house now."

"How did you know where we were, though?" Regina asked, still amazed.

"David called Reverend Whitfield, and he said the two of you were having dinner together. We took a chance and came down here. We figured Charles would try to soften you up by taking you to Zanzibar Blue, since it holds so many memories for the two of you," Yvonne said.

Regina pulled the car to the curb and turned and looked at her friends. Tears sprang to her eyes, and she didn't bother to try to hide them.

"Damn, I love you guys." She laughed through a sob.

"Oh, God, don't start blubbering," Puddin' said, swatting Regina on the head. "You know this is how we hang. Now drive the damn car. I have a date tonight."

Regina laughed and wiped her eyes.

"Am I dropping you guys at David's mom's house?" she asked as she restarted the car.

"No, don't worry about it. I'll call him and ask him to meet us back in New York City," Tamika said, pulling her cellular telephone from her pocketbook. "I think we should drive home together, don't you guys?"

"Damn straight. Now hurry up so Puddin' can make her date or we'll never hear the end of it," Yvonne said.

"Okay, but I just want to say again, that I love you guys," Regina said as the car pulled onto the highway, and headed home to Harlem.